Poisoned Vows
A Dark Mafia Standalone

M. James

PNK Publishing

Copyright © 2023 by M. James

All rights reserved.

No part of this book may be reproduced in any form or by any electronic or mechanical means, including information storage and retrieval systems, without written permission from the author, except for the use of brief quotations in a book review.

Lilliana

"This all depends on you. And you can't even remember which fucking fork to use."

My father's voice cuts through the air, sharp as a knife. A whip crack, lashing at me. I should be used to it by now—he's talked to me this way all my life. Being loved by a parent, cherished—isn't something I've ever known or experienced. There have been no moments of kindness or closeness. The moments I look forward to are the ones where he forgets I exist.

In the past few weeks, those have been nonexistent.

In his eyes, I have a chance to fulfill my purpose—the only purpose I've ever had. The only reason for him to ever be grateful that he has a daughter and not a son. I'm something to be molded, shaped, bent to his will. That's all I've ever been.

My beauty was the luck of the draw. The rest of it—any grace or intelligence or good manners I possess, any charm or seductiveness—has all been instilled in me. Taught, for this moment.

What I can't seem to learn is how place settings work at a fancy dinner.

"Do you really think they're going to care?" I blow out a harsh breath, exasperated. I'll likely pay for that later, but my nerves are stretched taut, humming with anxiety. "I'm meant to be this man's fuck toy, not his wife. What does it matter if I know which spoon is for soup and which fork is for dessert?"

I can see the moment my father wants to hit me. He might have, if we weren't so close to the day of reckoning. But he can't risk anything marring my face. No redness or bruising. Nothing that leaves a mark, and he can't be trusted to stop himself, if he unleashes that control. So instead, he makes a fist, glaring at me with piercing dark eyes.

I've been told I have my mother's eyes, soft and blue. But I wouldn't know. I don't remember her, and there are no pictures of her in the house. Nothing to remember her by.

"He may want you for more than one night," my father snaps. "And sometimes Bratva men take their mistresses to functions. You will impress them more if you behave like a mistress and not a whore. A woman who can hold her own among their associates."

Ah, yes. That distinction. I've heard it a thousand times. A whore lies on her back for one night and gets paid. Easy, simple. One and done. A *mistress* is beautiful. Polished. Elegant. For my father to succeed in installing his daughter as a mistress and not a whore means *more* for him. More of everything—but mostly the potential to rise higher...the only thing that's ever mattered to him.

"All daughters in these families manage to learn these lessons," my father snipes at me as I look down at the place setting in front of me again, struggling to commit to memory what I'm meant to do with the silverware. As far as I'm concerned, I'd rather shove the butterknife in one of these men's eyes than politely eat soup with them.

But it's not my choice. It never has been.

"I'm not one of those daughters." The words catch in my throat. "I'm no one." *You're no one,* I want to say, but that might earn me a beating no matter how hard my father tries to restrain himself. And then later, when he's realized what he's done and blames me for pushing him to it, days locked in my room without food or entertainment, only the charm school books that reinforce my place in the world.

Whether I'm on my feet or my back, I'm here for the pleasure of the men around me. To serve their whims. To make them happy.

"You're right," he says, his voice still cold and cutting. "You are no one. But you will make me into someone. You *will* please the *pakhan*, and you will earn me my rightful spot in the ranks. And then, when he's finished with you—"

He trails off, and I wait for the end of that sentence. The only thing that's kept me from stealing a kitchen knife and slitting my own wrists long ago, to escape the absolute hell of my own existence.

"Then you can do as you damn well please," he finishes. "And good fucking riddance."

At least there's no pretense. That's the only relief I have. My father doesn't pretend to be a good or kind or loving man. He isn't horrified that I'm afraid of him, rather than loving or respecting him. He relishes it, because no one else is afraid of him, and he so desperately wants to be a man that others fear. A man whose name makes others tremble.

I want to laugh at him. To tell him how pathetic it all is. But I have a healthy dose of self-preservation, so I don't.

I endure the rest of the lesson and his berating, and then I go back to my room. Hungry, which is ironic, considering that we spent the last two hours discussing silverware and dinner platings.

But my father wants me slender, which means I eat very little, and what I do eat is restricted. I'll have to come down for dinner later, where he'll eat as he pleases, and I'll be served the usual—a spinach salad, grilled chicken, and a medley of vegetables. Water, not wine, or anything else more exciting. I've never actually had a drink other than the few times I've been brave enough to sneak it from my father's liquor cabinet or an open wine bottle—on the occasions that he has others over for holidays or other celebrations, he makes the excuse that I'm too young.

Twenty *is* technically too young, but I don't think anyone else gives a shit. Neither does he, really, other than it's something else to prevent me from doing. Another edict, another form of control.

I close the door to my room behind me, leaning back against it, letting out a long breath as I allow the exhaustion to sink in. I've been up since five in the morning—exercising, doing my lessons, going to my hair and beauty appointments, and coming home for more lessons and more exercise. It's the same thing day in and day out, with the exception of the appointments on a biweekly rotation. I know my father doesn't really have the money that he spends on me, but he considers it an investment.

An investment that, should I fail to deliver the return he expects, will be taken out of my own flesh. I can't imagine what's in store for me if I fail to please the *pakhan*, the man that I'm going to be presented to very soon. What will happen if he doesn't want me—if he doesn't give my father what *he* wants.

Slowly, I walk to the bed, sinking down on it. There's little to do when I'm alone—I have a few books, and I've read them so much, the covers are falling off. Outside I can see the Chicago skyline rising in the distance, and I know there are streets full of people living their bustling, full lives—on their way home, or to see friends, or to go out on a date. The things that ordinary people do, in their ordinary lives.

I would like very much to be ordinary.

I *should* have been ordinary. My father is no one. As far as I know, my mother was no one, too. My father is a rank-and-file man in the Chicago Bratva, someone whose life means very little to the men far above him, the men he seeks to cozy up to. I was never supposed to be one of those girls bred and groomed for the pleasure of a high-ranking man, for marriage, for providing heirs. My future was supposed to be wholly unwritten.

Of course, I won't be marrying anyone. I won't be providing any children, thank *fuck*. I'll be *getting* fucked, and then once that's done, once my father has gotten what he wanted and I'm free, I can choose a different life.

I get up, open the window, and lean out. Our apartment is high up, on the twelfth floor, and there have been many nights where I leaned out just like this and imagined what might happen if I simply…tumbled out. I ran the calculations, trying to determine if there was a chance of survival. I was fairly sure that there wouldn't be.

Isolation and loneliness will do that to a girl. Growing up with a father obsessed with pushing his daughter into the bed of the most advantageous man will do that. *Everything* I've endured has pushed me to the very brink.

But now, if I can hold on just a little longer, my freedom might be very close. And with it, what will I do?

I'll get the fuck out of Chicago, that's what. I'll go as far away as I can—Florida, California, fucking Alaska, for all I care. I don't give a shit *where* I end up, as long as it's not this room, this apartment, this *fucking* city. As long as I never have to hear the words *pakhan* or *Bratva* again. As long as I get to choose who I fuck and when.

All I have to do is give up this one last thing. Endure for just a little longer. And then my value to my father—to all of these men—will be gone. I won't be a virgin any longer, and none of them will give a shit about me.

I've spent the better part of my life being tutored in anything that my father thought might give me an advantage over these men. It's been impressed upon me over and over how worldly they are, how cultured, how my intelligence could matter, if the pakhan decides he wants me for more than just a single night. If he wants me on his arm as a mistress for any length of time. Literature, world history, geography—I've had all that drilled into me, too, along with the placement of spoons and forks.

The result of that wasn't entirely what my father hoped for, though. I have some of those maps still squirreled away, some of those books with places highlighted, outlining a future in which I can travel to those places on my own, without anyone else to hold me back. Destinations I want to visit, a world I want to see with the freedom I've earned, and no one will tell me no.

Those plans are all ephemeral still, and I haven't decided where I'll go first. But that doesn't really matter.

Anything is better than this.

All that will matter is that I'll get to *choose* what I do next.

If I can survive.

Nikolai

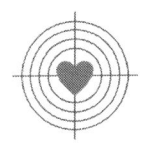

The man's screams and pleas are meant to move me. I know, objectively, that they are. But I feel nothing as I stand there, hands bloodied, setting the pair of pliers I'm holding aside as I stare at the man trussed up in front of me.

He's missing most of his teeth at this point and several nails, both on his hands and his feet. His answers, the ones I've managed to coax out of him, are spoken through blood and spittle, sobbing gummily as he cries between words.

The man is utterly pathetic, and I'm ready for this to be over.

"Tell me again," I say patiently, reaching for a filleting knife. "And perhaps I'll believe you this time. How many men did you say that we have watching tomorrow night's shipment? And what time did you tell them that it will be landing? And to whom?"

It's too many questions for a man in this much pain to remember, so I repeat them again, in between shaving off thin strips of skin. I know he's lying, and at this point, I'm not sure what it will take to get him to tell the truth. But lies are useful, too. If he's enduring this much, it means his treachery goes deeper than we knew. It means he's afraid of something more than my father and I—which could be very few men in this city.

I am brutal, but my father is terrifying. Merciless, even to those he loves. This, to me, is a job. A rote duty that I'm expected to carry out. My father has often told me that he leaves interrogations to me because while we're both equally skilled, my father enjoys it far too much.

That, and he's getting older. His hands are no longer as steady as they once were. But he would never admit that, and to suggest it would mean ending up where this poor bastard is, trussed up above plastic sheeting and being killed an inch at a time.

His end is quick, at least. When I'm sure there's nothing more to gain from him, I slit his throat. A gunshot would be quicker still, but I left my weapon on the other side of the room, and he only told me lies. He didn't earn the effort it would have taken for me to get it.

As I'm washing my hands afterward in a side room, rinsing the blood from around my nails while I listen to the steady thump of my father's lackeys removing the body and cleaning the room, my phone buzzes in my pocket. I dry off my hands and see a message from my father.

Meet me in my office as soon as you're finished.

Brief, and to the point. I chuckle to myself, because my father is nothing if not consistent. He could want to speak to me about anything, and the message would be the same, no matter his mood. He could be pleased or furious, hopeful or despondent, have good news for me or bad, and I would receive the same text.

Emotion, in his eyes, is something for a man to quell. To kill, lest it get him killed. And I have learned, over the years, to keep whatever emotion I feel buried to a fault.

Fortunately, it hasn't seemed to matter much. My life is a pleasant one. I have whatever I desire. I live in a Chicago penthouse, I want for nothing, I drink and eat what I wish and fuck who I please, and go where I want. One day, my father's empire will be mine. And all I have to do in return is follow his commands and, sometimes, spill a little blood.

A small price to pay for the life I lead.

My father, Egor Vasilev, is in his office as promised. He's leaning back in his broad leather chair, flicking through papers with a cigar burning in an ashtray next to him and a glass of vodka at his right hand. My father is a man who rarely stops working, and so he enjoys his pleasures when he wishes to take them, rather than saving them for the end of the day. If it had been anyone other than one of his children coming to meet him, he likely would have had a woman under the desk. I'm almost surprised that he doesn't, anyway. It's only my sister Marika's sensibilities that he concerns himself with, mostly.

"Nikolai." He doesn't glance up, waving at a chair with one hand as he reaches for his vodka with the other. "We've had an offer."

His expression doesn't change, but there's a hint of amusement in his voice. He sets the papers down, taking a long sip of his drink, and then looks up at me, at my blood-spattered shirt and trousers. "No time to change?"

"You asked me to meet you as soon as possible," I say calmly. There was a choice to be made between receiving that text and coming to meet my father in his office. I could change my clothes, and come to him fresh and appropriately dressed—or I could follow the letter of his instructions, and come as soon as I was finished. Knowing my father, I chose the latter.

"Very good. You're a good son, Nikolai."

Coming from him, that's the very highest praise.

He leans back, steepling his fingers as he looks at me. "The man you interrogated, he's dead?"

I nod. "As the proverbial doornail."

"And did he give us anything useful?"

"Not plainly. But he lied, right up to the end. Nothing broke him. That kind of pain is only endured when the fear of telling the truth is worse. Which means whoever he was reporting to, it can only have been a few of the men in the city."

My father nods. "Theo, maybe. Or Haruki."

"It's possible. We can try to find out more. Some of his friends may be more—forthcoming, once they know what happened to him. They'll be eager to avoid the same fate or be perceived to have helped him."

"We'll have to be careful to separate lies from truth. To make sure they aren't offering up false information to save their own skin."

"Someone will," I tell him confidently. "And that man's punishment will be enough to dissuade the rest."

My father nods approvingly. "Spoken like a true Bratva *pakhan*. No man among us, of our rank, should be afraid of blood on his hands. You bathe in it, and don't flinch."

The pride in his voice is evident. A rare thing, from him, and only in private. It's no secret that my father values me—as his only son and heir, it goes without saying. But anything else is kept between us and in this room.

There is no room for caring in our world. No room to love what can be lost.

"You said there was an offer." I clear my throat, banishing any thoughts of regret that I might like to be closer with my father. To feel more affection from him. Those sorts of ideas are a pointless weakness. "From who? And about what?"

"I'm getting to it." He takes another sip of his vodka, nodding to the decanter on the gilded bar to his right. It's a clear offer for me to pour myself a glass, and I take him up on it. An afternoon like the one I had makes a man need a drink.

I pour two fingers into a crystal glass and sit back down.

"One of our lower-level men has an offer for us. An Ivan Narokov."

The name doesn't ring a bell. "I haven't heard of him."

My father shrugs. "I don't know who the fuck he is, either. But he clearly heard that someone in our inner circle betrayed us. How he came about *that* information, I'm curious to know. Ordinarily, I might have had you simply torture it out of him. But his offer was —intriguing."

Now I'm all ears. My father's curiosity is rarely piqued, and he has a penchant for violence. If he's chosen to hear this Narokov out rather than simply taking pieces off of him until he gives up how he came to find out about this vacancy, *I'm* curious to know why.

"Apparently, he has a daughter. A very beautiful one."

"Oh?" I take another sip, even more curious now. "I'm sure many men who work for us have daughters. What does that have to do with anything?"

My father chuckles. "She's a virgin. Twenty years old. And he's offered us her innocence, in exchange for the place that the traitor you tortured today so recently vacated." He pauses, finishing his drink. "He offered *me* her virginity, specifically. Suggested that I might use her in any way I pleased, for as long as I pleased. No parameters on it, either—no pleas that I do not harm her. Honestly, I think I could have said I planned to strangle her after I fucked her, and he would have agreed."

"Hm." I take another sip, hiding the shudder that goes through me. The only kind of violence I abhor is violence that targets women. The idea of killing this girl, whoever she is—particularly in such a way—makes my skin crawl. But I don't let it show. "And you don't want her?"

He shrugs. "I considered it. A beautiful, innocent young woman entirely at my mercy? It's a pleasant thought. But you've done well. You are an exemplary son, a worthy heir. And I think you deserve a reward. It's good timing, actually. I'd been wondering—what does a father get a son who has everything? Well, now I see." An uncommon, satisfied smile spreads over my father's face. "A virgin that you can use as you please. That's quite a reward, isn't it? And if her father proves to be useless, as I expect he might, we'll simply have him killed after you've had the chance to enjoy her."

I'm not sure it's a reward that I want. I'm not in the habit of forcing women, and I doubt that this girl is going along with this scheme willingly. But I also know better than to refuse my father, especially when he's clearly so pleased with how it's all worked out.

I drain the rest of my glass. "And when will I be meeting this girl?"

"Tonight. Her father is bringing her here. I knew you'd like the suggestion, so I've already accepted the offer." My father's pleased expression spreads across his face, a jubilance I've only seen once or twice before.

The last time, there were more bodies than I could count around us.

"Well then." I stand up, setting the glass aside. "I suppose I'd better change clothes."

Lilliana

I stare down at the dress on the bed, wondering if I'm going to be sick.

Now that the moment is here, I'm not sure how I'm going to manage it. I'm on my own when it comes to getting ready, but my hands are shaking, and I feel so nauseated that I almost think I might have to lie down. My teeth are clenched together so hard that they hurt.

I heard my father's conversation earlier. Eavesdropping is something that could earn me days without food or water, but I had a feeling that I'd be *presented* tonight—or very soon, at least. The appearance of the new dress in my closet, more expensive than anything else I own and elegantly seductive, seems to be too big of a coincidence, coupled with a private phone call. So I risked it. And what I heard made me want to run.

Not that I'd get out of the house. The doors are all barred from the outside with a separate iron grating, unlockable only by a key that my father keeps on him at all times. The only window that I could escape through, via the fire escape, is in the living room—and that one is barred and locked as well. If I were alone at home, and there was a fire, I'd fucking burn to death, or have to jump from a twelfth-story window.

I've often wanted to ask my father how he'd feel if his meal ticket burned up in a fire, all because he's so intent on keeping me imprisoned. I've never had the nerve.

You can use her as you like. Those were the words that made my gut twist, the implications that made me feel as if I won't be able to go through with it.

I don't know why I thought there would be any other outcome. It's not as if my father cares for my personal well-being. It's been made very clear to me that the only thing that matters is that I please the *pakhan* enough to ensure he accepts my father's offer. My own happiness and safety aren't taken into consideration. So I don't know why I would have thought that my father might caution him not to hurt me in any permanent way.

If that's what pleases the *pakhan*, then that's what will please my father.

I've always known I had to manage to survive this until the end. It just didn't really sink in, I suppose, until right then.

I might not live through this. Hell, I might not live through tonight.

I know just how brutal these Bratva men can be. I've heard stories. And right now, as I stare down at the dress on the bed, a hundred violent scenarios are running through my head, each one worse than the last.

Just get dressed, Lilliana. That's the future. This is the present, and if you make him wait, you'll suffer now.

That's the only thing that gets me moving. I *know* how it feels to endure my father's anger, and keeping him waiting today of all days wouldn't be in my best interests.

Lilliana

The dress is pale blue, a few shades lighter than my eyes. It has a fitted bodice with a deep v that dips low, a few inches above my navel, the material tight enough to hold my breasts in place. The shoulders are a few fingers wide, held by silver rose-shaped clasps that can be flicked open easily, and the skirt is fitted to my shape, pooling around my feet and slit up to my thighs on either side. It's a dress meant to showcase all my best assets, a dress meant to put me on display.

I have no choice but to wear it. It's beautiful, but I feel bare in it, even though nothing is actually exposed beyond my cleavage and a long stretch of leg on either side. It's not indecent, but it feels more so than something skimpier might have, because it draws the eye to everything a man could want to look at.

It doesn't help that, per the instructions I was given, I'm wearing nothing underneath it. No bra, no panties. It's the dress only, and beneath that, I'm bare.

I'm an offering, all of me made accessible to the man I'm being sacrificed to.

I try not to think about it as I go through the rest of the motions. Light makeup, curled hair left long and loose around my shoulders. A dab of rosy lipstick to accentuate my full lips. Thin liner, gold shadow, and mascara to make my eyes look wider. My nails have been done, my hair cut and highlighted. There's nothing else that could be done to make me look any more beautiful. I'm supposed to feel honored by this, pampered and polished to be given over for my father's elevation.

I feel disgusted. And tonight, I'll have to try to hide that.

Or maybe I won't. Maybe he won't care.

My father is equally well-groomed when I meet him downstairs. He's waiting by the door, hair combed back, in a pressed suit. His gaze rakes over me in a way that no father should ever look at his daughter, assessing how fuckable I am. How likely I am to make the Bratva *pakhan* get a hard-on he can't ignore.

"Lovely," he murmurs, circling me. "Absolute perfection." And then, he faces me once again as he tips my face up into the light, examining my makeup. "As long as you keep your mouth shut until he requests otherwise, this night should go perfectly."

Of course, he couldn't compliment me without also cutting me down. It's also a lie—I've been taught to be charming and well-spoken all my life, for this exact night. Although—I also have a sharp tongue, when I can't force myself to control it any longer.

Tonight I'll do my best to keep it under wraps. For my own sake, if nothing else.

There's an Uber waiting outside for us. My father locks the door, his hand on my elbow as he steers me towards the waiting SUV—black with tinted windows—and it's all I can do not to laugh. It's the perfect allegory for my father's entire life—something very much like what he wishes he could have, but a cheap imitation of it. Not a bulletproof SUV of his own to be driven around in, but something to let him imagine that one day he could have that.

I want to tell him that even if this all goes off flawlessly, he'll never be anything but someone in service to more powerful men. That he'll never be a *pakhan*, not even a second-in-command. He'll still be a lackey, even if he's in the inner circle. And one day, his ambition will outstrip his machinations, and he'll end up in pieces at the bottom of the Chicago river.

But I keep my tongue leashed. After all, I'd like for it still to be in my mouth when this is all over. And I wouldn't put it past my father to give the *pakhan* ideas about what kind of depraved things he could do to me while he enjoys me.

I breathe slowly, in and out, as I slide into the car. The interior is cool and smells of clean leather, and there's a bottle of water in the back of the seat in front of me. I reach for it, and my father instantly snatches my hand away as the driver pulls away from the curb.

"I don't know how long the *pakhan* will keep us waiting," he says in a low, harsh tone. "I won't have you asking where you can piss in the meantime, and risk not being ready when he calls for us."

I clench my teeth against a response, but I don't fight. There's no point in it. My mouth is dry and my throat tight, and seeing the water and being denied it makes me want it all the more. But I know how my father likes control. I should never have reached for it in the first place.

Just endure, and it will all be over soon enough. One way or another.

I wondered where we would go—whether we'd be taken to a penthouse in the Gold Coast neighborhood or somewhere further out. It turns out to be the latter—we drive out to the edge of the city, down a long street full of manicured trees and lawns, with sprawling mansions, all the way to one street where there's nothing but a single mansion at the very end, secluded and walled in, with another fence beyond it and a guard hut.

I catch a glimpse of the driver's face in the rearview mirror. He looks uncomfortable, and who could blame him? He probably hadn't counted on driving up to a mansion guarded by men with guns for thirty dollars round trip.

I doubt my father is going to tip him well, either.

"Tell them Ivan Narokov has an appointment," my father says harshly from the backseat. "They can check if they like. My daughter is here with me."

I can *see* the driver's Adam's apple bob in his throat as he nods and rolls the window down. There's a rumble of thunder, and I see the rain start to drip down the tinted windows as a black-clothed guard swaggers up to the car, seemingly uncaring about getting wet. It's hard to say, between the angle that I'm looking from and the fact that the guard's clothing means he nearly blends in with the darkness.

The driver repeats what my father said. "I'm just dropping them off," he adds, his voice going thready. "I don't have any part of this."

The guard smirks. "Sure enough, son," he tells the driver, his eyes glinting as if he enjoys the other man's discomfort. The driver isn't that old—early twenties, maybe. This is probably his second job, putting him through college. It makes me feel sick to think that something bad could happen to him because he accepted this ride.

The guard says something I can't hear into the walkie on his shoulder. It crackles a moment later—or I think it does, it's hard to hear over the steadily-increasing rain—and the guard waves a hand at the shack. The iron gate to the outer fence slowly creaks open, and the guard nods. "You can go on ahead. I recommend dropping them off at the front and going on your way," he adds, and the driver goes a shade paler.

"Shit," he mumbles under his breath, but he hits the gas anyway, going through the gate and down the driveway to the second set of gates. His fingers are drumming on the steering wheel, and I can tell he wants to be out of here.

I don't blame him. So do I.

A fantasy flashes through my head, one in which I shove my father out of the car and bribe the driver with whatever he wants—pussy, head, anything I can offer—to drive me out of here and as far from Chicago as he can get me. The same offer the *pakhan* is getting—my innocence to use as he pleases…except I think this boy would be far gentler with me than the man I'm being handed over to tonight.

But there's no way to know. Given that kind of power, innocent-looking men can be just as violent. And it doesn't matter anyway; this kid doesn't have the balls.

It's a funny thing to think, considering I'm almost certainly younger than he is.

"Lilliana." My father's harsh voice cuts through the air, and I snap back to myself, out of fantasies of escape. The door is open, the rain is pouring down, and my father looks pissed. He looks around, and snatches an umbrella off of the floor of the SUV.

"That's mine—" the driver protests weakly, but anything else he might have been about to say dies on his lips as my father gives him a withering glare.

Umbrella opened and shaken out, my father slides out of the car, standing in the rain as he holds it for me. It's the kindest thing he's ever done, and I know it's not for my benefit. It's for his, because the *pakhan* won't be aroused by a woman who looks like a wet cat dragged in out of a storm, with mascara running down her face.

I pick my way down the driveway in my high heels as we walk, my father doing his best to share in the cover of the umbrella. Behind me, I hear the sound of the wheels squealing as the driver gets the fuck out of Dodge as fast as he can, and I don't blame him.

I would, too, if I could.

The doors to the mansion's entrance are huge—wooden and gilded, and they swing open as we approach, no doubt because someone saw us over a security system. We step into a marble-floored foyer, greeted by a tall, severe-looking man in a black suit, and just beyond, I see more guards flanking the exit of the foyer.

"I will take your—umbrella, Mr. Narokov," the man says, reaching for it. "Would you perhaps like a towel to dry yourself with, sir?"

He glances at me, his eyes never dipping below my chin, the picture of propriety. *The one man who probably won't take the chance to get an eyeful tonight*, I think to myself, pressing my lips together against a bubble of hysterical laughter. If I start, I won't stop, and that will do no one any good.

Least of all me.

"Yes, thank you." My father's voice has changed. There's an arched confidence to it that I personally think is entirely unearned, but he's playing the game. I stand there, waiting for directions, because nothing about tonight is my choice. I'm just a chess piece, and I wait to be moved like one.

The black-suited man leaves and returns with a crisp white towel. He hands it to my father, who dries his hair, face, and arms with it, before running his fingers through his hair so that it's slicked back darkly, dented in at the edges where his hairline is receding.

"Follow me, if you please," the man says, and my father obeys. He gives me a sharp glance, and I do the same, my heels clicking against the marble as we're led out of the foyer, past the guards, and down a hallway to another tall gilded door.

The *pakhan* is not inside. It's what looks like a formal living area—gleaming hardwood floors, tall bookshelves, and leather couches framing a stone fireplace. Huge glass-paned windows are on either side of the fireplace, rain streaming down them.

"Someone will come to fetch you when Mr. Vasilev is ready," the black-suited man says, and then he steps out, closing the heavy door behind him and leaving us alone.

I sink down onto one of the leather sofas, feeling my knees tremble a little. I don't know if I'm meant to sit down, but I don't care. No one was meant to stand in four-inch heels for long.

My father glances at me, but he doesn't tell me to stand up. I feel my heart beat in my chest, a hard rhythm, and I try to count each one, something to focus on beyond what comes next.

If I let my mind run away with itself, the horrors I'll come up with will be too terrible to manage. I've become very good at controlling my fear over the years. Counting heartbeats, counting breaths, counting the seconds until something is over. Counting the strokes of a belt against my skin.

I nearly jump out of that same skin when the door opens, and a harsh, strongly-accented voice carries into the room.

"The *pakhan* will see you now. Follow me."

I stand up automatically, without having to be told, smoothing my skirt under my hands.

The moment of reckoning has come.

Nikolai

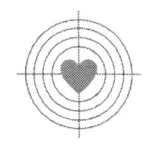

I'm barely out of my father's office before a delicate hand snags my shirt and drags me into the next room.

"Nikolai!" My sister, Marika, is staring up at me with a furious expression on her face. For all that she's a foot shorter than me, and a hundred pounds lighter, her anger is nothing to scoff at. Right now, she looks as if she wants to scratch my eyes out. "You're not actually going to go along with this, are you?"

"You should know better than to eavesdrop." I'd like to say that our father has a soft spot for his daughter, but I've long since known that my father has *no* soft spots, not where anyone is concerned. If he'd known Marika was eavesdropping, she'd be punished.

"I never get caught." She sniffs, brushing her white-blonde hair out of her face, blue-grey eyes the same shade as mine sparking up at me. "You can't be serious. You're going to take that poor girl, and—"

"You don't even know who she is."

"That doesn't matter." Marika stamps a petite foot. "What if it was me? What if our father was sending me off to fuck some man just so—"

"That would never happen, and you know it. You're the *pakhan's* daughter. Whoever you marry will be handpicked for you."

She wrinkles her nose. "You're still missing the point."

I run a hand through my hair, letting out a sigh. "Marika, be reasonable. Do you really think I'm going to hurt her?"

"You can't agree to this and *not* hurt her."

"If you were eavesdropping, then you heard all of the conversation. Our father is very pleased with himself for coming up with this idea. You know I can't tell him no."

She purses her lips. There's no comeback for that—she knows as well as I do that *no* is not a word in our father's vocabulary.

"What are you going to do?" she asks finally.

"You know I don't hurt women. I don't mind violence—but I won't do that."

"You're not going to—" Marika swallows hard. "Force her?"

My face twists, and I glare down at my little sister. "I've never forced a woman in my fucking life." The words come out harsher than I mean for them to, but I don't apologize. The very idea is insulting. "Of course, I'm not going to fucking do that."

"Technically willing doesn't mean—"

"Christ, Marika. I fucking know that." I drag my fingers through my hair again. "I'll figure it out. Maybe I'll just keep her for a few days, make them think I fucked her, and then let her leave. It sounds like her father doesn't care what happens to her afterward. I'll give her some money and then send her on her way."

"Like a whore?"

"Oh, cut the outrage." I glare at her. "I adore you, Mari, but you know as well as I do that there are very few choices in this world, and even fewer for girls like you and her. You might be on different ends of the spectrum, but it's the same goddamn thing."

"What if you want her?" Marika bites her lip. "Are you still going to leave her alone?"

I can't believe I'm having this fucking conversation, but Marika is like a bulldog when it comes to something she's fixated on. She won't let go until she has an answer that satisfies her.

"Then I'll find another woman I want," I tell her flatly. "I can have just about any woman I please willingly, and if I want something darker, I'll pay for it. I don't need to break my own moral code to fuck." I narrow my eyes. "Now, can I stop having this conversation with my goddamned sister?"

"Fine." Marika shoves the door open, stepping to one side. "But you better not be lying to me."

I roll my eyes at her and stalk out of the room.

The entire situation has me wound tight. I'm being offered something that few men would refuse. An innocent girl, entirely untouched, to do with as I please. To do *anything* I want with, and her refusal, if it came, wouldn't matter. She would be mine.

I can't pretend the thought doesn't excite me. Not the violence inherent in that, but the idea of divesting this girl, whoever she is, of her innocence. I don't even know what she looks like yet, but I don't doubt that she's beautiful. That would be enough. And she would be all mine, for as long as I pleased.

I can feel myself getting hard as I stride back to my room to change, just at the thought, aching for a girl I haven't even seen yet and have no intention of taking for my own. The idea of it—

I've gotten tired of fawning women who can't wait to fuck the billionaire heir to Chicago's most dangerous Bratva family, women who salivate and open their lips and legs for the idea of letting a killer fuck them raw. I've gotten tired of whores, too; the women I can pay to willingly let me enjoy the darker things I crave from time to time. There's no novelty in it any longer. It's begun to feel hollow, unfulfilling.

I don't want to hurt this girl. Not really. I have my kinks, but the women I enjoy them with submit willingly. A man like me, one steeped in violence and blood, has to have a code. A line he won't cross, or he becomes nothing but a monster. A sociopath.

Shoving open the door to my room, I try to push the idea of her out of my head. The picture of full lips opened for my cock, wide, pleading eyes looking up at me as I push myself into her mouth. The sound of a sweet voice begging as I slide into her tight, virgin pussy for the first time, begging for me to stop at first, and then to *not* stop, once I show her just how good it can be. And later, her ass—

I could take every part of her. Exercise every filthy desire and fantasy I've ever had. I could open up an entire world of pleasures to her, show her how deep the darkness can go, and how *good* it can be at the bottom of that deep well. But first, I'd have to overcome her resistance.

And that's where the fantasy stops, because she wouldn't be with me willingly, and I can't reconcile that.

Every other woman I've ever shown that darkness has begged for it—but only because they hoped that if they pleased me, I'd reward them…with money, with connections, or for the most delusional, my hand in marriage. Rarely because they truly wanted *me*.

This girl would be no different, I remind myself, rubbing my palm over the stiff outline of my cock. *She would submit because she's being forced to. Not because she desires you.*

My cock throbs under my hand, and I unbutton my shirt with the other, still stroking myself on the outside of my trousers. It does little to relieve the ache, but I have time. And I intend to go into this meeting with a clear head, rather than a stubborn hard-on like a teenage boy touching a pair of tits for the first time.

I'll accept my father's offer, of course. I'll take the girl away and keep her until enough time has passed, without touching her. And then I'll give her some money and set her free.

A little rabbit in a trap that the wolf will choose not to eat.

God, I bet she'd taste fucking delicious, though.

My mouth waters at the thought of that, of tying her to the bed and teasing her to her first orgasm with my tongue, listening to her beg for it until *I* grant her her pleasure. I toss my bloodied shirt aside, striding into the bathroom as I unzip my trousers and free my aching cock.

I'm already stroking it by the time I step under the hot spray of water in the shower, thumb pressing into the swollen head as I groan. I haven't moved past the fantasy of eating this girl's virgin pussy, and I can almost taste it on my tongue; how sweet she'd be. How eager, once she discovered that pleasure.

What she looks like is a blur in my head. Blonde, brunette, redhead, it doesn't matter. I can almost feel the softness of her skin under my hands, the way she'd arch up, grinding against my tongue, begging. The quick thrum of her clit, the flood of arousal over my tongue as she comes. My cock drips pre-cum against my hand, my hips thrusting into my fist as I imagine it.

She'd be frightened once she realized what came next. I have no delusions that I'm anything but large. She'd be more than a little afraid of my cock, but I let myself indulge that idea, picturing her wide-eyed fright as I line it up against her virgin entrance, too thick for her, even with her arousal easing the way. I have no intention of acting on the fantasy, of allowing myself that. It's only that, a fantasy—the squeak of terror as I push against her, stretching her, that wide-eyed moment of pain before I allow her to adjust. My little rabbit, caught in a trap, with no choice but to submit.

Fuck. I don't get past that image, her full lips parted on a mingled cry of fear, pain, and the beginnings of pleasure as I push my too-big cock into her untouched pussy. I spasm in my fist, a spray of cum hitting the shower wall as my hips jerk, my fingers curling against the tile where I've braced myself as I thrust into nothing, imagining a tight, clenching pussy around my cock instead. Imagining how good she would feel as I filled her up with my cum.

I feel almost dizzy as the last drops of cum spill from my cock, my fingers stroking along the shaft as I squeeze the last of it out, wanting myself drained dry. I want a clear head when I meet this girl. I want no chance that I might betray my own moral code, the only vestiges of humanity that I have left to cling to in a world that demands I be a monster for the sake of power and family.

If I hurt her, I've become exactly like my father. I've tried all my life to keep from being that. I have no intention of letting one woman break me.

My head does feel clearer, as the pleasure ebbs. I finish showering, stepping out, and drying myself off, choosing a suit for the evening's meeting. My father will expect nothing less than perfection from me —the impeccable heir that he's raised, sophistication and elegance, brutality and violence, all wrapped into one perfectly honed man.

I don't see Marika again as I go downstairs, and I'm glad. I don't want to listen to another of her lectures, not when I'm focused on the night ahead. All I have to do is convincingly accept the offer, and then I can stash the girl away in one of my apartments, out of sight and out of mind, until enough time has passed that I can send her away.

I stride down the hall to my father's study. It's a heavily masculine room—mahogany bookshelves, another long mahogany desk, a gilded bar cart, and leather wing chairs next to a fireplace. He's in front of the unlit fireplace now, sipping a glass of vodka as he stands facing away from me. He doesn't look up as I walk in, and I go to pour myself my own drink, not bothering to wait to be invited.

He says nothing about that, either. Slowly, he turns to face me as the bottle of vodka clinks against the crystal, and I see a contemplative look in his eyes.

"Narokov and his daughter are being brought to us now." He narrows his eyes at me. "I've considered taking her for myself after all. An offer like this is so tempting. But I can have any virgin daughter I like. I could command any of my men to give up their daughters to me, and they would, for fear of me. It's more interesting to give her away to someone that she doesn't expect, don't you think?"

I'm not sure what game my father is playing at, but I nod.

"You've never asked for anything like that." He takes a sip of his vodka, appraising me. "You could have any of them as well. You are the *pakhan*'s son. Is that not something you crave? A virgin at your beck and call? A girl ordered to go to your bed? It's a singular pleasure."

A warning pings in the back of my mind. My father prides himself on the brutal son that he's raised, on how I don't flinch from violence and blood. I have a sudden, deep fear that he plans to test my limits. To see how far he can test the limits of my depravity.

I steel myself. Surely there are some lines even my father won't cross. Things that he won't demand his own son do. I will only have to agree, not prove that I'm willing to violate her.

I hear the sound of footsteps in the hall and the click of heels against the hardwood. *She's outside the door.* There's a tight curl of anticipation deep in my gut that I can't ignore. I'd fantasized about this girl less than an hour ago, coating the wall of my shower with my cum as I imagined her. Now I'll find out who she is.

It will be a test of my will. But I've never been one to break when challenged.

The door opens. Her father is first, a tall, lanky man with a face that looks as if it would crack easily under my fist, if I so chose. A man who stinks of weakness from the moment I look into his eyes.

I dislike him from the start. But then he steps aside, and I hear the click of heels again.

The door opens a little wider, and *she* steps inside.

Lilliana

There are two men in the room when I walk in.

One is clearly the *pakhan*. He's older than my father, with iron-grey hair carefully combed back and a clean-shaven jaw that might once have been strong, but has jowls beneath it now, in his older years. His suit is carefully tailored, the lines of it attempting to hide the fat that's taken over what was once likely muscle, and his face is craggy. His eyes, however, blue and cold, are sharp and alert. He looks at me, and I see a lust that sends my stomach roiling with nausea as his gaze rakes down my body, taking in every inch of it.

The other man is younger. Not *young*, he's in his mid to late thirties, most likely, but he looks enough like the man next to him that I know this must be the *pakhan*'s son, without being told. He's the picture of handsomeness that I expect his father once was. He has thick dark hair, a chiseled, gorgeous face, and those same blue eyes. His body is all hard muscle poured into a bespoke charcoal suit, and everything about him screams power and control. His gaze sweeps over me too, but more dispassionately. As if he's disinterested in me and what I have to offer.

I find myself wishing I was being given to this man, the one who doesn't seem to want me. Maybe then I'd be spared the fate waiting for me. But I can see the naked desire in the *pakhan*'s face, and I wonder if I'll even make it out of this room without getting fucked. He looks as if he wants to devour me whole, a filthy old man salivating over a girl likely forty years his junior, if not more.

I don't know how I'll make it through my deflowering without vomiting. That, if nothing else, will probably be the reason I end up murdered at the end of it.

My father inclines his head respectfully. "*Pakhan*. Allow me to introduce my daughter, Lilliana Narokovna."

I know what I'm expected to do. I clasp my hands in front of my skirt, inclining my own head, keeping my eyes fixed on the gleaming wooden floor in front of me. "A pleasure," I murmur, though it's anything but.

This is likely to be the worst night of my life, and that's quite an accomplishment.

"Hmm." The *pakhan* grunts. "And you've come here to offer her up to me, Narokov? For a place in my inner circle, eh?"

"Yes, *pakhan*." My father's voice is ingratiating. I find myself wishing the *pakhan* would be offended by it and shoot him on the spot. Even if it ended in my own death as well, it would be satisfying to know that all this was for nothing. That my father won't get what he wants in the end.

"It's quite the offer." The older man walks towards me, a crystal-cut glass of vodka held in one hand. His gaze rakes over me again, like a dog salivating over a raw steak. He circles me, and it's all I can do to stand straight and still under the weight of his appraisal.

The other man does nothing. He says nothing. He stands very still. I keep my eyes on the floor, but I find myself wondering what I would see in his face, if I looked up.

"I'm tempted to agree and take her for myself," the *pakhan* continues, and my heart stutters in my chest. *What does that mean?* I'm being offered to him. What other possibility is there? There's denial, but the thought of that makes me as sick as the possibility of acceptance. I won't survive my return to my father's house, if the *pakhan* turns him down.

The *pakhan* retreats, returning to his spot in front of the fireplace. I feel my father's tension, the anger beginning to radiate off of him as he considers the possibility that all his work and investment have been for nothing. I almost like the *pakhan* more for making him sweat. *Maybe that can be what gets me through this, if he takes me.*

"But my son, Nikolai—" the *pakhan* gestures at the dispassionate man next to him. "He has earned a reward, I think. So I will accept your offer, Narokov. On behalf of my son, if he wishes it. But I think he should take a closer look at the girl, first. To be sure that she is up to his standards." He motions to the man next to him—Nikolai. "Go closer, son. Look at her and tell me what you think."

There's no hesitation, but I sense that Nikolai doesn't want to. I'm not sure why, and it unsettles me. Being given to the *pakhan* would be bad enough, but I at least know what he wants. This man is behaving strangely, and that frightens me more. A moment ago, I wished it would be him. Now that it seems as if it might be, I wonder if that was a mistake.

Nikolai stops in front of me. He reaches out, tipping my chin up so that I'm looking at his face, and his touch is surprisingly gentle—restrained, as if he's making an effort to be so. His fingers hold my face aloft, and my gaze meets his.

His eyes are stunning up close. Blue-grey, I realize, not entirely blue, and now stormy with an emotion that I can't read. His face is even more handsome than I noticed at first, the picture of stony masculinity, and I have a sudden urge to reach up and run my fingers over his sharp jaw.

What is wrong with me? I stifle it immediately, clenching my fist at my side, and immediately regret the motion. I should have known it would have consequences.

"She looks as if she has a little fire in her," the *pakhan* rumbles, a pleased note in his voice, as if he's enjoying the show. "I imagine you might enjoy that. Isn't that right, son?"

"Of course." Nikolai's voice is smooth and smoky, wrapping around me like velvet. Something tightens deep in my belly, something that I don't understand. It coils tighter when he rubs his thumb over the side of my jaw, up to my full lower lip, pressing against it as something in those stormy eyes heats up.

His hand drops to his side. "I will accept." His voice is flat and emotionless, and the *pakhan* narrows his eyes.

"How can you be sure?" He nods towards me. "You've inspected very little of her. Perhaps she should take the dress off, so you can be certain that her body is pleasing to you."

Oh god, please, no. How had I not thought of this possibility, in all of my macabre imaginings? I hadn't thought of being forced to strip naked in front of my father and these other two men. The shame of it burns hotly in my belly, rising up into my throat, tears pricking at the back of my eyes. There's nothing beneath my dress, and I realize with a sick sensation that it was for precisely this reason. My father *had* anticipated this.

Nikolai's jaw tightens, and I feel the smallest flicker of hope, foolish as it is. *What if he's not as bad?* The possibility seems ludicrous, but I cling to it.

"If I'm being given her innocence," he says calmly, "then I would prefer to be the only man who sees her bared. After all, a piece of art so beautiful is best viewed by only one set of eyes." He looks at me, the heat in his gaze darkening. "If she is my reward, then I will be the only one who enjoys her charms, in all their many forms."

The *pakhan* makes a grunting noise, taking another wet swallow of his vodka. My heartbeat slows, relief washing over me, but only for a moment.

"Then test her, at least," he growls. "I will not take this man's word for it that she's untouched." An anticipatory look settles on his face, as if he's waiting to see what happens next.

Something flickers in Nikolai's eyes. *What the fuck does that mean?* I wonder, my heart racing again, as Nikolai steps closer to me. He stands in front of me, his body blocking mine from the view of the other two men in the room, and he fills the space, his muscular body radiating heat.

I've never had a man like this so close to me. Everything about him screams danger. He looms over me, those eyes thunderclouds now, and one hand rests on my waist, long fingers pressing into me as he looks down at my face.

"Don't move, little rabbit," he murmurs, and the nickname startles me into absolute stillness as I feel his hand fist in my skirt, raising it so that he can slide his hand beneath it.

Oh god. My heart is galloping in my chest, the sensation painful. I feel like I can't breathe, as if I might pass out and crumple onto the hard wooden floor. I have no idea what this man is going to do to me.

Terror fills me—and something else, too, as I feel his hand slide under my skirt, the material draped over his muscled forearm. A heat that I've never experienced before, creeping over my skin.

His fingers brush over the taut skin of my abdomen, just above the apex of my thighs. I realize what he's going to do, and those sharp tears of shame burn at the back of my eyes again.

I want to beg him not to touch me like this, not in front of my father and his—not at all, if I could somehow talk him out of it. But I know it's useless. I was brought here for the *pakhan*'s pleasure, and it seems that his pleasure is both in giving me to his son, and having his son humiliate me here in this room, one way or another.

Begging will only add to my shame.

I tilt my chin up, looking defiantly at Nikolai as his fingers brush lower. I was instructed to shave bare, and I did. My pussy is soft and smooth, and I see his jaw tighten as he touches me, his lips pressing together as one finger slides over the seam between my thighs.

Heat blossoms over my skin again. He hasn't even delved between my folds yet, and I can feel something prickling over me, an unsettling sensation that makes me want to fidget. But I hold myself ramrod-straight and still, refusing to so much as flinch as his finger taps against my outer folds, his eyes narrowed as he looks down at me.

"Well?" the *pakhan* demands. "Does she seem untouched?"

"Are you, little rabbit?" Nikolai's voice is low and rough, hushed as it is. I wonder if I looked down, if I would see that he's aroused. I feel a strange, wicked temptation to do just that. But I force myself to hold his gaze. I don't want him to see the slightest bit of interest from me. Only my refusal to be cowed by this. "Are you as innocent as your father claims?"

I try to swallow, but my mouth is bone-dry. I nod speechlessly, my tongue sticking in my mouth.

"Use your words, rabbit." Nikolai rubs his finger back and forth. "Are you untouched?"

"Y-yes." I manage to force the word out. "I'm a virgin, if that's what you're asking."

"Untouched by anyone?" His finger pushes between my folds, and I feel the tip of it graze my clit.

I almost gasp. I barely manage to choke back the sound, forcing myself to remain silent. His finger taps against me, in that sensitive spot, and his eyes narrow. "Have you touched yourself here, Lilliana?"

It's the first time he's used my name. The shock of it, growled in that deep, accented voice, jolts me, and to my everlasting humiliation, I feel myself pulse against his fingertip—and for the first time in my life, I'm wet.

"Answer me," he murmurs, his voice a warning. "You'll find that no one here has infinite patience, rabbit."

I don't want to answer him. But I force the words out, knowing that I can't test my limits here. Not tonight. If I'm sent home, my life will end before the sun comes up.

My urge to survive is greater than my sense of shame.

"No," I whisper. "Never."

Nikolai's eyes widen ever so slightly, as if I've managed to surprise this man. There's a hint of satisfaction in that, if it's true. His finger presses a little harder against my clit, and once again, I swallow back a gasp.

"Never?" His finger rubs back and forth, just a little, and I feel another shameful flood of arousal, wetness gathering around his finger. I think I can feel myself starting to drip down my own thighs, and my cheeks flame. I can feel eyes on us, his father's and mine, and I begin to wonder if death is preferable after all.

"I find it hard to believe you've never touched this pretty pussy. Never made yourself come." A second finger slips between my folds, and they slide lower, towards my entrance. "But then again, from the way you're soaking my hand—"

"I've never wanted to," I whisper fiercely, the words cracking and sticking in my throat. "I don't care if you believe me. It's true."

It's my only bit of bravado, all I can manage. And it *is* the truth. Since I've been old enough to understand what sex is, I've been taught that my body, my sexuality, would be wielded as an instrument of my father's advancement. Sex has always been a threat. A promise of a horrifying end to my innocence. I've never touched myself. I've never wanted to, because even if I felt the smallest hint of arousal, I've always remembered what would happen when a hand other than my own touched me.

I've never had any reason to want it.

Nikolai looks at me, as if he's determining whether I'm lying to him or not. His fingertips press against my soaked entrance and dip inside the tiniest bit, looking for resistance. For proof.

They rest there for the briefest of seconds, and to my everlasting horror, I feel myself *clench* around him. I tighten around his two fingers, as if I *want* them inside of me, and I see his gaze darken with a sudden, instantaneous lust that terrifies me.

And then, just as quickly, it's gone. He pulls his hand from under my skirt, letting it fall back into place, and he nods as he turns back to face our fathers.

"Narokov is telling the truth," he says flatly. "She's a virgin, I'm sure of it."

"Well then." The *pakhan* looks almost regretful, as if he's reconsidering giving me away. He takes another deep swallow of his vodka, his gaze raking over me one last time. "Do you accept the offer, son? Or should I send her back with her father?"

I tense. This is the moment that decides whether I live or die—or at least whether I live a little longer, past the time it will take for my father to take me back home. I don't know what Nikolai will do with me.

But I think it might be better than what his father would.

Nikolai looks at me. His stormy gaze runs over my body, but it's not lecherous like the *pakhan*'s. There's lust in it—but it's different. Darker, as if he's fighting something within himself. As if he doesn't *want* to want me. I don't understand it.

"No," he says finally, and I feel my stomach drop to my toes. *I'm dead. I'm fucking dead.* My father's expression is carefully blank, but I know what hides under it.

"I won't accept the offer of her virginity," Nikolai continues, and I stare at him, confused. What else is there?

"But," he says, his voice suddenly hard and firm. "I will accept her as a bride."

Lilliana

I don't think I've heard him correctly at first. I can't have.

A bride? My head swims with confusion. It makes no sense. I feel stunned, frozen to my spot in the study, my knees weakening with the shock.

I'm not the kind of girl who marries a Bratva heir. My father is no one. *I'm* no one. I can offer him nothing except what's been offered up tonight, and beyond that, I have no worth. It's the lesson that's been taught to me since I was old enough to understand.

There's no reason why a man like him would want to marry me.

My father looks startled, but he inclines his head. "This is an unexpected honor," he manages. "If this is what you wish—"

"It is," Nikolai says sharply, cutting him off. "And as long as she pleases me, your head will remain intact. As will the rest of you."

I look at Nikolai's father, the *pakhan*. His face is carefully blank, and my heart races with terror as I wonder what he thinks of what his son has said. He can't be pleased with it. Even I know how unusual this is. How illogical.

I don't understand why Nikolai would do this.

I'd prepared myself, to the best of my ability, for the prospect of a night with the *pakhan*. I'd tried to brace myself for whatever that meant. I'd steadied myself, again and again, with the reminder that if I survived it, I would have my freedom when it was all over.

That was the deal I'd been promised. My virginity, for a life of my choosing, when I was no longer of use to the man I'd been given to.

This isn't freedom. This is a permanent prison.

"No." My hands fist at my sides, the word choked out through my panic. "No. I won't marry you."

The instantaneous reaction from both my father and the *pakhan*, turned on me in one terrifying moment, tells me what a mistake that was. The *pakhan* glowers at me, mingled anger and disbelief on his face, and my father steps forward, fury flaming on his as he raises a hand to strike me.

"Get down on your knees in front of your betters, girl," he hisses. "And be grateful for what they give you."

His hand carves a path through the air toward my cheek, prepared to put me on the floor before I even have a chance to obey. But Nikolai is there before the blow can strike, his broad hand shooting out to grab my fathers.

He closes my father's fingers into a fist, surrounded by his, and I see the pain flash across my father's face at the strength of his grip.

"Give me a moment with her," Nikolai growls, and before anyone can respond, he puts his hand on my waist and steers me toward the back of the room, away from either of the other men.

"There's nothing to fear, rabbit," he says softly, that strange nickname sounding oddly hoarse on his lips. "But there's no point in trying to refuse, either. I *will* marry you. But I won't harm you. You don't need to fear that."

I laugh. I can't help it. I close off the sound behind tightly pressed lips, choking it back. "You marrying me *is* hurting me," I tell him, the words choked and smaller than I want them to be. "You can't *not* hurt me. It's who you are. Who you *all* are."

He doesn't smile. His face hardens at that, and his hand tightens on my waist. "There is no refusal, Lilliana," he repeats, and once again, the sound of my name in his heavy, accented voice sends a flush of heat through me that makes no sense. "You will marry me, if I have to have guards march you down the aisle and hold you there while I say your vows for you."

My mouth drops open a little. I can't help it. There's a vicious certainty to his words that makes me feel—strange. I don't understand what's happening. "Why do you want to marry me?" I whisper, looking up at him and fighting both the urge to try to run and the urge to lean into him all at the same time.

Both seem as if they could be equally dangerous, and I only understand one.

His mouth tightens, and his other hand lands on my waist as he leans in, drawing me against him. Through the layers of fabric between us, I feel the hard shape of him against my pelvis, a warning of what's to come.

Literally, I think, and have to swallow back another burst of hysterical laughter.

"Because, little rabbit," he murmurs against my ear, his breath warm against the shell of it—

"I want to decide the nature of your trap for myself."

—

Trapped.

It's certainly how I feel right now.

After Nikolai pulled away from me, leading me back to where his father and mine were waiting, it was decided that we'd be married in two weeks. Why that particular length of time, and why the rush, I don't know.

Nothing makes sense.

A contract was signed, in ink and in blood. A quick swipe of a knife over my thumb, Nikolai's, and each of our fathers'—the witnesses—pressed below each of our names. Barbaric, I thought, but I hardly felt it. I was too confused. Too numb.

I thought Nikolai would take me to some other room and fuck me after that. That he'd want to enjoy the prize he claimed. But instead, his father rang a bell, and a black-uniformed woman showed up in the doorway. She escorted me up a winding staircase, to the third floor, and left me in the room I'm standing in right now.

I heard it lock behind her. And now I'm frozen in front of it, trying to make sense of what's happened.

I'm going to marry Nikolai Vasilev. The heir to the Vasilev Bratva.

It feels like a nightmare. Like it can't possibly be happening. My thumb throbs where it was cut, and I look down at it, seeing small drops of blood still beading from the cut.

Angrily, I swipe it over the skirt of my dress, ruining the pristine fabric. It stings, and I squeeze my hand into a fist, leaning into the pain. Into anything that can help ground me in what feels like a fog of impossibility.

I was supposed to be free when this was over. But there is no freedom from this. No possibility of escape from a marriage into the Bratva.

No visiting the Hollywood sign in California or roller-skating down Venice Beach's boardwalk. No dipping my toes into bright white Florida sand. No wandering among old buildings in England or looking at ancient art in Italy. Or at least, if I go to any of those places, it won't be on my own, to wander as I please and spend my days however I choose. It will be with a man who has his own agenda, who will want my time and attention for himself. It won't be the way I dreamed it.

Nikolai will possess me forever, and there's nothing I can do about it.

Somehow, my feet propel me forwards. I grab the doorknob and rattle it, but it's locked, just as I thought. I'm every bit the rabbit caught in a trap, just like he said. Panic overwhelms me, thick and hot and bleeding through me until I lose the control that I've been clinging to all night with my fingertips.

Clenching both my hands into fists, I start to bang on the door. I slam my fists into the heavy wood, again and again, and when no one comes, I add screaming to it. I scream my throat raw, beat my hands bruised, until the pain becomes too much and I taste blood, and then I crumple to the floor.

I lean back against the door, hot tears welling in my eyes. *I'm trapped.* The words repeat in my head, over and over in a miserable loop, and I try to force myself to accept them, as I've accepted everything else in my life so far.

What will it be like being married to Nikolai Vasilev? I don't understand him, and that frightens me more than being given to his father would have. I know men like his father. He would have taken everything he pleased from me, and it would have hurt me, maybe even killed me, but it would have been predictable. I would have known what to expect.

But Nikolai makes no sense to me. I have no doubt that he must be as brutal of a man as his father—he must be, to be the heir in such a cutthroat world—but it seemed as if he were trying to…restrain himself. Like he wanted to keep himself away from me.

He refused to strip me down in front of others. He touched me—but something told me that he didn't really want to be doing that, either. That he was doing it because he knew he had no other choice. That it would be worse for him if he didn't.

Are we alike in that way?

I shake the thought away. There's no possibility that Nikolai and I are alike, in any sense of the word. He's the heir to a powerful crime family, a billionaire, a man with enough power, influence, and money to have and do anything he wants. And I'm at his mercy.

Little rabbit.

The memory of the strange nickname, rasping over his lips, sends another unfamiliar flutter of heat through me.

You're going to have to fuck him. Not as his whore, but as his wife.

There's no difference, really. I've been sold to him either way. But my thoughts linger on it. I try to focus my mind away from it, to think about something else…anything else. But I keep feeling the echo of his fingers between my thighs, softly rubbing, bringing sensations and feelings out of me that I've never experienced before.

That I never thought I *would* experience.

My hand slides down to grip my skirt the way he did before I can think twice about it, slowly raising it up my thighs. I reach beneath it, tracing my fingers up the soft inner flesh. I can feel the stickiness there, my arousal clinging to my skin, and I can feel the heat from between my thighs.

I've never touched myself there. Not even for a moment. I've never had an orgasm.

I don't have to give him that.

There's a small moment of rebellion that sparks and catches flame. I press my finger against the seam of my pussy, like he did. I rub it back and forth, against the outer flesh, and I feel myself throb from within.

The promise of pleasure against my fingertips.

I gasp when I push my finger between my folds, tapping my fingertip against my clit. I'm still soaking wet, and the sensation that darts through me is startling and new, flooding my veins. Tentatively, I rub my finger back and forth, testing it.

Oh god. I bite back a whimper, my head tipping back against the door, my hips arching into my hand. I circle my clit, rubbing it harder, wanting more of the pleasure without any real idea what I'm doing, only that it feels so fucking good. All of these years, I could have been doing this. It's so good.

I'm drenched. I can feel myself dripping, soaking my skirt, and I hesitate, bringing my other hand between my legs. I don't dare push my fingers inside of myself, don't dare to risk the possibility of ruining my virginity. Still, I trace the outside of my entrance, delving the very tips of my fingers inside, like *he did*.

I don't want to think about Nikolai while I do this. But once I do, I can't seem to stop. I remember his long fingers stroking me, the way they felt smooth against my drenched, hot flesh, and the pleasure he sparked in me. I wonder what his cock will look like, if it will be big or small, thick or slender. I wonder how he'll fuck me.

I wonder if it will feel as good as this.

He'll make you do everything, a small voice in my head warns me. *He'll make you let him fuck your mouth, too. Your ass. He'll take all of you as payment.*

But with my fingers circling my now-swollen clit, it doesn't seem so bad. My mind feels foggy with pleasure, things that were once horrifying are now arousing me instead as my back arches. I resist the urge to push my fingers deeper inside of myself, my hips grinding a steady rhythm against my other hand now.

I can feel the mess between my thighs, my fingers sticky, drenched with an arousal that I know will humiliate me later. I'm dripping for a man who has bought me, who has told me I can't refuse, that he'll have me marched to the altar one way or another, all so he can claim my virginity under the sanctity of marriage for some unknown fucking reason. But right now, I don't fucking *care*.

For the first time in my life, all I care about is an orgasm, and I drive myself toward it relentlessly, the vision of Nikolai looming over me with his fingers pushed between my folds, the thing that finally pushes me over the edge.

I yank one hand out from beneath my skirt, clamping it over my mouth to muffle the ragged, filthy moan that tears free from my lips. I can smell my arousal on my fingers, *taste* it on my lips as I come hard, bucking against my hand as I orgasm for the first time in my twenty years of life. It feels like the pleasure will tear me apart at the seams.

This is what I've been missing.

And then the thought right on its heels—*what if he makes me feel like this?*

I shake it off, hot embarrassment rapidly replacing the flush of desire as the pleasure fades, and I realize what I've done. I've given myself the first orgasm of my life while fantasizing about a man who's trapped me. Who's forcing me to the altar.

Who is turning the rest of my life into a prison, I'll never escape.

I sink my teeth into my lower lip—I taste the tang of my arousal from my fingers on it all over again. Tears of shame burn in my eyes, and this time I let them fall, streaming down my face as I lean back against the door and close my eyes, my shoulders, and then my entire body wracked with sobs.

I hadn't realized just how hard I'd clung to that promise of freedom until it was gone. How much I'd relied on the idea that I'd only have to endure belonging to someone for a little while, and then the rest of my life would be my own.

There's no chance of that now. Death is my only way out, and I realize with a fresh wave of shame that I very much want to live— even if it's not on my own terms.

I shouldn't care about that. I should want any way out of this that I can find. But apparently, my will to survive is stronger than I knew.

Exhaustion washes over me, and I feel my eyes close. There's a bed in the middle of the room, huge and comfortable and inviting, but I can't find the strength to get up. I can't even move.

The weight of the day crashes over me, and I slump against the door as I fall asleep where I sit.

Nikolai

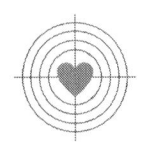

"What the *fuck* is wrong with you?"

There's a fury in my father's voice that I've never heard directed at me before, and I know I should be terrified. For him to break composure means that I've crossed a line too far. But I can't find it in myself to regret it.

Truth be told, I don't know what came over me. All I know is that I touched Lilliana Narokovna and knew I had to have her. I knew I wouldn't be able to take her home—take her *anywhere*—without making her mine. Without fucking her in every way available to me —which would be all of them.

I refused to force her. Refused to cross that line. *I will not become a man who violates women.*

There was only one way out of it that my muddled brain could come up with. So I spoke before I thought.

I said I would marry her.

No, I *demanded* that she be given to me to marry.

My father looks like he wants to murder me.

Hers has already been escorted out, promised a meeting with the Vasilev inner circle to discuss his promotion. Now I'm alone with mine.

No.

I'm alone with the *pakhan* of the Vasilev Bratva, and he's furious with me.

"What has come over you?" Egor demands. "You are the fucking *heir*! Your marriage is meant to make alliances. To bring another family into the fold and bend them to our will. To bolster our wealth and our power. *That* is the way of things. You know this. Marika knows this. And yet you say that you will marry this..this—"

"Be careful," I warn, and I don't recognize the voice speaking, or the words that come out of my mouth. No one would dare speak to the Vasilev *pakhan* like this, not even me, and yet I am. "You're speaking about my fiancée."

Egor's mouth tightens. I can see that he's considering the consequences if he murders me. What the repercussions for the family would be. If he can marry Marika to someone who would be willing to forsake their family name for ours and carry on the bloodline that way. I see all those thoughts and more cross his face, and somehow, I'm not moved.

I'm not afraid of my father. It's a strange thing to realize, especially at a time like this, when I can see he wants my blood.

"Explain it to me," he says, his voice low and dangerous. "Make me understand, *son*."

"You offered me a reward." My voice is every bit as tight and angry—but I'm as angry with myself as he is. I can't understand what came over me. It was a foolish thing to do. It made no sense.

"And *this* is the reward you seek? A worthless piece of cunt who will bring our family nothing but shame? I offered her to you to fuck, not to wed!"

"Careful," I warn again, looking him directly in the eyes. "She is my fiancée. The contract was signed in blood. Speak of her that way again, and the rest of your blood will join it."

I know what kind of threat that is. The consequences it could have. "Will the *pakhan* go back on his word?" I ask, each of mine sharp and cold. "Will you break a binding contract and send her home to her father? Or will I go to the altar in two weeks' time?"

"You know I can't allow you to do this without punishment." Egor's eyes narrow. "You've defied me, son. The first time in your life that you've chosen this path. I have to set you back on the correct one."

There's something almost like regret in his voice. Like he doesn't want to hurt his child. I can't quite believe that's true. I'd be more likely to believe it if it were Marika. I don't think he'd take pleasure in beating her.

I think he wants to remind me of my place. Always one rung below him, until he's six feet under the ground.

"I hope she's worth it," is all he says as he walks behind his desk, opening a drawer and pulling out a length of coarse, thick rope, knotted evenly all the way down it. "I best not hear a sound from you, son."

I reach for the buttons of my shirt without needing to be told. It's been many years since my father punished me. Not since I've been a man. But what I've done tonight could have earned me far worse.

I don't intend to let him know the pain this causes me. Just as I hope I can stop myself from taking it out on Lilliana later.

I just hope she's worth it, too.

―

The hot spray of the shower is painful as it washes the blood from my back, seeping into the cuts and torn flesh left from the knotted rope. My back is already bruising, turning purple and black, and I have a hot, violent need to take the same pain and inflict it on someone else. If we had any prisoners or anyone needing torturing, it would be an easy urge to find a release.

But the only man we had right now I dispatched earlier today.

My fingers itch for a blade, a pair of pliers—or something else. A paddle, a flogger, a cane. A woman squirming and begging as I take my pain and anger out on her soft flesh, but a woman who is willing nonetheless.

Even if it's because I paid her.

That, at least, I can satisfy. I won't even have to undress, so I won't have to endure the pitying look that the bruises on my back would earn, and result in further violence.

If there's one thing I can't fucking stand, it's pity.

I dress stiffly after I get out of the shower, throwing the blood-stained towel in the trash. Black pants and a black shirt to hide any further bleeding. Pain radiates through me every time I move, but I lean into it. Accept it.

Life is pain. I'm no exception to that, not always. In our world, you get what you take. Violence is a requirement, not an option. I took something more than what I was meant to be offered, and I should have known there would be consequences.

I call my driver and tell him where to take me. One of our family's clubs, a particular place called the *Ashen Rose*. A dungeon where the women who work there will accept anything. Some clients have more depraved desires than I could ever imagine having. They appreciate when men like me show up, men whose kinks lean towards violence, but not as…creative as others.

When I walk in, I'm pleased to see that one of the women working is my favorite—a pretty, slender blonde who calls herself Asha and looks like a porcelain doll, but can take more than any other woman I've ever been with—and genuinely enjoys it. I've rarely seen a woman come so hard on the other end of a flogger. She sees me and sways towards me, her eyes widening with pleased recognition.

"Nikolai." Her voice is a sensual purr. She's wearing black latex from her tits to her toes—literally. She's encased in a corset, a garter belt, and a strip that runs between her thighs, those same thighs dipped into tall black latex boots. She looks like a dominatrix, which tells me that's the side of this she's working tonight.

She's also the only woman I've ever met who gives as well as she takes. Not that I've experienced it—I don't get off on receiving. But I've heard.

"I'm a domme tonight," she tells me, and I can hear the regret in her voice. She likes when I come asking for her. She always has.

"You'll be what I want you to be, so long as I'm paying," I tell her, and I see the instantaneous reaction she has to that, the flush on the high points of her sharp cheekbones. Asha is one of the few women who I know genuinely wants me. It's what keeps me coming back to her.

But I still don't know that she'd fuck me if I didn't pay her. *Never give away what you can make a dollar from.* I know that's her mantra. I know her very, very well.

"It's your club, boss," she says with a seductive smile, her tongue tracing the edge of her full, red-painted lower lip. "If you want me to swap the latex for lace, I can do that. Or whatever else you'd like."

Anything I'd like. I know that's what's on offer here. I've been taking advantage of it for years. I *own* this place—or at least my family does—and by virtue of that, every woman who works here.

Lilliana springs into my mind, unbidden. A scared little rabbit in a trap, but a defiant one. I'll own her too very soon, by the letter of the law—and according to the law of the Bratva, I already do. But I know she doesn't see it that way.

She's going to fight me until I teach her to submit, until I make her *want* it, and the appeal of that has my erection dying before Asha's seductive expression can bring it to life.

"Actually, on second thought, don't let me take you away from your night's work." I give her a casual, affable smile. "I know how much those Chicago politicians will pay to have you step on their balls, after all. I see the books."

"Hopefully, you don't see the little bit extra I pocket, then." She flashes me a flirtatious wink, as if she doesn't give a shit that I turned her down, but I can see the hint of disappointment on her face. I know she wanted me. Normally, that would be enough for me to take her downstairs and give us both what we want and need.

But tonight, it's not what I want. The woman I want is back in my family mansion, locked away in one of the many bedrooms, awaiting the day we say *I do*. And while I don't intend to give in to temptation and fuck her tonight, I do want to see her.

I *need* to see her, and that's something I'm going to have to figure out what to do with, before it gets me into more trouble than it already has.

"Have a good night," I tell Asha, and she blows me a kiss as I leave, her expression unfaltering. I respect that about her—she hides her emotions as well as I do, keeps them locked up behind sex and seduction, as well as I keep mine locked behind the cold, brutal outer shell that I've so carefully honed. She'd never let me see her flinch, not for more than a second.

I tell myself to go to bed, as the driver takes me back to the mansion. Not to find Lilliana and look in on her. Better yet, I should have my driver take me to my penthouse on the Gold Coast, so there's distance between me and the woman who is not yet my bride.

But I don't like the idea of leaving her in my father's house while I'm not under the same roof. I don't *think* he'd touch her, not considering the rightful consequences if he laid a finger on my wife-to-be. But there's a part of me that wouldn't necessarily put it past my father to think himself above any consequences.

I want her to be safe. From him—and from me. It's an urge I don't understand, but it keeps me from telling my driver to take me elsewhere, all the way until I'm back in the familiar foyer of my father's mansion.

It's nothing, of course, to find out which room they gave her, or to get the key. No one would deny me anything here except my father, and he's already gone to bed. Thankfully, so has Marika. Once again, I can't stand the idea of facing her censure or dealing with her reaction if she's already found out what I've done.

I know part of my father's worry is that my rebellion will feed hers. That because I've done something outside of our traditions, she'll start to think that perhaps she can, too. That whatever marriage he's been crafting for her behind closed doors won't go as smoothly as he's planned.

I don't think Marika has that kind of rebellion in her. But I've been wrong before.

Before tonight, I wouldn't have thought I did, either.

Lilliana's room is on the third floor, towards the back of the long hall. I slide the key into the lock, turning the knob—and meet resistance.

I frown, confused, and push the door open. I hear a thump and a low moan, and I shove myself through the opening, peering down in the dim light to see a shape on the floor.

"What the fuck?" I realize she's crumpled on the floor, and my first terrified thought is that she's found some way to kill herself. That the idea of marrying me was so horrifying that she opted for another way out.

I crouch down next to her, fingers against her slim throat. I feel her pulse, like a trapped butterfly under her skin, and let out a breath as relief washes over me. I don't care about her—not like that—but it seems I care enough to not want her dead.

She lets out another low, soft moan, and I realize that she's not passed out—not exactly. But she's clearly so exhausted that even being pushed over from where she must have fallen asleep against the door hasn't woken her up. I look down at her and feel a wave of unfamiliar pity wash over me.

I wonder if she'd hate being pitied as much as I do.

She curls into herself, another of those low moans slipping from her lips, and my cock swells. It's easy to imagine her making that sound for a different reason, one that has to do with me. I feel myself lengthen along my thigh as I reach down, scooping her into my arms and lifting her off of the floor. She's still in the dress she wore to come here, and the fabric slides dangerously against her chest, threatening to reveal her breasts to me.

As I lift her against me, I smell the sharp tang of feminine arousal, and my brow furrows.

What the hell?

I carry her across the room, laying her back on the bed. Her head lolls to one side, her body sinking into the softness of the mattress, and I know I should cover her up and leave her like this. Anything else will only lead down a risky path, one that threatens to come very close to that line I've drawn for myself.

But I can still smell the scent of her. I *know* it's her, because I had her on my fingers earlier. I can still feel the slick, wet heat against my hand. She'd been angry and terrified, and to hear her tell it, so innocent that she'd never even made herself come. But she'd gotten wet for me. For *my* touch.

I want more of it. Desperately.

No woman has ever made me feel this kind of lust. This kind of *need*. My hope is that by legitimizing it, by making her my wife so that taking her to bed is no longer by force, I'll quell that hunger. I'll have her, and I'll grow bored of her, like everything else. I'll put a child in her, and then I'll go back to my own diversions, without ever having delved too deep into the kind of darkness there's no coming back from.

Fuck. The thought of my cum in her, taking root, has my cock aching. I reach for her hand before I can stop myself, bending over her sleeping body so I can breathe in the scent on her fingers, to find out if my suspicion is correct.

Oh fucking hell, it is.

I can smell her all over her fingers. I don't think she was lying when she said she'd never touched herself—I know when someone is lying, after many years of honing that particular skill—which can only mean one thing.

She hated what I had to do to her downstairs in my father's study. But it also turned her on enough that she couldn't stop herself from making herself come for the first time in her life.

I'm aroused and furious all at once. The thought of pretty, innocent Lilliana on the floor with her hand up her skirt, stroking her clit until she came all over her hand, has me throbbing to the point of pain. But at the same time, I'm angry beyond reason that she stole her first orgasm from me.

I'd had the chance to be the first one to make her come, *ever*, and now she's felt that pleasure. I won't get to see her surprise as she experiences it for the first time. I won't get to watch her discover it.

"I'm going to punish you for that," I murmur, and the words startle me. I've said them before, certainly, but to women who wanted to hear them, paid or otherwise. I've said them in the middle of a scene, negotiated and agreed upon, with a safeword in place. I've never said it to an innocent, defenseless, *sleeping* woman, locked in a room in my house, with nowhere to escape from me.

The thought makes my cock *ache*. I can feel pre-cum dripping from the tip, sliding down my shaft, creating an excruciating friction in my jeans as my shaft slides along the fabric it's trapped in. It feels like I've been hard all fucking night, since the moment I saw her walk through that door, and I don't know if I'm going to be able to make it back to my own room without doing something about it.

I won't fuck her. Not like this. I'll wait until our wedding night if it fucking kills me, just so I can live with myself. But I need *something*.

I slip my hand under her skirt, and I feel the damp patch of fabric beneath her. "Oh, you *filthy* girl," I groan, my cock throbbing as I reach to undo my buckle, so I can free myself. "I bet your pretty pussy is such a mess. Dirty girl."

The words slip out of my mouth, crooning, as I slide my fingers between her thighs. I'm right—she's fucking *soaked,* her entire pussy and her inner thighs drenched, sticky from it, and when I slip my fingers between her folds, I'm greeted by a goddamn *lake* of arousal.

"Oh *god*." I drag my fingers through her pussy as I free my cock hastily with my other hand, feeling her hips twitch as I stroke her clit. My cock springs free, the cool air of the room striking my swollen, heated flesh, and I draw my hand away from her as I use her wetness to lube my shaft, mingling it with my pre-cum as I wrap my fist around my aching length.

My left hand slips under her skirt, where my fingers were a moment before, and I find her swollen clit easily. I can't imagine how exhausted she must be to sleep through this, but though I can see the rise and fall of her chest, her breathing quickening a little as I slide my finger in slow circles over her sensitive flesh, she doesn't wake up.

Her full lips part, and she moans, softly. Her hips twitch under my hand, her clit throbbing, and my fist tightens around my cock, stroking as my palm rubs over my swollen head.

I'm going to come so fucking hard, and I'm going to leave the taste of it on her lips. A reminder of who owns her now. Who she belongs to—who she'll submit to.

She might have taken her first pleasure from her own hand, but I'll be the only man who ever gives it to her. And before the first night is over—

I'll have her begging for more.

I stroke myself faster, my balls tight and aching. It takes everything in me not to climb onto the bed with her, to push her thighs apart and her skirt up, to put my mouth on that sweet wet pussy and make her come with my tongue before I fuck her hard. If she were anyone else, I would. If she were *willing*.

But she's *mine*. My innocent, defiant bride-to-be—and I refuse to be ruled by my desire for her. I refuse to let her make me do things that will make me hate myself later. That will make me wish I'd chosen otherwise.

This is bad enough. I know that, even as I feel her squirm under my hand in her sleep, her body arching towards her pleasure unawares. But I need *something*. And from the way her body is responding, so does she.

My cock is rock-hard, on the verge of bursting. I slide my hand along it in long, firm strokes, passing over the head with each slide, at the very edge of my pleasure. I'm so fucking close. It's like I never jerked off in the shower today. Like I haven't come in months. I think of her arousal on my fingers, of her rubbing herself to her first frantic orgasm, of that same wetness on the shaft of my dick right now, easing my hand as I stroke myself, and I rock forward as I feel the pleasure well up, my cock hardening and swelling as I come in my fist—

—and I feel her come, too. *God*, I feel her come. I feel her clit throb under my fingers, feel her clenching lower down, and I can imagine what that would feel like around my cock. It sends another jolt through me, my cock spasming in my fist as I feel her pussy flood over my hand, and somehow through it all, she never wakes up.

As far as she knows, she's having a wet dream. One that she'll wake up from wondering what happened and what the taste on her lips is.

The thought sends one more jolt through my cock, cum arcing over my hand and hitting the side of the duvet, splattering over her skirt. Another shudder goes through me at that—the sight of my cum streaked over the otherwise pristine fabric of her dress—and then I see something else, too.

A streak of blood over the pale blue.

I reach for her hand again, my half-hard cock still outside of my slacks as I look at her thumb in the dim light where it was cut. It's scabbed over now, and I know I'm tempting fate, risking her waking up and finding me here.

I don't want her to know how much I want her. The power she seems to have over me.

If all goes according to plan, I'll have it out of my system before she ever realizes it.

But I can't stop myself. I lean down, pressing my lips against her wounded thumb, sucking it lightly into my mouth until I taste her blood.

I wipe my hand against her skirt, more cum streaked across it. And then I take my fingers, still damp with my release, and press them against her lips. I trace my cum over that full lower lip, seeing it glisten in the low light of the room, and I let go of her.

I reach for a soft blanket at the foot of the bed, and cover her up—as much to keep myself from touching her further as out of any sense of wanting to care for her. She already feels like an addiction. Like she could make me do things whether I wanted to or not—overcome my better sense.

She has twice already, in just one night.

My entire body feels as if it's throbbing. It takes physical effort for me to back out of the room, leaving her there as I walk out, closing the door and locking it behind me.

If only it could keep me out, as well as it keeps her in.

I was supposed to enjoy her and then discard her, nothing more. If I'd been able to do that, it would have made things a great deal easier for me.

But there's something about her that made me speak out. That made me determined to marry her, instead of only fucking her. And deep down, despite my efforts to deny it, I know it's something more than just my determination to keep myself from crossing a line that I can't ever go back from.

She'd displayed strength and bravery in the face of something terrifying. But she's fragile, too. I can see it. It made me want to protect her, as I've wanted to protect very little in my life.

It's a dangerous thing to want, in a world like mine.

For her and I both.

Lilliana

I wake up with my head aching, feeling as if I've been run over by a truck. My entire body hurts, and I rub one hand over my face, licking my dry lips. They taste oddly salty, and I wonder if I cried in my sleep. I feel—strange.

I remember having strange dreams of being touched—pleasurable, fretful dreams that make me feel hot and embarrassed remembering them. I push myself upright, tossing the blanket that I must have covered myself up with at some point off of me, and I gape down at my skirt as I see the utter mess on it.

Did I touch myself again in my sleep? It's the only conclusion I can think of, that I'd rubbed myself to another orgasm on account of the dreams—or that that's where the dreams came from—and gotten my own arousal all over my skirt.

My face flames hotter still, and I reach for the zipper of my dress, wanting to be out of it. I don't know what's come over me. In the space of one night, I've gone from having spent my entire life dreading and abhorring the thought of sex to seemingly being ravenous for pleasure. If I didn't know better, I'd think they drugged me with something.

But I didn't eat or drink a single thing since I left home last night. My stomach rumbles, reminding me of that fact, and my mouth is still dry as sandpaper. I glance towards the door on the left side of the room, hoping that it leads to a bathroom.

I desperately need a shower, and to pee.

To my relief, it does. I turn on the water to let it heat up as I use the bathroom, splashing cold water on my face afterward and looking at myself in the mirror. I'm slender to the point of skinniness, but other than that, I can't find anything objectionable about my appearance. I also can't find anything particularly thrilling, the kind of thing that would drive a man like Nikolai to make the kind of decision that he made last night.

One that I suspect isn't in line with the choices he was expected to make.

The hot water is a relief. I stay in the shower for as long as I can, washing my hair and making thorough use of the expensive toiletries lining the shelves. When I've scrubbed myself pink, I sit on the tiled floor, letting the hot water run over me until it turns cool. It's not until then that it occurs to me that I have nothing to wear other than the stained dress I left on the bedroom floor.

Surely Nikolai doesn't intend for his wife to go around naked?

I dry off with one of the fluffy, thick towels—one benefit of my imprisonment, at least, is the improved amenities—and wrap it around myself as I walk back into the bedroom…and stop dead in my tracks.

There's a very pretty blonde girl in the middle of the room, a few inches shorter than me and very petite, with blue-grey eyes that instantly remind me of Nikolai. She's setting a pile of clothes on the rumpled bed, and when she looks up and sees me, a smile flashes across her face.

"You must be Lilliana! I'm Marika, Nikolai's sister." She gestures towards the clothes. "I brought something up for you to wear. I think we're probably close to the same size. Not exactly—but close enough, until your things can be brought over from your house. I think Niki is sending men over to collect them today. We're going shopping, too, so if you want to buy anything new—"

She pauses, taking in the expression on my face. "I know what Niki did last night," she says gravely. "*Papa* is pretty pissed about it. But he won't break a binding contract. So you're going to be my sister-in-law." She presses her lips together. "I know this is probably not what you wanted. Actually, I'm sure of it, from what I've overheard. But Niki isn't a bad man—"

"They said the wedding was in two weeks." I cut her off, unable to stand her cheerful monologue any longer. "Is that still what's happening?"

Marika sinks her teeth into her lower lip, worrying at it. "Yes," she says finally. "And I've been put in charge of getting you ready. We're going shopping today—"

"You said that." I know I'm being rude, but I can't bring myself to care. I don't know how I'm expected to spend a day picking out things for my unwanted wedding with a complete stranger as if nothing were wrong. "Why doesn't someone just plan it and tell me where to show up? That's about as much choice as I've been given so far."

"I know." Marika gives me a sympathetic look, and somehow I hate that even more than her cheerfulness. I don't want her pity. I don't want that from any of them.

I'd prepared myself to be a fuck-toy for the *pakhan*. I'd even braced myself for the possibility of being his mistress for a period of time—having to attend events on his arm, pretend to be pleased by his attentions. But in the end, it would have bought my way out of all of this.

I wasn't prepared to get married. I hadn't planned on becoming a part of this fucking family. And I sure as hell don't want to be

Marika's sister-in-law, no matter how sweet she probably is. I don't want to be close to any of these people.

My entire life has revolved around this family and how I was going to be used by them. Now I've been given a life sentence, and I refuse to plaster a smile on my face and whistle *here comes the bride,* all the way to my doom.

"Niki has given us an unlimited budget," Marika says, as if that makes things any better. As if the extravagance of the wedding somehow changes the fact that I'm getting married by force.

"Can I use it to buy back my freedom?" I snap, and a shadow crosses Marika's face, but she doesn't respond. She just looks at me, and the sympathy in her eyes is almost as bad as if she'd told me to go fuck myself.

"I'll make sure to spend as much of it as possible, then," I tell her crossly, and her face softens, the smile returning, as if we're co-conspirators.

"Perfect." She nudges the clothes. "Get dressed. There's breakfast downstairs. I'll be waiting outside for you; I'll show you around."

She's definitely nothing like her brother, I think to myself as I pick through the pile of clothes. Nikolai had been terse and controlled last night, only those stormy eyes of his hinting at any emotion. Marika is as bubbly as popped champagne.

The jeans she brought up fit me, although they're several inches too short, so I roll them up instead, slipping my feet back into the high-heeled sandals I wore last night, despite the complaints from my sore toes. I slip into a black sleeveless chiffon shirt that fits me as well. It's also a little short, but the jeans are high-waisted, so all in all, I look at least decently put-together. I won't be an embarrassment to myself, at least.

"Can someone throw my dress from last night away?" I ask Marika as I join her outside. "I really don't want to ever look at it again."

"It can be dry-cleaned, if you—" she looks at my expression and shrugs. "Sure. I can tell the maid assigned to your room to toss it."

I don't ever want to see the dress again. Just the thought of it makes my face burn hot with shame, remembering what I did. What *he* did to me in it, in front of his father and mine in that office.

At first, I don't think I'm going to be able to eat. Marika takes me to what I'm guessing is the informal dining room—the table could still seat at least twelve people, and the room is huge, decorated lushly with heavy curtains drawn back at the windows and carved chairs around the mahogany table—but it's not as grand as what I imagine their dining room for dinner parties must be.

I've never been in a mansion like this before. This room alone could fit more than half of the apartment I grew up in inside of it. I've also never seen so much food—and definitely not food that I'm allowed to have.

There are covered plates across the table, and Marika takes the lids off, peering at them. There are two place settings—one for her and one for me, I imagine, and I stop a few feet away, feeling uncertain and confused.

"Is Nikolai not eating with us? Or your father?"

Marika laughs. "*Papa* gets up very early in the morning. He has breakfast alone, usually. He has ever since our mother passed away. Niki usually eats on the go. Just a protein shake or whatever he has on the way to the gym." She rolls her eyes. "So it's usually just me and all of this. I'm glad to have the company. Sit down."

She points at the chair, and I gape at the food, astonished at the waste that must occur every day. There's no way a girl as petite as Marika eats more than a small portion of this.

"Eat whatever. Help yourself." She gestures again, looking at me as if she doesn't quite understand my reaction, and then starts to spoon scrambled eggs mixed with some kind of cheese and herbs onto her plate.

My stomach growls audibly, and I swallow hard, reaching for my plate. I've been on my father's strict diet for so many years that I don't know what to do with the literal buffet in front of me. "Nikolai is fine with this?"

Marika looks at me as if I have lost my mind. "Why would he care?"

Because he won't want his wife to get fat. The thought crosses my mind, even as I realize exactly how ludicrous it is. I have a long way to go before I could even come close to that—and even then, I'd be fit as long as I kept up with my usual routines. I'm painfully thin now, and exercising according to the regimen I've been on for as long as I can remember usually leaves me dizzy and tired.

He wanted me like this.

"Lilliana." Marika blows out what sounds like a frustrated breath. "Eat. We have appointments to get to."

I put some of the eggs and a piece of dry toast on my plate, picking at it. Even as hungry as I am, my anxiety closes my throat and makes it hard to swallow anything. None of this feels real.

Last night, I was bracing myself for the loss of my virginity. Now I'm staring down the barrel of an unwanted marriage.

I couldn't have imagined how quickly things would change.

Marika plows through her own plate of food, and then waits for me until it's clear that I'm not going to eat anything else. She pulls out her phone, tapping out a quick message, and then gets up. "The driver will be around in a minute. Let's go."

The driver. I feel a moment's small satisfaction as we walk out to the steps in front of the mansion, and a black SUV pulls up in front of us. It's exactly the kind of thing my father aspires to—a driver and a car, being chauffeured around, enough money to spend without limits. I don't want this—but there's something just the tiniest bit vindicating about the fact that I'm getting this kind of treatment, when my father had intended for nothing other than to sell my body to gain a pathway to it for himself.

Marika sits across from me, and she reaches over to a wooden panel, pressing it open. I see dry ice and small bottles of champagne and orange juice. She pulls out two flutes, handing one to me as she makes herself a mimosa, and then fishes out another of each bottle and passes them to me.

"Maybe you're not feeling very celebratory," she explains, "but it'll take the edge off one way or another."

I can see that hint of sympathy in her eyes again, and I look at the small bottle of champagne. I've never had the opportunity to drink like this. I've never been allowed. A flush of rebellion washes over me, and I think, *why not?*

It's not as if Nikolai told me I can't drink. And who cares, anyway? What could he do to me that hasn't already been done, or won't be done very soon?

My father isn't here to tell me no, and I don't belong to him any longer.

Fuck it. I make the mimosa and take a long sip.

The champagne bursts over my tongue. It's dry and tart, tinged with the sweetness of the orange juice, and I'm pretty sure it's one of the best things I've ever tasted.

"You like it?" Marika grins at me, and I realize she's enjoying this—introducing me to new things.

She seems excited to have a sister. A friend, even. It makes me feel a little guilty for how cold I've been to her. It's not her fault my father groomed me to sell to her family, or that her brother is forcing me into an unwanted marriage.

She's probably going to be forced into one, too, eventually.

"It's good," I tell her, and she smiles. "Really good."

"Well, there's plenty in here, if you want another." She tips her glass back, draining it, and then clinks it against mine. "Here's to spending my brother's money."

Three mimosas in by the time we reach the bridal boutique, the world is a little fuzzy around the edges, and I feel a little more capable of handling what's ahead of me—until I see the wall of white silk and lace surrounding me when we step inside, and I feel my stomach churn.

"I can't do this," I whisper to Marika, as if she's my confidant instead of a part of the enemy's plan, and she gives me that sympathetic look again.

God, I hate feeling pitied.

"You can." She pats my hand. "We all have to deal with it, eventually. My turn is coming up soon enough, I'm sure."

Except I wasn't supposed to have to! I want to scream at her. I'm not the daughter of an influential family born to this fate. I was supposed to have my freedom. I was only supposed to serve a term, not a life sentence.

I wish I knew why this was happening to me.

Marika is speaking to one of the sales associates, a pretty brunette woman with a cheerful smile on her face.

"Ah! Ms. Narokovna. We're expecting you. You and Ms. Vasilev, come with me, please."

She takes us back to a private dressing room, already filled with sample gowns. There are several pink velvet chairs scattered around a three-way mirror, a rack filled with sashes and veils, and a bar cart with the fixings for more mimosas on it.

"Feel free to enjoy," the brunette woman—I see a name tag that says Anita on it—says, waving her hand at the bar cart. "I'll be back in just a moment; I think Denise is helping you today."

Denise, I find out a few minutes later, is the owner of the boutique—which makes sense, I suppose, since I'm marrying a Vasilev. I have no doubt she was informed just how much money was probably going to be spent here today.

I'd had reservations about it, but with the champagne fizzing in my blood, I start to wonder just what the most expensive dress here *is*, and whether or not I might like it.

"Look at that." Denise beams at me. "Anita already filled up a room for you. We'll see if you like any of these, and if not, we've got a lot more for you to try. You have the run of the place, so whatever you see, feel free to let me know, and I'll grab it for you."

I realize as she's speaking what she means—why the rest of the store is empty. At first, I just thought we had the first appointment of the day, but then it dawns on me that the store has been closed for us. This is a *private* appointment. I literally have the run of the boutique.

Why is he doing this? I don't understand. I can't understand his motivations for marrying me at all, but spoiling me like this? It makes no fucking sense. He could have sent his personal assistant to give someone my measurements, pick something out, and told me to wear it.

I don't understand Nikolai Vasilev at all, and the more I realize that, the more terrified I am of him. I can't fight against what I don't understand.

"You have a lovely figure. I can't think of anything that won't look good on you," Denise praises as I strip out of my jeans and top and stand there anxiously while she takes the first dress off of the hanger. I'm wearing borrowed underwear, too, which feels uncomfortable, but at least they're clean. Marika is apparently almost my cup size—the bra only gapes a little at the corners. Strapless, which was thoughtful, considering she knew we'd be shopping for wedding dresses.

Under other circumstances, I might actually like her. I might want to be her friend—although I've never *had* a friend, so I wouldn't even really know how to go about it. But I can't let myself forget that she's Nikolai's sister. She's not my ally, no matter how kind she seems.

I step into the first dress Denise holds out for me, a slinky off-white satin gown that clings to me, highlighting just how very thin I am. I know she was bullshitting me when she said I have a lovely figure—there are plenty of silhouettes that won't suit me. But I'm here with Vasilev money, so she's going to suck up to me.

It feels strange. I've never been in that sort of position. I'm not sure I like it.

But if I'm marrying Nikolai, I'm going to have to get used to it.

I don't hate the dress. The neckline drapes over my slight cleavage, the gathered straps sitting flatteringly on either side of my sharp collarbones, and the skirt pools around my feet. I look a bit like a marble statue in it, I think, and I don't mind it.

It makes me think of what Nikolai said about me last night—calling me art so beautiful that I should only be seen by one set of eyes—and just as quickly, I'm not so sure I like it any longer.

Denise does up the last of the buttons in the back, clipping it so that it fits me perfectly, and then opens the door. "Go look in the mirror," she encourages, and I hear Marika's soft intake of breath as I step out.

"Oh, you look beautiful!" she exclaims, her mimosa glass tilting a little as she leans forward to look at me. "Try on a veil with it!"

Denise gets out a simple fingertip-length veil with a raw edge, sliding the comb into my hair as I stand in front of the mirror. I look like a bride; there's no doubt about that. It's magazine-perfect.

"Try on a few others," Marika encourages, seemingly realizing that I'm on the verge of saying this is the one just to be finished with the entire ordeal. It's on the tip of my tongue to say it anyway, but for some reason, I feel bad disappointing her.

So I go back into the room, let Denise take me out of the satin gown, and lace me into a strapless, corset-backed gown with a full skirt and lace applique spilling from the strapless bodice down the heavy satin skirt.

I don't like this one as much. The silhouette is too much over me, overwhelming my slender frame, swallowing me up. It occurs to me that maybe I should choose one like this instead. That perhaps I shouldn't give Nikolai the satisfaction of seeing me in a dress as perfect as the first one.

"I liked the first one better," Marika says pensively when I walk out. "Maybe try something with a more slender silhouette, but all lace? See how you feel about that?"

In the end, it comes down to three dresses—the draped satin one I tried on first, an all-lace pure white gown with scalloped lace straps, a sweetheart neckline and a trumpet skirt, and a strapless mermaid gown that's cream-colored heavy satin, with lace around the edge of the skirt. I try on all three of them again, at Marika's urging, and end up with the one I tried on first, along with the raw-edged veil Denise had suggested with it.

I didn't bother looking at any of the price tags. My jaw almost hits the floor when, after taking my measurements, Denise tells Marika the price of what seems like such a simple dress. But Marika whips out a heavy black credit card without blinking, handing it to Denise, and before I know it, she's whisked me out of the shop and onto the sidewalk.

"We should look for shoes next. Jewelry, maybe? You should have a piece for your something new. And then some clothes—I know Niki was sending men to get your old things, but you should pick out something new—"

She keeps chattering as we walk down the sidewalk, but my mind has already run off in a different direction. It occurs to me that we're downtown, in the middle of the city, a place I've never been allowed out into before. What's stopping me from simply running away? I don't have any money on me, but I could hitchhike, if I got far enough. It's not the safest plan of action, but is getting murdered by a person who picks up hitchhikers really worse than marrying the Vasilev heir?

I won't be able to run far in these heels, but if I can get away from Marika before she sees which way I've gone, I could stop and get them off—

I turn to see what's behind me, poised for flight—and see three muscled, black-clothed security guards behind us, guns at their hips, watching us both with an eagle eye.

My heart drops. I could try to run, but I don't think I'd make it far. They don't look like they can run very fast, but I've been surprised by less. If I could even make it around them. They all but block the entire sidewalk.

When I turn around, Marika is looking at me with that sympathetic expression that I'm rapidly coming to hate. "I know what you're thinking," she says, looping her arm through mine as she tugs me down the sidewalk, and I recognize it for what it is—as much a gesture to keep me in sight as it is a friendly one. "But there's no point. You wouldn't get far. My family owns most of this city, and the parts they don't are owned by men who would find you and hurt you to get back at us in ways that would make even my brother shudder." She pauses and stops in front of the jewelry store, her long-fingered, slender hands wrapping around mine as she looks up at me.

"I know you don't want to be a part of this, Lilliana," she says gently. "But you are now. You're betrothed to my brother, in ink and blood, in the tradition of our family going back generations. I know this isn't what you expected, but I promise you, my brother is not the evil man that I know you think he is. He can be brutal and violent, but that's the way of our world. He will try to do right by you—but you would do well to not make that any harder than it needs to be."

She looks at me as if she's pleading with me to understand, and I let out a long breath. "Fine," I tell her, the word coming out a bit more sharply than I intended, and Marika looks faintly relieved.

But inwardly, I take all the anger that had been dulled earlier by the champagne, now heating my blood again, and clench it into a hard ball, letting it settle in my gut.

I refuse to give in to this. I refuse to let Nikolai, or his family, think that they can change the rules of this game whenever they please and bend me to their will.

I can't escape this marriage. But I don't have to be fucking happy about it.

Lilliana

Without really meaning to, I do spend a considerable amount of money. I've never been out like this, with an unlimited credit card and an enabler at my side. I choose heels for my wedding dress without looking at the price tag and nearly pass out when I realize they cost over a thousand dollars. At the jewelry store, I found a sapphire bracelet that Marika insisted I buy, telling me that it would be both my something new *and* my something blue, and how could I resist what was, essentially, a two-for-one deal? The bracelet was beautiful—dark oval sapphire surrounded by delicate milgrain beading and linked by small round diamonds, and Marika's argument sounded convincing—until I actually purchased it, and it was nearly five figures.

I'd never owned anything so expensive. Never even *dreamed* of it. If I'd ever had anything worth almost ten thousand dollars, I would have sold or pawned it for a ticket out of Chicago, away from my father, and to get started somewhere else. The idea of wearing that much money on my *wrist* feels insane.

But I can't take it back. And even after that, Marika dragged me clothes shopping, insisting I should add some new things to my wardrobe. By the time we're finished, I'm at least able to change out of my high heels into a pair of designer sneakers, and that eases my guilt a little bit at how much we've spent today—easily fifteen thousand dollars on shopping in a single afternoon. I look at the new leather handbag next to me as the car drives us home, feeling slightly sick with guilt.

Until I remember that the man who gave Marika that heavy black credit card had his hand under my skirt last night before pronouncing that he was going to marry me, upending my entire life's plan in an instant, and the guilt vanishes.

After the life I've had leading up to this moment, maybe I deserve a fifteen-thousand-dollar shopping spree.

When we walk back into the mansion—sans bags, Marika informed me that a member of the staff would take them up to my room— we're immediately stopped by the black-suited man who greeted my father and me last night, who I now understand must manage the household. "You're wanted in the informal dining room, Ms. Narokovna," he tells me primly. "Ms. Vasilev, your father has requested your presence for dinner in his private sitting room."

What is this, a fucking palace? I feel like I'm in the middle of royalty, like I've been swept away into an entirely different century, let alone a different life, where all the things I grew up with and the world I knew doesn't apply any longer. I feel out of place, unsettled, and as I follow the black-suited man to the dining room, I don't know what to expect.

I'm left at the door, and as I walk in, Nikolai stands to greet me from where he is seated at the head of the table. There are two place settings at the ridiculously long table, as there was this morning, and I remember my father's lessons with no small amount of irony. I hadn't thought I would need the fucking lessons on table manners, but it looks like I was wrong.

I've been wrong about a lot of things in the last twenty-four hours.

"Lilliana." My name sounds sinful on his lips. Like he's savoring it. Heat pools in my belly unexpectedly, and I almost trip over my own feet, feeling my cheeks flame. *What the fuck is wrong with me?*

Nikolai shouldn't have this effect on me. I *hate* that he has this effect on me.

"I'm not dressed for dinner." I look down at my sneakers, my rolled-up jeans, and the shirt that threatens to ride up and expose a sliver of pale stomach despite the high waist. "I should—"

"It's fine. Truly. Please, sit down." He pulls out the other chair for me, and I see that he's dressed impeccably—black suit trousers tailored to him perfectly, flattering muscled thighs and an ass too perfect for any man to have, and a dark blue button-down that sets off his eyes. The top two buttons are undone, showing a hint of chest hair, and my mouth goes dry.

Seriously, what the hell is wrong with me?

"I really feel underdressed—"

"Lilliana." My name is sharper on his tongue this time, and my cheeks burn red. I sit down in the chair, hard, and try not to think of his hand under my skirt. His voice, whispering to me as he asked me if I'd ever touched myself.

You wouldn't be able to answer that question the same way now, would you?

"We got off on the wrong foot." Nikolai reaches for a decanter of red wine, pouring us both a glass. "I arranged a private dinner for us tonight. I thought perhaps we could get to know each other a little better."

"A date." My voice is flat.

"A dinner." He smiles at me, nudging the wine glass towards me. "I hope you like red. This is an excellent vintage."

I don't know what kind of wine I like. I don't say it aloud, because I don't really want him to know just how sheltered I am. I don't want him

Lilliana

to realize that I've been essentially kept a prisoner all my life, and now I'm just trading one type of cage for another.

I take a sip of the wine, trying to look as if I appreciate it. It *does* taste good, rich and earthy, but I couldn't say what the notes are, or if it's better than any other kind of wine.

The door opens, and a staff member sets salads in front of us, an arrangement of greens studded with dried berries and bits of soft white cheese. I look at the table setting in front of me, hoping I remember which fork to use.

If I choose the wrong one, Nikolai doesn't say anything.

"Did you enjoy your day out today with my sister?" He looks at me, taking a bite of his salad. "I know Marika can be—extroverted. But she's very excited to welcome you to the family."

"She was very nice." I keep my tone flat and diplomatic. "It was fine." *Fine* seems like the wrong word to use for a five-figure shopping trip, but a part of me wants to undersell it. I want Nikolai to see that I don't care about any of this. That I'm not impressed or won over.

Setting me free would impress me. Letting me go would make me like him. But that wouldn't be to his benefit, so it's not going to happen.

To my surprise, he makes no mention of the credit card or asks how much I spent, as if it truly doesn't matter to him. He takes another bite of his salad, as if considering what he wants to say.

"Is that something you like to do? Shopping?" He asks, and I have to fight not to roll my eyes at what feels like a painfully banal line of questioning.

"Why are you asking me?" I ask him bluntly, taking another sip of my wine. "Why do you care?"

Nikolai lets out a breath, tapping his fingers against the edge of the table. "I'd like to get to know my new wife-to-be before we're wed," he says simply. "What you like to do—your interests."

"Why? So you know if we're a good match?" My tone is every bit as mocking as I mean for it to be. "Did you not think to find out before we signed a fucking blood contract?"

I regret cursing as soon as the words are out of my mouth. That sort of tone would have earned me a slap from my father, or at the very least, a few days locked in my room. But on the other hand, I almost want to push him. I want to find out how violent my new husband is going to be. At least then, I can prepare myself for what's coming.

Nikolai doesn't flinch. "I understand this is difficult for you," he says finally. "But it could be worse. My father seriously considered taking you for himself."

I stare at him, realizing that he means it. He thinks this is better. "I would have rather had your father," I say finally, my tone cutting. "He would have fucked me and gotten tired of me. Then I could have left and lived my own life. This is life in prison, Nikolai. It's not a fucking favor."

Nikolai's mouth twitches. His fingers tap against the table, and I wonder if these are his tells. If this is how I know he's reaching the end of his patience. My father has those.

If I want to survive, I'd be wise to learn Nikolai's.

"My father would likely have killed you," he says finally. "You wouldn't be the first. And your father was very clear that he could have done anything to you that he liked. It all would have depended on his mood. And with that sharp tongue of yours, he might have cut it out of your mouth before he finished with you."

The way he says it, so dispassionately, as if he's talking about the weather, makes me feel sick. I can't take another bite of my salad, so I reach for the wine instead.

"Just let me go." The words come out before I can stop them. I don't want to beg him, but I also don't know how I can bear to stay here. This world isn't for me. This family is everything I despise. "I can't marry you. Please just let me go."

Nikolai looks at me for a long moment. "No," he says finally, and it feels like cold water thrown in my face. I think I actually flinch.

"You were given to me," he says after another moment. "I plan to have you in every way."

Again, he says it so calmly. As if it were a normal thing to declare over salads and wine. A normal thing to say as a staff member comes to sweep our bowls away and replace them with a soup course.

I feel like I've entered some kind of alternate dimension.

"You *will* be my wife, Lilliana," he tells me. "But I won't be cruel to you. I can be a cruel man, it's true, but not to my bride. You will be cared for. You will enjoy the privileges that the wife of the Vasilev heir should enjoy. You will have everything you want."

"I want my freedom."

"No one is keeping you prisoner."

"Can I refuse you?" I challenge. "Can I refuse this marriage, say it was contracted under duress? Will you give me money for a plane ticket anywhere I want to go? Let me start a new life and not come after me?"

He remains silent, and I shake my head, fighting back useless tears. "Then I'm a prisoner," I tell him flatly. "A gilded cage is still a cage."

"I won't hurt you." He says it as if it matters. As if it makes things better that he thinks he's a kind jailor.

"You're hurting me by keeping me here. By touching me when I don't want you to. By making me marry you."

"Don't you? Want me to, I mean." His voice lowers, like smoke wrapping around me, seductive over my skin. Reminding me of how he touched me in his father's study. How he tapped his finger against my clit, and I was wet for him in an instant.

I *hate* that he's reminding me of that. I hate him for it.

"Fuck you." I stare down at my soup, my appetite gone.

"You will." His voice keeps that same silken tone. "But not until we're wed."

"Why?" I look up at him. "Why not do it right now? Why not just bend me over and fuck me while your servants bring the main course? You could even eat dessert while you do it, if you can last that fucking long."

Nikolai lets out a sigh, as if I'm being a petulant child. "There's no need to make this harder, Lilliana."

"Fuck you," I repeat and drain my glass of wine.

He goes silent, and it drags out for several long minutes, interrupted only by the clink of a spoon against porcelain and the sound of wine glasses being refilled. "Did you go to college?" he asks finally, as if none of the preceding conversation happened. As if we're actually on a fucking date.

"No." The idea is laughable. My father would never have let me so far out of his sight. Never risked the chance that I might see some boy I liked and let him steal away my carefully guarded virginity. "I had a tutor at home. So I'm not an idiot."

He ignores that, as if it's immaterial to him. "Do you have any hobbies?"

"I thought about taking some up, once I could live my own fucking life." I narrow my eyes at Nikolai. "But no."

He presses his lips together, and I can see he's fighting for control again. There's something stormy in those blue-grey eyes once more, an emotion that I don't recognize. I wonder if he wants to hit me. I wonder if I'd prefer it if he did, over this manufactured courtesy.

"You've barely touched your food." He gestures at the plate in front of me, the perfectly arranged main course of lamb chops and garlic potatoes, whipped finely with a pool of rich gravy in the center, bordered by roasted vegetables. I've never had anything so fancy.

I don't want to give him the satisfaction of eating it.

"You like the wine." He looks at my glass. "Eat your dinner, and I'll refill it."

I glare at him. "I'm not a child being bribed to eat my dinner with the promise of dessert."

"Then stop acting like one." His voice deepens, growing harsher, and I see his control slipping, the brutal man beneath the mask. "You were brought here for a purpose, Lilliana. I have decided what that purpose will be. That is the way this world is."

"Not the world I want to live in."

He sighs. "Eat, Lilliana."

I want to refuse. But god, I'm so fucking hungry. I've been hungry my whole life. And the food in front of me looks like heaven.

I don't think a hunger strike will sway Nikolai. So I eat. He refills my glass, as promised. And when dessert comes, a whipped mousse with strawberries, I eat that too. There's really no point in fighting it. *Maybe if I get fat, he won't want me.*

"Come with me," he says when the dishes have been whisked away. "The night isn't over yet."

Oh, goody. I look at him with an expression that asks him how he possibly thinks that I would *want* that, but he ignores it, leading me away from the informal dining room and to the room that my father and I were first brought into to wait for the meeting. Or at least, I think it's the same one. It's hard to be sure in this massive house.

The fire is lit, crackling, and there's a thick, furry rug in front of it with a tray set up on the hearth. I realize that it's *not* the same room—my mind nonsensically remembers that there was no rug in the room we were taken to—and before I know it, Nikolai has led me to the rug and is tugging me down to sit on it next to him, reaching over to the wood and slate tray to uncork the bottle of expensive whisky sitting there.

"Do you like whisky?" he asks, and I look at him.

"I have no idea," I tell him flatly, suddenly very tired. I see the rest of my life stretching out in front of me, being this man's wife, and I wonder how long it will take before he gets tired of playacting. Before he comes around to the idea that we're enemies, and no amount of pretending to be the good guy will ever make me not hate him for taking away my chance at freedom.

"This is an especially good one," he informs me, pouring a little into each of the cut-crystal glasses. "My father prefers vodka, and I like it too, but a good whisky is a treat. Don't tell him I said that, of course—he hates the Irish, and the Scots, too, though the latter has never really set up business here, so I don't know why." Nikolai hands me the glass. "Notes of peat and vanilla. A little hot on the back of the throat, but it smooths out nicely."

There's that seductive note in his voice again as he says it, rubbing over my skin like the wrong side of velvet, and it makes me flush with a heat that I know isn't from the fire. I resist it, trying to push back. He can force me to marry him, but surely he can't force me to want him.

There has to be something that's within my control.

I take the glass from him. I want to refuse it, but something tells me that he'd push the issue—and I'm curious. He makes it sound like a delectable treat.

Choose your battles, Lilliana. The thought startles me, as I take the crystal glass out of his hand. If I'm going to have to marry this man, my life is going to be a long war of attrition, studded with battles that I suspect I will largely lose. If I fight them all, I'll be exhausted before we're six months in.

I take a sip of the whisky. It stings my tongue, a line of fire to the back of my throat, and I cough when I swallow it, the liquid sloshing in the glass as I lean forward sharply. Nikolai takes the glass out of my hand, his other hand suddenly on my back as I cough again, and I see a small smirk on his face as he looks down at me.

For a brief second, I almost think I see a glimmer of concern, too, through the amusement. But I'm certain I've imagined it.

"It can be a little startling the first time you try it." His voice is still smoky, a hint of innuendo there under the words, like he's not entirely referring to the drink. "I can get you wine instead, if you like."

"No, it's fine." I reach for the glass, suddenly determined to finish it. I don't want to give him the satisfaction of knowing I can't handle something so minor.

So much for picking your battles.

I take another sip, this time forcing myself to hold it in my mouth for a second before I swallow, bracing myself for the burn. I try to taste what Nikolai told me—the peat and vanilla, to feel the way it smooths out after that initial wave of heat.

The second taste doesn't give me that, or the third. But by the time I get to the fourth swallow, I start to taste what he meant.

It *is* good. Not my preferred drink, I still think I like the wine better —but there's something seductive and masculine about it that makes me feel more confident, sitting here and sipping the whisky next to this man. Like maybe I can hold my own in this situation.

Until I look at him and see his eyes on my mouth, and a tremor of fear ripples through me again.

Who am I kidding? Nikolai will take what he wants. He always will. I can fight against it—and I plan to—but all of this is just a game to make me think that he's something better than a brutal thug who has stolen a wife against her will.

I set the glass down. There's a bit of amber liquid in it still, but I've lost my taste for it.

"This is all unnecessary," I tell him flatly, gesturing at the drinks, the fire, and the thick, soft rug beneath us. "All of this—window dressing. I'd rather just get it over with, if there's no way out."

Nikolai's gaze flicks up to mine, and I see those blue-grey eyes darken. There's something heated and violent in them, something that I can see he's holding back, and his voice is low and rough when he speaks.

"And what do you mean by that, *krasivaya devushka?*"

Beautiful girl. I speak Russian as well as anyone else—my father is first generation, and he instilled the language into me along with English. I know it's meant to soften me. To compliment me. I refuse to let it do either.

I hold his gaze. It's the best I can do—to not back down. His full lips part, and he reaches out, his hand on the side of my face as he draws me towards him.

I should try to pull away, to jerk back and avoid his kiss. But I feel like a deer in headlights, frozen as he tugs me forward, his thumb brushing over my jaw almost delicately.

This man has had his fingertips inside of me, but this is our first kiss. It's all so ridiculously backwards.

And then his lips touch mine for the first time, and every thought flies out of my head.

I'll think later about how much I hate myself for that. How much I wish that the kiss—my first kiss—had been disgusting, that it had turned me off. But instead, I feel a flush of heat as his warm mouth presses against mine, the taste of whisky on his lips, on his tongue as he slides it over my lower lip. I hear his soft groan, deep in his throat, feel his other hand on my waist as he pulls me closer across the rug, and I'm suddenly so aware of *everything* that I feel—of the thick fur under my hands as I grip it, closing my hands into the rug so I don't give in to the urge to reach out and touch him, the flickering heat of the fire across from us and the intimate awareness of his big, muscled body so close to mine.

In two short weeks, that muscled body will be atop mine. He won't just be kissing me, he'll be *inside* me. He'll take what has been prepared for him, what I've been taught my whole life that I was meant to give over. But instead of one night, or a few—it will be forever.

The thought makes me tense up, chasing away the building pleasure, the sensation dancing over my skin as he started to deepen the kiss, his tongue teasing between my lips. My hands clench in the thick fur of the rug, and I stiffen. I pull away, all the budding softness in me gone.

I wait for him to push the issue. To pull me into his lap. To spill me back on the rug and strip away my clothing and take what he's claimed. When my gaze flicks downwards, I can see the evidence of how much he wants to, straining against the front of his finely tailored trousers. He's hard—and *huge*. I feel a different kind of fear, seeing the thick ridge against the fabric of his pants. I have no idea how that is going to fit inside of me. Especially not if I don't want him there.

I'm not an idiot. I have some idea of how this all works. And I know that it makes a difference if I'm turned on or not.

Well, you didn't have much of a problem getting wet when he fingered you in front of an audience, did you?

The thought sends a hot flush up my neck, racing into my cheeks, embarrassment overtaking me in an instant. I let go of the rug, wrapping my arms around myself as I turn away from Nikolai.

"I'm tired," I tell him stiffly. "It's been a long day. I'd like to go to bed now."

I expect him to refuse. To tell me that I'll go to bed when *he* says I will, when he's finished with me. But instead, he stands up without another word, holding out a hand to me.

I'm eye-level with his cock for a moment, and I stare for the briefest of seconds. I can't help it. It's not that I've never seen an aroused man before—but not *this* close. Not literally close enough for me to touch, if I wanted to.

But I don't want to. I don't.

When I look up, there's that smirk on his face again. He saw me looking. And I hate him all over again for it.

I don't take his hand. I push myself up to my feet and tilt my chin up defiantly, glaring at him. "I can find my own way back to my room."

"I'll walk with you anyway." There's a note of command to his voice that tells me this is not a battle to pick. I'll lose it, and it will be pointless.

So I let him walk with me. He doesn't touch me again, not even a hand on my back as we go up the curving staircase to the floor that my bedroom is on, not when he opens the door to let me in. He doesn't follow me inside, and I see the glint of a key in his hand as he stands there, looking at me.

He's going to lock me in again. I'm not surprised, but my stomach clenches with a mingled fear and anger that rattles me.

"You said you weren't keeping me prisoner." I nod at the key, and he shrugs, his face carefully blank.

"Maybe you convinced me otherwise." His eyes still have that stormy quality, but there's nothing else on his face. "Good night, Lilliana. I'll see you in the morning."

He closes the door, and a moment later, I hear the click of the lock.

Nikolai

My new bride-to-be is infuriating.

I hadn't expected her to be willing. But I had expected her to be pliable. I had expected her to come to us prepared for her fate. Even when I saw her in my father's study, I hadn't realized just how much spirit there was in her.

I'm quickly finding out. And the problem is that as maddening as she is, it doesn't make me want her less.

Normally I'm up quickly in the morning, dressed, and on my way to start my typical routine—which hasn't changed in years. But I find myself lingering in bed, thinking about my bride-to-be, considering that she's only one floor up and a few doors away. I've stayed at the mansion instead of my penthouse since she was brought here, unwilling to leave her so close to my father without my presence there.

I feel possessive, protective over her already, and it's a feeling that's so wholly unfamiliar that I don't know what to do with it.

I've thought more than once about visiting Asha. She'd be willing—eager, even, to help me drain away the tension and built-up lust that

Lilliana has been making steadily worse with every day that I see her. But every time I consider going to the dungeon and enjoying the company of my favorite submissive, I find that the lust tapers off. It fades, and I don't fucking understand it.

There's never been a moment in my life where I've been a one-woman man. I've never had a fucking *relationship*. I've had women I fucked for an extended period of time on and off—Asha is one of them—but I've never fucking *dated* anyone. There have always been multiple women I've been seeing at once. The idea that one woman could make me want her so much that the idea of anyone else disinterests me is ludicrous.

But every time I get hard, all I can think of is Lilliana. Her smart mouth and her soft pussy, how wet she got against my fingers despite herself. How I can put both of those to use, once she's my wife. How I'll make her mine, how I'll make her *beg* for me before I'm finished with her—on our wedding night, if I can manage it. I want to make her realize how completely she belongs to me from the very first night.

It's made me feel like a fucking horny teenager. I haven't used my own hand so much in years—there's no point, when a willing woman is a phone call or a short drive away. But I find myself waking up every morning for the two weeks between signing that contract and our wedding day with a hard, aching cock that refuses to deflate until I wrap my hand around it, stroking myself almost resentfully until I come in my fist. And it's not just the mornings, either.

I've kept a steady routine for years. I get up, grab breakfast to go, and go to the gym. Afterward, I address whatever business my father has for me, whatever meetings I need to attend, or people that I need to pay a visit to. Later, sometimes there are business dinners, and sometimes there's time to relax—which means a night out with a good dinner, good drinks, and a woman to warm my bed by the end of the night…or a visit to a place where I can indulge my darker tastes.

Now, it feels disrupted. The gym is a good distraction from the constant, low-level burn of arousal that Lilliana seems to have sparked in me. I find myself pushing harder than ever—but by the end of it, I find myself in the shower, hand fisted around my cock again as I imagine her pressed against the tiles, her smooth pale skin under my hands as I fuck her hard and fast, her undoubtedly musical cries of pleasure filling the air.

I'll be past this soon enough, I tell myself as I finish with a groan, cum splashing over the tiles as I think of the night I slipped into her room, the way I left a little of the taste of me on her lips. *I'll marry her and fuck her, and then I'll put her out of my head.*

I'll exorcise whatever the fuck this is, and things will go back to normal.

The most infuriating thing about her is how she throws every single thing I do to try to make this easier on her back in my face. I said I'd marry her because I knew I couldn't refuse my father's 'reward,' and I knew I wouldn't be able to keep my hands off of her once I took her away. It didn't matter where I stashed her. I could have sent her to fucking Antarctica, and I'd be on a plane the next day to fuck her. There was nowhere far enough away.

There was only one way to keep myself from violating her in an unforgivable way and keep from being on the wrong end of my father's wrath. I'd known he would be angry about the offer of marriage, but refusing the reward and appearing ungrateful, especially in front of a nothing piece of shit like Narokov, would have been worse. It was the only solution, so far as I could see.

But Lilliana can't seem to grasp that. That sharp-tongued conversation at our first dinner together wasn't the end of it. Since then, I've tried a few different ways to get her to open up. To realize that my intent in all of this, is to prevent her being hurt as much as possible.

I've arranged a few more private dinners. Tried to set up a night for the two of us in the private theater in the mansion with a movie.

Attempted to do things that I've never even fucking considered doing for a woman before, just to soften the blow of this for her. To soothe it, until we can consummate the marriage, I can fuck her out of my system, and then she can settle into the life of being the pampered and ignored wife of the Vasilev heir.

It seems like a good bet for her. She'll want for nothing. She'll have everything she desires, without having to indulge my company or my cock, once I'm sick of her. I don't understand why she's so fucking pissed about it all.

For the last week, I mostly leave her alone. She both makes me want to fly into a rage and fuck her senseless every time I see her, and I decide it's better for us both if we have some space before the wedding day. I planned to ignore her entirely until I see her walking down the aisle.

But two nights before the wedding, I end up standing in front of her door again, even though I know better. Even though I know this is only going to end up leaving me both angry and unsatisfied.

I knock heavily on the door, and for a moment, I think she's already asleep. It doesn't matter; I have the key. But a few seconds pass, and I hear her sharp voice through the wood.

"You know it's fucking locked, right? If you want to come in, you have to open it."

I slip the key into the lock and push the door open. "I was trying to be a gentleman, little rabbit. But I can come in unannounced if you like." I don't bother hiding the innuendo in my words, and I see her flinch from where she's sitting, curled up in a chair by the window with a book in her lap. "I see someone brought you something to do."

"Marika was nice enough to bring me something to read. She asked me what I like, even."

"I've tried asking what you like." I glance at the book. It's a romance novel. I try to summon some kind of disdain for it, but all I feel is a sort of vague curiosity about why she'd choose that for her reading material. *Is she trying to get an idea of what's coming in a few days? Imagining a different kind of future for herself, one where she ends up with a hero instead of a villain?* I'd gotten the impression from her that she had no interest in romance at all.

"Not because you really care." She sets the book down, looking up at me with a flat, bored expression on her face.

"And you think Marika does?"

She shrugs. "She does seem to actually give a shit, yes. I think she likes having me around. She seems—lonely."

"Maybe I like having you around."

Lilliana snorts. "I piss you off. You think I can't tell? You don't want me here. You don't want to marry me. And I can't for the life of me understand why you are."

Something dark and heavy spirals through me, filling my veins like smoke. She's been driving me insane for going on two weeks now, making me angry and aroused and driving me up the fucking wall. I've kept a hard, tight grip on it—and myself—but now, just on the wrong side of too many expensive whiskies and with the knowledge that in two more nights, I'll be showing her a different use for her smart mouth, I feel my control wavering.

I stalk towards the chair, and I see the brief moment where her defiance wavers too, a flicker of uncertainty on her face. I grab onto that as I loom over her, hands on the arms of the chair as I look down into her lovely, delicate face, illuminated by the light from the lamp next to her.

"Let's get this straight, Lilliana," I growl, trying my best to keep the words from blurring together, the whisky swimming in my head. "*I* am the one in control here. You can fight me all you like, but in two days, you *will* be my wife. Nothing is going to change that. *You* can't change that. And once you are mine, I won't have to feel bad any longer about what I'm going to do to you. Do you understand what I'm saying?"

I swear I feel a quiver go through her at that, vibrating in the air between us. I swear I can see her breath catch in her throat, like she fucking wants it, like saying that turns her on. I wonder if I slid my hand down her tight leggings and under her panties right now, if she'd be wet.

The thought makes my cock twitch and swell, a throb of need pulsing through me.

She tilts her chin up, her bright blue eyes glaring into mine. "Do you want to hear what *I* know, Nikolai?" she asks, her voice soft and sharp, and I smirk, looking at her soft, plush lips as she speaks.

"Sure," I tell her, half-mockingly. "Tell me what you think you know, little *krolik*. Say what you want to now, because in two days, those pretty lips will be around my cock."

She tries not to flinch at that, and fails. "You can force me to marry you," she hisses sharply. "You can make me be your wife. But you can't make me love you. And I will *never* belong to you."

I laugh at that, a short, sharp bark of a sound. I can't help it. "I don't want you to love me, pretty little rabbit," I tell her, reaching up to touch her cheek lightly. I can feel her stiffen, trying not to flinch away. "I don't care if you do. But you *will* belong to me. You can do what you like with your heart; I don't give a shit about it. But the rest of you—"

I drag my gaze slowly down her body—down her pretty face, her pert breasts in the tight tank top she's wearing, noticing that she's not wearing a bra. I can see the soft, small shapes beneath the thin fabric, her nipples pressing softly against it, and my fingers itch with the desire to touch her, to pluck the sensitive flesh until it's taut and stiff, until she's begging me for more.

My eyes flick lower, to the apex of her thighs, where I suspect she's warm and wet right now, no matter how much she'd deny it. "I'm going to show you all the ways that a man like me can use a girl like you," I tell her, my voice rasping as I look back up at her face. "You will be mine, in every way that matters. You and I will say our vows, and sit at our reception, and dance and cut a cake and eat our wedding meal, and then I will whisk you away for the night, and I—"

The words stick in my throat, a fierce arousal throbbing through me at the thought of it. I want it *now*, to yank her out of the chair and bend her over, my fist wrapping in her hair as I drag that tight fabric down her hips and thighs and thrust my aching cock into her. It would feel so fucking good. I've never denied myself anything I wanted like this before, not in my entire life. I've never had to.

But if I do this now, if I take her before our wedding night, I'll cross the line that I've determined separates man from monster. I'll hurt her in an unforgivable way.

Somehow, I leash that desire again. I look down into her delicate, defiant face, and I let go of the chair, stepping back an inch, and another, until I feel like I can breathe again.

I see her gaze flick down to the front of my trousers, the way her eyes widen briefly, seeing the force of my arousal. I doubt she's ever seen a cock before in person, let alone one of my size.

"I'm going to fuck you," I tell her, low and rough, and I see her eyes widen a little more. She's afraid. *Good*. She needs to be. She needs to understand that whatever her father taught her when it came to men like me, he should have taught her how to keep a better leash on her tongue. "On our wedding night, and as many nights as I want to, afterward. *However*, I please. And you will not tell me no. You will *enjoy* it."

She laughs. I can't fucking believe it. She tilts her head back a little and laughs.

"Of course, that's what you're going to do," she tells me, her tone the one that's almost mocking now. "But you can't make me enjoy it, Nikolai. You can't make me want it. That's the one thing you can't do."

I wonder if she knows how wrong she is. She must, after what happened in the study—after how wet she was on my fingertips, even though I know a girl like her would never have wanted that to happen. She must know that I control more than just whether or not she agrees to marry me.

But she *looks* as if she believes it. Or maybe she's just forcing herself to try.

"You will be the wife I need and want," I tell her flatly, pushing the arousal out of my tone. I deliver it like an edict, a command, because I have to put some distance between us now, or I'll snap. "You just don't know it yet. You *will* belong to me, and you will be what *I* tell you to be. On your knees or on your back, for as long as it pleases me."

Lillian's mouth tightens. "I hate you," she hisses. "You know that, right? How does that feel, knowing your wife-to-be hates you? That I'll hate you for every second that you—"

I step towards her again. I can't help it. She draws me in like a magnet, and I want to wrap my hand around her throat and drag her lips to my cock. But instead, I reach for her hand, my fingers closing around her small wrist as I plant her hand against the front of my trousers.

She can't hide the gasp that slips out of her mouth as her palm presses against the ridge of my cock. I know she can feel me throb under her touch. I'm so hard that it fucking hurts, hard enough that she can probably feel the fucking veins through the fabric, and for a moment, I think I might actually come just from the warm pressure of her hand against me, like a green kid with no self-control instead of a grown man.

"Does it feel like I care if you hate me?" I ask, holding her hand there. I want to rub her palm across myself, see if she gives in to the urge to curl her fingers around me, but I don't dare risk it. I can feel the dampness of my own arousal sliding down my shaft, worsening the friction, and

I'm so close to losing the upper hand in this argument. I can only imagine what she'd say if she made me come in my pants like this.

Lilliana licks her lips, and *god*, I want to believe that it's because she wants me in her mouth. But I know that it's out of fear. "No," she says softly. "It doesn't feel like that at all."

"Remember this," I tell her. "This is what you're going to feel on our wedding night. It doesn't matter what you say. It doesn't matter how much you hate me. I am *saving* you from a worse fate, Lilliana Narokovna. And you will understand that, eventually. But in two nights, I won't stop."

I let go of her hand, stepping back for a second time, despite the fact that every cell in my body screams for me to keep going, to use her for my pleasure. I desperately need to come.

She stares at me, speechless for once. And I use that moment to force myself to walk out of the room.

I don't make it off of the third floor. I duck into the nearest bathroom, two doors down, shutting the door behind me as I lean against it, reaching feverishly for my zipper. I don't even bother turning on the fucking lights. I wrap my fist around my cock, and my mind is full of Lilliana—her defiant eyes, her full lips, the feeling of her hand pressed against me. I drag my fist down my length, hard and fast, and in my mind's eye, she's on her knees, that same defiant look blazing on her face as I feed my cock between her lips on our wedding night.

I come in seconds, cupping my other palm over the head of my cock as I thrust against my hand, imagining that it's hers, that I'd unzipped myself and made her feel my hot flesh as I came in the palm of her hand.

It's only when the dizzying rush of pleasure has ebbed, and I'm standing there, panting and sweating in the dark with a handful of my own cum, that I realize exactly how that statement sounded in my mind. Exactly what I thought, as I let myself go.

Our wedding night can't come fast enough. The sooner I've had her, the sooner I can forget her.

Before she becomes something I can't shake.

Lilliana

The morning of my wedding day dawns bright and beautiful, and it feels entirely wrong. It should be storming, thunder and lightning, dark and angry, the way I feel about this entire farce that's been thrust upon me. Instead, the sunshine is streaming through the curtains when I wake up. I press a hand over my face, wondering what would happen if I simply rolled over and disappeared beneath the blankets.

Instead, there's a knock at the door—everyone insists on knocking politely, which seems utterly ridiculous to me, considering the fact that I'm always locked in here—and a moment later, Marika pushes it open and steps inside.

"Lilliana?" Her voice is tentative, and I can tell she's wondering if I'm going to try to resist. I want to—but what's the point? I'm going to end up married to Nikolai if they have to drag me there, I have no doubt.

If nothing else, he was very clear when he came to see me. After today, as far as he's concerned, I'll belong to him. And there's no one who is going to do a damn thing about it.

I haven't so much as heard from my father. If Nikolai changed his mind, or if he hadn't gotten what he wanted, I'm sure I would have in some way. But it's been only silence. I've served my purpose, and whatever happens to me now isn't his problem, as far as he's concerned.

"I'm having breakfast and mimosas sent up," Marika says, her voice as encouraging as she can manage. She throws the curtains wide, flooding the room with light, and I press one hand over my eyes.

"The ceremony is later this afternoon. I can't sleep in?"

"It's after eleven a.m. already, silly." She smiles at me, but even I can see it's taut at the edges. She's wondering how difficult this is going to be—if she's going to be able to be my friend, or have to be part of forcing me to the altar. "It's going to take a while to do your hair and makeup."

My bedroom becomes a steady flood of people, in and out. The staff member who brings up the breakfast Marika mentioned, which I pick at once I'm out of the shower and in the silk robe she left hanging on the bathroom door. The hair and makeup artists that someone hired, fuss over me as Marika watches, curling my hair and dabbing at my face until I'm transformed into the very picture of perfection for my *special day*.

And I do look lovely. That, I have to admit. My hair falls around my face and shoulders in thick, glossy, Hollywood-siren blonde waves, and the makeup is flawless. I look better than I ever have in my life, even on the night when my father brought me here to present me to the *pakhan*.

I've never been more disappointed to be beautiful.

I can see Marika smoothing out my wedding dress as the woman doing my makeup attaches thin, individual eyelashes to each of my lids, and I try desperately not to blink. This entire thing feels ridiculous, like playacting for a performance that everyone around me knows the truth of. I don't understand why we can't just sign some paperwork and call it a day.

Although, of course, I do. Nikolai's family is the head of the most powerful Bratva organization in Chicago, and he's the heir. It has to be a spectacle. And I will have to play my part, or pay the price for it later.

Marika brings my dress over, shooing the others out. She undoes the buttons on the back while I shrug out of my robe, my movements feeling almost robotic at this point. I'm wearing only the white lace thong that we'd purchased underneath the robe, nothing to leave any unsightly lines under my silk dress. Still, Marika barely glances at me, even though I feel vulnerably bare and exposed. She just holds the dress up so I can step into it, drawing the silk straps over my shoulders, and starts buttoning up the back.

"You're going to be the most beautiful bride," she tells me gently, as if that makes any difference. As if that makes this better, and not worse. "My brother is very lucky."

No, your brother is high-handed and demanding. Luck doesn't factor into it. My father made a play for power, and Nikolai made his own play in return. That's all that's going on here.

I don't say it, though. My "sharp tongue," as Nikolai has referred to it, is stilled, if for no other reason than that there seems to be no point. Nothing I say will change what's going to happen. The time to hope that I might get a reprieve is past.

Marika lets out a sigh as she does up the buttons, her fingers moving quickly and nimbly up the back of my dress. "There's no point in acting like you're going to your execution," she tells me, although her voice is kind as she says it. "He won't hurt you. He'll try to be a decent husband. And you'll be treated like the wife of the heir should be. You won't want for anything."

"I know." My voice sounds flat and hollow, not really like my own. "He's told me all of that."

"You can try to make the best of it—"

I think Marika feels the way I tense, my jaw tightening as I bite back what I want to say in return, because she goes silent after that, buttoning the last few buttons up the illusion lace in the back of my dress and then stepping back.

"I'm going to go get into my own dress," she says finally. "I'll come back and get you, and then we'll go down to the car."

I hear the door lock behind her as she leaves. I sink down onto the edge of my bed, not really caring if I wrinkle my dress, and run my fingers over the smooth silk.

I've imagined so many scenarios over the years, knowing what was coming for me eventually. But I'd never imagined this one. I imagined it ending in my freedom or my death, but never a wedding.

It sounds dramatic to say that it feels worse. But at that moment, it does.

I'm not sure how much time passes before Marika knocks on the door again and opens it, dressed in a pale rose bridesmaid's dress, her hair pulled to one side with a diamond clip and her makeup carefully done. She's holding my bouquet and hers in her hands, and I have to stifle a near-hysterical laugh at the sight of it. It all feels so incredibly stupid to put on such a show for something that we all know is fake.

Or is it? I might not want this, but the marriage itself is real. I will be Nikolai's wife, very soon. I'll go to his bed, and eventually, I'll have to give him an heir. I'll be expected to play the part of his wife at all times, in all ways, when he expects it.

It's pageantry—but that doesn't mean it isn't horribly, awfully real.

―

I feel hyperaware of everything as we arrive—the brightness of the late-afternoon sun, the click of my heels on the church steps, the thick scent of the flowers, the sound of the music trickling into the nave as Marika and I stand there, waiting for my father to arrive and the doors to open so we can start our procession down the aisle.

I haven't seen my father since the night he took me to the meeting with the *pakhan*. I don't know what I expect when he walks in. Actually, I *expect* nothing. I hope that I might get at least an acknowledgment of what this is getting him. Some sign of affection. Some reward for being the dutiful daughter that he raised—even if I haven't been given much of a choice. Some recognition that I didn't make them haul me in here kicking and screaming.

Instead, I get nothing. His face is blank as he walks towards me, as if he doesn't even recognize me. And then, as his arm slides through mine, hooking my elbow into the crook of his, I feel the tight grip of his other hand on my forearm as he leans in to whisper into my ear, like a father dispensing wisdom to his beloved daughter on her wedding day.

"Don't fuck this up," he hisses, his breath hot against my cheek. "The meeting went well, but I can tell I'm on thin fucking ice. You make him happy, whatever you have to do."

He pulls away, and I catch a glimpse of concern on Marika's face. Just a little—but not enough to make a difference. Not enough to make her put a stop to all of this—as if she could. It's the only thing that makes me not hate her. I know at the end of the day, she has as little power as I do in all of this, and eventually, they'll come for her too.

The doors open, and the bridal march pours down the aisle toward us. Marika starts walking, and I look down at the bouquet spilling over my hands as I count the steps. For a moment, when it's my turn, I think my feet aren't going to move. That I'm going to stay rooted to this spot on the carpet, and remain here, frozen.

But my father propels me forward, as I'd known he would. "Fucking *walk*, Lilliana," he hisses at me. Then he's all but marching me down the aisle, in step with the music but with a purposeful stride that has the clear intent of getting me to my bridegroom before I can decide to put up a fight.

I don't look up. I keep my eyes on the bouquet in my hands as we walk, dreading the moment when I'll see Nikolai. I pick out the names of the flowers I know—roses, that's obvious; daisies, I think, peonies. Some burgundy flowers in the spray of pink and white that I don't recognize. Greenery interspersed throughout—and then I see the bouquet being taken out of my hands by Marika's, and a broad, masculine hand taking one of mine as my father passes it over.

There are men's shoes in front of me. Expensive-looking ones, polished leather, with dark grey suit trousers above them. I can't bring myself to look up. All that time staring defiantly back at Nikolai, and now I don't want to see his face. It will be real, if I do.

His finger touches my chin through the delicate lace of the veil covering it. He tips it up, and I see him, as the priest starts to speak.

"Just repeat the words, Lilliana," he says quietly, and for a moment, I almost think I hear sympathy in his voice.

But that makes no sense, because if he had any sympathy for me at all, he'd have let me go.

I don't know how I make it through the ceremony. Nikolai says his vows in a strong, sure voice, and I repeat mine rotely, like a bird parroting words it doesn't really understand. He slips the wedding band onto my finger without a hitch, but when it's my turn, I almost drop it. I barely hang on, managing to push it onto his third finger as I repeat the vows the priest tells me to.

With this ring—honor, cherish, love—

It's all such utter bullshit. I won't be cherishing Nikolai, and he won't love me. I won't be worshiping him with my body, and while he might be endowing me with all his earthly goods, he isn't going to be honoring me. I find myself wondering when I missed the part where the priest asks if anyone objects, and wishing I'd both heard it, and had the nerve to speak up. To say I'm being forced into this —as if it would make a difference.

The priest probably wouldn't skip a beat. And there's nothing I can say to change any of it.

Dimly, I hear him say that Nikolai can kiss the bride. And I realize, in that exact moment, that Nikolai *is* going to kiss me, for the first time since he tried to manufacture that "date" with dinner and whisky in front of the fire.

His hands lift the veil over my face, letting it fall down the back of my hair, and his mouth brushes against mine, light but firm. I can feel the possessiveness in it, the ownership. A reminder that tonight, he will kiss me much more intimately. That I'm his now.

Long fingers thread through mine, our palms pressed together. "It's almost done," he says quietly, his voice low and rough, and once again, it almost sounds like he's trying to help me through this. Like he has some sympathy for my situation.

It makes no fucking sense.

But he's right. This part is almost over. All I have to do is walk with him down the aisle, a smile forced onto my lips as the guests clap politely for us, through the doors to the church nave, and out into the sunlight where a car waits for us, idling at the curb to take us to our reception.

I don't breathe until I'm inside, until there's cool leather under my hands, and I suck in the artificially-chilled air, the smells of roses and incense fading and replaced by Nikolai's cologne as he slides into the car next to me.

"There. First part is finished." He flashes a toothy smile at me, and I resist the urge to slap the pleased expression right off his face.

"Fuck you," I mutter, wrapping my arms around my waist as I look out of the window; the car starting to pull away from the curb.

"That's no way to talk to your new husband." His hand brushes against mine, fingertips touching. "This doesn't have to be so bad, Lilliana. We could even enjoy the evening—"

"No." I grit my teeth, trying to breathe through the urge to cry. I feel panicky, trapped, and I have a momentary intrusive thought of opening the car door and flinging myself into the passing traffic. I could do it. Whatever Nikolai is expecting from me, it probably isn't that. I could put an end to all of this, with the added bonus that it might haunt his family forever. I can see the newspaper headline already, if they didn't manage to squash it in time.

Crime family heir's new wife commits suicide only minutes after their wedding!

I can see Nikolai's jaw tighten out of the corner of my eye. "You need to be more careful, Lilliana," he says flatly. "If you ever speak to me like this in front of someone like my father, I can't always help you. I'll be forced to punish you, or I'll have to stand back and let someone else do it. There are rules in this life. Your father should have taught you that before he thrust you into it."

"I wasn't meant to be a permanent part of it," I hiss at him, swallowing hard. "None of this was supposed to happen. So fuck you."

Nikolai lets out a sharp, frustrated sigh. "Fine," he says sharply. "We can do this the hard way."

I don't say anything else. I focus on breathing shallowly, keeping myself from losing control, as it all sinks in, the gold of my wedding band glinting up at me from my lap. I don't have an engagement ring—Nikolai didn't bother buying me one. Which makes sense, of course—engagement rings are for *proposals*. No one asked me. An engagement ring would have been more of a ridiculous farce than this entire production has already been.

We're going to go to the reception, and eat an expensively catered meal, and dance so that everyone can see how happy we are, and then—

I swallow hard, knotting my fingers in my lap. I don't want to think that far ahead.

The reception is on the top level of one of the most exclusive, expensive restaurants in the city, the entire place cleared out for the Vasilev family and their guests. It's gorgeous—slate walls with one of them entirely glass, overlooking the city, and the rest of it all black and marble tables and decor, smooth and elegant. It's decorated lavishly with white flowers everywhere, a sweetheart table set up for Nikolai and me, and a space cleared out for a dance floor with a live band already beginning to play behind it. I can see the open-air kitchen from where we walk in, where the staff is preparing to bring out the beginning courses.

If I wanted any of this, it would all be perfect. The space is beautiful, the food is exquisite—all plated like those pretentious Michelin-starred courses in the movies—the wine perfectly paired with every course. I nibble at it, barely tasting the food, and I see a sea of guests that I don't recognize in the room—and, of course, one that I do. My father, who is dressed in a more expensive suit than I've ever seen him wear before, drinking the Vasilevs' expensive liquor and making conversation with everyone he's ever wanted to get access to—and all at my expense.

My stomach shrivels at the sight of it. I set down my fork, staring numbly down at a sea scallop prettily plated in a polished shell, with some sort of pea tendrils and an airy mousse around it.

"Is the food not to your liking?" There's that faintly mocking tone to Nikolai's voice again, and I swallow hard, trying to bite back the sharp response that immediately leaps to my tongue.

"I'm tired," I say flatly, looking out at the dance floor. The thought of going out there and swaying in Nikolai's arms makes me feel genuinely exhausted, and there's so much night left to deal with after that.

"I wouldn't expect to get to sleep anytime soon." His hand finds my thigh, thumb brushing over the silk, and I stiffen under his touch.

"But you'll sleep in the lap of luxury tonight, when you do. I've picked out the nicest hotel in the city just for you, little rabbit."

I've never felt as thoroughly caught in a trap as I do right now.

"Who planned all of this?" I ask idly as the next course is brought. "No one asked me about any of it."

Nikolai shrugs. "Marika, probably? My father's assistant? Mine? Who knows. I certainly don't."

"I haven't met your mother. I assume—"

"She's dead," he says shortly. "It's just my father, Marika, and I." He cuts a glance sideways at me, his fork sinking a little too viciously into the thumb-sized filet in front of him. "Which you would have known if you'd engaged with any of the conversations I've tried to have with you over the past two weeks."

If he wants me to engage with him *now*, I'm not doing it. I keep my lips pressed tightly together, cutting off a sliver of my own food and slipping it into my mouth, if only to have a reason not to speak. I don't know why he cares that I haven't had a conversation with him. Why it could possibly matter to him.

I'm not spared from any of the pageantry of the reception. A huge multi-tiered cake is wheeled out as the band plays a sweet-sounding song, one I don't recognize. Nikolai stands next to me with his hand over mine as we slide a knife through layers of chocolate and fondant.

"Open your mouth, little *krolik*," he murmurs, fingers closing nimbly around a small chunk of cake, and I wrinkle my nose at him. I hate that nickname already. *Rabbit*. I hate even more in Russian than I do in English.

"Wiggle your nose, little bunny, but it won't do you any good." He lifts the cake to my mouth, his blue-grey eyes fixed on mine, and I open my lips before I can stop myself. I want to fight him, but nothing good will come of it. If anything, it will only make what's going to come later tonight so much worse.

The cake bursts over my tongue, sugary and too sweet, and I reach for my own bit of cake, to keep his fingers from lingering against my lips if nothing else. I felt the pressure of his finger against my lower lip, the intimate way it stayed there a moment too long, and I wanted him to stop touching me.

Even if it meant touching him instead.

I lift the cake to his lips, and the moment his eyes lock with mine, I know he's going to make it uncomfortable for me—if only because he gets some sick pleasure out of it. I push the sugary sweetness into his mouth and feel his tongue brush against my fingertips, his lips closing around them, and I want to spit in his face. Not only because of the wicked glint in his eyes, but because of the shiver that runs down my spine as I feel the warmth of his tongue flicking against my fingers.

I don't want to desire him. I don't want him to make me feel anything but disgust, and every time I do, I hate him all the more.

I pull my hand away as quickly as I can, reaching for a napkin to wipe away both the stickiness of the cake and the warmth of his mouth. I can see that satisfied smile on his face again, but when I glance back up at him, I see something else too.

Something that makes me quiver with fearful anticipation.

There's a hunger in his eyes that's terrifying—and, I tell myself, *unwanted*.

"You're going to be as sweet as that cake, *krolik*," he murmurs, his voice a low, sensual purr as his arm goes around my waist and he pulls me into him.

This time, when he kisses me, he lingers. His lips press against mine, in front of everyone, and I hear a smattering of approval through the room, and why not? Nikolai is a husband kissing his new bride in front of our wedding cake. He's putting on the show that they all expect.

I want to slap him, when he pulls away. My hand forms into a fist at my side, resisting the urge, and he must see it, because his hand catches mine, raising it to his lips as he kisses the back of my whitening knuckles.

"Careful there, pretty rabbit," he murmurs. "I won't have you doing anything untoward in front of all of our guests. Imagine what could happen to your father, if you did."

"You're assuming I care about what happens to him," I hiss, and Nikolai's eyes widen the smallest bit.

"But you care about what happens to yourself, I'm sure." He pulls me in as the music swells, leading me toward the dance floor for our first dance. "So you can keep that in mind, instead."

Do I? I wonder, as Nikolai leads me out onto the floor in front of everyone, his hand on my waist and arm. *What's the worst that he could do? Kill me?* My sense of self-preservation has kept me alive this long, but that was when I thought I had a life to live after this, that I'd earn my freedom on my back in the *pakhan's* bed.

And yet, I can't quite summon the courage necessary to find out if he'd take it that far.

Maybe there's a way out, I think to myself as he spins me, pulling me back in a moment later, his hand warm on the small of my back. *He can't keep me locked up forever. Maybe I can escape.*

I cling to that as we dance and try to use it to distract myself from how it feels to be so close to Nikolai. I want to think about the possibility of escape, not the sharp, spicy scent of his cologne in my nostrils, or the broad, muscled shape of him in the finely tailored suit, or how it feels to have him so close to me. His hand is pressed possessively to the small of my back, fingers tracing the silk along my spine, and I *hate* how it makes me feel. I do.

I really do.

He spins me again, pulling me back into him with a sharp jerk of his wrist, his arm sliding around my waist. He leans in, his breath warm against my ear, and I stiffen to keep him from feeling the shiver that goes down my spine.

"Not much longer, little rabbit. I can feel you quivering. We'll be leaving before you know it."

That's what I'm afraid of. This is bad enough, being forced to put on a smile and pretend as if his hands on me don't make my skin crawl, as if I don't want to scream in front of everyone gathered here that this is against my will—as if anyone would care. But what comes next—

That will be worse.

It comes too soon. Before I know it, there's a line to bid us farewell as Nikolai leads me to the door, out of the restaurant, to another waiting car. This time, when his hand lands on my thigh, it's more possessive than before. Anticipatory. There's hunger in his touch, and I see his blue-grey eyes shining in the darkness as he gives the driver directions.

I'm well and truly trapped.

Lilliana

The room he takes me to is as beautiful as everything else has been, a gorgeous honeymoon suite. He lets me go inside first, always pretending to be the gentleman, and then closes the door behind us.

There are two double doors leading out to a balcony, and I walk over to them, looking out at the city beyond. I can hear Nikolai behind me, the rustling as he slips off his jacket and loosens his tie, the clink of ice in a glass as he gets himself a drink.

"Do you want something to drink?" His voice is so casual, as if this is nothing. As if he's enjoying drawing it out.

I clench my teeth, swallowing hard. "No," I manage. "I'm fine." I had enough wine at dinner to take the edge off; anything else will only make it harder to keep my composure.

"Suit yourself." There's the sound of liquid in a glass, and I resist the urge to turn and satisfy my curiosity as to whether it's vodka or whisky. I'll find out soon enough, when he kisses me.

The thought sends another ripple of fearful anticipation down my spine, and I grit my teeth against it. *I don't want this. I don't want any of it*. That moment when he slipped his fingers under my skirt and I was slick with desire for him, when he kissed me in front of the fire and I wanted more, that wasn't me. It wasn't because I *wanted* it.

That's what I tell myself. But as I hear his footsteps across the carpet, feel his presence behind me, the quick beat of my heart in my chest threatens to betray that.

His hands settle on my waist, the only part of him touching me so far. "It's just us now, little rabbit," he murmurs. "I can make this good for you, if you'll let me."

Acid leaps to my tongue before I can stop it, the anger in the words as much for myself as for him. "I don't *want* it to be good," I hiss, still facing away from him. "I don't want *you*. I don't want any of this."

"We'll see." His fingers stroke my waist through the silk, slow and patient, and my heart sinks.

I'd hoped he'd be too ravenous to go slow, that two weeks of our back-and-forth, of him waiting for something he so clearly wanted, would result in him tearing my dress away and ravishing me like a kidnapper in an old Harlequin romance. That he'd fuck me hard and fast, and it would probably hurt, but it would be over just as quickly. That he wouldn't have time to make my body betray me. That he wouldn't be able to make me want it, because of his own greed.

But it's clear that Nikolai is controlling himself—perhaps even enjoying making himself wait a little longer. His fingers stroke my waist for a moment more before he reaches up with one hand, brushing my hair lightly away from the back of my neck with a flick of his fingers.

"You're mine now, pretty rabbit," he murmurs. "I can have you as many times as I like. If you don't like it the first time, there's always the second, or the third. I've never had a virgin before, but I hear it takes some time to warm up to it."

"You'll be waiting until hell freezes over," I snap, keeping my gaze fixed on the city lights beyond. "I already told you. I know you're going to fuck me. You can't make me want it."

He chuckles, trailing his fingertips down the back of my neck. My skin pebbles under his touch, and he laughs again, low and dark. "Oh? Can't I?"

"It's cold in here."

"Of course." His fingers drift lower, toying with the top button of my dress. "The sooner you're out of this and in bed, the sooner we can heat things up."

The first button comes loose. Another, and another. His fingers brush over my spine with each one, lower and lower, and I feel my skin prickle and my breath catch. I'm lying—I'm not cold at all. My skin is flushing with heat, the unfamiliar sensations tingling over my flesh as it's exposed bit by bit. I'm suddenly very afraid that I'll lose the battle even sooner than I originally feared.

I hate Nikolai Vasilev with everything in me. I do. But somehow, he makes me respond to him so easily.

When the dress is open to the small of my back, he reaches up, gently sliding the straps off of my shoulders, his fingers tracing my collarbones, the tops of my shoulders, as he pushes the silk away.

The draped neckline falls, catching on my stiffened nipples as it slides away, and I hear his low groan of pleasure as the dress falls to my hips. "So little underneath it. And all for me."

"Lines under the dress would have ruined it," I snipe, wanting desperately to break the moment, to keep him from drawing me under with that smoky voice, the sound of it wrapping around me and making me want to melt into it.

"That would have been a shame." His hands dip beneath the silk against my hipbones, fingers tracing around to the small of my back. I sink my teeth into my lower lip, hard enough to taste blood, refusing to do anything that might make him think I'm enjoying this. I refuse to gasp, refuse to moan. And then I feel his fingers wrap around the open sides of the dress.

His lips brush against the shell of my ear, his knuckles pressing into the flesh of my sides. "I was always going to ruin the dress, little rabbit."

And then he *rips* it.

It tears easily down the back, buttons flying across the carpet as the remainder of the dress comes apart, fluttering down around my feet. I'm left standing in nothing but the lacy thong, a gasp torn from my lips despite myself, my heart pounding in my chest.

Nikolai grabs my waist, and turns me to face him.

His gaze is dark and stormy, filled with a lust that terrifies me and heats my blood at the same time. I don't *want* to be aroused by it, but there's a magnetism to him, a beautiful violence that threatens to drag me down like an undertow, and I'm flailing to keep my head above water as he pulls me to him.

He's still fully dressed, aside from the jacket and tie he'd shed when he got his drink. I feel more vulnerable than ever, nearly naked, as he pulls me closer, one hand leaving my waist to take my chin in his fingers, keeping me from looking away.

"I'm not going to let you close your eyes and hurry through this, *krolik*," he murmurs. "You're going to remember every second of tonight."

Why? I want so desperately to ask it, but I can't make my mouth form the word. I can't make myself say anything at all. My throat feels closed over, and as his hand slides into my hair, his fist knotting in it as he drags my mouth to his.

Whisky. It was whisky in the glass. I taste it on his lips as he presses them to mine, his fist against the back of my head as he kisses me.

It's not a gentle kiss. There's nothing soft or romantic about it, but I can *feel* how much he wants me, the heavy hand he's still holding his desire back with.

"Just do it," I hiss, twisting my lips away from his. There's nothing but a breath between our mouths—I can't get further away than that, not with his hand knotted in my hair. "There's no point in making a big production out of it. All of this—"

"—is what *I* want," he finishes for me, his other hand tightening on my waist, pulling me hard against him. I can feel the thick, rigid length of his erection in his suit trousers, pressing hotly against my bare thigh, the thin strip of lace between him and me, nothing that can protect me. "I want to take my time, Lilliana. I want you to *feel* everything that I'm going to do to you. Every touch—" his hand on my waist skims up my spine, tracing upwards. "Every kiss." His lips graze over mine again, his fingers tugging at my hair as he bends my head back, his mouth finding the edge of my jaw, dipping lower still to the smooth skin of my throat. I feel a flush of desire as his tongue grazes over the soft spot just beneath my ear, trailing a path lower, and my skin prickles under his lips.

"You like that." It's not a question, murmured against my skin.

"No," I insist. But I'm starting to wonder why I'm still trying to insist otherwise. Nikolai is no fool, and he's definitely not a virgin. He knows how a woman who wants him responds, I'm sure of that. And while my mind might be screaming for me to be let out of here, my body wants to arch into him, unbutton his shirt, and find out what that hard, muscled body feels like under my hands.

What am I thinking? In two weeks, I've gone from being someone who's never even fantasized about having sex, dreading the very thought of it, to quivering with desire at the memory of his fingers beneath my skirt. And now—now he's going to do so much more.

His hand cups my breast, palm warm against my skin, his thumb brushing over my stiffened nipple. "Every inch of your body is perfection," he murmurs, and suddenly his hand releases my hair as he steps back, his gaze sweeping over my nearly-nude figure.

"I didn't need to have you strip for me to know it would be. And I'm glad I didn't." His eyes are hungry as they take in my face, my breasts, my narrow waist, and the slender swell of my hips, dropping lower to the apex of my thighs. "Take off the panties, Lilliana. Let me see the rest of you."

I shudder. I can't help it. Up to this point, he's undressed *me*; I haven't had much of a say in the matter. But now he wants more. He wants me to assist in my own debasement. In my submission to his desires.

"Take them off yourself." I tilt my chin up, summoning the last of my defiance. "You know what you want, after all."

"I want my new wife to obey me." His gaze darkens. "I could have made you strip, you know. In front of my father, in front of yours. I could have demanded just about anything, and you would have been forced to do it. My father loves the idea of humiliation, when it comes to beautiful, innocent young women."

"But you didn't want him to see me. You'd already decided I was yours, and yours alone. So *make* me." I glare at him. "Take what you stole, Nikolai. I'm not giving you a damn thing."

He closes the distance between us in a moment, his hand wrapping in my hair again as he looks down at me with blue-grey eyes gone steely. "Be careful what you ask for, Lilliana," he growls, and my name sounds like sin on his tongue, like he says it with a lust I've never heard or imagined from anyone.

"I'll never ask you for anything." I breathe the words through clenched teeth, fighting back the wild tangle of emotions inside of me. I don't know what I feel any longer, my mind and my body entirely at odds with each other, and as Nikolai backs me towards the bed, I feel my heart galloping in my chest.

"No," he murmurs. "You're going to beg."

And then he spills me back onto the bed, his fist grabbing the side of the panties as he rips them away from me with a tearing of lace that sends a shudder through me from my head to the tips of my toes.

"Open your legs," he demands, and I ignore him. My thighs are pressed together, because I don't want him to see that I'm wet, my skin flushed and beginning to swell with arousal, my body starting to pulse with an ache that I've only recently learned the meaning of.

"I told you I'm not doing anything that you don't make me." I grit my teeth against the fear of pushing him. *What's the difference between this and what would have happened with the* pakhan? If I let Nikolai get the better of me now, no matter what danger it might put me in, it will set a precedent for our marriage.

He might hurt me, if I make him angry. But I was always prepared for pain. What I wasn't prepared for was to be caught in a trap I could never escape.

If I make this frustrating enough for him, maybe he'll even decide he's done with me, after tonight.

Nikolai hisses through his teeth, and I can see his cock straining against the front of his trousers. His hands land on my legs just above my knees, fingers digging into my flesh with barely restrained violence, and he pushes them apart, hands sliding down my inner thighs until they're closed around the soft skin as he pushes my knees apart and back. He spreads me open for him, so he can see all my soft pink flesh bared and vulnerable, and I feel my cheeks heat with shame and unwanted arousal as he lets out a low, satisfied groan.

"That's what I wanted to see, *devochka*," he murmurs, his eyes hard and dark with lust.

"What is that?" I choke out the words, fighting back humiliated tears. This somehow feels worse than what happened in the study. He'd kept that a secret between us, the shameful arousal that I'd felt as his fingers teased my clit. But this—

Why did I think he wouldn't know? He was always going to touch me eventually.

"The truth." His hands slide higher, holding me open, and his fingers stroke along my outer folds, so close to where I'm beginning to swell and throb, the ache spreading through me. "You can lie to me all you like, Lilliana. There will be consequences, but your pretty mouth can spill all the untruths you desire. But your body—" he groans again, his fingers parting me, his gaze hungrily taking in the sight of every inch of my pussy, spread open for his pleasure. "Your body will tell me the truth."

His finger touches my clit. It's a slight touch, the fingertip rolling over the hard pebble of flesh, pushing the hood up as he rubs back and forth with the lightest of grazes. But my entire body jerks, my hips arching into his fingers, and he chuckles—that low, satisfied sound again.

"You want me. And when you find out how much pleasure I can bring you, you will *beg* for me."

"No," I whisper. "I'll never beg for anything from you."

His finger rolls over my clit again. He seems to know exactly the right pressure to make me twitch and arch under him against my will, even though he's only ever touched me like this once before. It's not enough to make me come, not even if he did it for a long time—at least I don't think so—but it's enough to make me breathless, to effectively steal my ability to snipe back at him, which I think is exactly what he wants.

"Maybe not tonight." His other hand goes casually to the buttons of his shirt, undoing one at a time as if he weren't stroking me intimately with the other. "But I'm going to make you come tonight, tomorrow night, and again the night after that. You'll be addicted to the pleasure, Lilliana. You'll *crave* it—crave *me*. And eventually, I'll withhold it. And then—"

He makes himself sound like a drug. And I don't want to believe him.

But the pleasure slowly heating my blood makes me wonder, at that moment, if he could do exactly what he threatens.

His shirt falls open, revealing his muscled chest and abs, a light dusting of dark hair across his thick pectorals and trailing down over the ridges of abdominal muscles, over his navel, and disappearing beneath the buckle of his belt. When he shrugs it off, letting the shirt fall to the floor, I see muscled shoulders and biceps that would be hard to wrap my hands around.

I remember Marika saying something about him going to the gym—and she wasn't kidding. My mouth goes a little dry as I look at him, forgetting for the briefest second that this is a man I'm supposed to hate. A man that I *don't* want—because he's gorgeous. Absolutely fucking stunning.

His hand goes to his belt, the other still stroking me almost absent-mindedly now as he takes off his clothes, and fear sparks through me again as my gaze flicks down to his erection.

He's *huge*—unless the shape in the front of his trousers is an optical illusion. I don't know how it's physically possible for him to be inside of me, if he's that big. I want to look as if I don't care, but I can *feel* my eyes go wide as he flicks open his belt buckle, and a slow, satisfied smirk spreads across his lips as he moves his hand away from my pussy.

"Don't close your legs," he says, the words in a clear, sharp order. "Hold yourself open for me, Lilliana, or you won't like what happens when I open you up again myself."

"I won't like it anyway," I snap at him, but the retort doesn't sound as sincere as it did before. It doesn't matter what I say, I realize. He's seen that I *do* want him. That my body is already craving more of the pleasure he's given me. I can feel how wet I am, how my clit throbs and flutters as he takes his fingers away, wanting him to keep stroking. My fingers tremble, pressed against the bed, and I watch as he reaches for his zipper.

"You've never seen a naked man before, have you?" His eyes narrow, his hands reaching to push his suit trousers off his hips.

"Of course I have." I swallow hard. It's the truth, actually—but he doesn't believe me. I can see it in the smirk on his face.

"Is that why you're staring at my cock like you're afraid it might attack you? Or is it just because you can't wait to find out how it's going to feel inside of you?"

He slides the pants down as he speaks, and as they fall, leaving him as naked as I am, his cock springs free, slapping against his abdomen and leaving a faint trail of pre-cum against his skin, he's so hard.

It wasn't an optical illusion. He's fucking *huge*. His hand wraps around his shaft, bringing it down so that swollen head is pointed at me, and I swallow hard. Whatever desire I felt, it's at least momentarily replaced by fear once more.

"I can't take that." The words slip out before I can stop them, because I feel certain that if he tries to fuck me, he'll tear me apart. "That's not—that's not possible."

"Yes, you can." He steps closer, between my legs, and for a terrifying moment, I think he's going to thrust into me fast and hard, the way I thought I wished he would. I'd thought I wanted him to fuck me and get it over with. But if he had, I think I'd be in the emergency room.

If he cared enough afterward to take me there.

His hand slowly slides down his thick shaft. There's a pearlescent bead of fluid at the tip, dripping downwards, and he rubs it down the underside of his cock, easing his fist as it slips over his straining flesh. He reaches out with his left hand this time, his fingertips grazing my clit again before sliding down to my entrance.

"You'll be surprised what you can take, pretty little rabbit," he murmurs. "My tongue, my fingers…my cock. You'll be surprised *where* you can take me. And you *will*, because you're going to be my good girl. My obedient bride."

Two fingertips slip inside of me, just faintly, the way he had in the study when he touched me for the first time. He leaves them there for a moment, as if he's letting me get used to the sensation, his hand still sliding slowly up and down the length of his cock.

His gaze is hungry as it settles between my legs, and I realize, with a sort of detached shock, that he's doing this *for* me. I can see from the look on his face that he's barely hanging on to his self-control, that he wants to be inside of me now, instead of readying me for him like this.

That's what he's doing, I realize dimly, as he slowly pushes his two fingers into me. The stretch is startling at first, a sort of raw burn as I feel the strange sensation of something inside of me for the first time. It's only strange at first, and then as he slowly starts to move his fingers, it feels—good.

I feel myself tighten around him involuntarily, and my cheeks flush hot. I see from the gleam in his eyes that he knows what he's doing to me. His hand slows on his cock, as if he's trying to maintain his control, and his fingers push deeper, his thumb pressing against my clit as he adds to the pleasure.

"This will be my cock soon, my pretty little bride," he murmurs, his fingers stroking inside of me. It feels strange and good all at once, the pressure turning into something better, stronger. "And it will feel every bit as good. It will feel *better*."

I suck in a breath, summoning every bit of presence of mind that I have left, and look him straight in the eye as I spit out: "Go fuck yourself."

His hand goes still. His thumb presses down, hard against my clit, and a smile spreads across his face.

"Oh, Lilliana. I won't need to."

Nikolai

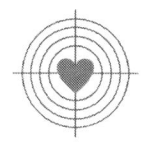

Lilliana Narokovna—now Vasilev—is going to make me lose my fucking mind.

I should have just fucked her. I should have ripped off her wedding dress, tossed her on the bed, and fucked her the way I've been imagining it since the night she walked into my father's office. But my decision not to was two-fold.

I told myself it was just because I didn't want to hurt her. I've never hurt a woman, and I didn't plan to start on my wedding night. Besides, I wanted to enjoy her more than just once, and I couldn't do that if she was damaged.

But it was more than that. I wanted to make her *want* me. Not just permit me to do what I wanted to her, but to *submit*. I wanted her to get wet for me, to desire me. I wanted her to learn to crave me.

By the end of the night, I wanted to have her begging for more. But she got under my skin, too.

I hadn't planned to rip her wedding dress off of her. I hadn't realized how hard it was going to be to dance that delicate line between violence and care, between wanting to devour her and making certain not to break her.

Even now, it's incredibly hard not to thrust myself into her, to forget that she's not ready. Her warm, wet core clenches around my fingers, velvet heat against my hand, and I can feel her twitching under my thumb. I'll make her come before the night is over. She thinks I won't, but I know better. I can feel the way she reacts to me.

There's a new kind of pleasure in that. I'd told her the truth when I said I'd never been with a virgin before. And Lilliana is mine—all of her. No one else has ever touched her—and no one else ever will.

I slide my fingers deeper into her, enjoying the way her eyes widen. She thinks that she's hiding her pleasure from me, convincing me that she doesn't want it. She thinks she can make me believe that she isn't responding to me. But everything I see and feel, tells me otherwise.

I want to taste her. But I plan to save that for later. I plan to teach Lilliana *all* the ways that I can make her body crave mine, until she realizes that there's no escape. That she can't flee from what she truly wants.

That she can't flee from *me*.

I have to take my hand off my cock, or I won't last long enough to enjoy her the way I really want to. I move my two fingers inside of her, letting her feel the stretch of it, hearing her soft intake of breath that she tries to keep quiet.

She's so fucking beautiful. Her body is every bit as perfect as I knew it would be, her blonde hair falling around her face and shoulders in a way that begs for me to sink my hands into it. I want to kiss and touch every inch of her, learn every soft curve and line. And I will—when she submits to me.

When she *earns* it.

And then, when I've learned all of her, I'll grow tired of having nothing new, and I'll be rid of the obsession that is Lilliana Vasilev.

She will live the rest of her life enjoying the benefits of being my wife as she does her duty to me, and I'll go back to enjoying the pleasures of being rich and powerful—and beholden to almost no one.

Her head tips back as I roll my thumb over her clit. Her full lips are parted, and I want to feel them against mine again, the heat of her mouth, her tongue, as I slide into her. My cock throbs, pre-cum sliding down my shaft, dripping as I push my fingers into her pussy. I angle my hand upwards, adding a third finger as she lets out a sudden, startled cry that goes straight to my cock.

"That's it. You make such a pretty sound when you're stuffed full." I roll my thumb again, easing the pressure of my fingers inside of her. "Are you ready for my cock, *krolik*? Or should I make you take my whole hand, just to be sure?"

Her eyes fly wide, and I smirk at her. "I take it my cock is the better option?"

She glares up at me stubbornly, and I consider making her take a fourth finger just to show her that I don't make idle threats. But I don't think I can wait much longer. I haven't ached for a woman like this in so long. I *need* to bury myself inside of her.

Lilliana's innocence is my reward, and I can't wait to claim it any longer.

I slip my fingers out of her suddenly, and I hear her gasp as I step away, my cock still jutting lewdly out in front of me. I yank the covers down, reaching for her waist as I maneuver her back onto the pillows.

"Nikolai—"

It's the first time she's said my name all night. A strange pang strikes me in the chest at the fear that threads through it. I don't want her to fear me. Submit to me, yes. Beg for me, yes. But *fear* me?

I married her to protect her. She has nothing to fear from me.

"My family is old-fashioned," I tell her as I lay her back atop the sheets, her head sinking into the pillows. "They will expect to see the bedsheets in the morning."

"The—*oh*." Her eyes fly wide again with shock, and I'm reminded that she wasn't prepared for a marriage. She was prepared to be given to a man who would fuck her and throw her away.

I don't know why the thought of that makes me angry. It shouldn't. I've tossed aside plenty of women in my day. But Lilliana—

I push the thought away as I lean over her, brushing her hair away from her face with more care than before. I can feel her starting to tremble, and the idea of her fear doesn't turn me on. I want her to *want* this.

My other hand slips between her legs, caressing her lightly, my fingers brushing over her clit. "This can feel good, if you let it," I murmur, dipping my head to let my lips trail over her ear. "You don't have to fight me, little *krolik*."

I *feel* her stiffen underneath me, and it's all I can do not to let out a frustrated sigh. "You're so wet, little rabbit." My fingers slip into her again, stroking, thumb grazing her clit. Her hips twitch, and I know she wants more. "So wet for *me*."

She opens her mouth as if to protest, but I don't want to hear it. What I want, I can't wait any longer for, and I lean down, silencing her with a kiss as I guide myself between her thighs, the tip of my cock nudging against her as I keep one hand pressed against her jaw, keeping her from breaking the kiss.

For a moment, I think it won't be enough. She's so tight—so much so that I think she might not be able to take me after all. I'm determined not to hurt her—I did this to *keep* from hurting her—and I hover on the edge of indecision, feeling her tense body trying to keep me out.

"*Krolik. Devochka.* Lilliana." I breathe her name against her lips, my fingers moving between us again, my cock rubbing against her as I start to stroke her clit. I need to make her come; no matter how much she fights it, I *will* make her come.

It's easy to learn her. Even as she tries not to respond, her body can't keep from reacting to the new touches, the new sensations. She's quivering beneath me as I roll my fingers over and around her clit, not teasingly like before, but with purpose this time. Every time I stroke my fingers upwards, her hips jerk, and she turns her face to one side, her eyes stubbornly closed.

I reach for her face, turning her back to me. "Eyes on me, Lilliana," I murmur, my thumb pressing into her lower lip. "I want you looking at me when you come for me."

"I'm not—" the words break off on a gasp as I speed up, increasing the pressure of my fingers as I roll them over her sensitive flesh again and again, feeling the way she tenses beneath me. She's close, her pussy drenched as I slide my fingers down, gathering her arousal on my fingertips before I rub it over her now-slick clit, increasing the pleasure as Lilliana clenches her teeth against a moan. "I won't—"

"Yes, you will, little rabbit." I lean in, brushing my lips along her jaw, giving myself one more taste of her before I watch her come apart for me. "Come for me, Lilliana. Come on my fingers so I can fuck you."

I *see* her unravel. She stares up at me, her face taut with horrified pleasure as those last filthy words trigger something deep within her, and she comes *hard*.

Her hips jerk up, and my cock, still nestled against her entrance as I've stroked her to her climax, starts to slip inside of her as she tightens around me, fluttering as she comes on my fingers—and now on my cock.

The pleasure is overwhelming. I have to keep myself from thrusting into her as deeply as I can go, the rippling of her wet, velvet heat around me nearly making me lose control. She's still arching against my fingers, her teeth sinking into her lip as she forces back a moan, and I promise myself, as another inch of my cock slips into her, that one day I'll hear her scream for me.

She feels fucking *incredible*.

I keep my hand on her jaw, forcing her to look up at me as I slide deeper. "How does that feel, *wife*?" I breathe, a strange jolt of pleasure going through me at the word, at all that it implies. That she belongs to *me*—her innocence, her body, *all* of her, mine for the taking, and now I have. No one else has ever had her. No one else will ever touch her.

The thought of anyone so much as *looking* at her makes me murderous.

She doesn't say a word at first. She glares up at me, her angry expression at odds with the way she's trembling beneath me, her hips still arching into mine as she takes more of my cock, squeezing around me. "It's—" she swallows hard, realizing that I'm not going to let her get away with complete silence. "It's so much—"

Pleasure rips through me at that, a sort of satisfied thrill as my hips rock forward, so close to being entirely buried inside of her. "You're taking it so well," I murmur, my thumb stroking over her cheekbone. "Such a good girl. Taking my cock. You just needed to come first."

Her eyes narrow, and she goes very still underneath me. "I didn't—"

"Yes, you did. I felt it. Don't lie to me." I give in to my urges, just once, to show her just how serious I am. My hips snap forward, burying the last inches of my cock in her tight, wet pussy, and she gasps despite herself, a cry slipping past her lips as her hands curl into the sheets.

"Do you want to come again?" I hold myself there, despite the tortuous pleasure, giving her a moment to adjust to my cock. "Do you want to come on my cock, *krolik*?"

She gives me a mute, rebellious glare, and I slowly start to move.

She feels like heaven. She's drenched despite her protests, and I slide in and out of her more easily than before, rocking my hips so that I grind down onto her clit with each thrust. I can feel her starting to lose control, the way she arches up a little each time, wanting more of the friction, the way her lips part on a gasp that she tries to hold back. She's gorgeous like *this*, and I can't begin to imagine what it would be like if she let go, if she gave herself over to the throes of desire and let me see her completely undone.

"*I* want you to come again," I tell her, leaning forward so my lips are nearly touching hers. "So you will."

I kiss her before she can say anything. A part of me is beginning to like her snappy comebacks, her defiance, if only because it's more interesting than the women who fall all over themselves to please me in any way they think I might like. But right now, I don't want to hear her sharp tongue. Soon enough, I'll show her a different use for it.

My hips snap forward again as I kiss her, my tongue tangling with hers as I drive my cock into her, and this time I stay deep inside of her for a moment, rocking my hips against hers, letting my pelvis grind down onto her clit. She's still excruciatingly tight, but I can feel her twitch every time the swollen head of my cock brushes over a certain spot inside of her, and I know she's enjoying it. She'd deny it if she could, but I know what I'm feeling.

I kiss her until I feel her starting to tremble around me, the sharp rise and fall of her chest quickening as she nears the edge—and then I break the kiss, leaning back on my knees as I slide my hands down the backs of hr thighs, lifting her legs up.

"What are you—" she breaks off with a gasp as the new angle changes how my cock pushes inside of her, making it feel as if I've somehow gone deeper, even though I already had every inch buried within her. I lift her legs over my shoulders, angling her so I can see between her thighs, and the sight is enough to make my balls tighten and push me very close to my own climax.

She's stretched tight around me, the sight so lewd that it makes my cock throb. Her small, swollen clit is visible above where I've impaled her. I reach down, starting to stroke it again as I pull out just a little and slide back in, for the sheer pleasure of being able to see it.

Her jaw tightens, and I know she's trying not to make a sound. Her hands are fists in the sheets now, and she turns her head away again, trying not to look at me.

"I told you," I growl, drawing my cock out of her again, tearing my eyes away from the sight of her wrapped around my length long enough to look at her stubbornly set face. "Eyes on me, little rabbit."

"I hate you," she hisses, but her back arches as she says it, as my fingers roll over her clit again. "You're a—"

"What?" I bite off the word on a groan as I sink into her again, my other hand holding her face so she's looking at me still. I tilt her chin down, forcing her to look at where I'm thrusting inside of her, the sight of my cock splitting her open. "If you hate me so much, *devochka*, scream it for me when you come. But you'll look at me while you do."

Her eyes are murderous, but they're looking at me. She holds my gaze as I rub her clit faster, feeling my cock harden inside of her, knowing I'm not going to make it much longer. I *need* to come inside of her, my balls at the point of feeling bruised from how long I've drawn this out, my cock painfully hard. I need the release—but she's coming with me.

"Tell me how much you hate me, little rabbit," I murmur, and I flick upwards on her clit as I drive my cock into her, feeling her sweet, wet heat envelop me once more.

I think she might bite her tongue off before she screams for me. I see her teeth grinding together to keep from letting out even a hint of pleasure, even as her back arches, her hands twisting in the sheets as she comes apart. I couldn't have pulled out if I wanted to—her already tight pussy has me in a vise as she ripples along my length, squeezing me again and again with a pleasure so good it's almost too much.

"I'm going to come in you, *krolik*," I murmur, the words strangled as my cock throbs, and I let go of her jaw to dig my fingers into her hip, hard, as I feel the first flood of my cum start to erupt from my cock.

She might have told me to go fuck myself again. I can't be sure. I can't be sure of anything except how fucking *good* she feels, how I'm coming harder than I think I ever have in my life, hard enough that my vision blurs at the edges as I rock against her, feeling the heat of our climaxes mingled as she squirms beneath me, finally sagging back against the pillows.

I don't want to slip out of her. I have a moment's thought that I could get hard again, if I stayed inside of her—I remind myself that she was a virgin a few minutes ago, and my cock is large. I don't want to hurt her.

Slowly, I ease out of her, hissing through my teeth at the feeling of it along my over-sensitive shaft. "You're lucky I don't take you again right now, *krolik*," I murmur, rolling away from her onto my back as my cock drops against my thigh, still half-hard and soaked from her. "I could be hard again in a moment, just thinking about it."

"Lucky me." She rolls her eyes, pushing herself off of the pillows and towards the edge of the bed. Before I can think about what I'm doing, my hand shoots out, fingers wrapping around her wrist.

"Where are you going, little rabbit?"

"To shower." Her lips press together tightly. "Don't worry, I'm not going to try to escape my trap. What's the point, now?"

Her shoulders droop slightly, and I know what she's thinking. She'd told me that she wanted her freedom, after her virginity was sacrificed. I've made that impossible for her. But surely she must see that this is better.

"You'll be alive tomorrow, Lilliana." I turn my head to look at her, my long fingers still wrapped around her wrist. It's small and delicate, and I shudder to think what a man like my father might have done to a girl so fragile-looking. "You might not have been, without me. In fact, you might already be dead. My father would not have given you two weeks to become accustomed to the idea of going to his bed."

"Do you understand what you sound like?" She twists around, glaring at me with those bright blue eyes. *"Oh, Lilliana, you're so lucky! You're forced into an unwanted marriage and onto a different unwanted cock, instead of being fucked and then murdered!* My hero," she adds sarcastically. "Fuck you, Nikolai."

Once again, I act before I can think, her words striking me somewhere that I've never felt such a sharp, angry pang before.

I yank her back onto the bed, onto her back, with my muscled bulk leaning over her before she can wriggle away. "Is that what you want, *krolik?*" I purr, running my fingers over her slightly swollen lips. "To fuck me? Because it can be arranged."

My cock jerks, hardening instantly as I lean over her, the tip brushing against her belly. I feel her shudder, and I smirk down at her. "You wanted my cock." I reach between us, touching her sensitive folds. "I felt it. You were wet for me. *Soaked.*"

I shouldn't fuck her again. I should let her body rest. But she glares up at me with those defiant eyes, lips pursed as if she wants to spit in my face, and the urge to make her beg for what she claims to hate is overwhelming.

I nudge my cock downwards, the thick head pressing against her entrance. "I could fill you up with my cum all over again, right now." I nudge against her, and I see her eyes flare wide, hear the quick hiss of her indrawn breath—and I know she's sore. Hurting, even, from the size and stretch of my cock earlier.

It takes everything in me to pull away. Every single part of me is screaming to bury myself inside of her again. I'm as hard and aching as if I'd never fucked her at all. But somehow, I pull myself away.

I roll onto my back, cock jutting lewdly up in the air as I force myself not to look at her. If I see her pretty, delicate body spread out for me right now like a dessert table at a buffet, I won't be able to stop myself from devouring her.

"What are you—"

"Go take a shower." I bite out the words, and out of the corner of my eye, I can see her hesitating. "Now!" I snap. "Before I lose control and fuck you again."

She's off the bed in an instant. I don't let myself look until I hear the sound of the bathroom door closing behind her, and then I glance at the bed where she was.

There's the necessary bloodstain on the sheets. Thank *fuck* for that. I'm intelligent enough to know that not every virgin bleeds on the first night and that this archaic practice is so much bullshit, but especially in *these* circumstances, when her father has bought a place at our table with her virginity, my father would insist on it. I wouldn't have let her face the consequences if she hadn't bled—I'd have found a way to fake it, but it's easier all around now.

I wouldn't have doubted she was a virgin, either way. That was plain as day to me. But not any longer.

Fuck. My cock is still rock-hard, and I wrap my fist around it, trying not to think about the irony of the fact that my pretty new wife is one room away, naked and wet in the shower, and I'm still jerking off. But I saw the pain in her face when my cock touched her again. She's too sore for more tonight.

My length is still wet from her and from my cum. My fist slides easily over it, and I close my eyes, imagining her wanton and moaning for me, begging for more. I can get her there. She came twice for me tonight—and there's so much still for me to show her.

So much for me to introduce her to that will teach her how much pleasure can be had.

I could break her. I could force her to beg for me, hurt her until she gives me what I want. But I don't want it that way. I don't want her broken; I want her willing submission. I want her to give herself to me, in spite of what she thinks she wants.

A new fantasy starts to fill my mind as I stroke myself in the middle of my marriage bed, my thumb pressing against the swollen head on each pass, as if it's her tightening around me. A fantasy of having her alone, somewhere secluded, with no distractions. Nothing but her and I, and the chance to immerse her in pleasure until she's addicted to me.

I don't let myself think about how obsessive that sounds. How much that makes it seem as if *I'm* the one addicted to *her*. Like I want unfettered access to my fix, with no other demands on my time.

A honeymoon. I'll take her on a fucking honeymoon. But not to the Caribbean or some shit where we can go on excursions and spend time doing things other than enjoying each other in bed. I want there to be nothing for her to do except for me.

My cock throbs in my fist eagerly. There had been no plans to take her away on a honeymoon, but the more the idea takes shape, the more I like it. It feels like a good plan. One that could work.

Maybe by the time it's over, I'll have worked her out of my system.

The bathroom door clicks open, and I realize how long I've been lying here, stroking my cock while fantasizing about taking my new bride away. It should set off a ping of alarm—I've never focused so much on any woman for so long—but that thought isn't anywhere near the forefront of my mind right now. What *is* on my mind is the gorgeous picture of my new bride stepping out of the bathroom, a thick robe belted tightly around her—and the way her eyes go wide when she sees me jerking off.

"What are you doing?" Her voice isn't as snappish as before, but she sounds shocked. "What the fuck—"

"You're too sore to take my cock again." Something about the sentence sends another jolt through me, and my hand spasms around the stiff length. "But I'm hard, and I need to come. So either come over here and put your pretty mouth on it, or let me finish."

Her lips part, but I know it's not to come over here and suck my cock. She won't willingly do that yet.

"I could order you to do it." I slide my hand up, squeezing the head as she stares at me. Her shocked gaze watching me stroke myself, increases the pleasure, and I grit my teeth, suddenly wanting to last longer. "I could tell you to come kneel between my legs and use those pretty lips to get me off and swallow my cum. But you were such a good girl tonight—"

I run my hand slowly down the straining length, letting her see it. "You took my cock so well. So I'll have some mercy on you and finish like this instead."

She swallows hard. I see her throat move, and *god,* I want to be fucking buried inside of it. I reach down, cupping my balls, showing off for her a little—and she starts to turn to flee back into the bathroom.

"Oh no, you don't." The words come out a little more strangled than I'd like them to. I'm close to the edge, pre-cum sliding down my cock as I stroke, and I'm battling back the climax until I'm ready for it. "Come here, *krolik*."

"You said—"

"I'm not going to fuck you or make you suck me. But you're going to watch." I pat the bed next to me, my hand sliding down to the base of my shaft and holding myself there stiffly. "You're going to see exactly what you do to me."

She hesitates, and I narrow my eyes at her. "*Now*, Lilliana," I growl, and something about the use of her name propels her forward.

She doesn't take off the robe as she climbs into bed next to me, and I'd known she wouldn't. My hand slides over my length again, and I know I'm not going to make it much longer.

I roll over, getting up on my knees as I reach for the tie of her robe. Her lips part to argue with me, and I shake my head.

"I'm not going to fuck you," I repeat. "But I'm going to look at what's mine."

She wants me to think she hates me. Maybe she does. Maybe she just *believes* she does. But I see the fine tremor that goes through her when I say that.

My hand moves over my cock, quick and fast, driving me towards the climax that I can't hold back any longer. I spread her robe open, looking at the pale expanse of her perfect body in front of me. I rock forward on my knees, my cockhead flaring as my balls tighten, and I feel myself about to come.

"Nikolai, no—" she exclaims as she realizes what I'm about to do, but there's no stopping it now.

I groan, a deep, pleasurable sound as cum spurts from my cock, landing hotly across her breasts, her stomach, and her thighs. My hand jerks and stutters over it, my breath coming in sharp gasps as I paint her skin with my cum. As the last drops pearl from the tip, I lean over her, nudging the head between her folds and against her clit as I rub my cock clean on her pussy.

"You fucking—" She's trembling with rage now; I can see it in her face. "I just fucking showered!"

She starts to get up again, but this time when I pin her arm to the bed, I mean it. There's something about her that's awakened a raw possessiveness in me that I've never felt before, and I know what I want right now.

She's not going to tell me no.

"You're going to stay right here," I tell her, my voice low and dark. "You're going to sleep covered in my cum, little rabbit. My pretty wife, next to me, with my cum marking her skin. You can shower in the morning—if you're a good girl."

The look in her eyes is murderous once again. But I think she knows just how serious I am—or doesn't want to test the limits of what happens if she defies me—because she swallows hard and doesn't move.

I slide back in bed next to her, feeling as if I can finally fall asleep as I switch off the light. "Good night, *krolik*," I murmur as I lay back next to her, but she doesn't make a sound, nor does she move.

The shape of her name is on my lips as I fall asleep.

Lilliana

I wake up to a knock at the door and the sound of a voice calling out that there's room service waiting.

My entire body feels stiff and sore, the ache between my thighs magnified. My skin feels taut and sticky, and I don't realize why at first, until the last events of the evening before come rushing back to me, and I clutch the sheet to my chest, realizing someone is about to come into the room while I'm still naked in bed, covered in my new husband's cum.

That new husband is getting up, reaching for his boxers as he walks casually in front of me, nude and rock-hard. His cock tents the fabric as he slips them on, and I stare at him, horrified.

"You're going to answer the door like that?"

He smirks at me. "Why not? Would you rather answer it in your—state?" He gestures at me, knowing full well what's under the sheet, and I glare at him.

"I'll take that as a no." He strides across the room, glancing back once more with a wicked expression on his face. "Who knows?

Maybe the woman outside will see this, and want it more than my pretty new wife says *she* does."

He gestures at his erection and my face flames. I feel an instant, white-hot burst of jealousy at the thought of another woman seeing, touching, getting fucked by Nikolai, and it makes me feel insane, because I don't *want* him. I should be thrilled at the idea of any other woman taking him off my hands. It would mean the end of his attention being focused on me.

But the thought of him fucking someone else the way he was with me last night—

I push the image out of my head, because I suddenly feel hot, irrational tears burning at the back of my eyes, and I hate myself for it. I hate all of it.

He opens the door, and the server outside—a man, I realize—wheels it into the room. The man pauses briefly, his gaze flicking towards the bed, and I'm suddenly very aware of my bare shoulders above the sheet, and how obviously naked I am beneath it. I wonder if the man has any idea that I'm covered in cum.

The server looks at me a second too long, and I *see* Nikolai's face tighten with rage.

"Get the fuck out!" he snarls, taking a step toward the man, and I've never seen someone move so fast in my life.

The door shuts behind him, and I glare at Nikolai.

"You didn't even tip him."

"He's lucky I didn't strangle him, the way he was looking at you."

"Stop acting like you give a shit." I wrap the sheet more tightly around myself. "You don't care about me."

"I care about someone looking at what's mine." His gaze slides over me, and I can see a hunger that has nothing to do with the food on the cart next to him.

I open my mouth, but no retort comes out. I don't know why that affects me, the way he says it when he calls me *his*. I don't want to be his. I want to be free. But something about it tightens my belly and makes me flush hot every time.

"I'll strip the sheets after we eat and dress," Nikolai says, picking up a plate. "They'll have to be delivered to my father."

"Do they *have* to be?" My voice is smaller than I'd like as I say it, and Nikolai looks up, his expression startled. It's one of the few times I think I've ever caught him off guard.

My cheeks are flaming hot at the idea of the blood-stained, cum-covered sheets being displayed in front of the *pakhan*, for him to see the evidence that his son fucked me. It's not as if he doesn't know anyway—there was a goddamn *wedding* yesterday—but something about the idea of Nikolai's father casually looking at the leftover evidence makes me feel sick to my stomach.

"It's tradition," he says shortly.

"Is it tradition for you to marry the daughter of some no-name Bratva soldier?" I spit out. I know there's no real point in fighting this—it's going to happen regardless, but I can't seem to stop myself.

"You don't have to argue over every little thing." He sets the plate down, walking towards the bed. I can still see the shape of his cock in his boxers, still half-hard. "There's no choice about it, Lilliana. Put it out of your head."

I can feel the heat in my cheeks intensifying, hot tears burning at the backs of my eyes. I'm not entirely sure why this particular thing is affecting me so much, but I *hate* it. I hate the thought of Nikolai's father seeing the bloody sheets. It feels like parading my shame in front of him, my imprisonment, like I've been reduced to nothing but a stain on a wedding bed.

"There's nothing to be embarrassed about," Nikolai says, almost gently, as if he can hear my thoughts. "You don't even have to be there. It's nothing, *krolik*."

"I wish you'd just fucked me and let me go." I can hear tears threatening in my voice, and I hate that too. I've tried so hard to fight him, to keep from showing any weakness, but I feel so tired after last night. It's sinking in, all over again, that this is permanent. The thin gold band on my left hand might as well be steel manacles, for how tightly it keeps me locked away.

"I would never have been satisfied with only once."

There's a deep, rough lilt to his voice as he says it that I'm beginning to recognize as desire. Something tightens deep inside of me when I hear it, a response that I can't help, but I set my teeth against it, still holding the sheet tightly to my chest.

I see his cock jerk inside of his boxers, pushing against the fabric, and I shake my head when I see him push them down. "I can't," I whisper, knowing how very close I am to begging—not the way he wants me to, but begging nonetheless, and I don't want to beg him for *anything*. "I'm too sore. I can't take it again."

His cock looks even bigger now, in the daylight of the room, close enough to touch. I can see the throbbing veins, the thick girth of it nearly touching his abs, and I feel a jolt of pain at the idea of him pushing it inside of me again. I can't do it.

"That's fine," he says, moving to get onto the bed, and I flinch away.

"I really can't." I swallow hard. "I'm not playing hard to get, Nikolai; I can't—"

"I know." He pushes me back onto the pillows with one hand on my chest, his fingers curling around the sheet and pulling it away from me, despite my attempts to grasp it back. "I'll soothe you instead."

I don't understand what he means at first. I'm too focused on trying to stay covered—the robe has long since been lost, and I had nothing but the sheet—but Nikolai pulls it away, revealing my bare, cum-soaked skin to his hungry gaze.

He kneels between my legs, his hands pressing almost gently against my inner thighs as he opens them, and he lets out a low groan.

"You do look tender." His fingers lightly stroke my outer folds, and I grit my teeth against a gasp that could be pleasure or pain; I'm not sure which. It all feels muddled right now. "I can help you with that."

"I don't—" I swallow hard as he leans down, his fingers lightly stroking my bruised inner flesh as he holds my legs open—and then I feel the warm caress of his tongue as he presses his mouth gently between my thighs.

It startles me into silence. I hadn't expected gentleness or pleasure. I saw how hard he was, and I didn't think he would put off his own need to tend to me—or do *this*. I'd honestly never imagined anyone doing this to me.

I didn't think the man I was sold to for my father's advancement would care enough to pleasure me with his mouth. I couldn't imagine it was something men really liked doing. And I certainly didn't think Nikolai would.

But he *moans* as his tongue slides over my pussy, as if it's turning him on. His tongue slides against my entrance, licking lightly, as if he is trying to soothe away the soreness. It feels warm and wet and so fucking *good*, and I feel myself tremble as I try to hold back any sign that I'm enjoying it.

Nikolai lets out a slow sigh, his mouth leaving my pussy for a moment as he looks up at me, his hair falling messily into his face. "There's no point in pretending you don't like it, *krolik*," he tells me, his voice almost exasperated. "Just let it feel good."

But I *can't*.

He doesn't understand that admitting to the pleasure would be giving in. It would be giving him an inch that I know he'll run with, demanding more and more of me until he gets me to admit that I want his cock, that it feels good, that I *like* when he fucks me. He'd push and push, if I gave him the slightest satisfaction in admitting that the hot, wet slide of his tongue over my pussy feels like fucking heaven.

I'm *definitely* not admitting that.

But I also know that if he keeps doing this, I'm not going to be able to stop myself from coming. And he'll *know*.

He knew when I came for him last night. My cheeks burn all over again, remembering it. How his fingers felt on my clit. He knew just how to touch me, and I hate that the thought that he knows because he's pleasured so many other women makes me jealous.

It's just because it's not fair, I tell myself. *It was so important that I be a virgin, but god only knows how many women he's fucked. It's not because I care that he's done this to someone else.*

I'd tried so hard to keep from responding. But it had felt so fucking *good*. Better than my own fingers. He'd found exactly the way I liked it, when I barely even know. And when he'd done it again while he was inside of me—

His cock had hurt. I'd been right that it was too big. But something about that stretch, the fullness of it, had felt *good*, too. I can see how in time, after getting used to it, it could be incredible.

Except I don't want to get used to it. I don't. I don't want to come again with his cock filling me up and his fingers on my—

Nikolai picks that moment to run his tongue over my clit, swirling it in a way that makes my back arch and my mouth drop open as I suck in a sharp breath, and I feel his lips curl in a smile against my flesh.

I can just imagine the self-satisfied look on his fucking face.

But I can't think of anything to say. He's still fluttering his tongue over me, circling it, repeating the pattern until the muscles in my thighs tense and my hands claw at the sheets, and I *know* I'm giving him what he wants, letting him see how good it feels—but I can't stop.

I can't stop, and I can't fucking tell him to stop either, because I want to come.

I want to come on his face while he licks me.

His tongue keeps up the slow circles, better than my fingers, better than anything I've ever felt in my life. My head falls back against the pillows, my lips parted on a gasp, and I feel the moment I come unraveled on his tongue.

It's all I can do not to moan his name. I clench my teeth, fighting back the cries of pleasure, and the worst part is that I *know* he's right, that if I let myself go, it would feel even better than this. It could be even *more*, and I want it so badly. I want to know what that feels like—

The orgasm crashes through me, my thighs tensing around his head as he keeps stroking his tongue over me, extending the pleasure, making it more than I ever thought it could possibly be. His hands grab my inner thighs, forcing them down on the bed, forcing me to lay there spread open for him, and as I buck against his face, I feel him take one hand off of my leg and thrust two fingers inside of me.

It sends a jolt of pain through me from the soreness, but there's pleasure, too. He curls his fingers inside of me, stroking more gently than he did with his cock last night. I feel the orgasm ebb and then build again, his tongue still sliding over my hot, swollen flesh throughout all of it, sending me into a second wave of pleasure as he expertly plays my body like a well-tuned instrument.

My jaw hurts from how tightly I'm clenching my teeth, trying to keep from moaning, crying out his name. A whimper slips from between my lips, my hips bucking upwards, and Nikolai keeps me pinned there, forcing the pleasure on me until I'm limp and breathless.

The fingers inside of me slip free as I look up at him, still panting as he pulls away from my oversensitive clit, his hand wrapping around his stiff cock. For a second, I think he's going to push inside of me anyway, but instead, he starts to stroke, looking down at me with a heated expression on his face.

His fingers still have my arousal on them, stroking over his cock, and something about that sends a jolt of desire through me that I know I shouldn't feel. I'm trembling from a mixture of exhaustion, fear, and arousal. I can't move as Nikolai's hips jerk forward and shudder, his body leaning over mine as his cum splashes over my belly for the second time since last night.

He arches forward, rubbing the head of his cock against my clit as hot cum spills over me, and I see the satisfied expression that spreads over his face along with the pleasure as he groans, his hand sliding along his length.

"*Fuck*," he breathes as he pulls back, the last drops of his cum dripping from his cockhead onto my pussy. "You look fucking gorgeous like that."

I don't feel gorgeous. I feel tired and haggard, with my cum-covered skin and tangled hair. I want to shower and go back to sleep, and as Nikolai slides off of the bed, I glance toward the room service cart and wonder if I'm even going to be able to eat when I feel like this.

He looks at me, and something about the expression on my face must be apparent to him, because he shrugs. "Go ahead and shower if you want," he says carelessly. "We'll be going home after this."

"Where is home?" I ask tentatively. "Back to the mansion?"

Nikolai smirks. "No. I'm taking you to my penthouse in the city. And after that—"

He trails off, and I swallow hard, wondering what he means. What comes after? I don't like the silence that hangs in the air after he says it.

"We'll talk about it later," he says finally. "Go shower."

I don't give him a chance to change his mind. I slide off of the bed, and as I start to walk past him, he grabs my arm, his gaze raking over me again.

"Don't get so in your head about it," he says, and I narrow my eyes at him.

"I don't know what the fuck you're talking about."

"Of course you do." He lets go of my arm. "You're pissed that you came. You're mad at me for making you come, but you're also mad at yourself for coming, even though you couldn't have helped it. Not when I was eating your pussy like that."

"You arrogant—" I can feel my cheeks flushing hot and red.

He laughs, cutting me off. "You're my wife now, Lilliana. You belong to me. When I want you, I'll have you. But I want you to want it too. That's why I didn't make you take my cock again this morning. You were sore, and I wanted to make you feel good."

"You didn't." I turn away from him, wrapping my arms around my waist and feeling my sticky flesh brush against my arms. "Nothing about you feels good."

"If that makes it easier for you to live with this, then tell yourself that. But you can't lie to yourself forever."

Nikolai turns away from me, going back to the bed. I can't bring myself to look at him, and I hurry towards the bathroom before he can decide that he wants something else from me and keeps me from showering.

All I want is him off of me. I don't want any trace of what we've done since last night. I want to forget this is happening for a little while.

But I'm not sure even a hot shower is enough to wash away the feeling of Nikolai's tongue on me.

Nikolai

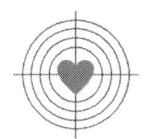

"I have some things I need to do before I take you home," I tell Lilliana as we leave the hotel, once the sheet on the bed has been stripped away and tucked into my bag to be taken to my father. "I'll leave you at the mansion for a little while and then come back and fetch you."

"Like a dog with his toy," she mutters under her breath, and I choose to ignore it. It feels like the wiser choice.

The breakfast had been cold by the time she got out of the shower, but she'd eaten anyway, choking down some dry toast and a little fruit. I'd given her as much space as I could, trying to ignore the way she looked at me, like I was a monster that might pounce on her at any moment.

After I'd made a point of not forcing myself on her earlier, it felt like an insult.

Taking her away for a little while will make a difference, I tell myself as we ride the elevator down to the lobby. Lilliana is on the other side of the elevator car, dressed in jeans and a t-shirt, her arms wrapped around her slender waist. She looks exhausted, and I resolve to give her a night to rest at the penthouse before I take her on our honeymoon. *I can keep my hands off of her for one night.*

I feel a flicker of desire even as I think it, though, just looking at her leaning against the opposite wall, and it unsettles me. I've never met a woman who makes me feel like this, almost unhinged with need. I've never met anyone who makes me feel less than in control of myself.

I want it—*her*—out of my system.

She's silent all the way to the mansion, sitting as far away from me as she can in the backseat of the car. I can feel the anger radiating off of her, and it frustrates me to no end. I haven't hurt her. If she'd been given to my father, things would be much worse for her. And yet, she's treating me like the enemy.

"I'll be back in a few hours," I tell her as I escort her up the stairs and back into the mansion. "You can do what you like, but I recommend staying out of the way of my father, unless you want to have an uncomfortable conversation."

Her cheeks pinken, and I know she's thinking about the sheets. "I'll just go up to my old room," she says stiffly, and I smirk at her.

"If you're going to hide away, I'll take you to my room. I like the idea of you waiting there for me when I get back."

Lilliana glares at me, but she says nothing. For once, she isn't fighting me, and that's better than the alternative.

"Take a nap," I suggest. "We'll have dinner and go back to the penthouse when I'm done."

"Do I even want to know where you're going?" she asks acidly, and I shrug.

"Probably not," I tell her honestly, as I take her up the stairs to my suite on the second floor. "But if you decide you want to know, maybe I'll tell you, depending on how nicely you ask."

She wrinkles her nose, and it's a more adorable gesture than it should be. I shouldn't like it the way I do. I shouldn't give a shit either way. But as I step into the room with her, I can't resist tugging her towards me, my hand on her elbow as I lower my lips to hers.

A goodbye kiss is more intimate than I want to be with her. But I can't resist the pull of her soft mouth.

She stiffens under my touch, not returning the kiss, and I force myself not to react. To behave as if I don't care.

"I'll be back," I tell her, and then I shut the door behind me. I don't bother locking it. She's mine now, and I don't think she'll try to run. I'll have to trust her to stay put at some point. I can't keep guard over her forever.

The business I have to take care of involves one of the family businesses, a lower-end bar outside of the city that is mostly used as a money-laundering front. The ledgers have been turning up a bit short lately, and since the warnings the manager has received don't seem to have taken root, it's my job to go and look into it.

It's a reminder of who I am—the brutal man who does the dirtiest of work for my father, when I'm the only one he can trust with it. I'm not a soft man, not an emotional one. Whatever Lilliana makes me feel, the temptation to be gentler, to want something that softens me, it can only make me weaker in the end.

And if there's one thing I know my father can't stand, it's weakness. I can't let him think that my choice to marry her has made me less capable.

Even so, Lilliana is on my mind as the car makes its way toward the part of town where the bar is located. I already want her again, my palms itching to touch her. The way she'd felt under my hands, the *taste* of her—she was intoxicating. And taking her innocence—

If it was only that, I'll know soon enough. If I don't enjoy her as much, now that she's not untouched, even if it's only me that's touched her. But from the way my cock is throbbing against my thigh, I don't think that's the case.

I force my mind away from her and last night as I walk into the bar, looking for Marcus, the man in charge of it. I find him in the back office, poring over those same ledgers, and I walk in, closing the door behind me with a click.

The look that passes over his face before he regains control of his expression is enough to let me know that my father's suspicions aren't unfounded.

"Marcus. We need to have a talk."

The man's face turns a greyish-white as I lean back against the door, motioning for him to get up. "I'd like to take a look at those ledgers," I continue, and he pushes himself up out of the chair, swallowing hard.

"Sure thing, boss. No problem. Take a look."

I sit down in the uncomfortable office chair, flipping through the pages, one eye on the now-sweating man to make sure he doesn't make a break for the door. He's trying to keep a poker face, as much as a terrified man can. Everyone knows if I come down to take care of business and you've been doing something wrong, the rest of your day will be one you won't soon forget.

If you live long enough to have a chance to remember it, that is.

Four hours later, my hands are soaked in blood in a warehouse ten miles away, Marcus wriggling like a fish on a hook as he tells me everything I need to know. It wasn't him cooking the ledgers, but the fact that he kept it secret is bad enough. He's good at his job, so instead of killing him, I take three fingers. The left hand, so he can still write—but as a reminder to keep his figures straight from now on.

The man responsible for it will be at the bottom of the Chicago River by morning, but I won't have to be the one who does that. I'll send a few guys that I know I can trust to take care of it.

I tell myself that it has nothing to do with Lilliana. That I'm not passing that part of the job off because I want to be back with her, instead of dealing with the traitors and thieves who think they can pull one over on our family.

There's always been a certain amount of satisfaction in what I do, in my capabilities both as the heir to my father's empire and the one who is able to exact his will on those in need of reminding. But right now, I don't feel that satisfaction. I feel like I want to get the blood off of my hands and into a clean shirt before I go back to check on my new wife.

My phone buzzes as I go out to where the car is waiting for me, and I reach for it. I already know it's going to be my father before I even light up the screen.

Meet me in my study when you get back.

I bite back a groan of frustration. I'd planned to go straight to Lilliana and take her back to my penthouse, but it's clear that's going to have to wait. There's no rescheduling a meeting that my father demands.

He's waiting in his study when I arrive back at the mansion, exactly as expected, standing in front of the fireplace. It's reminiscent of the night that Lilliana was brought to meet us, and I think, from the sheet draped over one of the chairs, that he's set up this little tableau on purpose.

"Are you pleased with your new bride?" He asks the question without turning around, and it's hard to tell from the tone of his voice what mood he's in. He says it flatly, without any inflection.

"Yes." I don't elaborate further. I don't particularly want to discuss Lilliana with him—it feels like a minefield for which I have no guidance.

"We have proof that her father wasn't lying, at least." He gestures towards the sheet. "You don't need to keep her. There are ways to—"

"I'm pleased with my bride," I tell him, a hint of force in my tone. "In fact, I'm going to be taking her away for a few days. Up to the hunting cabin. I think the two of us could use some time alone together. To get accustomed to each other."

My father turns, and I see a small smirk at the corners of his mouth, a knowing expression. "Well. If she happens to meet with an accident, I'm sure we'll all be devastated. I know I would, to lose my new daughter-in-law so soon."

He says it with a hint of concern, as if he means it, but I know him too well not to know what underlies those words. I can feel my shoulders stiffen.

"I'm sure Lilliana will be very careful. And she'll have me there to watch over her, after all."

The last isn't a threat, not exactly. I don't think my father would go over me to harm my new wife. But he is the leader of our family. His authority supersedes me. He can do as he likes. And I know he isn't pleased with the choice I made.

"You have your proof that her father didn't lie." I gesture at the sheet, which somehow looks even more lewd, displayed here in my father's elegant study. "I'd prefer if you dispose of it, now that you've seen it."

"Of course." He glances at it, and his face is as impassive as ever. There's no way to know if he regrets giving me Lilliana, if there's jealousy there, if there's a thought that he could have been the one to enjoy her. But it's enough to make me uneasy, all the same. "Her father has what he wanted. A place in our inner circle, just under one of our brigadiers. We will see if he lives up to the challenge."

I nod. "And if he doesn't?"

My father shrugs. "We'll dispose of him."

I don't ask what that means for Lilliana. As my wife, she should have complete protection. I shouldn't have to worry about her.

But my father is not a man to turn your back on, and trust that he won't find a way to still stab you in the heart.

Lilliana

As much as I don't want to give Nikolai the satisfaction of doing anything he says, I do take a nap while he's gone. I'm too exhausted to do anything else. I fall into the huge king bed, trying not to think about whether or not he's ever brought any other women here, and I'm asleep almost the moment my head hits the pillow.

I'm woken up by the sound of the door opening. I peer through cracked eyelids, and see him walking in, an almost irritated expression on his face.

"Wake up," he says, walking to the closet and opening it. "We're leaving in an hour. You need to pack."

"Pack what?" I ask groggily, pushing myself up on my elbow. "None of my things are here."

Nikolai gestures impatiently to the closet, and I push my hair out of my face. I have that feeling that comes with a particularly deep sleep, where everything feels foggy and slow at first. It takes me a minute to see what he's talking about.

Hanging in the closet is a row of feminine clothes, and I see more folded on the shelf above it. There are shoes in a rack below, and I realize that someone shopped for and put these things away. I don't have the slightest doubt in my mind that it wasn't Nikolai—probably a personal assistant—but it startles me nonetheless.

"What is all this?" I sit up, blinking. "I don't understand."

"I had someone pick out things for you." He says it casually, as if there's no reason why I might dislike that he assigned someone to buy things for his new wife. "Anything else you might need is here as well. There are toiletries in the bathroom, an assortment of them. Whatever else you might desire can be acquired, if you want. But if you need anything, let me know before we leave. We won't be close to civilization for a few days."

I feel a knot in my stomach at that. *Is he taking me somewhere remote to get rid of me?* The possibility that he might want to dispose of me hadn't crossed my mind. I'd feared it from his father, but why go to all the trouble of marrying me just to kill me?

Truthfully, I don't understand why he went to the trouble of marrying me at all.

"Did luggage come with it?" I ask, and Nikolai raises an eyebrow.

"Still that sharp tongue." His voice is casual, offhand, as if he doesn't really care. "I'm looking forward to softening it up a little."

"You didn't answer my question." I feel a little more awake now, and my irritation with him is creeping back in.

"There's a suitcase in the closet. And lingerie in the top drawer, some of it even chosen by me." His gaze darkens, that stormy look in his eyes again. "Feel free to bring some of it along, or don't. I like you naked just as well."

I think it's meant to be a compliment. And maybe another woman would be pleased to hear him say that. But I'm not another woman. I'm the woman he chose to marry, and I have a feeling he's going to regret that choice before too much longer.

I get out of bed, ignoring my rumpled clothes and tangled hair. *I shouldn't care what he thinks of what I look like,* I remind myself as I walk to the closet, peering at what's inside as he goes to the dresser to pack some of his own things. It feels uncomfortably intimate, being in the room together, packing. Like we're a married couple—which we are…but I have no desire to actually feel that way.

Whoever did the shopping did an excellent job. The clothes are all beautiful, in my size, and it makes me wonder if Marika had a hand in it at all. Nikolai spared no expense in spoiling me; that much is clear. There's everything I could possibly need and more, and it confuses me all over again.

He wasn't expected to do any of this. I was supposed to be a fucktoy for his father, something to be enjoyed and thrown away. But now I'm Nikolai's wife, looking at a closet full of designer clothes, about to be taken away somewhere on what I can only assume is a honeymoon.

At least if he bought me all of this, he's probably not planning on taking me somewhere and murdering me. It seems like a waste.

I don't pack any of the lingerie, out of sheer stubbornness if nothing else. He can make me fuck him, but he can't make me bring clothes to dress up in for it. "Where are we going?" I ask as I put three pairs of jeans into the duffel. "I have no idea what to bring with me."

"A cabin," he says offhandedly. "Bring what you want to wear that will be comfortable. There won't be any fancy dinners or shopping excursions."

He says it almost derisively, as if he's expecting me to be disappointed. As if I care about any of that. Like my life was ever any of those things before.

"I didn't expect that," I tell him flatly, taking two of the pairs of jeans out and replacing them with leggings. If he says comfortable, I'm going to be fucking comfortable. If he has an attitude about having to see his new wife in lounge clothes, I'll remind him of what he said. I have no desire to swan around a cabin in a cocktail dress and diamonds.

"The car is going to be here soon." He looks at his phone. "Hurry up."

"I'm hurrying." I shove a handful of T-shirts into the bag. "Is a plane leaving or something? Don't you have a private jet?"

"We're driving. I'm ready to get out of here, that's all."

There's something tense in his tone that I don't like, though. If we don't have a plane to catch, there's no reason to be in such a rush, and my stomach knots with cold anxiety as I walk to the bathroom to toss whatever I might need into a bag. It takes me longer than I think he likes, but I don't actually know what's been purchased for me, so it takes me a minute to find it all.

"Are you done?" He's all but tapping his foot as I walk out with my bags, and I narrow my eyes at him.

"Maybe you do need a vacation. Are you always this tense?"

His face doesn't change. "Let's go, Lilliana."

I've started to learn that when he uses my actual name, and not one of the nicknames I despise, it means that he's serious about whatever he's saying. All it does is make me want to buck against it more, because I don't want him to think he can Pavlov me into doing what he wants by using my name.

The way he's in such a rush is starting to make my skin crawl, though. The entire idea of going out to a remote cabin with him after the way he's been acting is making me more and more uncomfortable. But I don't see how I have a choice. There's no getting out of this. If I tried to run, his security would grab me. Or he'd grab me himself, and I think I'd prefer getting tackled by the guards.

"Lilliana." His voice cuts through the air again, and I glare at him.

"Alright! Let's go."

When we walk out front, a car is there, but with no driver. I look confusedly at Nikolai as he takes my bags and gestures at the passenger's seat.

"I said I was driving."

"No, you said—" I break off, feeling that knot of anxiety tighten. He'd said *we* were driving, which I'd interpreted to mean we were being driven. But now, seeing the Maserati parked there and the lack of a driver, it's clear that he's taking the two of us to this cabin himself.

Am I coming back?

None of it makes sense. He didn't need to marry me if he was just going to off me the day after the wedding. He certainly didn't need to buy me a department store's worth of clothes and other items. But it still makes me feel as if something is wrong.

"You can't buy my affection, you know," I tell him as I slide into the car, and he starts the engine. "Designer clothes and a sports car aren't the way to my heart."

"I told you I wasn't interested in your heart." The engine purrs as he turns down the long driveway, and I fight the urge to rub my hands over the buttery soft leather seats. I've never been in a car this nice before.

"Just my body." I don't bother trying to keep the distaste out of my voice. I want him to know just how much I don't want this. *And I don't. I really don't.*

"Better me than others." He doesn't look at me as he pulls out onto the highway. "I won't hurt you."

"You and I have different ideas about what constitutes *hurt*." I push my hands between my knees. "You're making me do things I don't want to. I think that's hurting me."

"Then you have no idea what pain really is."

"And you have no idea what you're talking about," I snap back, gritting my teeth as I try to hold back the instant flare of anger that swells up in my chest. *How dare he?* He has no idea what my life has been like, what I've been through.

"I might if you told me, instead of throwing these cutting words at me constantly." Nikolai's jaw is set, and I can tell he's getting equally pissed. *Good. If we're a married couple, we might as well fight like one.*

"I don't think you really care."

"Believe what you want. But we're going to be together for a few days, and if you don't want to spend them talking, I know what else we'll spend them doing." He looks over at me, a heated glint in his eyes. "But we'll be doing a good bit of that regardless."

My stomach ties itself in knots all over again—out of dread, I tell myself, not any sort of anticipation. I don't want to go to bed with him. I don't want anything to do with him.

But I have a flash of memory of this morning, of his mouth between my legs, soft and wet and hot, and my thighs tighten involuntarily, a low throb pulsing between my thighs.

The further away from the city we go, the more visibly winter it is. There's snow by the time Nikolai tells me we're close to the cabin, and I look apprehensively out at it as he slows the car on the winding roads. The last thing I want is to be snowed in with him.

It occurred to me that I might be able to use this as an opportunity to escape. That there's a chance that I might be able to slip away from him more easily here. He didn't say if there would be security or not, and if there isn't, then it will be just him. If I could steal some money or the car—or even if I can't, I still might be able to get *away*. I can figure out the rest later.

I know that's not really a plan. Not any sort of decent one, anyway. But I have no idea what else to do. If I go back to the city with him when this strange honeymoon is over, I don't think I'll get another shot. Not for a long time—if ever.

The cabin isn't what I imagined. I'd pictured something tiny and rustic, but what rises up in the middle of the trees and snow to greet us is much more luxurious. It's made of pale wood, two stories with a dark-colored gabled roof, and a porch wrapping around. The door, I see as we drive closer, is a deep forest green, and there's snow scattered over the ground, making it all look like something out of a magazine.

Nikolai glances over at me. "Welcome to our honeymoon."

Lilliana

Nikolai kills the engine, getting out to come around and open my door. I tug my coat a little closer around me as I get out, feeling the wind pick up. It's not so much that it's colder out here than it is in the city, but it feels different. The air feels crisp and sharp, and the snow crunches under my feet as I follow Nikolai up to the front of the house.

He flips on a light as we step inside, and the house is instantly flooded with a warm, buttery glow. The floors are gleaming hardwood, a woven rug leading out of the foyer into the hall, and I kick off my boots, hanging my coat up as Nikolai slides it off my shoulders. He's being a gentleman, but I still feel anxious about all of this. I didn't see any other houses around for miles, and it feels very alone out here, just the two of us.

But there's also no security that I've seen. Which means that my tentative plan to make a run for it at some point might just be a possibility.

Is this really so bad? The thought flickers through my head, and I immediately push it away. I meant it when I said he wasn't going to buy my compliance, and I have every intention of sticking to that. *I've never needed any of this*, I remind myself as we walk into the living room of the house. *I'm not going to start now.*

Nikolai flicks on another light, flooding the room with that same warm, cozy glow. The house is furnished and decorated in warm woods and soft textiles, and there's a huge stone fireplace against the far wall, between two large windows looking out to the snowy night beyond.

"I'll get a fire started and get us something to drink. Sit down." He gestures towards one of the soft-looking dark brown couches.

"Do you ever say anything in a way that doesn't sound like you're giving orders?"

I expect an irritated retort from him, but instead, he suddenly turns, stepping closer to me. He moves smoothly, faster than I expected, and his fingers are under my chin, tipping them up so that I'm looking up into those blue-grey eyes.

"If I'm giving you orders, *krolik*," he murmurs. "You'll know it."

My heart skips in my chest. It shouldn't. But he looks down at me, his voice suddenly smooth and smoky, and I feel my breath catch in my throat and my pulse quicken.

"Sit down," he says again. "Or you'll be sitting on my lap."

Somehow, I make my feet move, pushing past him to the couch. I see the smirk play on his lips, and I hate him for it. He makes me feel as if it's *my* fault for not wanting this, as if I'm the one being difficult, when he's the one who forced me into a marriage I didn't want.

He crouches in front of the fireplace, taking sticks of wood out of the brass holder next to it and sticking kindling in between—and it makes me forget for a brief second how pissed I am, because I'm so surprised to actually see him building a fire. I'd assumed there would be security and staff here just like the mansion, that someone as wealthy and powerful as Nikolai wouldn't do anything for himself. But it really does appear to be just the two of us here.

The room is quiet, and I sit there, hands knotted in my lap, as I watch him work on the fire. I don't know what comes next, but I can't imagine it's anything good. I don't understand why he bothered bringing me here. He could have fucked me just as well at the mansion, or his penthouse that he keeps mentioning. He didn't have to take me away to the middle of nowhere.

Nikolai stands up, brushing his hands off on the dark jeans he'd changed into before we left, and I'm struck all over again by the muscled size of him. He's tall, with broad shoulders and visible muscle in his arms and thighs, the dark denim of his jeans and charcoal fabric of his t-shirt stretched tautly over them. He flexes his hands, and I remember what they felt like on my skin.

I don't want to want this. But a flush of heat spreads through me, tingling over my skin, and I feel my mouth go dry as he walks towards where I'm sitting on the couch.

"Hungry?" he asks, and I realize I am. I haven't eaten all day, except for the dry toast and fruit that I picked at while we were at the hotel. But I'm nothing if not stubborn, when it comes to Nikolai. I don't want to give him something else to use against me.

I shrug. "I'm fine."

He glares at me, letting out an exasperated breath. "How many times do I need to tell you that you don't have to fight me on *everything*, Lilliana? I know you're hungry. I asked as a courtesy, but I know you barely ate this morning, and I'd be willing to bet you didn't ask for lunch at the mansion."

He's right about that. The idea of having staff still makes me feel uncomfortable, and there was no chance I was going to find my way downstairs to the kitchen and find someone who would get me a meal. I didn't think I'd be allowed to cook for myself.

More than that, I'd been afraid of running into his father. But I'm not about to admit that aloud.

"Where are we getting food?" I cross my arms over my chest. "I don't think there's sushi takeout here in the middle of nowhere."

"I despise sushi," Nikolai informs me. "But there's plenty of food here."

"Who's going to cook? You?" I'm actually a fairly decent cook, but I'm not about to tell Nikolai that. I refuse to be his stand-in maid while he has me trapped here.

"That was the plan." Nikolai gestures for me to follow him. "Come with me. I'll get you a glass of wine while I start dinner."

"Is it going to be poisoned?"

Nikolai looks as if he's struggling mightily to hold onto his patience, which just pisses me off that much more. *He* has no right to feel impatient, irritated, or anything else. He's the architect of this entire situation.

"Just come with me, Lilliana."

He's called me Lilliana, and not one of his nicknames, more since we got to the cabin than since we met. That feels like a sort of victory, especially since it means I'm getting under his skin. I haven't given up on the idea that if I irritate him enough, maybe he'll just divorce me when he's tired of me in bed.

So I give in to this one thing, and follow him out of the living room.

He takes me into a huge open kitchen with a large island in that same pale wood with a black granite-topped counter and a rustic-looking iron rack hanging above it that holds all sorts of pots and pans. Nikolai motions for me to sit down at one of the leather-topped barstools, and then crosses to a black granite countertop on the other side of the kitchen, where there's a wine rack made out of the same rustic iron.

"I seem to recall you liked the wine we had at dinner that first night." He slides a bottle out of the rack, smoothly opening it and sliding a glass decanter toward where he's standing. Everything he does seems effortless and practiced, and I wonder how much time he spends here.

"Do you come here a lot? To be alone, or—" The question comes out without thinking, and I stop myself halfway through, cursing myself for showing any interest in all in what he does. I regret it even more when I see the small smirk that appears at the corner of Nikolai's full lips.

"Ah. Finally showing an interest in your new husband, I see." He reaches up, opening one of the wooden cabinets, and gets out two wine glasses before crossing to the black metal refrigerator, where he pulls out a white paper packet and sets it on the counter, all without answering me yet.

Nikolai turns, looking at me as he leans one hip against the counter. "Is there anything I can get you while the wine breathes? Some water?"

"What are you, the fucking wait staff?" I glare at him. "Can you not answer one single question? I already regret asking at all."

"You don't answer very many of mine." He reaches up into another cabinet, getting out a glass, and filling it with water before pushing it across the island to me. I am actually thirsty, but I don't touch it.

"Fine. I don't really care anyway." There's a droplet of condensation on the glass, and I'm reminded that my long nap this afternoon means I've drank as little as I've eaten today. I reach for the glass, hoping he doesn't make a big deal out of it.

Nikolai unfolds the paper packet, and I see two thick steaks. "I hope you eat meat," he says casually, as he starts to move about the kitchen. "I suppose I don't really know if you were just being polite at the dinners before and our reception."

"If I didn't eat meat, I wouldn't have been polite." I feel slightly feral, looking at the steaks and the other food that Nikolai starts to set out on the counter—small red potatoes, a bundle of fresh-looking asparagus, butter, lemon, and herbs. I'm not going to be able to pretend not to be hungry once he starts cooking, if he's any kind of a decent cook at all.

"Of course. That was foolish of me. When have you ever spared my feelings?" There's thick sarcasm in his voice as he walks over to where I'm sitting, and sets the wine glass next to me, the decanter in the center of the island as one of his long-fingered hands curls around the edge of the barstool, his arm pressing against my back.

"You're mine, *krolik*," he murmurs. "We can find out more about each other over time, if you like. We can try to make some kind of peaceful marriage out of this—determine a truce, if you will. But I will only tolerate your behavior for so long. I'm giving you plenty of rope, Lilliana, because I know this is difficult for you. But in time, if you don't reign in this seemingly natural obstinacy of yours, you'll hang yourself with it."

My skin chills at that, and I have to force myself to keep my face blank, not to react. "Is that a threat?" I ask, tipping my chin up to look into those blue-grey eyes, and Nikolai laughs softly.

"Again, *krolik*. If I were threatening you, you would know it."

I don't doubt that's true. I can feel the powerful bulk of his body leaning over me, the looming presence of him, and I know he could make me do anything, do anything *to* me, that he wanted.

I have to get out of here. I have to find a way out.

The most obvious answer is to get him to drop his guard. There's no security here, no one except Nikolai to keep me trapped. But if he's on edge because I'm constantly baiting him, he's going to be watching me very carefully.

If I'm suddenly sweet and compliant, though, he'll also suspect that something is up. This isn't a game I can win without thinking through every move I make.

He steps back, pouring wine into both of our glasses. "Maybe this will help you relax a little. It's our honeymoon, *krolik*. A vacation."

Nikolai goes back to cooking dinner, and I take a sip of the wine. It's delicious, and I'm pretty sure it really is the one we had at that first dinner he arranged for us, although I'm not certain. My palate isn't that refined.

As I'd expected, it smells amazing. The kitchen is filled in minutes with the scents of butter, garlic, herbs, citrus, and cooking meat. I bite my lip to keep from making a sound that would let Nikolai know just how much I'm looking forward to the meal.

Gourmet food, a closet full of designer clothes, and a gorgeous man who wants to fuck your brains out? Maybe you really are protesting too much.

It's the principle of the thing, though. I haven't chosen to be here. I've been forced. And none of this was ever part of what I'd been prepared for. This wasn't the *deal*.

It doesn't matter what he bribes me with, I remind myself sternly. *I'm not giving in.*

It's much harder to remember that when Nikolai slides a blue stoneware plate over to me, refilling my wine before he sits across from me at the island, refilling his own glass as well.

It's heavenly. The steak has a crust on it of blue cheese and garlic, the mashed potatoes are velvety and creamy, and I thought I hated asparagus—but evidently not roasted like this, with herbs and lemon. I've never had a meal like it—it's even better than what the staff at the mansion made for us or what was catered at our reception—and I end up complimenting him before I can stop myself.

"This is incredible," I blurt out, and Nikolai looks up at me. I expect a sarcastic smirk, a cutting remark, but he just watches me for a moment, almost as if he's enjoying seeing me eat the food.

"I'm glad you like it," he says finally, and I hear myself speak again, even as I'm screaming in my head that I'm supposed to be withdrawn. I'm not supposed to care about any of this shit.

"Why did you learn to cook? It's not like you don't have an army of servants waiting on your every need." *There, that last part was better. Deprecating. A little rude. What he's come to expect from you.*

Now Nikolai does smirk, shaking his head as he takes another sip of his wine. "Everyone needs a hobby," he says with a shrug.

"Yours isn't pulling off fingernails or something?" I roll my eyes at him, stabbing another piece of asparagus with my fork.

Something flickers across his face that I can't quite understand. "Well, some days everyone's fingernails stay intact, and I need something to do," he says finally, but a little of the humor in his voice is gone.

"Why did you bring me out here?" *I might as well just say it. Even if he's not going to answer.*

Nikolai frowns, refilling his wine glass and mine. "It's a honeymoon, Lilliana. You know, the thing you do after a wedding."

"So you brought me out here into the middle of nowhere?"

"Is it not nice enough for your refined tastes?" He gives me a challenging look, and I have to admit, he's got me there. Even this supposedly rustic, isolated cabin is miles beyond what I grew up with. It definitely stretches the bounds of the definition of "rustic." I'd go so far as to say that it only applies to the aesthetic of the place, not the cabin itself.

"There's an indoor/outdoor hot tub," he says after a few moments, taking another bite of his steak. "Why don't you go upstairs and put on your bikini, once you're done with your food? I'll clean up."

I blink at him. "I didn't bring one."

He raises an eyebrow, and I can see that goddamned smirk at the corners of his mouth again. "No? Why not?"

I grit my teeth together to keep from shouting at him. "Remember when you told me you were taking me to a cabin in the woods in the middle of winter? I didn't pack for a tropical vacation."

The smile spreads across his face, and I realize I've ended up right where he wanted me. "Well, I suppose you'll just have to skinny dip, then."

"Or I could go to bed." I once again regret the words as soon as they come out of my mouth, seeing the expression on his face.

"Well, if that's where you want me, then—"

I glare at him. "I meant to sleep."

Nikolai laughs. "Oh, you won't be sleeping for a while, Lilliana. I plan to enjoy as much of the night with you as I can, until we're both too tired to stay up any longer."

"Is that supposed to be enticing?"

"It could be if you let it."

We look at each other from across the table, and Nikolai lets out a long breath. "I'm going to clean up," he says finally, as we finish our food. "And since you don't have a swimsuit, you can sit right there until I'm done, and I'll show you the hot tub."

It's clear that I'm not getting a say in how the night goes—not that I really thought I was getting one anyway. I also know I'm going to have to try harder if I want any chance of being out from under his gaze long enough to escape.

I keep sipping the wine while I wait for Nikolai to finish, hoping that a little bit of a buzz from the alcohol will make the night more bearable, and trying not to think about how it feels like I'm seeing a different side to him here. The man who cooked dinner and is currently loading a dishwasher doesn't seem like the brutal, arrogant Bratva heir that I was introduced to. He seems almost—normal.

He still forced you to marry him. He isn't letting you go. And he's still someone who insists you obey his every whim. Doing a few dishes doesn't change that.

But when he takes me to where the hot tub is, it's almost enough to make me forget that resolve I had earlier.

Hot tub isn't an accurate description for it, just as *remote cabin* isn't a good way to explain where we're staying. There's a large room at the back of the cabin, spanning the width of it, with a wet bar built into one wall, a large television and seating area on the other side, and then, along the wall facing the woods that is nothing but one floor-to-ceiling glass window, there's a black granite pool built into the length of it. That's the only way to describe it—a *pool*, not a hot tub. It's narrow, the width of maybe two people side by side if they were broad-shouldered, and as Nikolai and I walk closer, I see that the glass window opens out into the snowy landscape beyond the cabin, with the pool extending outside. Steam is rising off of it, and the inner portion has glowing fairy lights strung along the ceiling, creating a star-like effect above the heated pool.

I can't control the expression on my face. I've never seen anything like it, and I know Nikolai can see.

"I can tell you like it." There's almost something pleased in his voice, as if he's *glad* that I like it. As if that somehow matters to him.

He's a mystery to me. So much about him doesn't make sense. And I can't let myself start to want to unravel it.

Nikolai strips off his shirt, and I try not to look. But I *can't*. For all that I hate him, that I don't want to be married to him—he's fucking gorgeous. His muscles stretch and flex as he takes off the shirt and tosses it over a nearby seat, all that tattooed flesh on display, ink curling over his chest and down his abdomen, over his shoulders, and around his arms in patterns and designs that I haven't allowed myself to really look at. I never want him to catch me staring. But he looks deadly and beautiful like this, and for a brief second, I let myself just look.

His hands go to his belt, and he motions at me. "Take off your clothes, *krolik*," he says in that low, smoky voice, and I feel my pulse stutter in my throat.

I don't move. "I don't want to," I say in a small voice, hating myself for it, but if defiance doesn't work, then I can try for sympathy. I can try to appeal to whatever other side of him seems to have come out here.

Nikolai's jaw tightens. "Do you remember earlier, when I said you would know if I gave you orders? Take off your clothes."

His belt comes undone, and his hands linger on it. I have a sudden vision of that leather folded over, striking my skin, and I'm not sure where it comes from. He's never directly threatened anything like that.

Worse still is the odd prickle of heat I feel at the idea.

"We're going to enjoy the water together," he says smoothly, his fingers drawing down his zipper. "And I'm going to enjoy you with your clothes off. So do it, *krolik*. This time I'm not doing it for you."

I don't have a choice. I *know* I don't, and that makes me even angrier. "Fine," I hiss, grabbing the hem of my t-shirt and yanking it over my head. I'm not going to strip sensually for him.

I can feel his eyes on me as I toss the t-shirt onto the floor. "The bra next," he says, his voice low and smooth.

"You're going to decide what order I take my clothes off in now?"

"You're doing it for my pleasure, Lilliana." There's my name again, but it sounds more decadent on his tongue now, his accent thickening, as if he's savoring saying it. It sends a shiver down my spine and makes something low in my belly clench, and I try to fight the sensation. It feels as if it's slowing me down, pulling me under. Drawing me towards him.

If I try to please him, maybe I'll have more of an opportunity to escape.

I reach behind my back, unhooking the bra. I hear the low sound he makes in his throat as he sees my breasts, almost a growl of anticipation, and I force myself to look at him, eyelashes lowered as I drop the bra to the floor and reach for the button of my jeans.

"Slowly." His voice is thicker now, full of a lust that makes my hands tremble. His gaze sweeps down my body, and I can see how much he wants me.

There's something a little heady about that—the idea that this powerful man wants me so much. It's something I could get caught up in, if I'm not careful. Something that could drag me down, if I let it.

Slowly, I push my jeans down my hips, taking my panties down with them, as one final act of rebellion. I know he's going to want me to do it separately, but I'm not willing to cede all of the control to him.

"Good girl." The words are smooth as molasses on his lips, and I feel that prickle of heat over my skin again. "But you should have left the panties on."

He's still half-dressed, and I know what it is—the power that comes with him still being partially clothed while I stand there bare. I know he enjoys it. And I *shouldn't*—but if I don't, then why do I feel that wet heat gathering between my thighs, that ache spreading through me as I stand there under the weight of his gaze?

I know the answer to that, and I don't like it.

"You were going to tell me to take them off anyway."

"Of course." He starts to push his own jeans down. "But when *I* decided."

He's half-hard when he steps out of his pants, and I see him stiffen as he looks at me, his cock rising as his gaze sweeps over my naked body again. "Come on, little rabbit," he murmurs softly as he steps towards the pool, gesturing to me. "I won't eat you. Yet."

God. The memory of his tongue between my thighs has my knees weakening. I suck in a breath as I follow him, and one of the worst parts of it all is that I *don't* hate *this*. Of all the time I've spent with Nikolai so far—and it's been much less than I'd think someone should have spent with the person they were going to marry, but what do I know? This isn't a world I belong in—tonight has been by far something that I would have liked the best…if I liked him.

It's all something I wish I *could* let myself enjoy. The secluded cabin, the romantic atmosphere, the delicious dinner he cooked himself for us, and now skinny-dipping in a luxurious heated pool with the snowy vista just beyond us—it's all something out of a fantasy. Not a fantasy I've ever had—but one that maybe I could have had, if I'd ever felt like this kind of a thing was a possibility for me.

It would be so easy to let myself fall into it. To accept that this is my life now. This is my future. To try to find some form of happiness in it.

But that would be ceding the victory to him. And clinging to my refusal to enjoy anything he offers me is all I have left. Certainly not my own free will or choice.

"Lilliana." I can hear the exasperation in his voice. "Come here."

There's a clear order in the words, and it makes me defiant all over again, but I go anyway. I step into the water, the warmth wrapping itself around me as it comes up around my waist, and I can feel Nikolai's eyes on me.

"Feels nice, doesn't it?" He steps towards me, the water swirling around his hips, and he reaches for me, pulling me closer.

"Yes," I admit. There's no point in lying. It's probably one of the best things I've ever experienced—and he knows that.

Why? I ask myself all over again, as he draws me in and lowers his mouth to mine. *Why seduce me like this? Why even try to be romantic? What's the point?* He's gotten what he wanted. He has me—for as long as he wants me. I can fight him, but I can't outright refuse.

Seduction, I always thought, was for men who couldn't simply take. Nikolai *has* already taken me. So all of this feels so pointless.

Unless it's simply because he wants me to give in and fall into his trap. He wants to catch his little rabbit.

I can't stop him from kissing me. But I don't kiss him back. I stand there in the water, his fingers pressing into my waist as his full, soft lips slant over mine, and I pretend that none of this is happening.

He can have some of what he wants. But not all of it.

Nikolai

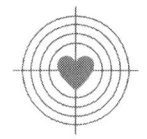

Why am I doing this?

The question sticks in my mind as I kiss her, and feel her go wooden under my touch. Why am I even bothering?

If it's pleasure I want, I can have it. I don't have to seduce her to have her in my bed. I don't have to do any of the bullshit I've done tonight just to fuck her.

But I want something *more*.

I want her submission. I want her desire. I want her to admit what she can't even admit to herself, that she wants me. That she wants what I can do to her, what I can give her.

You said you weren't going to hurt her. Isn't that the cruelest thing of all, to make her give in and then take it away?

I'm not taking anything away. She'll still be my pampered wife. I'll just be the one in control. The one who decides if and when she gets my attention. I won't feel so—unhinged. Feral. Needy.

A man like me shouldn't be needy. Not for anyone or anything. The world bends to me, not the other way around.

She's going to bend to me.

"There's a lot I want to do to you tonight," I murmur against her mouth, my hands stroking along her waist. I want her to soften against me, to moan, to let me know that she's enjoying this. "But we'll start with this."

I lift her up out of the steaming water, setting her on the edge of the pool. She lets out a small, involuntary gasp, her full lips parting, and there are so many fucking things I want from her. So many things I want her to do with that mouth, that I haven't demanded yet.

My hands slide up her legs over wet skin, pushing them apart. She has the prettiest pussy I've ever seen, soft and pink and tight, and I want to taste her again. I want to show her just how much pleasure I can give her if she lets me.

I turn my head, pressing a kiss to her inner thigh. It's more tender than I mean to be, but maybe that's what she needs. A little tenderness to soften her.

It doesn't work. If anything, she only stiffens more under my lips and hands, and I fight back a wave of frustration, and the urge to simply pull her back down into the water and onto my cock. I don't have to be so patient with her. I don't have to give her so much room. I could simply take what I want.

But if I do, I'll never get what I really want in the end.

I lean in, brushing my lips over the soft outer folds of her pussy. Her hands clench against the sides of the pool, her body rigid with the effort of not reacting. She does her best not to let me know that it feels good, but she doesn't understand that I already know. I know *exactly* what I'm doing, and maybe it's arrogant, but I don't ever have any doubt that I can make a woman come.

Lilliana is going to come for me whether she wants to or not.

I slide my hands upwards, tracing my fingers over her soft folds, parting her for my tongue. She's still rigid under my touch, but I ignore it, flicking my tongue out to stroke her clit, focusing right on the spot where I know it will please her the most.

Her body jerks when I lick her, and I feel a jolt of satisfaction. *There. Not so wooden now, are you?* I feel the small muscles in her thighs tremble where they're pressed against my arms, and I stroke my tongue over her again. She tastes sweet, and I turn my head, licking and nibbling gently at her soft flesh as she sucks in an involuntary breath.

"There you go, little rabbit. Enjoy it. There's no harm in that."

"You said you weren't going to eat me," she whispers, her voice trembling, and I laugh.

I can't help it. It's the first bit of humor I've gotten from her, even if it's said in a voice that sounds as if she's afraid, and I kiss her thigh again, rubbing my hands over her. "I said 'not yet.' *krolik*," I murmur, kissing my way back up to where I want my mouth on her the most. "And I couldn't wait any longer."

I run my tongue up her pussy, sliding it between her inner folds, and I hear her suck in another sharp breath as I push my tongue inside of her. Her legs stiffen, her back arching as she grips the sides of the pool hard enough for her knuckles to turn white.

"Nikolai, *stop*," she moans, and I pull back, but not because I plan to listen to her.

I stand up to my full height, leaning over her as I slide my hand around the back of her neck, wrapping her hair in my fist.

"There's no stopping, little rabbit," I murmur, leaning close. "You're mine now. I married you, and you belong to me. But I plan to make this trap a very pleasant one for you, if you let me."

"Nikolai—" There's something almost close to pleading in her voice now, and I wonder what I'll do if she begs me to stop. I don't want to. I'm not sure that I *can*—the taste of her has me rock-hard, and I've only kept myself from fucking her because I want her to come on my tongue first. But if she begs—

I slide my fingers against her pussy. She's wet, both from my tongue and her pleasure, and I trace my fingertips around her entrance. "Let me make you come, rabbit," I murmur, pushing my fingers inside of her, up to the first knuckle. "Just give in. It will be so much better for you when you do."

When. Not *if,* but *when.* She *will* submit to me. No matter how long it takes.

The ferocity of the thought startles me. But Lilliana clenches around my fingers, tight and wet, her mouth opening on a plea that turns into a startled gasp of pleasure as I curl them inside of her.

"There you go, *krolik*," I whisper, bending my head to run my lips along her ear as I keep her head tugged back. "Squeeze my fingers. You like being filled. I know you do. I felt how tightly you gripped my cock last night."

She clenches her jaw, glaring up at me, and I laugh—a low, dark sound that rumbles against her ear. "Fight it all you want, little rabbit. But I can feel what you don't want to tell me."

I keep sliding my fingers inside of her, stroking that tight, hot wetness until I feel her start to shudder. I bend my lips to her throat, kissing and sucking lightly against the soft flesh, but I don't want to feel her come on my fingers. I want to feel her come on my tongue.

I hold her in place with one hand hard on her thigh as I slide back down into the heated water, and I slide my fingers out of her in one swift motion, replacing them with my tongue.

Her entire body jerks again, and she lets out a small cry of shock, her hips arching upwards against her mouth. I stiffen my tongue inside of her, curling it, licking her from the inside out as I fuck her with it like a smaller version of my cock, and her breathing quickens, turning into short gasps as I drive her towards the edge.

I press my thumb against her clit, rolling it beneath the soft pad, and she falls apart.

I can't describe how it feels to have her clench around my tongue. I can feel her squeezing and fluttering, and I want to feel that around my cock so desperately that I nearly come on the spot, my cock jerking in the water as I feel her arousal flood my mouth.

She tastes so fucking good. I could eat her out all night, and as her spasms start to lessen, her body loosening around me, I swipe my tongue upwards as I replace my tongue with my fingers again.

Her second orgasm is almost instantaneous. I can *feel* the anger radiating off of her, but it's almost as if that intensifies it for her. Her hips buck against my mouth, small whimpers squeezing out between her clenched teeth as she fights the pleasure, and the more she fights it, the harder she comes.

I need to fuck her. I let her ride out her climax, wait until she's nearly stopped shuddering and writhing on my tongue, and then I yank her towards me, catching her mouth in a deep, hungry kiss as I pull her back into the water and spin her around so she's facing away from me.

"Hold onto the edge," I order her, my arm sliding around her waist as I move her into the position I want. My other hand squeezes her perfect ass before lining up my cock with her drenched entrance.

I hadn't planned to fuck her in the pool. But I can't resist her.

She's still fluttering when I push inside of her; the stretch is almost too much, even after she's come twice. She's so fucking tight that it's almost painful the way she grips my cock, but I slide deeper anyway, taking her a little harder than I did last night. I don't want to hurt her—I know she's still sore, and this is only the second day—but I can't go as slowly as she might need. I want her too much for that.

I hear the sound she makes behind her clenched teeth, and it almost sounds like my name, bitten back so that she won't moan it aloud. Her back arches, her hips pushing back into me, and I know I'm winning this battle. She's still fighting me, but her body wants what her mouth claims it doesn't.

"That's it, *krolik*," I murmur, sliding my hand over her hip. "Good girl. You take my cock so well. So tight and wet for me."

"Not for you." She pants out the words, her pussy squeezing around me again despite herself. "Never for you. I won't—"

"For who, then?" I grip her ass, squeezing hard as I thrust again, sinking deep this time, enough to make her cry out a little with the hard jolt of my cock all the way inside of her. "If you're thinking of someone else, rabbit, I'll have to find him and kill him."

"No one." She spits out the word. "I'm not thinking about anyone. But definitely not *you*."

"I don't believe you." Another hard thrust. *God*, she feels fucking incredible. I rock my hips against her, sinking myself as deeply as I can go.

"I don't care." Her head drops forward, her hands gripping the sides of the pool in a death grip. "I don't care what you think."

It's almost difficult to slide back out, just because it feels so fucking good to be in her like this, every inch of my cock buried, her hips rocking back against me despite herself. I grind into her, the heated water splashing around us, and when I finally manage to find the will to thrust again, I slam myself back into her, unable to resist the urge to take her as hard as I want, just for a moment.

The instant I thrust back into her, the hard, rough slide sending a jolt of pleasure down to my toes, she lets out a cry that stops me. It's clearly a cry of pain, and I let go of my hold on her hip, still buried inside of her, as I feel her shudder.

"I'm sorry, *krolik*." I run my hand along her waist, trying to soothe her. "I didn't mean to hurt you."

"You're always hurting me." She turns her head away, and for the first time, I feel some of my arousal lessening. Her insistence that I'm hurting her is starting to get to me, even as I try to shove it away.

"I don't mean to hurt you like that." I keep still inside of her, giving a moment for the pain to fade, before I start to move again—slowly this time. I slide my hand over her belly, down between her thighs, and stroke my fingers over her clit, wanting to feel her come when I do. I want that feeling of her gripping my cock again as I fill her up.

Another small moan slips from her mouth, as if my touch is soothing away the pain, and I like that more than I should.

"That's it, little rabbit. Come for me." I rub her clit a little more firmly. "Let me make you feel good."

Her back arches, and I can tell she's losing control. "I don't...want to," she pants, and I shake my head, thrusting into her again and holding onto control of my own climax for dear life as I roll my fingers over her swollen clit.

"Yes, you do, *krolik*. Stop fighting it. Stop fighting *me*."

She lets out a sound that's half moan, half sob, and her entire body spasms as I feel a sudden flood of heated wetness over my cock, her body clenching and pulsing around me, rippling down my hard shaft as I groan aloud and rock forward, thrusting into her as deeply as I can without hurting her again. I can feel how tightly she's stretched around me, how her orgasm pushes the boundaries of what she can take, and feeling her like this drives me insane.

The pleasure is too much. At the sound of her moan, her losing control, the *feeling* of her around me, my cock swells and throbs harder than I think I've ever been in my life as I thrust into her once more, feeling my balls ache with an exquisite pleasure as I fill her with my cum.

She lets out another of those sounds, another sobbing moan as she feels the hot rush of my cum. It sends another wave of release through me, prolonging my orgasm at the sound of her moaning because of my cock.

Her hands are still gripping the edge of the pool as she stands there, her head hanging down, and as I slide out of her, I reach for her, tugging her away and into my arms. The slide of my cock out of her is a sweet pain, my oversensitive flesh wanting more and unable to take it. Still, it's overshadowed by the fact that I don't know why I feel the urge to soothe her, to comfort. I've always wanted space from whoever was in my bed after I came, but now I want her in my arms.

"Come here, little rabbit." I stroke a hand over her damp hair, and for one brief second, she leans against my chest, her hands pressed against me as if she wants the comfort, too.

And then she pushes herself away, arms crossed over her breasts as she swallows hard.

"Happy? Feel better? Can I go upstairs and go to sleep now."

The momentary softness I felt towards her is instantly replaced by a sharp stab of irritation. "No, *krolik*," I tell her as calmly as I can manage. "We're going to enjoy the evening as I planned. And then, afterward, we'll see what we do in bed. But I don't believe it will be sleeping."

Lilliana grits her teeth, but she says nothing. And I wonder if, for the first time, my bride might not be dreading the idea of being in my bed as much as she'd like for me to believe.

Nikolai

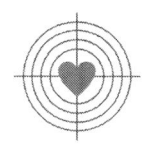

While she stands there in the pool, glaring at me as if I'd kicked her favorite puppy, I get out and go to the wet bar to get us drinks.

"Do you want wine, rabbit? Or something else?"

"What will it take to get you to stop calling me that?" she grinds out between her teeth, and I can see that her attitude is back in full swing.

"Nothing," I tell her calmly as I get out a crystal glass, pouring a splash of good whisky into it. "I like the nicknames I've chosen for you. They seem fitting."

"Only to you."

"Well, that's what matters." I take a long sip of the whisky and add another slug of it. Lilliana is likely to make me need it before the night is over.

Unfortunately, it's part of what draws me to her. Her defiance, her rebellion, her smart mouth—it's all so different from what I'm used to, from the way women usually treat me. I never thought confrontation would arouse me, but every time Lilliana mouths off to me, it feels like it goes straight to my cock.

"You can tell me what you want, or I'll pick something for you," I tell her, and I hear the sigh she lets out.

"Wine," she says finally. "You really want to stay out here?"

"You don't?" I gesture to the pool and the view beyond, and I can see that she doesn't have an argument for that. It's truly stunning, and I see her gaze flick out to the snowy landscape past the windows.

I don't bother with a towel when I get out to fetch our drinks, and I can feel her eyes on me as I uncork and pour the wine, entirely naked. My cock has softened, but it's still thicker and longer than most men, even when I'm not aroused, and I know she enjoys looking at the rest of me, too. I've seen the way she's looked at me when she thinks she has enough time that I won't notice—or when she just can't help herself.

I like to think I'm not a particularly arrogant man, but I've always enjoyed women's attention. Something about Lilliana being unable to *not* look at me feels better, though. Like something I've won, if she can't stop herself from ogling.

This girl is really getting under your fucking skin, Vasilev.

I bring her the wine, wondering idly if she might smash the glass and stab me with it. I'd almost be impressed if she tried, but she just takes it from me as I sit on the edge of the pool nude, sipping my whisky as she takes a slow drink of the wine.

"I'll make a wine connoisseur out of you yet," I tell her, slipping back into the water and setting my glass on the edge.

"I think it would be wasted on me." She takes another drink. "I doubt they'd taste all that different."

"Well, there's only one way to find out." I watch her as I say it, and her expression doesn't change. I don't know why I feel the urge to introduce her to new things, show her how this life she's now a part of doesn't have to be the prison she thinks it is. No matter how I try to not care, it feels as if she keeps working her way back in.

I finish my whiskey, and then I motion to the floor-to-ceiling window. "Let's go outside."

Lilliana looks at me as if I've lost my mind. "It's freezing out there. *Below* freezing."

"It feels nice when you're in the hot water. Trust me."

As soon as I see the look on her face, I realize what a ridiculous statement that was. Of course, she doesn't trust me. I can see the moment that she considers whether or not to argue, and then shrugs.

"Fine. But if I feel like I'm freezing my tits off, I'm coming back inside immediately. *And* going up to bed."

"Such crude language." I let my gaze sweep over her bare chest, letting her see just how much I enjoy looking at her when she's naked for me like this. "You have a deal, *krolik*. But if you go up to bed, I'll be coming with you. So just remember that."

She doesn't argue with me again about it. She follows me out through the cut-glass opening that leads to the outdoor part of the pool, the steam rising up off of the water, and I can see a light prickle of gooseflesh over her arms and upper shoulders. I almost want her to beg off, saying it's too cold, so I can take her back to bed.

I see her gaze flick around the view, and I want to see her reaction. It's beautiful out here—the ground misted with snow, the trees rising as a backdrop, the dark sky studded with stars. I have the sudden urge to tell her how much I love coming out here, how relaxing I find it, away from my father and the responsibilities of our family. How often I like to come here alone when I can—and how having her here has made it…

Made it what, exactly? I can't say more pleasant—Lilliana is not a pleasant companion right now, at least not conversationally. *Interesting?* I don't think she'd take that as a compliment. And she already knows how much I enjoy fucking her.

"It's beautiful," she says softly, and it might be one of the first sincere things I've heard her say that isn't tinged with sarcasm or a biting comment. I think she realizes as soon as the words come out of her mouth what she's said, because she looks away, wrapping her arms around herself. "And cold," she adds, as if she's remembered that she's not supposed to enjoy any of this.

I move through the water towards her, reaching for her waist as I pull her back against me, and I lean down, brushing my lips over her shoulder where the skin is prickled. "You do look a little cold," I murmur. "Should we go upstairs and warm up?"

She tenses instantly. "It's not that bad."

"You'd rather freeze than have me fuck you again? It's not *that* bad, Lilliana. I've made you come more times than you have in your entire life. After all, you did say you've never even touched yourself."

I wait for her to admit that she did the first night in the mansion. I have no idea how many more times she made herself come in the two weeks between that night and our wedding—and it drove me insane to imagine it—but I know she did that night, after I touched her in the study. Whether or not she'll tell me remains to be seen.

"You're full of yourself," she says tightly, her arms still wrapped around herself. "Maybe I faked it."

"I know the difference. But if you don't—" I let one of my hands slide over her stomach, down lower, just above where I imagine I might find her hot and wet if I touched her there. "I could help remind you. And don't worry," I add, my fingers stroking over the smooth, bare flesh at the top of her pussy and feeling her shiver. "Soon enough, you'll be full of me."

She wrenches away from me, gliding through the water until several arms' lengths are between us. "Do these lines normally work on women?" she demands, the words thrown over her shoulder at me as she turns away to try to keep me from looking at her bare breasts. "Because they're not working on me, Nikolai."

"Sometimes." I follow her, and I feel a flicker of heated excitement. It's a low-effort chase, but it's a chase nonetheless, and out here in the dark silence, with nothing but the snowy woods beyond, I feel as if she's my prey. A pretty little rabbit, waiting for me to catch her and gobble her up.

She tries to move away from me, but I grab her by her waist, pulling her back against me, letting her feel that I'm hard all over again as I press my cock against her ass. "Maybe it is time to go upstairs," I murmur into her ear, and I feel the faintest twitch of her hips, her ass moving against me involuntarily at the sensation of my cock before she catches herself.

Lilliana can pretend she doesn't want me at all, but little by little, she's giving herself away.

I lead her back inside, giving her a towel as I gather up our clothes. She balks as we start to walk towards the stairs, and I look at her, shaking my head.

"I can carry you upstairs, Lilliana, but you're not going to like it nearly as much when we get up there if you make me do that."

She glares at me, her lips thinning, but she follows me up. There's an odd tug-of-war here that I don't entirely understand, one that leaves me constantly off-balance, and I don't like it. I can never tell what will make her give in, and when I *want* her to give in, she seems to know and fights harder.

She makes me feel as if I'm losing my mind—and all because I couldn't leave her to my father's nonexistent mercy. All because I wanted her. Because I couldn't make myself force her and then throw her away.

I flick the light on to the bedroom, and I'm once again rewarded by a small, involuntary gasp from Lilliana. She looks around, her eyes widening slightly as she takes in the huge, rustic four-poster bed, the knotted pine floor, the thick fur rug in front of the stone fireplace, the iron chandelier hanging over the velvet wing chairs next to the bookshelf and window that look out over the view beyond. There's a balcony out there too, but it *is* too cold for that.

"I'll build a fire," I tell her. "There's a robe in the closet, but don't bother with it. I want you naked for me tonight. You can unpack your things tomorrow."

She stares at me as I walk to the fireplace. "How do you say that so casually?" she demands. "You can't just *tell* me that I'm going to be naked. It's supposed to be—"

"What?" I turn and look at her as I crouch in front of the fireplace. "How is it supposed to be, Lilliana? Because I can guarantee that my father wouldn't have given you a choice, either, and he would have been much less gentle about it."

She swallows hard at the reminder. "You could have let me go," she says softly. "You could have fucked me and let me go."

"No, I couldn't," I tell her simply, and leave it at that.

She stands there for several long seconds as I start to build a fire, and then I see her out of the corner of my eye, starting to walk around the room as she takes it in, still clutching her towel to her chest. She doesn't come close to me again until the fire is roaring in the hearth, and then I stand up, dropping my own towel as I clear my throat.

"Come here, *krolik*."

Just giving her the order hardens my cock. I can feel myself swelling and stiffening as she turns, and by the time she's facing me, I'm hard for her all over again. I see her gaze drop to it instantly, and the look of apprehension that crosses her face.

"You don't need to be afraid of me, rabbit," I tell her gently. "As long as you obey. So come here."

I see the moment where she considers trying to defy me, and then, slowly, she walks towards me. She stops an arm's length away and reaches up to brush some of her long, damp blonde hair nervously out of her face. It's a sweet, adorable gesture, and it makes me feel a strange stirring in my chest that I've never felt before.

"Drop the towel," I tell her as gently as I can manage. "Don't make me ask twice, Lilliana, and you'll enjoy this much more."

Once again, I can see the moment that she considers retorting, undoubtedly something about how she won't enjoy it regardless, but she stops herself. To my surprise, she reaches up, loosening the towel where it's tucked above her breasts and letting it drop to the floor.

The willingness of her gesture, as much as her naked body, arouses me beyond belief. As much as I seem to enjoy her contentious nature, seeing her submit to me in even the smallest way makes me ache, and I have to resist reaching for her and taking her directly to bed. I have other things I want from her, first.

I step back, so there's plenty of room for her on the fur rug, the fire crackling next to us. "Kneel down, *krolik*," I tell her, and I see her eyes widen.

"Nikolai—"

My cock throbs at the sound of her saying my name. "I wanted your mouth last night. But I wanted to give you time. I'm not waiting any longer, little rabbit."

She hesitates. Just looking at her mouth makes me ache, pre-cum pearling at the tip of my cock. I see her eyes flick to it, the way her throat convulses, and I *need* her.

"Now, *krolik*." My voice is a little sharper this time. "Don't make me tell you again."

She looks as if she's thinking of something—remembering something. A moment later, to my surprise, she steps slowly forward, until she's standing in front of me.

And then, wonder of wonders, she sinks down onto her knees.

Fuck. She looks so fucking beautiful like that, kneeling on the fur rug entirely naked, her blonde hair around her face and those wide blue eyes looking up at me. Her hands are resting on her bare thighs, and she looks up at me with a carefully blank expression.

"Are you going to tell me what you want?" she asks, but there's not as much venom in her words as I'd expected there would be.

It feels like something is off. But my mind is foggy with lust, my cock throbbing an inch from her lips, and I can't think entirely straight. *She's finally worn out with fighting,* is all I can think, and even as I have a feeling it's wishful thinking, I find myself simply looking at her.

She's like a fucking piece of art, waiting to suck my cock.

"I want your mouth on my cock, *devochka*," I murmur. "We'll go from there."

She leans forward, those wide blue eyes looking up at me as she tentatively flicks her tongue out over the tip. It's a light touch, almost not enough to feel, but there's a jolt of sensation through me anyway, simply because of the sheer eroticism of it. She looks so beautiful, so innocent, and even more than that, she looks as if she's submitting to my desires at last.

"That's it." I step a little closer, the head of my cock brushing against her mouth as I trail my fingers over her hair. "Lick my cock like a good girl."

She flinches the tiniest bit. But she slides her tongue over me again, a little more firmly this time, swirling it around before slipping it beneath the head and stroking the soft skin there with the tip of her tongue. It startles me a little, because it feels a little too— experienced, for a girl who's never sucked a cock before.

The thought lingers for only a second before it's gone, because her lips are pressed against my cockhead now, her tongue still rubbing that sensitive spot, and she slowly pushes her lips around me, her gorgeous eyes still fixed on me as she takes the first inch into her mouth.

"There you go. Nice and slow." I stroke her hair again, fingers curling around the back of her head. "You don't have to go fast, little rabbit. Take your time. You can have my cum when you're ready."

I *feel* her intake of breath at that, and my lips curl in a smirk. *My little rabbit likes it when I talk dirty to her.* She'd never admit it, but she does.

She takes my permission to go slow to heart. I would have thought that having her just playing with the first inch of my dick, licking and sucking without a great deal of skill, would have made me lose my erection. I'm used to women who know how to swallow a cock like a professional, or who *are* professionals, but something about just having Lilliana touching me keeps me hard as a rock, throbbing against her lips as she starts to experiment with taking me deeper.

She's a novice, that's for sure. There's the occasional scrape of teeth and awkward movement of her mouth, as she learns what it's like to have a cock there for the first time. But what throws me off here and there, cutting through the fog of pleasure, is how she seems to *know* what she's trying to do. Like she's watched a bunch of porn and is trying to mimic it.

Maybe that's what's happening. Maybe in an effort to learn to please who she was going to be given to, she tried to learn how all of this works.

To learn to please my father.

That thought pisses me off. The idea of her trying to learn to suck a cock to please another man sends a hot rush of anger through me, and my fingers tighten in her hair, tugging her mouth further down my length.

She chokes a little, her lips stretched around me, and I instantly feel a flash of guilt. I shouldn't punish her for what wasn't her fault. But at the same time—why do I *care?*

Her eyes are watering a little, and I reach down with my other hand, thumbing a little of the dampness away from the corner of her eye. "You look so pretty with your mouth full of my cock," I purr, loosening my grip on her hair so the long strands are just draped over my fingers. "Take your time, *krolik.*"

She nods, sliding down a little more, her tongue moving over the shaft. She rubs the tip of it along the pulsing veins, as if she's learning me, testing out what it feels like, and I find that I like the way she explores me. I like the feeling of her playing with my cock, even if she does it inexpertly.

Lilliana slides back, her cheeks drawn in as she takes a breath, my cockhead still resting damply against her lower lip. I can't resist wrapping my hand around my shaft, stroking lightly as I tap it against her mouth, rubbing the tip over her full lower lip. Pre-cum glazes over the soft, reddened flesh, and my cock throbs in my hand.

God, she's fucking beautiful. I've never had a thing for innocence, but Lilliana seems to have changed all of that.

Her tongue slides out again, swirling around my tip, licking up the pre-cum. She doesn't moan at the taste, but she doesn't show any sign of not liking it, either. She licks me for a moment, as if she's getting her breath, and the sensations rush over me, more of my arousal dripping onto her tongue as she teases me.

I can see that it's getting to her, too. She'd deny it if I said anything, but I can see the way she's fidgeting on the rug, one hand pressed hard against her thigh as she licks and sucks my cock, her legs squeezing together now and then. If I reached between them, I'm certain I'd find her soaked for me.

Don't worry, little rabbit, I think as she takes me in her mouth again, working her way down the first inch. *I'll make you come again before the night is over.*

She gets partway down my length before she starts to choke again, her eyes watering as she struggles to take more. I run my fingers through her hair, and it's a struggle not to push myself down her throat. The sensation of her choking against my cockhead feels fucking incredible, and I can only imagine how much better it would feel to have her throat wrapped around me, squeezing.

"You can take more, *krolik*," I encourage her instead. I could force it, but I want for her to want it. I want to see her *try* to struggle to fit me down her throat. "Just a little at a time. Good girl."

I can't tell how much she likes the praise, but I think it gets to her. I see her shift on the rug again as she looks up at me, struggling to take a little more. There are still inches of my shaft that she hasn't taken in her mouth, and I wrap my fingers around it, stroking lightly as her lips brush against my hand with each pass.

She drags her mouth backward off of my cock, panting. "I can't," she whispers. "It's too much."

I can tell she means it. I could force her—could keep going until she swallows it all, and come down her throat. It's tempting. My cock is aching, my balls tight with the need for release, and her swollen lips look so good around me.

But I also know that if I don't push her, she might be more likely to give in to me. To admit what she wants. Maybe not tonight—but sooner.

"That's alright, *devochka*," I murmur, reaching for her. I lift her up off of the rug, my cock throbbing in protest at the loss of both her mouth and my hand, but I have other plans.

I turn her towards one of the wing chairs, reaching for her hands and planting them on the arms, gently pressing her fingers into the velvet. "Stay just like this, *krolik*," I murmur to her. "Legs apart."

She swallows hard, and I can see the nervousness on her face, but I want her vulnerable. I run one hand down her back, fingers sliding along her spine, down to the small of her back. "Arch for me, little rabbit," I murmur. "Let me see how pretty you are with your ass in the air for me."

Lilliana makes a small noise, one that might be of shock or protest, but she does as I tell her. It startles me—I'd expected her to fight. But she arches beneath my hand, and I move to stand behind her, sliding my hands over the smooth curves of her ass and squeezing lightly.

I want to fuck her so badly that it almost hurts. But I want to teach her that her efforts are rewarded. That if she pleases me, I'll give her pleasure in return.

Slowly, I kneel down on the fur rug behind her. I hear her sharp intake of breath and see the way she twitches as she looks back at me, her eyes startled. "Nikolai—"

"That's it, *krolik*. I love hearing you say my name." *In time, I'm even hoping it will be in something other than protest.*

I smooth my hands down her legs, feeling the softness of her skin under my palms as I nudge her legs apart, wide enough for me to see her soft folds part for me. "Wider," I urge her, gently moving her legs further, and I feel her slight resistance as she looks back at me again. There's a plea in her eyes—for me to stop or for more, I'm not sure. But either way, I already know what I intend to do to her.

"Nikolai, don't—" she whispers, but I'm already looking at her, spread wide and vulnerable for me, her ass and pussy on full display.

"You look delicious, *krolik*," I murmur, pressing my thumbs into the soft flesh of her inner thighs as I hold her legs apart, refusing to let her close them. "Good enough to eat."

And I plan to.

I lean forward, running my tongue along her folds. She's as drenched for me as I imagined she would be, and that makes my cock throb, thinking of her being aroused by having me in her mouth. I feel her twitch, shuddering under my hands as I push my tongue into her for a moment, curling it and licking, feeling her tighten around me. I want to hear her moan. I fuck her with my tongue a little longer, enjoying the wet heat dripping over my lips and chin as her hips arch backward against my face involuntarily.

I reach between her thighs with one hand, stroking her slick clit as I thrust my tongue again, and I hear her gasp. Her legs tremble, her knees buckling slightly, and I steady her with my other hand on her hip, keeping her balanced as I pleasure her with my tongue and fingers.

When I finally pull back, still rubbing her clit, I can hear her panting. Her hands are clenched so tightly around the arms of the chair that I can see the indentations her fingers are leaving in the velvet, her hair falling around her face as her hips twitch and shudder.

"Will you ask me to make you come?" I murmur, my fingers still rolling over her swollen clit. "I want to hear you ask, Lilliana."

"No," she chokes out, the word strangled in her throat. "I'm not going to ask you for anything."

"Except for me to let you go." I rub a little faster, wanting to feel her body's submission. I want to feel her come for me, for her to understand that there is no escaping this. That she wants me, whether she likes it or not.

"Are you going to let me go if I come?" she pants, and I laugh, my other hand wrapping around my cock and giving myself a few quick, sharp strokes to ease the ache.

"No, little rabbit. You're well and truly trapped. But I'll go easier on you when I decide it's time to fuck you."

I see her jaw clench. "No," she hisses, and I nearly laugh again, because I know exactly why her answer was so brief. It's all she can manage when she's so aroused.

"You'll come for me anyway," I tell her. "But when I decide, then."

And I pull my fingers away from her clit.

I *see* how hard she has to clench her teeth to keep from letting out a moan of protest, and even so, a whimper slips out despite her best efforts. Her body shudders, her back arching, her body lost in her need even as she struggles to control it.

She had her chance. And now I'm going to torment her with pleasure until she either gives in or I decide I can't wait any longer and make her come.

I do exactly that. I tease her clit with my tongue and fingers, alternating, flicking my tongue over it with quick strokes of my fingers, waiting until I can feel her starting to tense before I pull away. I edge her like that, over and over, until she's a sticky, dripping mess, her skin beginning to sheen with sweat from the closeness of the fireplace, and when I pass my tongue over her clit again, I see her shaking.

"Ask me," I murmur, and she shakes her head.

"I'm never going to ask you for *that*," she spits out, and I chuckle, sliding my tongue over her dripping pussy again.

"Don't be so sure," I warn her, and then I give her what I'd planned on if she refused to do as I asked.

I press two fingers against her clit, rubbing as I push a thumb inside of her, giving her something to clench down on as I roll her sensitive flesh beneath my fingertips. And then, just as I can feel that she's on the verge of falling apart, I tilt my chin up, running my tongue over her tight asshole.

"Nikolai, *no!*" she cries out, her neck and face flushed with shame—because in the same instant that I slide my tongue over her tight little hole, she comes for me, *hard*.

Her entire body bucks, her hips thrusting back, pushing herself onto my tongue and trying to grind down on my fingers at the same time, and I know beyond a shadow of a doubt that if I hadn't licked her ass, she wouldn't have come as hard as this.

"Good girl," I murmur, still rubbing her clit as she shudders, her knees buckling against the chair. "Come for me, Lilliana. Good girl."

She lets out a helpless whimper, a sound that's almost a moan, and I run my tongue over her ass again, pushing the tip against her as she writhes under my mouth and hand, her arousal dripping over my fingers.

"*Fuck*," I breathe, and I can't wait any longer. I can feel her clenching around me, and I need to be inside of her. I've had her from behind once already today, but the seat isn't wide enough to get her on top of me, and I can't wait long enough to get her to the bed.

I push myself up to my feet, gripping her hips as I thrust my cock into her drenched pussy. She's so wet that even the stretch of it is a little less than before, the sensation curling my toes as I rock into her, pushing as deeply as I can go—and the shock of it makes her cry out.

"Nikolai!" My name spills from her lips, half-moan, half-scream, and I lose all control at the sound of her crying out my name.

My cock throbs as she clenches down around me, a hot rush of cum filling her, and my fingers dig into her hips, holding her on my cock as I grind into her. She feels exquisite, and I wrap her hair around my fist, pulling her head back as I lean over her and press my lips to her throat, breathing in the warm scent of her skin as I empty myself into her.

She's letting out small, helpless gasps as I pull out, and the sight of my cum dripping from her small, wet entrance nearly makes me hard all over again. She stays like that for a long moment, bent over, and I don't think it's for my pleasure.

"Lilliana?" I can hear the hint of concern in my voice. It's not like her to stay like that for so long.

"Fuck you," she breathes, swallowing hard. "Fuck you for making me do that."

"Lilliana." I try to hold back my frustration, but I can't restrain all of it. "There's no shame in enjoying it. You're my wife."

"I don't want to be." She's still frozen there, and I reach for her. Something about her stiff anger makes all of it much less erotic. "None of this is my choice."

"It doesn't have to be like this."

She turns away from me, her legs pressed close together, her arms over her chest. "I want to go to bed." She's looking at the four-poster across from us, and I can feel that she's as far away from me as she can get while still having to be physically in the room.

What I don't understand is why I give a shit.

When I don't say anything to stop her, she strides to the bathroom, shutting the door hard behind her. I hear the shower turn on, and the part of me that wants to master her, to make her submit, wants to tell her to get the fuck out of the shower, to go to bed with my cum still in her.

The part of me that wants her to *want* this leaves her alone.

I lay in bed as she showers, thinking back over what's happened since I brought her here. I can tell there's something off about her every time we're together, and it goes beyond just the fact that she doesn't want to be married to me. It feels as if she shuts off some part of herself whenever I'm intimate with her, a part that's covered up with the anger that she flings at me.

She seems to know more about sex than she should, too. I have no doubt that she was a virgin—she was telling the truth about that—but I can't help but wonder if she's done other things. The thought makes me murderous, and I'm still rolling it over in my head, getting more and more pissed off by it with every passing minute when Lilliana comes out of the bathroom, wrapped up in a thick terry-cloth robe.

"You know how you're meant to come to bed, *krolik*."

She narrows her eyes at me and yanks open the robe. For a brief moment, I think she's actually doing as she's told, but then I see she has cotton shorts and a tank top underneath it.

I should be pissed at her for her attitude, and for refusing to get naked for me—but somehow, she looks as delicious in that little sleep outfit as she does when she's entirely bare, just in an entirely different way. But then I think of someone else touching her the way I have, someone who didn't take her virginity, but might have come close, and the rage floods my veins again.

"Tell me, *krolik*," I murmur, my voice low and dark as I reach for her wrist and pull her into bed. "Who else touched you before me?"

She flinches, trying to pull her wrist away from me, but my fingers tighten around her. "No one," she snaps. "I told you. I'd never even touched myself."

"I'm not sure I believe you." My thumb rubs over the base of her wrist. "I think you might know more about what you're doing than you're letting on, *krolik*."

"I don't know anything." She tugs at my grip on her wrist again. "Not anything that you haven't shown me, anyway."

Her lips press together, and I still feel certain that there's something she's hiding.

"I was a virgin." Her words are clipped, angry. "No one has ever touched me besides you. No one would have been able to."

Her arms are wrapped around her waist, and she looks away from me. For the first time, I feel uncertain about what I should do.

I could try to drag it out of her. I could try to force her to tell me what she's hiding—and I know there's something. But if I do, I know it will close off any possibility of there being anything between us other than the tense, antagonistic relationship that there is now.

Why the fuck do I care? I can't tell why I do. But I feel as if I want to be careful with her, when it comes to this.

"We're going hunting tomorrow," I tell her, changing the subject. "Have you ever been?"

"Hunting?" Her eyebrows shoot up into her hairline. "No, of course not."

"I'll teach you. Just be careful. It's one of the few things there is to do around here, besides—" I raise an eyebrow, and she flushes. "But of course, if you'd rather stay in and enjoy more…indoor activities."

"No, it's fine. We'll go hunting." Her voice trembles a little as she says it. "I'm sure it will be…fun." She licks her lips nervously, glancing over at me. "I'm surprised you'd trust me with a gun."

I smirk at her. "I sleep beside you, *krolik*. If you wanted me dead, you'd find a way."

She stares at me, as if she can't believe how cavalierly I said it. "You don't think I could?" she says finally, and I laugh.

"No. I don't think so, little rabbit. But you're welcome to try."

Something about the look on her face makes me think I ought to handcuff her to the bed. The idea has certain merits, and I don't entirely rule it out. But for now, I'm going to let it be.

And I'll see what happens next.

Lilliana

I'd done my best to hide my fear from Nikolai last night, when he first brought up the topic of a hunting trip. I hadn't wanted to give him the satisfaction of seeing me even more terrified than before—I think a small part of me had hoped that if he didn't get the reaction he wanted, he might drop the idea altogether. After all, doesn't a predator want their prey to be afraid? Isn't the fear part of the thrill?

But when I wake up the next morning and see that Nikolai has taken the liberty of setting out clothes for me—on the same wing chair where he fucked me last night—that cold wash of terror chills me down to my bones.

To my surprise, he's not there next to me. I'd expected to wake up to him still in bed, expecting me to satisfy his desires. I'd braced myself for his body leaning against mine, hard cock nestled against my ass, hands roving over me as he demanded more pleasure—and more of mine that I didn't want to give him. But instead, I wake to an empty, peaceful bed—or at least as peaceful as it can be when I see the clothes laid out and realize that he wasn't joking about it—he hasn't changed his mind.

There are jeans and a heavy, cream-colored wool sweater folded neatly on the chair, with a durable work-style coat draped over the arm and lace-up hiking boots in front of it. Something about how intentional it is only amplifies my fear. Like he's dressing me up for whatever he has planned.

Is he going to hunt me? It feels like the most insane thing I could possibly imagine. What kind of man marries a woman and then takes her out into the woods to use her as prey? But what kind of man is Nikolai Vasilev, anyway? I don't *really* know him, and the kind of man who would do that is the same kind of man who would play sick mind games with me—who would cook me a meal with his own hands and pretend to play house, all the while planning to hunt me down in the woods for sport.

Krolik. Little rabbit. The nickname feels ominous now, rather than just his idea of a bad joke. My thoughts start to spin out of control, thinking back over everything that's happened. Nikolai is a brutal man; I know that. Did he see me in his father's study and imagine me as the perfect prey—naive, innocent, and sheltered? Was he aroused by the idea of making me think he'd married me out of lust or to keep me out of his father's hands, knowing that, ultimately, we'd end up here?

Has he ever done this before?

I clutch the blanket to my chest, my heart racing so hard that it almost hurts. I feel frozen, staring at the clothes, as if getting up and putting them on will start some ticking clock that ends with me running for my life through snowy woods, playing hide and seek with a psychopath. But what is the alternative? I can't just sit here and wait for him to come for me. One way or another, I'll end up out of this bed, dressed, and on that hiking trail. I have no doubt about that. The only choice I have is how that plays out.

I can go along with it, keep my dignity, and—maybe try to find some way to escape? I don't know exactly where we are, and running from a man with a gun who might want to hunt me sounds like playing exactly into his hands. So—what? I pretend to go along with this little hunting trip until he tips his hand?

There's no real plan that I can think of that ends in any good outcome for me. But fighting or running sounds like it might be exactly what he wants. I have to try to play it against him, if that's really what's happening here.

Quickly, I get out of bed and get dressed, before he can come up and see me naked and get any ideas. The fact that I woke up this morning without his hands on me feels like a reprieve, and I don't want anything to change that.

Don't you? That small, needling voice speaks in my ear as I dress, poking at me. *Don't you secretly enjoy what he does to you? Doesn't it get you wet? You can't pretend that it doesn't.*

It's just a physical reaction, I tell myself firmly as I slip into the jeans and sweater and lace up the boots, pulling my long hair back into a ponytail. *It doesn't mean anything. I can't control it, but I can control what I think and say. That's what matters.* I can keep trying to resist him.

Although, if he really has in mind what I think he might, I don't know what I'm going to do.

It's hard to fight back the fear as I go downstairs. I can smell the food as soon as I reach the stairs, and I pause for a moment, reminding myself not to show how afraid I am. If he doesn't think he's gotten a reaction out of me, maybe that will buy me time.

Nikolai is in the kitchen, making breakfast, and I'm once again startled by the sight of him cooking. I'd never imagined the brutal Vasilev heir making me bacon and eggs.

He pushes a plate in front of me almost as soon as I sit down at the island. "Orange juice?" he asks, nodding towards what looks like a fresh-squeezed pitcher. I narrow my eyes at him, forcing myself not to think about my suspicions. To treat this like any other morning, any other meal I've had to spend with him.

"What's the deal here?" I pour some into the glass anyway. Despite my fear, I'm starving. I've never been allowed to eat anything I want, and everything I've had since I came to stay with Nikolai and his family is delicious. I've given up trying to pretend that I'm going to hunger strike my way out of this. "Why are you playing house-husband?"

"I like cooking for myself here." He adds bacon and eggs to another plate for himself and goes to sit across from me at the island, the same way he did the night before at dinner.

"You like playing normal?" I raise an eyebrow at him. "There's no one to fawn over you out here."

"Maybe I enjoy that." He cocks his head at me. "Have you ever considered that?"

"No." I stab a piece of bacon with my fork. "Men like you always like to be fawned over. You feed off of it. The attention. The fear."

"You don't know anything about me, Lilliana." His voice lowers, and there's a thread of something dangerous in it. It makes me want to push a little more.

"Maybe you should have told me more, before you married me."

"Maybe it doesn't matter."

We stare at each other from across the island, and he lets out a long breath. "We could try to enjoy today," he suggests. "Get to know each other a little."

"What would you tell me that I don't already know?" I narrow my eyes at him. "What could possibly make a difference?"

"You could ask." He shrugs, and I poke at my food again.

"What are we doing today?" I ask instead, trying to keep my voice as casual as possible. "You said hunting. What does that *mean*? Is there something—specific that you like to hunt?"

"We'll head out, do a short hike, and see what shows up." He shrugs. "We might not get anything. It doesn't matter; it's more about the activity. Deer are pretty common this time of year. Smaller things come around sometimes. It's more about being outside and the fun of it." He winks at me, and I feel vaguely sick. *This is fun for him.*

"Hiking in the cold?"

"You won't be cold for long. And if you are, I can warm you up." He smirks at me, and I roll my eyes at him.

"Do you ever think about anything else?"

Nikolai smirks. He stands up, leaving his food as he circles around to me, leaning down to brush my hair away from my neck, his touch sending a tingle down my spine that makes me furious that I feel it at all. "I gave you a break this morning," he murmurs, his fingers lightly stroking the back of my neck. "But I woke up hard. I wanted to fuck you, *krolik*. I wanted to slip my cock into you and feel you come on it. You feel so fucking good when you come for me."

"It's never for you." I twist away from him. "It's because I can't help it."

"So you're admitting you came." I can *feel* his smirk burning into the back of my head.

I twist away from him, feeling my face flush. "Fuck off."

"You keep saying that." He leans in, brushing his lips against my ear. "I can take you upstairs, and we can discuss the merits of different types of fucking, if you like."

I push away from him, getting up and putting space between us. "Let's go, if we're doing this."

Nikolai smirks at me. "Alright, then. Let's go on a hike."

He takes me to what looks like a guest house, but turns out to be the nicest shed I've ever imagined. He takes two rifles out of a cabinet, and I instantly feel my stomach clench with fear. *This is really happening*. I feel crazy all over again for imagining something so outlandish—but maybe that's what rich people *do* when they run out of ways to be entertained. But then he hands me one of them, and I can feel my forehead furrow with confusion. *Why is he arming me if he's hunting me? Is it part of the game to see if I can fight back? Why the fuck would he do that?*

I don't understand anything that's happening here.

"I'm going to show you how to use this," he says, "and you need to listen to me. This is not a toy."

"I know." I narrow my eyes at him, my fear momentarily pushed aside by his continuous ability to irritate the shit out of me. "I'm not a child."

"I just want to emphasize it." He steps away from me, showing me how to hold it as he demonstrates with his.

"Do I have to have a gun? What if I just…go with you?" I blurt the words out before I can really think about them. I don't like how it feels in my hands or the idea of being responsible for it. I think some small part of me hopes that if I just go along with his 'hiking and hunting' plan, he'll lose whatever predatory urge he's having.

Are you stupid? If you have a gun, you can defend yourself. But I don't have the first idea of how to actually use it. I'm more worried about doing his job for him and accidentally shooting myself with it.

Nikolai frowns. "Is that what you want?"

Do I say yes? Do I tell him I don't want to be responsible for a gun? Or do I take it and maybe play into exactly what he wants? I take a breath, still not entirely sure of what I'm going to say—then suddenly, an idea starts to form in my mind.

If what he really wants is to hunt me, I don't think he's going to be dissuaded just because I don't take his offer of a weapon. But maybe, if I'm careful and don't set him off too soon, I can do more than just defend myself if he attacks first.

Maybe I can actually get out of here.

"No, I'll try. It'll be something for you to show me." I flash him my best attempt at a smile, trying to be convincing. "You wanted us to get closer on our 'honeymoon,' right?"

Nikolai raises an eyebrow, and for a moment, I think he might have picked up on what I'm thinking. But then he nods and comes to stand behind me, helping me adjust to how to hold the rifle.

He's standing very close. I hate myself for the leap of my pulse in my throat, the way it feels when his hands touch mine. I should hate every time he touches me, now more than ever. The rabbit isn't supposed to want the wolf to eat her. But my breath catches the moment I can feel him brush against me, the heat of his body sinking into mine.

I don't want him, I repeat over and over in my head, but something low in my belly tightens as he murmurs near my ear the instructions that I know I'm supposed to remember.

I'm going to have to do my best.

"Are you not an outside person?" Nikolai asks as we start to walk down the trail, boots crunching in the snow. It snowed again overnight, and my boots sink into it a little as we walk uphill.

"What gave you that idea?" I narrow my eyes at him as we walk, well aware that I'm already a little out of breath. I've had a gym membership for as long as I can remember, but being outside on an uneven trail in the snow and cold is something different altogether.

"You just don't look like it's something you're used to." He glances at me curiously. "You did say that you didn't have any hobbies."

"I didn't get out much." I shrug, trying to make it seem as if it's no big deal.

"By 'not get out much—'" Nikolai eyes me. "You prefer walking in a park? Working out inside?"

"Yeah, I went to the gym." I press my lips together, hoping he'll find a different line of questioning. I don't want to talk about my life growing up or how sheltered I was with my father.

"Well, I mean—I do the same." He laughs, a short, sharp sound. "But outdoors is much more pleasant, I think."

"Is it?" I shiver. Even the coat I borrowed is not enough to entirely stave off the chill.

"You'll warm up soon enough." There's something that almost looks like a genuine smile on his face. "Or—"

"I know. You'll warm me up." It's meant to be sarcastic when I say it, but it comes out almost like an inside joke between us. Like we're forming some kind of fucking connection.

Which is the last fucking thing I want.

He glances at me again. "That's really all you did? You just—went to the gym and went home? That doesn't sound like much of a life."

I should keep my mouth shut. I shouldn't let him bait me. But something about the way he keeps pushing frays my already raw nerves to the breaking point, and I glare at him, suddenly too angry to keep from snapping back.

"I was only ever allowed time for one thing," I bite out, pushing strands of hair out of my face with one hand. "Every second of my life was planned out, spent getting ready to be sold off to a man like your father. Like you. But my father didn't plan for that arrangement to be a marriage, or for my unexpected new husband to take me fucking hunting of all things. So no, I wasn't prepped for this particular trip."

Nikolai is silent for a long moment as we walk. "I'm sorry that your life has been so narrow for so long, *krolik*," he finally says. He stops suddenly, turning towards me with an expression on his face that I don't entirely understand. It looks almost—regretful. Like he's thinking over something and wondering if he could do it differently.

"Maybe we can change that," he says finally. "There's so much more than your world has been, Lilliana. It can be very different."

"It was supposed to be." The statement isn't as sharp as I thought it would be. It feels like that momentary flush of anger has started to drain out of me already, and I feel tired. Tired of the game Nikolai is playing with me. Tired of not understanding what is really going on here—why he married me, why he is so cold and lustful sometimes and seems shockingly normal at others. Tired of wondering when the other shoe is going to drop and the violence and abuse that I expected from whatever arrangement I entered is going to begin in earnest.

For instance, if it's going to start today, with Nikolai hunting his little rabbit.

He's still looking at me, standing there in the middle of the trail. "You look good out in the snow, little rabbit." His eyes flick over my face, and I see a familiar heat in them. "Your nose and cheeks are all pink. I like it when you blush."

I glare at him, but there isn't as much venom in it as there usually is. I don't want to enjoy his compliments. Now more than ever, I shouldn't. But I feel a warm flush when he says it, likely only adding to the pink in my face that he says he likes. I haven't received very many compliments in my life, before Nikolai. When my father did compliment me, it always felt tainted. It was never just about me for myself. It was always about what I would be able to do for him, one day down the line. Any beauty or intelligence or charm or grace or humor I possessed were only ever complimented in terms of how it could serve him, eventually.

The compliment sounds genuine. As if he's saying it because he really does like seeing me flushed and pink out here in the cold. And while I've never thought there would be a genuine bone in Nikolai's body—or any man like him—I can't help liking it.

He gestures for me to follow him, and I do. What turns out to be even more annoying is that he's right. By the time we reach the next layer of trees, I've started to warm up and even feel a little toasty in my sweater and jacket. I refuse to take it off out of sheer spite, but it's not the only thing he was right about. Despite the cold, the hike is actually enjoyable. The air is crisp, and there's the faint singing of whatever idiot birds are out despite the temperatures, and everything smells green and fresh.

"You really like it out here, don't you?" I look at him curiously. I don't *want* to see him as anything but the brutal, arrogant man I met that first night—as anything other than the embodiment of everything I've hated all my life. But he's making it difficult. So much of how he's been in just the day that we've been here *has* been different. And I don't know which one is the real Nikolai. Every moment I spend with him just confuses me more and more.

It doesn't matter, I remind myself. *Either way, he married you against your will. So it doesn't fucking matter.*

We round a corner, walking a little ways up a snowy hill where the trail narrows and roughens, and I see the tree stand. My stomach instantly clenches, my knees turning to water as I realize we're here. If Nikolai's intentions are as morbid as I'm afraid they might be, I'm going to find out very quickly—and I still don't know what I'm going to do.

I have to grab onto one of the trees, feeling dizzy with fear, and Nikolai looks at me with what appears to be genuine confusion— though I refuse to trust it. "Are you alright?" he asks curiously, and I force myself to nod.

"Just a little out of breath," I tell him, and it doesn't sound like a lie. My voice comes out high and weak, catching in my throat, and he laughs, shaking his head.

"I suppose we need to come out on more hikes like this, then," he says with a smirk. "It's one of my favorite activities, when I'm not—"

"Pulling off fingernails?" I suggest, trying for humor, if for no other reason than to try to keep from throwing up with sheer terror. I don't know if I can pass that off as just being tired from an uphill walk.

"I was going to say working," Nikolai says dryly. "Once you're recovered, we'll go up into the stand."

I blink at him. If we're both going into the stand, does that mean I'm not the prey? "Are we hunting to—eat?" I blurt out, hoping against hope that this is where he allays my fears, and this all turns out to be a massive overreaction on my part. "I don't like the idea of hunting for sport." Especially if the sport is me.

He raises an eyebrow. "I didn't know you had opinions on it."

The truth is, I *hadn't* had an opinion until a few minutes ago—not on hunting in general, anyway. I'd never had a reason to formulate one. But now I do—and I glare at Nikolai stubbornly, suddenly very certain of how I feel about it.

"Soft-hearted little rabbit." He leans forward, pecking me on the nose with a kiss, and I flinch back. It's an unexpectedly affectionate gesture, and I don't know how I feel about it. "Yes, I planned on using anything we kill up here for food. Ever eaten fresh rabbit?" He grins at me, and I stare at him in horror for a brief second.

All I can think is that I was right. I was right about all of it. He married me because he saw me as innocent prey, dragged me into bed with him so he could feast on my unwilling-but-still-willing body, and then took me out into the middle of nowhere so he could finish off his prize. So the Bratva wolf could hunt his little rabbit.

You're never supposed to run from a predator. Everyone knows that. If a dog or wolf or bear or mountain lion chases you, you're supposed to play dead. Drop and pretend like it's not happening. But there's no playing dead when my hunter is a flesh-and-blood human man. And the fear is too much for me to control.

So I turn and run.

The snow flies up around my boots as I dart into the trees. The gun smacks against my shoulder as I run, and I shrug it off, letting it fall into the snow. I'm not going to have time to use it to defend myself. I barely understood how to use it to begin with. All I can think about now is trying to get far enough away to keep Nikolai from catching me. And if I can get out of the woods—

I don't actually know where I'm going, though. I'm running in a blind panic, listening for the sound of footfalls behind me, waiting for the crack of a gun, the pain that will come after. Waiting for my wolf to catch me.

It's hardly any time at all before I can hear him coming after me, calling my name. Lilliana, Lilliana. He shouts it, not that hated nickname, not *krolik* or little rabbit, but my name. He sounds confused. Worried. But I can't let it stop me. I'm more sure than ever that it's just a ploy. A ruse. That if I stop, he'll be on me, and either that will be the end, or just the beginning of whatever other fucked-up mind games he has planned for the hunt.

My calves are burning, and my lungs are tight with the need for air. I've never run like this, flat-out for this far, through snow and over uneven ground. I can feel my footsteps starting to falter, and I slip on rough trail, nearly falling before I catch myself again.

He's closer. I'm sure of it. I hear him shout my name again, and I falter, a growing pain in my side intensifying. My feet catch on the rough ground again, and the toe of my boot slams against a snow-covered root, sending me pitching forward.

I sprawl in the snow, pain shooting up from where I catch myself with my hands, and I hear Nikolai behind me. I start to push myself up, my heart hammering in my chest, and I feel a strong hand suddenly grab my arm.

I flail in his grasp, twisting and thrashing, and it sends us both off-balance. We crash to the ground, Nikolai atop me, pressing me face-down into the snow, and I buck wildly underneath him, panicking.

Dimly, I realize he's hard. I can feel him pressing against my ass through my jeans, rock-hard from my squirming against him—or because he's aroused by the thought of what he's going to do to me next.

"Get off of me!" I shriek. "Get away!"

"I will as soon as you tell me why you took off running." Nikolai's mouth is very close to my ear, his breath warm against it, and I hate the shudder that it sends through me. Nothing about this should turn me on. But his body is hard and hot and muscled against mine, his cock pressing against me, and I can imagine him taking me here in the snow, thrusting into me like the animal that I've imagined him to be.

That shouldn't be something I want. What is wrong with me? Why does he make me think such awful, filthy things?

"Let me go!" I buck against him again, and he reaches out, pinning my wrists. That sends another hot jolt of arousal through me, and I kick at his shins, desperately trying to get out from under his weight. "I'm not going to be your fucking prey!"

Nikolai goes very still above me. His hands don't let go of my wrists, but he stays silent and unmoving for several long seconds, and then I feel him start to shudder above me. It takes me a moment to realize that he's laughing.

He pushes himself up, stepping back as he dusts himself off, looking at me with utter incredulity. "Lilliana—you're not trying to say— goddamnit, you thought I brought you out here to hunt you?"

He's looking at me as if I've grown two heads, and it infuriates me. God, he makes me so fucking angry *sometimes that* I could kill him. He's still laughing, his mouth twitching, and I glare at him from the other side of the space between us, shivering.

"Oh, like it's such a leap!" I shout at him, feeling all that anger starting to unfurl in my belly again. "You call me little rabbit, you tease me about eating me, you take me out into the woods on a supposedly impromptu hunting trip—"

"It's a hobby, Lilliana," he says patiently. "People have those."

"Not sociopathic organized criminals!" My voice is still echoing through the trees, but I don't care. I've stopped caring.

"Is that what you think I am?"

"It is what you are! You—" I trail off, breathing hard, and he shakes his head as he looks at me.

"I can't believe you thought I brought you out here to hunt you. That's fucked up." He's still fucking laughing as he says it, and it makes me feel unhinged.

"That's fucked up?" I lunge for him, shoving him hard in the chest—and as he stumbles back, I freeze, my stomach suddenly knotting.

I hadn't thought about what I was doing. It had been an involuntary reaction to what I thought was a horrible joke—and not only should I probably not have struck Nikolai Vasilev, I'm *more* horrified that this feels…almost like an ordinary argument. Like the kind of stupid misunderstanding a married couple has. Like we're having our first fight.

We've been together for two days. He's already getting under my skin. I feel a sharp bolt of panic, and it only intensifies when Nikolai smirks, his blue-grey eyes looking especially blue and mischievous as he reaches down and scoops out a handful of snow, packing it into his hands and flinging it at me before I can think to react.

It startles me so much that I don't move for a second after the loosely-packed snowball hits me, striking my shoulder and spattering over my clothes. And when I do react, it's not what I think I should have done.

Almost without realizing what I'm doing at first, I lean down and scoop up a handful of my own snow, squeezing it into a ball before I fling it at Nikolai. He stares at me for a brief second, as if he can't quite believe I actually did that.

I expect him to snap at me. To punish me. It can't possibly be alright that I slapped the Vasilev heir on the arm and then threw a snowball at him.

But instead, he *laughs*. And throws another snowball.

I don't entirely know what happens. For a few minutes, I forget that I'm supposed to hate him, that I *do* hate him. That a moment ago, I had horrific suspicions about him. That I don't want to be here. I've never really had fun with someone. I've never played around for the sheer enjoyment of it. But for a brief moment, I have a snowball fight with Nikolai Vasilev, and it's *fun*.

And then I stop, out of breath and startled at what's happening, and Nikolai is very close to me.

"You look like you enjoyed that, *krolik*," he murmurs, reaching up to brush a thumb over my cheekbone. His gaze drops to my lips and then flicks back up to look me in the eye. There's something softer in his gaze than has been there before, and it startles me. "Don't say you didn't," he murmurs. "I don't want to hear it."

The thing is—I wasn't going to say I didn't enjoy it. For the first time, I don't feel like lying to him and claiming that it wasn't fun, and that scares the shit out of me.

Nothing was supposed to change. And I remember the loose plan I'd tried to form, before we started the hike up here.

"Let's just keep going," I tell him, pulling back before he can kiss me. "I want to be in that tree stand, out of the wind." I want some space from him, but I know I'm not going to get it yet. More than anything, I want this entire strange, fucked-up day to be over.

"And closer to me?" Nikolai grins. "Are you sure I'm not going to eat you?"

"Let's just go?" I push past him, back the way we came.

"Do you know where you're going?" he calls after me, and I keep stubbornly going forward, refusing to look back at him

"I'll follow your huge, obvious footprints," I snap, and I hear him laugh behind me.

"You know what they say about huge feet—but it doesn't matter. You've already seen it."

Does he ever stop? I keep trudging forward, through the snow, all the way back to the tree stand. I'm fucking exhausted and hungry and more than a little pissed off, and I wonder how long this is going to take before we can go back to the cabin and eat. I wonder if he packed a lunch.

I wonder if there's the faintest possibility that I might still be able to pull off my plan.

What if I don't want to? What if—

Shut up. Stop it. You want to get out of here. You don't actually want to be married to Nikolai Vasilev. A snowball fight and a cute moment doesn't change that. Get your fucking head on straight.

I march up to the ladder and start to climb before realizing that going first means he's going to get the view of watching me. It's only *seconds* before I hear his voice behind me, and I don't have to see the smirk on his face to know it's there.

"I like the view, *krolik*," he says from the bottom of the ladder, and I climb faster, hoping he's not going to try to grope me. "I should let you climb up everything first."

"Am I going to be climbing up a lot of things?" I snipe back at him, hoisting myself into the tree stand. "I hadn't planned on it, so let me know."

Nikolai is right behind me, and he slings the rifles off of his shoulder, reaching for me. I realize he must have grabbed the one that I tossed aside, too, as he followed me back. "Come here, *krolik*," he murmurs, and I try to pull away.

"Aren't we supposed to be watching for something for you to shoot?" His hands are sliding under my jacket, and I have a feeling that this is going to progress to a place that I don't want it to.

"I already have my little rabbit trapped right here." His hand comes up to capture my jaw, holding me there as he leans in to kiss me.

"Are you going to try to shoot me if I run off?" I snap, but the words don't come out as angry as I'd meant for them to. His mouth is warm and soft, and the brush of it against mine sends a pleasant tingle over my skin that I know I should ignore. *You thought he was going to kill you twenty minutes ago, and now him teasing you about it is turning you on because he's using it to talk dirty? Are you insane?*

"You'd have to get away first." His voice is a low, rumbling purr, and it should terrify me. If he hadn't had such a blatantly disbelieving reaction to what I'd thought earlier, it would. But even now, I know it shouldn't have the effect on me that it does. Even with the immediate threat gone, it shouldn't make me feel hot and flushed to hear him murmur that as his hands squeeze my waist.

He spills me back onto the wooden floor, his hands roving underneath my sweater. His hands are cold to the touch, and I gasp, trying to twist away, but Nikolai is no easy man to get away from.

"I like it when you squirm, *krolik*," he murmurs against my ear. "Feeling you rub against me like that—god, it gets me so fucking hard." He shifts his hips, pressing into me, and I can feel that he's telling the truth. He's rock-hard, pressed against my thigh, and I feel a jolt of arousal at the sensation.

"We can't do this out here—" I try to squirm away from him again, out of habit if nothing else, even though I realize all too well that I'm only making it worse.

"Why not?" Nikolai bends, nipping at the soft flesh of my neck. "There's no one to see or hear us, little rabbit."

His hips lean into mine again, and I have to stifle a gasp. He reaches down, tugging at the button of my jeans, and for a brief moment, I wonder, despite myself, why I'm trying so hard to hide how he makes me react. It's not as if he doesn't already know.

Because you don't want to give him the satisfaction, I remind myself—just as his hand slips into my jeans.

I'm wet for him already. There's no hiding it, no way to pretend that the feeling of his hard, muscled body atop mine and the pressure of his cock grinding against my thigh didn't turn me on. I hear his groan, the way he chuckles as his fingers slide between my folds, and I wonder what he'd do if I bit him.

He'd probably like it.

I feel his fingertips against my clit, rolling over it as his other hand reaches for his belt, and I buck my hips upwards to get away. *I was going to try to get away. It's what I meant to do—really.* But I can't lie to myself. All I'm doing is grinding into his hand, seeking more friction, more touch, and I *feel* him laugh against me as he presses his mouth to my shoulder and moves his fingers faster.

"I'm going to be inside of you in a moment, little *krolik*," he murmurs. "So if you want to come before you have to take my cock, you should stop fighting it."

Fuck you. I don't know if I think the words or say them, because I'm losing the battle anyway between my desire to keep from doing anything that might please him and the arousal flooding me. The pressure of his fingers feels so good, and I can't help but roll my hips against his hand again, wanting more.

"That's it, little rabbit. Make yourself come on my fingers. I know you want it." His hand presses down, giving me more of that sweet friction, and I grit my teeth against a whimper as I rock helplessly against him.

I'm going to come. I just barely manage not to say it aloud, fighting back the moans as I feel the orgasm building, and I know I'm going to come all over his fingers. I can't help it. He seems to know exactly where to rub, to press, to stroke so that I'm flooded with pleasure, every inch of my skin tingling with it, and I feel myself clench, *wanting* to be filled up. Wanting his cock, and I hate so much that I do.

I feel that tight knot of pleasure coming unwound, feel my nails scratching against the wood of the floor. I dimly realize as I'm trying not to scream out my pleasure that he's using his other hand to drag his zipper down.

I'm startled by how huge his cock is, every time. I'm still shuddering from my orgasm when his other hand drags my jeans down, far enough that he can get between my thighs. I have to bite back another cry when the swollen head of his cock pushes against my entrance.

"God, you're so fucking tight," he breathes, rocking against me as his hips shove forward. It's just the first inch, but the stretch burns with a heated pain that turns almost immediately to pleasure, like the first night all over again. *How long is it going to take before it doesn't feel like losing my virginity every fucking time?* I'm soaked, and he's still almost too much.

I reach up, intending to try to push him away, but instead, I grip his shoulders, nails digging into the wool of his sweater as his hips rock forward again, pushing more of his impossibly thick cock into me. It feels so good—I wish it didn't feel so good. It could become addictive, the way it feels as he thrusts, filling me up as he pins me down against the wooden floor. It feels better than it did in bed, better than it did in the pool, something raw and frantic about fucking out in the woods, where anyone walking past could hear if they listened long enough.

It feels almost impossible to keep quiet. I know he doesn't want me to, that he's *trying* to make me cry out with every hard thrust. His hand slides under my sweater, under my bra, his palm cupping over my breast so it rubs against my nipple with every rock of his hips, until it feels as if there's a direct line of jolting pleasure between my stiff nipple and the hard slide of his cock.

He's going to make me come again. There's no way out of it. It feels too good, his swollen head rubbing over a spot deep inside of me that I didn't even know existed, over and over again, until the pressure building makes me feel as if it's going to burst.

My nails bite into the wool of his sweater, through the weave of it into his skin. I hear him groan, feel him shudder against me, and I have some wild hope that he might come first, that it might be enough to make this quick, even though I know it's going to leave me aching and unfulfilled.

I should have known better. He thrusts into me as deeply as he can go, grinding his hips into me so that every movement pushes him against my clit, his cock filling me, and I can't stop the pleasure that rushes up, lighting every nerve in my body on fire as I come apart at the seams.

I moan aloud. I can't help it. The sound tears out of me, a cry of pleasure as I come on his cock, squeezing around him as he lets out a groan of pleasure and thrusts once more, and I feel the heat of his cum filling me as he pins me against the wood of the floor and we come together.

Fuck. A shudder rushes over me at the realization. It feels horribly intimate, and I suddenly want nothing more than to be out from under him, away from him, to scrape the feeling of his touch off of my body. *Too close.* Today has all been too close. The jokes, the snowball fight, *this*—Nikolai is someone I don't recognize out here, and he seems dangerously close to being someone I might like.

I can't like someone who won't let me make my own choices.

The thought that I might be losing sight of the situation I'm in, falling into—something with him despite myself, sends me into a panic. I push at his chest, wanting him off of me, and to my surprise, he gets up, pulling up his jeans with one hand as I scramble back into mine.

"Is that it?" I snap, suddenly wanting very much to be angry with him. It feels like a different kind of release. "You just brought me out here for a new place to fuck me?"

Nikolai laughs, and that pisses me off even more. "No, *krolik*," he tells me. "I brought you out here for exactly what I said I did. If you want to think otherwise, that's up to you." He shakes his head, and I can see that mirth dancing across his face again. "Come up with all the crazy scenarios you like, little rabbit. This is just an ordinary trip out into the woods."

"I don't see any hunting happening."

"Well, I had to make sure you were satisfied, first. Couldn't have you panting in my ear while I was trying to line up a shot, being in such close quarters." He *winks* at me, and I know he knows exactly how much he's infuriating me with every word.

"You fucking—"

"Keep going, *krolik*," he says, his tone light. "I like it when you're feisty. Get me hard again, and we might end up back on the floor."

I glare at him, but say nothing else. After a moment, he shrugs and picks up the rifle, finding a spot at the small square window on the side of the tree stand.

"Keep quiet, little rabbit," he says in a low tone. "And tap me if you see anything out there."

A hush descends over the small space, and normally I would be grateful for it, but right now, I'd give anything to drown out my racing thoughts. Everything is a tangle in my head, a web of confusion over how good it feels to fuck him, how different he's been here, the theory I'd had that was so wrong, and the plan I'd started to tentatively form when I realized we were taking weapons deep into the woods.

This is my chance to get away. I don't know how, exactly—at least, I don't know how once I've gotten past Nikolai. I already ran out into the woods once, and I found out first-hand just how hard it will be to find my way out. To get away. But I can't just let this go. I can't just give up and let myself be caged.

Someone will be looking for me before long, if I succeed, and I don't have identification or money or anything else. If I go back to the cabin, I might find some money in Nikolai's things. I'll almost certainly have to risk it. But without identification, I can't buy a ticket anywhere. Not on a plane or train or anything else. I can't rent a car.

I'll figure it out, I tell myself quietly as I sit there, watching the snowy expanse beyond us with Nikolai. My rifle is close by, within reach, and I breathe through the nerves, waiting for the moment when Nikolai finally sees a deer, walking slowly through the snow.

Something in my chest clenches. It looks so innocent, so peaceful. It didn't do anything to deserve this. It is being hunted, and it doesn't even know it.

I want to grab Nikolai's arm and tell him to stop. But I need him distracted. I need to escape more than the deer does.

So I don't move. I don't speak. I don't do anything until I see his finger squeeze down on the trigger, the gunshot echoing, and I have no idea if he made his shot or not, because I'm already going for my own gun.

"Shit!" Nikolai exclaims, but he doesn't sound angry. "That was a hell of a shot. Look, *krolik*—"

His voice trails off as he turns and sees that I have my rifle aimed directly at him.

Nikolai

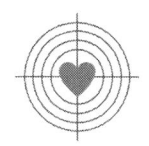

For a moment, I can't believe what I'm fucking seeing.

My pretty, innocent wife, Lilliana Vasilev *nee* Narokovna, is holding me at fucking gunpoint. She has a rifle leveled at my chest, and while I'm not at all confident in her ability to effectively handle the thing, I think it would be hard to miss at this range.

"Lilliana." I put every ounce of gravity into my voice that I can, making sure she hears just how fucking pissed off I am. "What the fuck do you think you're doing?"

"I'm getting out of here." Her voice trembles, but I'm pretty fucking certain she's not going to back down easily. This is what she's been demanding from the moment I put together that dinner for us. "Let me go, and I won't shoot you."

"You won't shoot me either way." I'm not entirely confident about that; as a matter of fact, I think there's a possibility she might shoot me just by accident.

"The fuck I won't." Her voice is a hiss through her teeth, and I can hear how angry she is. How desperate, how afraid.

Why can't she understand what I'm trying to keep her safe from?

"Lilliana. Put the gun down."

"Let me go, and I'll take it with me. You can do whatever the fuck you want after that."

"It'll be coming after you; believe me on that. And you won't get away."

"I'll take my chances." Her voice trembles again. "Let me go."

"No." I stand there, staring her down, and I know that anything I'm going to do, I'll have to do quickly. Her finger is near the trigger—not *on* it, thank god, I think she knows as well as I do how easily she could accidentally shoot—and if she manages to get to it, she could injure or kill me. Hell, she'll probably hurt herself with the recoil.

I hope, for a moment more, that if I wait her out, she'll give in. But it quickly becomes apparent that's not going to happen.

I've disarmed men with more gun sense than Lilliana has. I just have to move fast, and I do. Before she can react, I've grabbed the barrel and twisted it away, and she's not strong enough to hold onto the gun. I wrench it out of her hands, and she gasps, her eyes going wide and terrified.

"Nikolai—"

"No, we're past that. Get out. Go down the ladder. I'll follow you." I nudge the gun in her direction, and she lets out a terrified squeak that's more gratifying than it should be.

Good. She needs to be afraid. She needs to understand that this isn't a game.

"Go," I growl at her, and for once in her goddamned life, she obeys.

I hadn't seen the day going like this—walking my wife out of a tree stand in the woods with a gun to her back. I glance regretfully at the dead deer in the snow—it's a hell of a waste—but I can't go and get it now, and there's purposefully no one else at the house. It'll just have to be left for nature to handle.

Lilliana's gaze flicks to the deer as well, but I know she's thinking something very different. She's seeing herself there in that snow, bleeding out.

I step closer to her, the rifle nudging into her spine. "If you were anyone else and you pulled a gun on me," I tell her in a quiet, dangerous tone, "you'd be doing exactly what you're thinking of right now. You'd be bleeding out in that snow, and nothing would be able to help you. Do you understand me? You're only alive because you're my wife."

"Is that going to *keep* me alive?" she whispers, and I hear real fear in her voice for the first time. I hate it and love it at the same time—I never wanted to make her afraid of me, but something about the fear thrills me, too.

She underestimated me. She underestimated the kind of man I can be. And it might be time for her to learn.

I nudge her toward the trail with the gun in her back. "We're going back to the cabin. And then we're going to talk."

I don't know if *talking* is going to be a part of what happens for long. I'm going to punish her. It's what has to happen, what *needs* to happen—what should have happened when she started this arrangement off with a sharp tongue and biting words.

I'd tried to be gentle with her. Tried to be softer. I tried to make her understand that I was helping her. But it ended with a gun pointed at my chest.

So now, things are going to change.

"We don't have anything to talk about," she hisses, with surprising acrimony for a woman with a gun at her back. "There's nothing you can say that will make me want to stay here with you, Nikolai. Especially now that I know you're *exactly* the type of man you all make yourselves out to be. Brutal and rough and—"

I push the gun into her back again, just to remind her of her situation as we walk. "I'm not going to be convincing you to stay here with me, Lilliana. There is no world in which you *don't* stay here with me. And as far as what type of man I am—*you* pulled a gun on *me*. I'm reacting to that. And like I said—if you weren't my wife, it would have gone much differently."

She doesn't have an answer for that. In fact, she doesn't say a word until we're back at the cabin, at which point she digs in her heels at the prospect of going inside.

"Nikolai—"

"Go in the cabin, Lilliana. You're going to walk inside, and then you're going to go up the stairs, and we're going to go all the way to the bedroom. Then we'll *talk*."

"I don't like the way you're saying that."

"I don't care." I nudge the gun into her back again. "*Go*."

For a change, she does as she's told. I can see her hands trembling, and she clenches them into fists as she walks, slowly, through the house and up the stairs, all the way into the bedroom that I think of, unfortunately, as *ours*.

The moment she steps inside, very slowly, I set the gun down outside of the room. And then I close the door and lock it.

"Now. No weapons. Nothing for you to try to grab and threaten me with, and nothing for you to be afraid I'm going to use on you."

"You could hurt me plenty without a gun." Her gaze flicks over me, and I let out a sigh.

"Lilliana, I'm not going to hit you. Or punch you, or whatever you're thinking. I've never hit a woman. But you *have* to understand something."

"What?" She bites out the words, but it's beginning to lose some of its venom.

"There is no way out of this, *krolik*." I look at her from across the space between us, hoping she will somehow relent and understand.

I'll have to punish her regardless—she *has* to learn, or she will misstep at some point in front of someone important, in front of my *father*, even, and it will all be so much worse. But I could go easier on her, if she would give in and understand. "You are my wife, and you will continue to be so. You will behave in all the ways a wife should. You will learn to please me when I say and curb your tongue when necessary, and you will *not* threaten me." I shake my head, the frustration rising up again. "Your father taught you better than this, Lilliana. I know he must have, for what he had planned for you."

"Don't talk to me about my father," she hisses. "You have no idea what he did or didn't teach me. But what *I* know is that men like you are arrogant, brutal, self-involved fucks who get off on controlling others. On hurting others. So just fucking get it over with. Hit me, or force me down on my knees, or shoot me, I don't care. I want out. But you're not going to let me go. So how can you blame me for trying?"

The last words, especially, strike something within me. It's almost enough to make me change my intentions. I can feel the desperation in her voice, the fear, and I have a strange urge to reach for her and soothe her instead, to gather her in my arms and tell her that I could be good to her, if she would give this a chance. That it doesn't have to be so acrimonious. That we could enjoy each other until the lust burned out, and then she would be taken care of.

You've tried being gentle with her. You've tried patience, as much as you're able. And this is where it led.

"Whether or not I can blame you doesn't matter, Lilliana. You are my wife. You have defied me again and again, and I've been too lenient. I've put us both at risk by making you believe that it was acceptable. That you could get away with it. That changes now."

I nod at her. "Strip. One piece of clothing at a time."

She stares at me. "You have got to be fucking kidding."

I can't believe we're having this conversation. "I had a gun on you two minutes ago, *krolik*. You had one on me before that. I think we're past this song and dance about whether or not I can tell you to take your clothes off. Strip, Lilliana, or I will take them off for you, and it will *not* be to your liking."

She crosses her arms over her chest, and I wish to god I could be surprised when she spits out: "No."

"Fine." I stalk towards her in two quick, long strides, and grab her by the shoulders before she can dart away. I hold her there, one hand gripping her arm to keep her from fleeing, and I reach for the knife in my pocket.

Her eyes go wide when she sees it. "Nikolai—"

"I told you that you wouldn't like it. Now hold still, or you'll like it even less."

I've never cut a woman's clothes off like this before. Never threatened one with a knife—and I know Lilliana *feels* threatened, even if I have no intention of cutting her. I don't know how I feel about the odd thrill that it sends through me as I press the knife to the top of her sweater, the way my cock twitches in my jeans as I start to drag it down through the wool.

I've always been a brutal man. An efficient one, when it comes to pain. I do my job for my father well. But I've never gotten off on it.

The tip of the knife presses against Lilliana's flesh, and her gasp has my cock stiffening in an instant. I have no intention of drawing blood, but there's a faint pinkness as I draw it down, and my pulse leaps in my throat.

"See, *krolik*?" I murmur, slicing through the sweater slowly, revealing her bare skin inch by inch. "I have restraint."

"Is this your job?" she spits out, the words hissing between her teeth. "Frightening women into doing what you want?"

I laugh, low and dark, dragging the knife a little lower, exposing the inner curves of her breasts. "You don't want to know what my job is, little rabbit. It's not this. I don't hurt women."

"You're hurting me."

"No, I'm not." I press the tip into her skin a little harder, and I feel her shudder. A small part of me wonders if it's from fear or desire, and the thought that it could be the latter, or even *both*, makes my cock swell even more. "If I wanted to hurt you, Lilliana, you'd know it. I am not hurting you. And the fact that you think I am tells me you don't know enough about the world you've walked into."

"That you've *dragged* me into." She swallows hard. "I didn't want to be a part of any of this."

"Maybe not. But you were always going to be. I just made sure that your introduction to it didn't end in your death."

I jerk the knife down, slicing the rest of the way through the cream wool of her sweater, and it falls to either side. I can see the curves of her breasts in the light-colored bra she's wearing, the pale flesh of her taut belly, and I want to reach out and touch her. I want to run my hands all over her body, devour her—but that's not what I'm here for right now. She *has* to understand the situation she's in.

Don't pretend you're not taking pleasure in this. I want to think that I'm not. But as I motion with the knife for her to shrug off the pieces of the sweater, my cock jerks again against the fabric of my jeans.

She doesn't move, and I let out a sigh. "The harder you make this, the longer this will take, *krolik*," I tell her, reaching out and pushing the sweater off. With three quick motions, I slice through the straps of her bra, and it falls away, too, leaving her bare from the waist up, standing at the foot of our bed.

"You can take the jeans off, little rabbit. Or I'll start on those."

Her fingers are trembling when she goes to undo the button, her eyes on the knife. She jerks it loose, shoving the denim down her hips, and this time she leaves the panties on—not because she wants to obey me, I know, but because she doesn't want to be entirely bare before I make her.

"Those next." I gesture at the black cotton, and she glares at me.

"Alright." I shrug, stepping forward, and she shrinks away.

"Okay!" Her thumbs hook in the waistband. "I'll take them off. Don't—" she bites her lip, shuddering again as she looks at the knife, and I can't help but wonder if she's so averse to it because it frightens her—or because she likes it a little.

I'll find out soon enough.

Lilliana slides the black panties down her hips, revealing the rest of her to me, and I have my answer without even touching her. Her pussy is pink and flushed, the lips faintly swollen, and I can see a hint of her arousal glistening at the edges of her folds—and not just because she still has my cum in her from before.

That thought is enough to make me rock hard. My cock strains against my fly, and Lilliana sees it, her lip curling as she sneers at me.

"You *do* get off on frightening women. Look at you. You're hard as hell right now, from pointing that knife at me."

"I'm hard from making you strip." I glare at her, folding the knife up and putting it back into my pocket as she kicks the panties away. "But if you want to test that little theory of yours, we can try it."

She swallows hard, and I nod. "Good. You're starting to realize that mouthing off to me won't make this better. Now let's try the next step." I reach for my belt buckle, and I see her eyes widen. "Turn around, and bend over. Grab the footboard."

"No." Her lower lip trembles. "Wasn't fucking me out there enough for you—"

"I'm not going to fuck you." I jerk the belt out of the loops of my jeans, folding the leather in my hand, and Lilliana's eyes widen.

"Nikolai! You can't—"

"I can," I assure her. "And I'm going to. But if you want to keep saying my name like that while I do, I won't complain."

I see her chin jut out, her lower lip still trembling, and *fuck* if it doesn't make my cock throb and ache. I'd meant for this to be purely a punishment, not the kind of thing I get up to with the women I pay in the Chicago sex clubs. Still, the thought of seeing her ass reddened from my belt has my cock straining, pre-cum dripping down my shaft and soaking my boxers as I motion again for her to turn around.

She shakes her head, swallowing hard, and I let out a sigh.

"You're only making this worse for yourself." I step forward, my hand on her shoulder as I turn her around firmly, pushing her down so that she's bent over towards the end of the bed. "Grab the footboard and hold on. If you move, I'll find a way to tie you to it so you can't. You're not getting out of this, *krolik*."

"Stop calling me that," she whispers, her voice trembling as her fingers close around the footboard. I can see that she's terrified, but it's hard for me to think about anything other than how fucking gorgeous she looks bent over like that, the curve of her back and the slope of her ass making the prettiest fucking picture I've ever seen, the swollen lips of her pussy peeking out between her thighs. I can still see the pearlescent drip of my cum between those pink folds, and the fresh, glistening arousal that tells me that something about this is arousing her, too.

"Count, little rabbit," I tell her. "If you obey me, and don't fight, I'll stop at twenty."

"*Twenty?*" she gasps, and I step behind her, still far enough away that I can see the picture-perfect view of her from behind, but able to reach her with the belt. "Nikolai, please—"

"It's too late to beg now, *krolik*."

I don't bring the belt down as hard as I could on the first strike. She jerks in place anyway, letting out a gasp as the leather strikes her pale flesh, leaving a mark that makes my cock jerk, seeing the red stripe left behind.

She says nothing else, and I pause, waiting. When nothing else comes, I shake my head. "I told you to count, Lilliana."

"Fuck you," she spits out, and I let out a sigh.

"Lilliana, I will keep doing this until you start to count. And then it will be twenty from there. If you make me wait too long, I'll start raising that number." I reach out, running my fingers over the mark left behind, and she shudders under my touch. "You can't fight this, little rabbit. The trap hurts less when you stop squirming."

She lets out a slow, shuddering breath, her fingers clenching the wood of the footboard. When I bring the belt down again, she gasps again, but this time whispers: "One."

"Good girl." I bring the belt down on the opposite side.

"Two."

She keeps counting, and I bring the leather down again and again, watching the pattern it makes on her perfect flesh. By five, I can hear the sound of her beginning to sniffle through the count, and by ten, she's crying. But by twelve, I can tell something else is happening—something I'd suspected from the moment I cut through her sweater.

She's wet. I can see the arousal starting to drip down her thighs, her pussy even more swollen and flushed, a shade lighter than her reddened ass. And when I bring the belt down for the fourteenth stroke, the small cry she makes ends on a moan.

"Ah, there we go, little rabbit." I reach out, gently running my fingers over the marks I've left. "You like this, don't you? It hurts, but it feels good, too."

Lilliana shakes her head, and it doesn't surprise me. She was never going to admit it. But she can't hide it from me, any more than she's been able to hide how aroused she is in bed.

"It's alright to like it, little rabbit." I bring the belt down again, my cock jerking as she chokes out her count for fifteen. "Moan for me, *krolik*. Let me hear how much you like my belt against your pretty skin."

She shakes her head mutinously, her jaw clenched. I can see how tight it is from where I'm standing.

"You can't hide it." I bring down the belt, feeling another jolt of arousal when she moans out *sixteen*. "You'll have to admit it eventually, *devochka*."

She shakes her head again; the only sound she makes is the breathy moans as she counts out each stroke, again and again, until my entire body feels as if it's throbbing with desire. I know I shouldn't touch her when I'm done, that this isn't about fucking her, that she won't want me to—but I reach the twentieth stroke and look down at her trembling body, her swollen pussy dripping with her arousal, and I can feel the thread of my self-control fraying.

I can't remember ever being so hard. I can't remember ever needing anything as much as I need to be inside of her. And when she lets go of the footboard, twisting away from me before I tell her she can, something snaps.

I bring the belt down against her thigh. "Did I tell you that you could move, *krolik*?" I growl, my voice dark and deadly, and she lets out a small cry.

"Put your hands back on the bed. Spread your legs."

"Nikolai—"

I should hear the plea in her voice, how different it is from before. The defiance is gone, replaced by a tremulous fear. She *is* pleading with me now, pleading the way I'd hoped she would, for me to keep going, not to stop. But I'm past listening to her. My frustration boils over, mixed with the lust, and I step over the line that I'd sworn to myself I wouldn't.

"Spread your legs, Lilliana."

Her legs part, her hands clutching the foot of the bed, and I want to see her come from the belt. I want her to fall apart for me, before I thrust my cock into her, and I bring the leather down on the insides of her damp thighs, no longer asking her to count. I see her pussy clench on nothing, open and vulnerable for me with her legs spread like this, and I can see from the way the muscles in her thighs twitch and jump that she's close.

"Come without touching yourself, Lilliana, and I won't bring this belt down on your pretty little clit. Because when I do—"

"Nikolai, *no*—" she breathes out the plea, her head twisting around, those huge blue eyes looking at me fearfully. "You can't—I can't—"

"You can." I snap the belt against her thigh again, and I see her back arch and hear her helpless moan. "Come for me, *krolik*. I know you can do it."

"Nikolai, *please*—"

She's not pleading for more. But that's all I hear. I bring the belt up in quick succession, three times against her swollen pussy, the wet sound filling the room—and Lilliana *screams*, her knees buckling as she comes hard.

I drop the belt, the wet leather hitting the floor as I yank open my jeans, my cock barely out before I'm gripping her reddened ass and thrusting myself into her as hard as I can. It's primal, animalistic, every rational thought in my head gone as I slam every inch of my cock into her, and her scream only fuels the lust pounding through my veins.

She feels so fucking good. Hot and wet and tight, still clenching and fluttering around my cock from her orgasm, and I know I won't last long. The pleasure is indescribable, the feeling of her gripping me, the way she cries out with every thrust, her mouth open on a plea that ends with my name. I squeeze her ass, feeling the welted flesh under my palms, the memory of my belt striking her curves, the wet sound of it hitting her clit as she came apart—it pushes me over the edge faster than I'd hoped for.

My cock swells and hardens, erupting in her as I thrust into her once more, pounding as hard as I can. I fuck her the way I've always wanted to, hard and fast, still fucking her as I shoot spurt after spurt of hot cum into her, seeing it smeared over my cock as I keep fucking her until my erection starts to soften.

I pull out of her, panting, and she whirls towards me before I can catch my breath, as if she'd been waiting for the opportunity.

I don't even have time to try to grab her before she flings herself at me, nails clawing across my face.

Lilliana

He lost control. I know he did. But so have I.

All of the emotions of the last hour and a half or so—the fear and anger and unwanted arousal, the pain and pleasure all knotted together that I didn't want—it all comes surging up the moment I feel him slip out of me, and I spin around, flying at him like a furious cat with my claws out as I scratch at his face.

He dodges back, trying to evade my hand, but I don't stop. I all but yowl at him as I attack, nails raking down his cheek, the other hand slapping at him as I come unraveled. A sound comes out of me as he tries to grab me, an inconsolable scream, and I see blood on his face, on his chest, where I've scratched him.

"Fuck you!" I scream. "Fuck you, fuck you! I told you I don't want this! I don't want to be your wife. I don't want to stay. I don't want any of this—"

The words trail off, tears running down my face as I slap at him again, nails raking down his arm. I'm going for his cock next, and I think he knows that, because he backs away from me quickly, fending me off as he goes for the door.

"I'll talk to you when you've calmed down," he manages, his hand fumbling for the lock, and I let out a strange, high-pitched laugh, feeling as if all my nerves are frayed at the ends.

"I never want to talk to you again!" I scream, and Nikolai backs up quickly, one hand up to keep fending me off as he opens the door the slightest bit.

I try to bolt. I've forgotten I'm naked, sore from the spanking he gave me and the way he fucked me afterward, his cum still dripping down my thighs. I've forgotten everything other than my need to get away, and I try to get through the door after him, my fingers nearly getting slammed in it as he yanks it shut, and I hear the sound of the lock behind him.

"We'll talk later, when you're calm," he repeats through the door, and I scream again, slamming my fists into it.

"Fuck you!" I screech, and this time there's no quip from him, no remark about how he'll show me what it means to fuck him or anything like that. I hear his footsteps going down the hall, walking away, and I slam my fists into the door again and again, a mirror of the first night I spent in his father's mansion, as I cry and scream.

I've lost all control, and I know it. The punishment snapped something inside of me, and I gasp as the sobs take over, and I collapse to the floor, crying harder than I've cried in a long time. I'm trapped. I've never felt so trapped, and now I know what Nikolai will do to me if I make him angry. What he can make *me* do.

He made me come. Spanked me and whipped me between the legs with a belt, and I came for him. What's wrong with me?

A small voice says that nothing is wrong. That I have a kink, that's all. Something that I didn't know about, because how could I, the way I grew up? I was never introduced to anything like *that*. And there's a countering voice that says that's all well and good, but it doesn't matter if it turned me on. The problem isn't that I enjoyed it. It's that Nikolai *made* me enjoy it.

You held a gun on him. What did you think he was going to do if he got the upper hand? And how did you really think that was going to go?

I don't know how long I sit there crying for. It's dark outside by the time I manage to peel myself up off of the floor, and Nikolai hasn't come back. I don't know how long he plans on leaving me in here, or if he's going to bring me food, but I haven't heard his footsteps.

Slowly, I get up. My entire body aches, my ass raw and sore from the spanking, and I want a shower. I stumble to the adjacent bathroom, turning the water on as hot as I can stand it, and getting in, tears leaking out of my eyes all over again as the spray stings my abraded skin.

I wash every trace of him off of me that I can, until all of me is pink and feels faintly raw. I stay in the shower until the water runs cool, and I try to think of what I'm going to do.

I'd planned to run away. I hadn't cared about hurting him, hadn't planned on even shooting him, unless he stopped me. Which, of course, he had, and I still hadn't managed to shoot him. But the point of it is that I don't really want to *hurt* Nikolai. I want to get out of here. And my best chance is still while we're out here at the cabin, instead of back in the city.

Once we're back in Chicago, I'll never get away. There's too much security around him all of the time—and doubtless will be around me too, when he's not there—a doorman for his penthouse probably, layers of failsafes to get through to keep me from escaping. Out here, it's just him and I.

The room is locked. How the hell do you think you're getting away? Nikolai isn't going to give me an inch of free rein, after this. I wouldn't be surprised if he took us back to Chicago in the morning. Our "honeymoon" is spoiled, and he won't want to risk me trying anything else.

If I'm going to get away, it will have to be tonight.

I get out of the shower, slowly formulating a new plan in my head as I dry off and get dressed in clean jeans and another thicker sweater. I have a fleece-lined leather jacket, and I lay that on the bed as I find a pair of boots, watching the door every few seconds in case Nikolai comes in. I don't want him to realize what I'm plotting.

Leaning over, I peer out of the window to see how far up the bedroom is. It's hard to gauge in the dark with only the light from the front of the house, but I know I'm on the second story. It's just whether or not I can get down without hurting myself.

Once I start my plan, I have to move fast. If Nikolai comes in and catches me, it'll be obvious what I'm doing. And then—

I shudder at the thought of how he'd likely react. At the thought of him punishing me again. But I'm not entirely sure that it's just a shudder of dread.

I don't have time to analyze why his punishment turned me on. Why by the time the count had reached fifteen, I could feel that same tight heat washing over me that I feel when he touches me. Why I can't help but come every time he does *anything* to me. I have to get out of here.

I dig in the closet, finding spare sheets. As fast as I can, I strip the bed, knotting them together until I have a long rope of tied-together fabric. I feel like a ridiculous, obvious trope right now, about to climb out of a window on a rope made of bedsheets—but if it works, why do I care? If I can get away, it doesn't matter how I manage it.

He didn't think to lock the windows. I push it open slowly, poised to stop if I hear a squeak, but it's well-oiled and cared for. The window glides up, a burst of frigid air coming in, and I shiver as I reach for the sheets tied around the bedpost.

Fuck you, Nikolai, I think one last time—and I start to climb out of the window.

I immediately realize that it's not as easy as it looks. I *have* a gym membership—or had—but the treadmill and some light bicep curls five times a week isn't preparation for trying to rappel down the side of a house silently while holding up my own body weight, such as it is. For a brief, terrifying moment, I'm sure I'm going to slip and fall to the ground from the second story—or I'm going to make such a racket on the side of the house that Nikolai will come out and find me before I can get away.

I suck in a breath, clinging to the sheets and praying to anyone who might be listening that they don't give way—and try to move as quietly as I can. I don't let the breath out again until I reach the end of the rope.

There's still space between me and the ground, but it doesn't look like it's enough to injure me. I take another breath, curling in on myself, and let myself drop.

All the air is knocked out of me when I hit the frozen ground. It wasn't far, but my shoulder and hip strike the icy dirt, and the sharp pain is almost enough to make me cry out. I sink my teeth into my lower lip to stop myself, tasting blood, and I lay there for a brief second, wondering if this is worth it.

I could wait for Nikolai to come find me. He'd punish me again, but right now, I don't know if I can move. I'm afraid I've broken something.

Slowly, I move my fingers and toes. I try to push myself up, and I realize, to my relief, that nothing is broken. I'm just bruised and sore, and I scramble to my feet, realizing as I get my breath back and my vision clears that it's starting to snow.

Not just a light snow. It's starting to snow *hard*.

One more chance, Lilliana. Go back in and apologize. Tell Nikolai you're sorry. Sleep in a warm bed. Yes, it'll be next to him. Yes, he'll fuck you. But is it so bad? He makes you come. Just be a good wife, and it won't be so bad.

I can't do it. I can't make myself go back. For as long as I can remember, I've gotten through everything I've endured by telling myself that there was freedom at the end of this, so long as I could survive. Now I have a path to that.

I don't know how far it is to the road. But I start off away from the house, going into the trees, hoping that it will give me enough cover that Nikolai won't be able to see where I've gone. I have no idea how long it will take for him to realize that I've left.

By the time I make it a little ways into the trees, the snow is coming down harder. The wind has picked up, cutting through the leather jacket and sweater, and I wrap my arms around myself, shivering as I plunge deeper into the woods. I need to find a road, but by now, the light from the house has disappeared, and I'm not entirely sure which way I came from.

Fuck. I stop, looking around as I try to get my bearings. The woods are pitch black except for the moonlight filtering in through the trees, and I didn't bring any source of light. The snow isn't letting up, and the harder it falls, the more I realize what a stupid idea this was.

I'm so cold. Once I'm standing still, I realize just how cold it is— and it feels like the temperature is dropping. I didn't think any of this out—I didn't have *time* to think it out—but it begins to dawn on me how dire of a situation this is.

Okay. I'll try to find my way back to the house. I take a breath, trying to look for my footprints, but the snow is falling hard enough that the tracks are already covered. I'm surrounded by trees that all look the same, in a forest of white, and even if I could see the stars, I wouldn't know what the fuck to do with that.

I'm lost. The thought sends a cold bolt of panic through me. I'm shaking not just from the freezing temperatures but from fear now, and I try to calm myself down, to remember that the more I panic, the more likely I am not to make it out of here. But I'm not sure it matters anymore.

I start to try to walk back in the direction I think I came from, but it's only minutes before I realize it's impossible. I have no way of knowing which way is the right one. I can't find my way back to the house—not to go back and beg Nikolai's forgiveness if I wanted to, and not to try to use it as a guidepost for how to find the road.

I'm going to die out here. The realization doesn't hit me as hard as I think it should. I won't make it out here overnight; I'm almost certain. I have no way to keep warm. Eventually, I'll fall asleep, and from everything I know about exposure—which admittedly isn't much—I won't wake up.

A part of me isn't entirely sure that's so bad. *Maybe that's better than being married to Nikolai, spending the rest of my life as a Bratva wife.* I'd known, when I thought I was being given to the *pakhan*, that I might not make it out alive. This is just a different version of that. Maybe I wasn't ever supposed to make it out of this alive.

Freezing to death is probably better than what would have happened to me in that scenario.

I keep walking, because it feels like giving up to just stop. I keep hoping the trees will give way to a clearer path, to a road, a view of a highway. They never do. At some point, I think I might be walking in circles, but there's really no way to tell.

Eventually, I'm too tired to keep going. I don't know how late it is or how long I've been walking, but my legs are cramping from the cold. I trip and almost fall, and some part of me just…gives up. I sink down into the snow, crumpling into a heap, and I wonder dazedly how long it takes to freeze to death.

I'm somewhere on the edge of unconsciousness when I feel like I'm being lifted into the air. Hazily, I wonder if this is what dying feels like, if it's some sort of sensation of being out of my body, but I think I feel strong arms around me, the hardness of a broad chest against my cheek, a warmth sinking into me. It's not enough to bring me back to consciousness. Still, I'm vaguely aware of it in the last moments before the darkness presses in—and then there's nothing else.

Nikolai

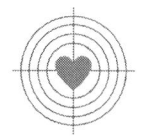

I'm cursing myself the moment I realize she's gone from the house.

How could I not have thought she'd find some way to try again? She'd found the nerve to hold me at gunpoint, and after I punished her, it makes absolute sense that she'd think up some sort of plan b. But I hadn't expected her to go out the fucking window.

And with a rope of bedsheets. She couldn't have picked a more trite way to go about it if she tried. It would be laughable if it didn't mean that she's out in the cold, alone, and probably lost.

I have to go after her, and for the first time, I'm cursing not just myself but the lack of security or anyone else at all out here with me. I don't have any help, anyone to assist in tracking her down. And if I'm not careful, I'll get lost out there, too.

There's a blizzard coming. I knew that—before I went up to check on her and found the window open and the room frigid, the makeshift rope hanging out of it—from the weather report. I'd been in the process of getting the house ready for it, making sure we'd be alright if the power went out, before I'd gone to see if she was asleep.

I'd half-hoped I'd find her on the ground outside. She would have been injured if she'd fallen, but that would have been better than being lost in the woods in the incoming storm. As it is, I have no choice but to hope I can find her, even with her tracks already covered up.

I take a few handfuls of red plastic ties with me, shoving them in my coat pockets after I bundle up and go out to the shed, taking a rifle with me for good measure. I doubt there'll be any dangerous animals out in this weather, but it's better to be safe than sorry. I bring a second coat with me, too, to wrap her up in if she went out without a jacket. I don't think she's that foolish, but I can't be sure. She'd been upset when I left her, and I have no idea what other sorts of irrational decisions she might have made.

I should have thought it through. I should have been more careful with her. The regret burns hot enough to keep me warm as I head out into the cold, tying the red strips of plastic around the tree branches as I go to mark my path. The snow is falling thick and heavy, and there's no chance I'll be able to simply retrace my steps on the way back. The wind is strong, buffeting against me, and it stings the scratches on my face where Lilliana clawed me.

It's a long time before I find her, long enough that I'm afraid I might not be able to—or that when I do, it'll be too late. When I finally do spot the shape in the snow, already half-covered with a thick dusting of it, I quicken my pace, heart in my throat, as I walk up to it.

It's Lilliana. She's all but unconscious as I reach for her, carefully picking her up, her head lolling to one side with a low moan as I gather her against my chest. She's cold to the touch, and I walk as quickly as I can, following the path I left behind back to the house.

By the time I get back to the house, Lilliana is unconscious, her head against my shoulder. *This is my fault,* is all I can think as I bring her inside, carrying her up to the bedroom and laying her down atop the blankets.

She still has a pulse, but it's shallow. I cover her up, going to the bathroom to heat a washcloth, bringing it back to gently dab it over her forehead and cheeks. I know I need to warm her up slowly, but other than that, I'm not entirely sure what to do.

She needs a doctor. No sooner do I have that thought than the lights go out.

Fuck. There's a backup generator for the house, but it doesn't come on. I'd been in the process of double-checking everything when I realized she was gone, and now I'm torn between going down to try to find out what's happened to it and staying here with her. I have a growing, irrational fear that if I leave her for even a moment, I'll come back up to find that she's dead.

This wasn't how this was supposed to go. There's no heating up the washcloth again, so I go to the linen closet in the hall for more quilts to pile on her. The room is dark, so I switch on the flashlight on my phone and go in search of a camp lantern and candles to light it. It keeps me busy briefly, but it's not long enough before I have nothing to do but sit at Lilliana's side in the dim light, feeling the crushing pressure of the guilt weighing down on me.

I care about her. It's a hell of a time to realize it, but over the brief time we've spent together, she's managed to make me give more of a shit about her than I ever have about anyone. If she were awake to hear it, I could list off all the reasons—her nerve even in the face of circumstances that would terrify most people, her toughness, even her wit, despite the fact that it's often aimed at me. If she could get past her resentment at the circumstances of our marriage, she'd be the kind of woman who would make a better wife for me than I ever could have expected.

I'd meant to fuck her until I got bored and then leave her as a pampered trophy, to trot out when I needed a wife on my arm. But she could be so much more than that. She's smart and well-educated, clever and not easily frightened, and she could be a real partner. The kind of wife that men like me don't often have the opportunity to find.

I hadn't thought I wanted that. I'd never even imagined it. I'd always pictured my life lived on my own terms, not shared equally with someone. But in a very short time, Lilliana has done more than just get under my skin and make me lust for her. She's made me *care*.

If I'm being honest, something about her made me care from the moment I saw her, as ridiculous as it sounds. I'm not the kind of man who ever believed in anything like that. But she struck me from the moment she walked into my father's study—not just her beauty, but her presence. Her refusal to let my father, or hers, or anyone else break her.

Until *I* broke her. The same woman I'm realizing now that I care more for than I ever have for anyone. And I'm terrified that it might be too late.

I have a feeling she's likely not to forgive me anyway, no matter what I say or do, if she makes it through this. She didn't seem inclined to forgive me before I punished her, and I haven't made things better. But there's only a chance if she lives.

After a while, it gets cold enough in the room that I get into bed with her, tucking myself under the pile of blankets with her, still fully clothed, in an effort to keep us both warm. And that's when I realize that while her skin had been cold to the touch before when I'd brought her into the house, she's burning up now.

Careful to let as little heat out as possible, I get back up, going to run cool water over a washcloth this time. She lets out another of those low moans when I dab it on her forehead and cheeks, and I find myself missing when those moans were for a different reason. Not out of discomfort, but out of pleasure that *I* was giving her. Pleasure she wouldn't let herself fully enjoy.

Frustration wells up in me as I sit there, cooling her face with the cloth while still trying to keep her warm, watching her shiver under the pile of blankets, occasionally trying to get her to take a sip of water. I've never needed to care for anyone. My business has always been the exact opposite of that—of taking people apart, not putting them back together. In this situation, I'm totally at a loss.

Lilliana is the only person I've ever wanted to protect, besides Marika. And at this moment, I realize how entirely helpless I am to do that in any situation that doesn't call for violence.

I had thought I was her best hope. But now I see that she deserved much better than me.

Lilliana

When I start to come back to consciousness, I've never felt more like shit in my life.

The room is filled with a hazy dawn light when my eyes flicker open, and I realize that there's someone in the bed with me. I have enough blankets on top of me that it's an uncomfortable weight, and I'm drenched in sweat.

I flinch to one side, looking over to realize it's Nikolai, propped up next to me, asleep with his head lolling to one side. He looks exhausted even in sleep—purple circles under his eyes, his face a little paler than usual. I can see the half-healed scratches on his face where I clawed him before he got out of the room.

Slowly, I try to push myself up to a sitting position. I feel weak and drained, like a kitten trying to walk, and I make it about a quarter of the way up before I slump back onto the pillows.

There's a camp lantern and candles scattered around the room, all blown out now. When I crane my head to look out of the window next to the bed, I see an expanse of white snow that blankets everything within sight.

Next to me, Nikolai starts to stir. His eyes flicker open, and then go wide when he sees I'm awake. "Lilliana!"

The way he says my name startles me. It sounds—*happy*. Relieved. Like he's been waiting for this moment with his breath held.

"What happened?" The words come out thickly, like my tongue isn't working quite right, and my jaw is sore, as if I've been clenching it for days.

Nikolai runs a hand through his hair as he sits up straight. I've never seen him like this—unkempt and messy, still dressed in jeans, a thick sweater, and a heavy work coat. "You got lost in the woods," he says slowly, his gaze sweeping over me in a way I've never seen before. It's appraising, but not in a lustful way. It's like he's trying to make sure I'm okay.

"I remember that." I rub a hand over my face, trying to remember the rest. "I think I—passed out?"

"You were close to it when I found you. I brought you back to the house and tried to keep you warm. The power went out—it's still out, actually—and the backup generators weren't working. Couldn't call a doctor."

"You came after me?" I'm not sure why that surprises me, exactly. I'm a valuable possession, like anything else he owns. He'd hardly let me be stolen or damaged or escape if he could help it. But I suppose a part of me thought that he might feel like he was well rid of me, if I died out there in the snow.

"Of course, I came after you." To my surprise, he reaches out, gently pushing a tangled bit of hair out of my face. "I wasn't going to let you die, Lilliana."

The way he says my name still sounds gentle. I don't know what to make of it.

"I'm sorry for what happened," he says slowly. "Before. I was—too rough with you. I let it get out of hand. I can't tell you how sorry—"

"That doesn't change anything." I wrap my arms around myself, pulling away from his touch. For a moment, I'd forgotten about the punishment. I'd forgotten about everything other than the fact that he'd come after me, that he looks as if he's barely slept waiting for me to wake up. I forgot who my husband actually is. "How long was I out for?"

"It's been two days. You ran a high fever. I thought—" Nikolai swallows, and I think I can see real regret on his face. I have to remind myself that it means nothing. That he's a liar, a man who has trapped and hurt me. "I thought you weren't going to make it."

"Well, I'm alive." I swallow hard, trying not to think about how close I really might have come to dying. Out there in the snow, exhausted and hopeless, I'd managed to convince myself that it wouldn't have been so bad. Now, the idea fills me with a cold, paralyzing terror.

"I feel awful. I need to use the bathroom. And—shower. Is the power back on?"

Nikolai shakes his head. "No. But I can heat up some water on a camp stove for you to wash off with if you like."

A bubble of laughter wells up in my throat that I think might turn into hysterics if I let it out. It all feels vaguely unbelievable—the idea that Nikolai, the powerful, wealthy Vasilev heir, is going to heat up water on a Coleman stove for me to take a sponge bath with, because we're stranded out in the middle of the woods.

He gets up, stretching stiffly. "I'll get something for you to eat, too."

I watch him go, still feeling as if this is all some kind of feverish hallucination. *How did we end up here?* He's making it hard to hate him. He has been since we came to the cabin—*with the exception of when he spanked you,* I remind myself. But even that—

I push away the thought of how he'd made me come with the belt. How the feeling of him thrusting into me, even though I hadn't wanted it—*I didn't, I really didn't*—had felt so fucking good. How he always feels so fucking good.

Nikolai brings up hot water and granola bars for me, exactly the way he said he would, leaving the hot water in the bathroom so I can have some privacy. It startles me, because I hadn't expected him to be that thoughtful.

"I'll be out here when you get done," he tells me, and I can feel his eyes on me as I walk to the bathroom—but it doesn't feel as lascivious as it usually does.

What I really want is a bath or a hot shower, to just sink into hot water for as long as I possibly can and wash away all of the aches, to actually feel warm down to my bones. But anything that makes me feel cleaner is something.

I strip out of the clothes that I've been running a fever in for days, shivering as I reach for a washcloth and quickly sponge myself off. I wrap a terrycloth robe around myself, still shivering in the cold room, as I wash my hair with the remainder of the water while it's still vaguely warm.

Nikolai is waiting for me in the bedroom, exactly like he said he'd be. He motions toward a glass of water next to the bed. "Drink some. I've been getting as much down you as I could while you were unconscious, but it was hard."

I nod, reaching for the glass and taking a sip. There's a strange awkwardness that's never existed between us before. I don't recognize this version of Nikolai, and I'm not entirely sure he recognizes it himself. He's trying to take care of me, and I don't think he knows how.

There's a long silence, and then when I set the glass down, he reaches out, pushing a piece of wet hair out of my face. "I thought you were going to die," he says quietly, almost as if he's reassuring himself that I'm still alive, and I don't know what to make of it.

I know even less what to make of it when his hand presses gently against my face, drawing me towards him as he bends his mouth to mine.

He's never kissed me like this before. It's soft and slow, his lips grazing over mine, as if he's worried I might break. I know I should pull away, tell him that I don't want him, but I've never been kissed like this before at all, and I *like* it. Somewhere in the back of my mind, I know I'm supposed to be horrified by that—but his lips feel good. They're soft and warm, his fingers brushing along my cheekbone as he cups my face. I unconsciously lean in, my hands sinking against the warm wool of his sweater as his tongue sweeps over my lower lip.

Nikolai groans, both of his hands sliding into my hair as his tongue slips into my mouth, and I'm jolted back to myself. I push against his chest, trying to squirm out of his hands. "Nikolai—"

"Please don't, *krolik*," he murmurs against my mouth, and I'm startled into absolute stillness for a moment. He's never asked me for anything before. Never said *please* to me. He's always wanted me to beg *him*. "I need—"

He groans, spilling me onto my back against the pillows, leaning over me as he reaches for a blanket to tug around us and block out the cold. "I need you," he murmurs against my mouth. "I want you so fucking badly, Lilliana—"

I can feel just how badly he wants me. He's rock hard against my thigh, his cock straining against the denim of his jeans, pressing against my bare thigh where my robe has been nudged aside. He's already fumbling with his clothes, shucking off the layers as he kisses me hungrily, and I can feel the tide of his desire threatening to overwhelm me.

It feels *good* to be so wanted. To feel how hungry he is for me, unable to get his clothes off fast enough, the hand not cupping my face fumbling between his clothes and my robe in a hurried urgency to feel skin against skin.

I should tell him no, even if it wouldn't make a difference. I should protest, tell him that I don't want this. But I *do*. I feel the same ache sweeping through me, the desire to feel his warm flesh against mine, the sweet, pleasurable stretch of his cock filling me, to be reminded that I'm *alive*. I'm still weak, feeling as if I can barely move, but Nikolai slides a hand down my side as he pushes my robe away, groaning as he kisses me again.

"I'll be careful," he whispers against my mouth. "I won't hurt you. Please, Lilliana. I want—"

He sucks in a shuddering breath, kicking away his jeans as he strips his sweater off, the blankets tucked around us both as I feel his broad, muscled chest brush against mine, all of that hard, bare flesh sliding against me as his cock nestles between my thighs.

"God, Lilliana—" he groans my name again, his mouth slanting over mine as he reaches between us, his cockhead nudging against my entrance. "I'll go slow, I—"

I can feel the restraint it takes for him to do exactly that. He's so fucking hard, his cock thick and rigid as he starts to push inside of me, and I can't stop myself from moaning into the kiss as I feel him starting to fill me.

"Tell me that feels good," he breathes against my mouth. "*Devochka*—"

I shouldn't. I should fight him like I always do. But I can't find the energy to fight against what I'm feeling too, not right now. It *does* feel good, so fucking good, and I moan again as he thrusts, another inch of his cock sinking into me as his hand clutches the pillow next to my head, the other buried in my hair.

"It feels good," I breathe, my hips arching up into his, my body wanting more. Another inch and I hear the whimper that slips from my mouth, my pussy clenching around him, pulling him deeper. "Oh—"

"That's right." He groans, another inch sliding into me. "It feels so fucking good. Oh god, Lilliana—"

He's never been like this before. *It's* never been like this before, slow and romantic and sweet, Nikolai taking me in slow inches until I'm gasping with pleasure, my back arched, fingers curled into the sheets. I'm going to come, just from the slow, rocking friction of him against me, and I can't fight it. I don't want to fight it.

"Oh god, I'm—" I gasp against his ear, arching again, and Nikolai groans, thrusting himself into me as deeply as he can.

"That's right, *krolik*. Come for me. Oh god, come for me, *malysh*—"

I come unraveled underneath him, the pleasure crashing over me in waves as I cry out, clutching at his shoulders as my hips buck against his. The orgasm keeps going as Nikolai thrusts, rolling over me and making me feel as if every nerve in my body is on fire as I moan, writhing beneath him as I clench and flutter along the length of his cock.

"*Fuck*—" he groans, thrusting again, and I can feel his entire body go rigid. "I'm going to—oh *god*—"

I feel the hot rush of his cum as he fills me, his hips shuddering against mine, his mouth against my shoulder as he comes hard. It sends another rippling jolt of pleasure through me, the feeling of him hot and hard inside of me, nearly sending me over the edge into another climax.

Nikolai doesn't move for a long moment, breathing hard as he braces himself above me. "Lilliana—" he breathes my name, reaching over to run his fingers over my cheek, and I feel my heart skip in my chest as I turn my face away.

In the aftermath, it all comes rushing back. I remember why I'm supposed to hate him, why I've fought him for so long, why I'm supposed to try not to enjoy what he does to me. He forced me to marry him, made me say my vows, and dragged me into bed with him. He punished me, hurt me, and now I'm here, recovering from exposure because he frightened me so much that I ran away into a blizzard.

I'm not supposed to like him, or want him, or see him as anything but a devil, a brutal man who I should do anything to get away from.

I think Nikolai can feel me shutting down, because he pulls away from me, his cock slipping free as he rolls to one side, careful to keep the blankets tucked around him.

"Lilliana—" he starts to speak again, but I shake my head, swallowing hard as I refuse to look at him. I can feel his cum on my thighs, and I don't want to think about how good it felt, how much I enjoyed him touching me like that. How the sweet, slow sex threatened to undo all the barriers I've woven to keep between us, so he doesn't make me feel things I shouldn't for him.

"Clearly, I can't get away from you," I tell him tightly, still looking away as I tuck the blanket in tightly around my breasts. "But I don't have to love you. I never will. I don't want you, Nikolai, and that's not going to change."

He's quiet for a long moment, and then I feel him shift, pushing himself up a little as he looks over at me. "You're wrong, Lilliana," he says quietly. "I know you want me. I can feel it every time we're together. I can see it in the way you look at me sometimes, when you think I don't see. You can pretend all you like, fight yourself all you want, but I know the truth. And there's nothing wrong with it."

I press my lips tightly together, looking away, but I don't answer.

"We could be good together," he says quietly. "You and I. We could make a good partnership, if you would just let yourself see it, *krolik*—"

I shake my head, opening my mouth to protest—and we both freeze as we hear the sound of the power coming back on, the lights in the room flickering and brightening the early morning light already in the bedroom.

I should be glad. The power being back on means we'll be warm. I can shower, and Nikolai can cook food. We'll be able to leave soon. But I feel a strange flash of disappointment at the idea that we won't need to stay close any longer to stay warm.

"Well, give it a minute for the water heater to get back to normal, and you can take a real shower. Or a bath." Nikolai pushes the blankets back, reaching for his clothing. "I'll go look and make sure everything is in order. Just stay here and rest, *krolik*."

He doesn't touch me again or kiss me before he leaves. It should make me glad. I should *want* the distance between us. I don't understand why I feel a sinking pit in my stomach as he walks away, closing the door and leaving me there.

Lilliana

The next morning, we're able to head back to Chicago. Nikolai has cleared out the path to the road, and with the power back on, we're showered, dressed in clean clothes, and full of a hot dinner and breakfast. The entire ordeal has started to feel like a bad dream.

We're both silent on the drive back. Nikolai didn't try to touch me again last night or this morning, and it feels like something is off. He's never had any restraint before, and I don't entirely understand what's going on. It leaves me feeling unsettled. I understood how he was behaving before. He married me, and I belong to him. But now, he's treating me differently.

I can feel the knot in my stomach tightening the closer we get to the city. "Are we going to the mansion?" I ask him finally, and he nods.

"I need to talk to my father. We'll go to the penthouse after that."

Silence falls over the car again after that, and I knot my hands in my lap, swallowing hard. I'd almost rather things go back to how they were before, just so I don't feel so uncertain.

Nikolai pulls up into the driveway, killing the engine. He comes around to open the door for me, and I'm out of the car and reaching for my bag before we both freeze in place.

The door to the mansion is open. Not just open—the hinges are broken, the door hanging off of them, splintered where the locks were.

"Oh my god—" My mouth drops open, and Nikolai is already striding forward, his jaw set and a gun in his hand that I never saw him draw or even realized he had on him.

"Stay close to me," he snaps, and for once, I don't have any intention of arguing.

There are muddy bootprints in the foyer, a streak of blood across the marble. The entire house is in shambles—bullet holes in the walls, blood splattered across furniture, and the bodies of staff slumped over chairs. Nikolai moves faster, glancing over his shoulder at me with an expression on his face that I've never seen before, so hard and cold that it sends a wave of terror through me.

"I don't know what I'm going to find in the study," he says tightly. "But I need you to stay next to me, Lilliana. Don't leave my sight for a second."

I nod, feeling a lump of fear in my throat that keeps me from being able to speak. All that comes out is a strangled noise that I hope sounds like it's in the affirmative as I do exactly as he says, staying close to him as he pushes open the door to the study slowly, his gun leveled.

He nudges the door all the way open, raising the gun—but the room is dark and empty…except for a body slumped over the desk. There's a rich smell of something sickening in the air, and I clap a hand over my mouth, a strangled gasp coming out.

The body is Nikolai's father. And he's been dead for a little while.

"Stay right there." Nikolai motions to where I'm standing next to the wall. "Don't move."

"The smell—"

"I don't want you out of my sight!" His voice is sharp and rough, and he clears his throat, shaking his head briefly. "I'm sorry, Lilliana. Just please—I know. Just stay where you are."

From the smell, I don't think that whoever killed Nikolai's father is still in the house. But I understand why he's demanding I not move. I stand there, my hand clapped over my mouth and nose, breathing shallowly as Nikolai goes to investigate the body.

A moment later, he strides back towards me, that cold and angry expression on his face again. "I need to find Marika," he says sharply. "Come with me. Stay—"

"Stay close," I echo. "I know, Nikolai."

For a moment, I've forgotten that we're meant to be at odds. I have nothing against Marika—she was kind to me when I was first brought here—and the idea that we might find her in a similar situation to their father makes me feel sick, bile rising up to burn the back of my throat.

We go up to each floor, the second and the third, and walk through every bedroom. But Marika is gone.

"Fuck!" Nikolai shouts the curse, his jaw clenched, and I flinch back. "I don't know who the fuck did this—" he runs a hand through his hair, tugging at it. "They're fucking dead as soon as I find out."

He looks at me, his chest rising and falling visibly as he tries to get control of himself. "I'm taking you back to the penthouse," he says finally. "There's enough security there that you should be safe. And then I'm going to see what I can find out about this shit."

I don't know what to say. My heart is racing as we go back out to the car, a fearful lump still clogging my throat. Nikolai opens the door to the car for me, and I grip the sides of the seat, trying to ground myself somehow as he gets in on the other side, slamming the door and revving the engine.

I can feel the anger rolling off of him in waves as he drives. It's not directed at me, but it's still terrifying. I sit there trembling, trying to breathe, trying not to remember the stench of death in the house.

I've never seen a dead body before. Never even been close to one. I feel like I might pass out or throw up, and I don't think Nikolai is in the mood to deal with either, so I sit there with my fingers digging into the buttery leather of the seats, clinging onto the last shred of my sanity for dear life.

He weaves through traffic as we head downtown, darting in and out at a frightening pace, until we reach the building where his penthouse is, and he pulls into the underground garage. He comes around to open my door again, and I find that I can't move. I'm frozen in my seat, shaking.

"Lilliana." His voice is less harsh than I expected it to be. "I need to get you inside. Come on."

Somehow, I manage to peel myself out of the car. My legs are trembling so badly that I feel like they might give out on me at any moment, but I follow him to the elevator, realizing that his gun is in his hand again.

"You don't think—" My eyes flick towards the weapon, my heart hammering in my chest. I need it to slow down, or I'm going to pass out.

"It's better to be safe," Nikolai says curtly. "I go first when those doors open, Lilliana. You stay behind me until we're safely inside."

I nod mutely. For once, I have no desire to argue with him. *I* want to be safely inside, but I have no idea if even that will be enough to make me feel like I'm out of danger. This wasn't at all what I had expected to come back to.

The doors to the elevator open, and Nikolai strides out, gun held by his thigh as he looks out into the hallway. I peek around him a little, careful to still stay behind him as instructed, but all I see are the black-clothed security that I'd expected lining the hall.

"Let's go," Nikolai says sharply, striding forward, motioning for me to follow. Vaguely, I'm aware that under any other circumstances, I'd be furious with being summoned along like this. Still, I can't bring myself to care. I feel as if I'm wound so tight that as soon as I let go, I'll collapse like a puppet with my strings cut.

Nikolai opens the door quickly, walking past the security standing by it. "Go inside," he tells me. "I'll be there in a minute. I need to talk to my security."

I nod, mutely walking inside. I see a flicker of something that looks like concern over his features, as if he's confused by my acquiescence, but it's gone almost as quickly.

The penthouse is beautiful, if a little masculine, for my taste. Everything is black and grey and cream, iron and leather and wood, with one wall that's mostly window overlooking the city beyond. Numbly, I walk to the nearest couch, my shoes sinking into the thick cream rug stretched out over the gleaming dark hardwood floor, before I topple onto the black leather couch.

It's cool against the backs of my arms. I lie there, staring up at the ceiling, at the iron chandelier hanging to my right. There's a certain rustic industrialness to the style of Nikolai's penthouse that reflects the cabin, and I realize it must be something he likes. Hard edges, rough texture, softened by some plush textiles.

There's a painting on one wall above a grand piano, I'd be willing to fucking bet Nikolai doesn't know how to play, in a frame made of some black metal that looks like twisted iron. It's a watercolor, all browns and greens and whites, and I think it's one of those bullshit abstract paintings that you're not really meant to understand what it is, because everyone interprets it differently. Lying there, I start to understand what that's all about—because I see the blurs of browns turning into the shape of that deer in the woods, the white that snow underneath its hooves, as it stood there without an idea in its head that it was about to die. There'd been a gun trained on its head, and it hadn't even known it.

There's no red in the painting, but for a moment, I almost see it, a splash of it on the blurry white.

What the fuck am I even thinking about? I feel like I'm going insane. Less than an hour ago, I was staring at a dead body, and now I'm thinking about interior decorating. *It must be a trauma response.*

I don't know how long I lay there, looking up, before I hear the door open. I sit up in a flash, curling back against the sofa, but it's just Nikolai—and that thought makes a bubble of laughter escape from my lips before I drop my forehead onto my knees and start to cry.

I would never have thought there would be a day when I would be relieved to see Nikolai walk through a door.

"Lilliana." His voice is still gentler than normal as he comes to sit down next to me. He reaches out, touching my thigh, and I flinch back. I can't help it. "Lilliana, it's alright. You're safe here, as long as you stay inside."

"How do you know?" I wipe at my face, sniffing back tears. It feels like everything is catching up to me at once, and I want to curl into a ball and sob until there's nothing left. But I can't do that in front of him.

Not for the first time, I wish he would leave.

"I have enough security to keep just about anyone from getting in here." His hand is still resting on my thigh, but for the first time, it feels like it's out of comfort instead of lust. "I have more coming, too. There will be a goddamn army keeping this place locked down until I get back—until I figure out what's going on."

"Is it really going to do any fucking good?" I look at him blankly. "There was security at the mansion, too. What difference is there?"

Nikolai's mouth twitches. "My father was arrogant," he says simply. "He kept less security around him than he should, and I have a feeling whoever did this was in his company often enough to recognize patterns in it. I handle things differently."

"Why do you care so much about keeping me safe?" I sniff again, rubbing my hands over my face. "What does it fucking matter? Your sister is gone. Why are you even still here?"

Nikolai looks at me, letting out a slow breath. I can't read the expression on his face, but for once, I believe the sincerity in his words when he speaks.

"You are my wife, Lilliana. Your safety is every bit as important to me."

He stands up in one fluid motion. "I'm going to look into this, *krolik*. Stay here until I get back. Keep your phone near you. Do not leave the apartment for any reason, do you understand?"

His voice hardens on the last word, and I nod. The idea of fighting him for the sake of it feels foolish and far away now, after what's happened today.

"I'll stay inside," I say in a small voice, and he nods.

"Good girl." He leans down, running one hand over my hair, and presses a kiss to the top of my head. It's such an innocuous gesture that it makes my eyes well up with tears all over again, and I'm surprised when he doesn't try to kiss me on the lips. He could have—I'm frozen, utterly confused that, for once, he's the one I feel safe with. That I almost don't want him to go. I've never had that feeling for him, and the irony of it isn't lost on me.

But instead, he takes one more look at me, then turns away, striding back towards the front door.

—

I end up falling asleep on the couch.

I don't know how long I lay there crying before I fall asleep. By the time I do, my throat feels raw and my face swollen, my body aching from the tension that's been running through my muscles for hours.

I fall asleep out of pure exhaustion, into the deepest sleep I think I've ever had that wasn't actual unconsciousness.

I'm woken out of it by what sounds like a gunshot.

I jerk upright, hands clenched against the leather of the couch, and it takes the sound of footsteps moving quickly across the wooden floor towards me for me to realize that I think it was the slamming of a door. There's no weapon in the hand of the shadow coming my way.

"Get up, *krolik*."

His voice is like nothing I've heard before from him. Darker, angrier, filled with a venom that chills me to the bone with terror before I'm even fully aware of what's happening. I open my sticky eyes and see Nikolai looming over me, silhouetted in the lights of the city streaming through the windows, his face a tight mask of anger as he leans forward and wraps his hand in my hair.

This is the wolf, I think as he drags me up off of the sofa by my hair. *This is the Bratva monster. The Vasilev devil. And now he's come for me for some reason.*

"Nikolai—" I can't bring myself to feel any shame about the way I whimper his name. I've never been so afraid. The man holding onto me doesn't feel or look or sound like my husband. That version of Nikolai, the one I know, was frightening enough. But I think this version is the one his enemies see—the *last* thing they see. And every part of me turns liquid with fear as he pulls me to my feet.

"Your father is behind this." His voice is deadly quiet. His other hand reaches out, and I see in the dim light that it's covered in bloodstains. As he drags me towards the window, illuminating us both in the light, I see that there's blood everywhere. On his face, his throat, his clothes. He's spattered in violence.

"I don't understand," I whisper weakly. "My father? My father is no one."

I wonder if he can hear the conviction in my voice. The certainty. My father has always been no one, and worming his way into the Vasilev inner circle was never going to change that. He will be no one until his last breath, because that's the kind of man he's always been.

"He's someone enough to get into *my* father's house. To take *my* father's life. To take *my* sister from me. And all because he used you to get close."

Nikolai's other hand comes up, his fingers sliding around my throat. I realize with sudden, terrifying certainty that he thinks I know something about this. That he somehow thinks I was in on whatever my father has done.

"Nikolai, please." I've never begged him before, never *let* myself beg him, and I know he's wanted to hear it all this time. I don't want to start now, but I'm so terrified I can't help it any longer. "I don't know what you're talking about. I don't know anything—"

"Don't *lie* to me!" He shouts it, his hand starting to close around my throat. "I know what you've done. Coming into my home, my *father's* home, playing the wide-eyed innocent. You and your father planned all of this, didn't you? How to bring down the mighty Vasilev empire from the inside. You conniving bitch—"

Somewhere dimly, as if it's from outside of my body, I hear myself starting to laugh. My shoulders begin to shake, all of me trembling in his grasp, and the laughter starts to get louder, almost cackling, as if I'm losing my mind.

Nikolai is staring at me as if I already have. His hand on my throat and in my hair loosens for a brief moment, and then they both tighten again, his face a mask of such incandescent rage that for a second, I think he's going to snap my neck and finish me off here and now.

"This isn't funny." His voice drifts over me, cool and hard as ice. "You're foolish if you think it is. This isn't a joke, *krolik*."

The nickname sounds so much darker on his tongue now. His anger is so cold, so inflexible. It feels as if there's no escape from it, and I can't believe I'm going to die over something that I have absolutely no knowledge of.

He turns me around, so quickly that I gasp in fear and shock as he pushes me against the glass. It's cold against my cheek, and I suck in a breath, my heart pounding so hard that it hurts.

"I'm going to get the truth out of you one way or another, little rabbit," he growls in my ear. "You don't know what kind of game you're playing." His hand on my throat falls away, reaching down to grab my ass, which is still a little sore from the spanking he gave me days ago. "You think this hurt? You have no idea how it will feel when I punish you again."

"I don't—know—*anything*!" My breath is catching in my throat, tight from fear and his grip on it. I feel like I'm having trouble swallowing. "God, Nikolai! I don't know what my father was doing!"

"I don't believe you," he sneers. He twists me around, my back against the glass now, looming over me. His hand twists in my hair, pulling it so hard that I'm terrified that at any moment, it's going to start ripping free. "I don't believe a word out of your lying little mouth."

His hand leaves my ass, grabbing my hand, holding it up into the light. My nails are still manicured from the wedding, and he presses his thumb against one rounded tip, pushing it back. "Can you imagine how it feels to have these plucked off one at a time, *krolik*? Yanked away while you're tied down and unable to move?"

His fingers are bloody. "Was that what you were doing?" I choke out. "Torturing someone?"

"How do you think I know what's going on?" His thumb presses harder against the nail. Even that is uncomfortable. I don't want to think about the kind of pain he's describing. "I am a master of getting information, little rabbit. I don't shy away from blood, and screams don't touch me. Yours won't, either."

I try to find some measure of courage. Somewhere, there has to be something. I can't crumble in front of him. My tears won't help. "You can do whatever you want," I manage, forcing each word out even as my entire body starts to shake. "It won't matter, because there's *nothing to fucking tell*, Nikolai! My father has never told me anything! All I know is what I was meant to do—be a plaything and a bedmate for your father or whoever he chose to give me to. That's *all*. I swear—I don't even know who he was trying to replace. All he ever taught me, all he ever told me was what he thought would make me a better mistress. I swear—Nikolai, *please*. You wanted to hear me beg. Fine. Please believe me. I don't know what the *fuck* is going on…and you're going to tear me apart for nothing."

The words come out in a rush, tumbling over each other, and I feel him go very still. His face is still a mask, still full of cold anger as he looks down at me, but I feel the hand in my hair loosen ever so slightly.

And then he lets go of me—so fast that I slide down the glass as my knees give out onto the hard wooden floor. I land on my ass, looking up at him as he stares down at me with a mixture of rage and contempt—a look I've never seen him give me before.

"Get up, Lilliana," he says, his voice low and dangerous. "I'll give you one chance to explain yourself. That's it. So make it quick."

Lilliana

For a moment, I don't think I'm going to be able to. I don't think I can make my legs hold me. But slowly, I push myself up to my feet, swallowing hard as I face my husband—a man I don't even recognize right now.

He's never shown me this side of himself before. I don't even know if he's going to listen to me. If he's going to hear anything I'm saying.

"I don't know anything about what's going on," I tell him in a hushed voice. "If you say this is my father—I believe you. My father is a terrible, awful man. But I don't know what he was planning. I never imagined—"

"Don't fucking start crying," Nikolai hisses. "I swear to god, Lilliana—" His fists clench at his sides. "What I've lost today—"

"Is Marika dead?" I press a hand to my mouth, fighting back tears. I feel sure that if I start crying, it will tip him over the edge, and I won't have a chance to even try to explain before he starts taking pieces off of me. I can feel how close that thread is to fraying. "Nikolai—"

"Right now, she isn't." His voice is tight and hard. "But I don't know where she's being kept. I'm going to fucking find out. But I need to know what you know first. What you and your father—"

"Nothing!" I burst out. "I keep saying it—what do I have to tell you for you to believe me? I don't know what the hell he was thinking—"

"Then tell me what you *do* know," he growls. "Tell me why a girl barely in her twenties doesn't have a hobby outside of gym sessions and hair appointments. Tell me why you can name every city in every country on every continent, but you can't hold a conversation that isn't just parroting facts. Tell me why you were supposed to be a virgin—you *were* a virgin—who claims she never even touched herself, but you suck a cock like you know what I'm supposed to like." His hands, clenched into fists, flex and tremble. "Tell me, Lilliana, or I will make you tell me everything anyway."

I know he will. The hardest part is getting the words to come past my lips.

"My fucking father groomed me as a way to get deeper into the Bratva," I hiss, the venom in my words apparent from the moment I start speaking. I can't hold it back. I've been stifling the pain of all those years in his house, all the things he did, all the ways he made me feel, for as many years as I've lived there. I've hated him for just about as long. And I want Nikolai to understand that there's no love lost there. That I want no part of my father or his dealings—and that he only ever wanted me for one thing.

"I was only ever meant to be a distraction," I tell him. "Not a bride. He never *dreamed* that whoever I was given to—your father or whoever your father chose—would *marry* me." I swallow hard, trying to breathe. "I was taught everything he thought I needed to know to hang off of a *pakhan's* arm for as long as I was wanted. I was taught how to eat at a fancy dinner, how to carry on a conversation about any number of topics, when to be silent and when to speak, how to dress, and how to do my makeup and hair. And I was taught what men like in bed."

Nikolai's face darkens. "So you lied to me?" He takes a threatening step forward, and I shrink back, letting out a small cry when I feel the glass press against my back, a reminder that there is such a fragile layer between me and the long drop to the street below. "You weren't a fucking virgin?"

"No!" I hold up my hands, trying to ward him off, trying to force back the burn of tears in my eyes. "I was! I swear, I was. I told the truth. I hadn't even touched myself, just like I said. I *hated* the idea of sex. Nothing about it turned me on. I didn't want anything to do with it."

"Why?" Nikolai's jaw tightens. "What do you mean, then, you were *taught*? Did your father—did he touch you?"

I swallow hard. "No." I shake my head. "Not—himself. No one touched me. He was very clear on that point. But he would pay—people. Escorts. Men and women. He would have them come to the apartment, because he refused to take me out to any of those places and have them perform all kinds of—things."

"What kinds of things?" Nikolai asks, the words dark and slow. "Be a little clearer, Lilliana. You don't want any misunderstandings with me tonight."

"Sexual acts," I whisper. "How to give a man a handjob. A blowjob. How to fuck. All the different positions, all of it in excruciating close-up detail. The kinks a man might have, the things he might say, and how to respond. And I was quizzed on all of it. Made to watch over and over and then asked questions. My father would say the things he thought the *pakhan* might say to me, and…punish me if I didn't respond the way he thought would be…arousing enough."

The last sentence I have to force out. It's disgusting, horrible, the things he made me do and feel without ever even having to touch me. "So you can see why I didn't lay in bed at night and touch myself to imagined fantasies of the man who was going to eventually rape me with my father's encouragement." The words drip with bitterness, with cold anger to match Nikolai's, and I feel some of the tension drain out of me as I look at him. I'm not even sure I care any longer if he believes me. I feel suddenly exhausted from recalling all of it, from remembering just how terrible it all was.

Nikolai's face is set in hard, angry lines. "And he thought that would accomplish what he needed?" His voice is so careful, so taut, that I feel like he's a ticking bomb waiting to explode. Anything I say could set him off. But I have a strange feeling that it might not be me that he's angry with any longer.

"He wanted me to be good enough to please the *pakhan*. He assumed if I pleased him, then he would get what he wanted. It was just another part of my *education*." I spit out the last word as if I can't get it out of my mouth fast enough. "He was ambitious, and he used me for his ambitions. That's all I know. He controlled everything about my life. What I ate, what I wore, how I did my hair, the routines I did at the gym. Everything was perfectly thought out to turn me into the ideal *specimen* to be the fucktoy for your father. He abused me, and I had no choice but to let him."

I suck in a harsh breath, staring Nikolai down, feeling tears well up in my eyes despite myself. "Even when I left the house was controlled. So when you ask me about hobbies or make small talk when I've never even had a friend—" I shake my head. "Fuck this. I don't want you to feel sorry for me. But I need you to understand that I don't know a goddamn thing about what my father was thinking or doing except that he had ambitions, and he used me to get them. I was promised my freedom, and instead, I got marched into a different prison."

I shake my head, swallowing back a threatening sob. "I have no idea what he's capable of," I tell Nikolai. "But I imagine it's plenty."

And then I press my hand over my mouth, stifling the whimper that slips out, because I can't speak any longer. It's taking everything in me not to burst into tears.

Nikolai is still and quiet for a long moment. The first thing I see is his hands, relaxing out of the fists they were clenched into. His face is still taut, but when he speaks, what he says isn't what I expected to hear.

"I'm sorry," he says quietly. "I—understand now. It all makes sense—the way you've been. And I've made it worse."

I don't know what to say. The tears spill out of my eyes, down over my cheeks. He doesn't move closer or try to touch me. He just keeps looking at me, his face hard, but the words he's saying are softer than anything I've ever heard.

"I punished you—and I regret that, now. I know that doesn't make it better, and it doesn't fix it. But I would never—if I had known—"

"You shouldn't have needed to know." The words come out before I can stop them, and I flinch, expecting him to retaliate. But to my surprise, he doesn't.

"You're right," he says. "I shouldn't have. I should never have touched you like that. I should have understood. And I shouldn't have forced you to marry me. I should—" He takes a breath. "I should have accepted that I couldn't have you and found a way to get you away from all of this instead."

"What do you mean?" I look at him, confused. "I don't—I don't understand what you're trying to say."

"I wanted you." His eyes, when he looks at me, hold a depth of emotion I can't fully grasp. "I wanted you so badly that I couldn't see any way I'd be able to stop myself from taking you." A shudder goes through him, as if he wants to come towards me, wants to touch me, and is forcing himself not to. "I'd never forced a woman in my life. So I thought if I married you, it would be different. You'd be mine, then. We'd be expected to go to bed. I could have you without hurting you."

I stare at him, trying to wrap my head around that convoluted way of thinking. "You were always hurting me," I whisper. "Even when you weren't—you were still—"

"I see that now." His voice is low and quiet. "All I can do is ask you to forgive me, Lilliana. For tonight—and all the nights before that. I'm so sorry. If I'd known—but you're right. I shouldn't have had to know to do things differently."

A small part of me, a very small part, wants to say I forgive him. I *do* believe him. I think he sees now what he couldn't see before, all because I'd told him about my past. But I meant what I said—he shouldn't have needed to know. And even if he realizes that now—it doesn't change things.

"It doesn't matter," I tell him, struggling to keep my voice from breaking. "I don't care what happens to my father, and I'm sure you understand why now. If he's really behind all of this, I don't care what you do to him. But I also want nothing to do with you."

I wrap my arms around myself tightly, trying to keep myself from starting to shake all over again. "I can't escape you or this marriage," I tell him quietly. "But I'm not going to forgive you. And if you really understand, then you'll leave me alone."

Nikolai says nothing for a long moment. I wonder what he's going to do, or say—if he's going to touch me anyway, insist I forgive him, tell me that I'm his wife and that I belong to him. But instead, he just gives me a sad look—the saddest one I've ever seen on his face.

"The bedroom is yours, Lilliana," he says finally. "I'll sleep out here. And I'll be gone in the morning to take care of business. Just stay here, and stay safe. That's the only thing I'll ask."

And then, before I can say another word, he turns and strides towards the front door. He opens it, and I catch a glimpse of the security outside before he closes it, and I hear the sound of the lock.

He's gone. And for the first time, I don't entirely know how I feel about it.

I sink down to the floor, burying my face in my hands, and I let myself fall apart.

Nikolai

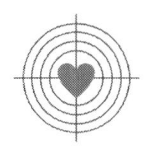

I want her forgiveness—and it's too late.

It feels ironic that I, who have spent my whole life making it my business to know what the people around me are thinking, doing, and wanting, that I missed all of those things when it came to my wife. I was raised to believe that those things didn't matter in a marriage—that all that mattered was obedience and docility—but I know that's no excuse. It's no excuse that I didn't understand what Lilliana has been through.

There's no real excuse for any of it.

If her father really is responsible for all of that—if everything she said is true, then maybe there is a way to earn her forgiveness. The thought enters my mind, as I'm driven to the office downtown where I can call the hackers who might be able to find information on where he's gone, and track Marika. There's no love lost for her father; I feel confident of that. If I can get vengeance for her, then maybe that will change things.

The scene keeps playing out in my head again and again—my hand in her hair, dragging her out of sleep and up off of the couch, the rough, violent way I handled her, so horribly sure of myself and my theory. I *hurt* her again. I have, as she said, been hurting her all along—the exact opposite of what I always meant to do.

I want nothing to do with you. I'm not going to forgive you.

How could I blame her? There's nothing I can say that could make up for what I've done. The only thing I can think of is to *do* something—and the solution that I have is one that will benefit us both.

Her father gone, saves my family, and gives her revenge. I can't think of a better way to accomplish two things at once.

I have a team that works on problems of tracking people I need to be found and other digital matters—accounts that need to be manipulated, digital tracing, online footprints. They're all top-school graduates with massive student loan debts and dubious moral compasses, and they haven't failed me yet—a mixture of skill and a knowledge of what happens if they do. Before the night is over, they'll have the information for me that I need—a location, or a list of possible locations where I might be able to find Marika.

In the meantime, I pace the office, restless and on edge. I don't like leaving Lilliana in the penthouse alone, but I know she doesn't want my company. There's enough security there that I feel comfortable she'll be safe from anyone who might come after her. And I realize something else as I pace the floor, something that's more than a little unsettling.

I—miss her.

I'd rather be home with her than here, fretting over what my hackers will find. I'd rather be getting to know her, learning things a husband should know about his wife. Or, alternatively, helping her find out the things that she doesn't know about herself.

It all makes sense now—her behavior about food, the way she'd never really tried any kind of drink before, her lack of hobbies. She'd never been allowed to develop any type of personality for herself outside of what a man might want her to be—and yet she still had to some extent, even if it was an acerbic one. It occurred to me, as she said all of it, that I could give her the freedom to learn all of that. She could learn who it is that she wants to be—try the things she hasn't tried.

And if that means she becomes someone you don't like? Or someone who likes you even less?

This all feels like uncharted territory. I've never cared about anyone, really, other than my sister. Marika is the only person who ever aroused a protective instinct in me, who ever made me want to be gentle or careful with my words or actions—until Lilliana. I'd never met a romantic interest who made me feel that way. But now—

She wants nothing to do with me.

I find it hard to believe that can't be changed. That I can't find a way to get her to come around.

I hear the sound of a voice coming over the speaker—David's, the man in charge of my digital team.

"Mr. Vasilev—we have coordinates. But you're going to need more than just you to get in. This is going to be a bigger operation than that."

When he brings up the security feed of the building—no, *compound*, that he traced to coordinates to, I force back an audible groan. It will take a force of men to get in there—and I know that very well, because I know where it is. It belonged to my family, and now Lilliana's upstart, traitorous father has tried to claim it for his own. A base of operations to run his little mutiny out of.

"I'll get men together," I tell him. "Keep eyes on it. I want a count of who you see coming and going, if it's anyone on the lists of men who worked for us. See if you can find a way to get the cameras shut down, before I go in. Tomorrow night, we'll stage an attack and see if we can't put an end to this bullshit."

"I hear you. I'll let you know what we find, sir."

The call ends, and I'm immediately up, texting my driver to let him know I need the car brought around. I'm going home to Lilliana, and she'll know what I have planned.

I want her to understand what I'm going to do. The freedom I'm going to get for her, as well as for Marika.

She's not in the living room when I walk in. I feel a twist of anxiety, but my security assured me that there was nothing wrong, that there hadn't been so much as a peep of hostility or a sign of anyone trying to get onto the penthouse level.

When I find her, it's out on the balcony of the master suite, and I feel that sharp pang of fear again.

"Lilliana," I say her name slowly, carefully, as I step out of the open door. I don't know if she was thinking of jumping or not, but I don't want to risk startling her so badly she falls. There's no surviving a drop like that.

"Nikolai." She doesn't turn around. Her voice is soft and flat, but it makes something inside of me jolt anyway, hearing her say my name. I want to hear her say it differently. I want to hear it whispered, moaned, screamed in pleasure. Even her biting wit is better than that near-emotionless flatness.

"I have something to tell you." I step out onto the balcony, still moving in slow, careful steps, like she really is a wild animal, a small rabbit that I don't want to frighten. She turns to look at me, those blue eyes wide and watery, and she laughs.

"Are you afraid I'm going to jump?" She runs her fingers over the railing. "You look like that's what you're thinking."

"I know you're emotional right now—"

"*Emotional?*" She lets out another sharp bark of a laugh. "I'm *emotional?* Oh, Nikolai, you have no idea what I am. But I'm not so desperate yet that I'm going to jump off of this balcony. If I was ready to give up, I'd have done it long before my father tried to sell me off to yours."

"You can't blame me for thinking it's a possibility."

Her eyes soften the smallest bit then, soft and sad, and she bites her lower lip, dragging it between her teeth. "No," she says quietly. "I can blame you for a lot, but I suppose not for that."

"I came to tell you that I'm almost certain I know where your father has gone—where he's taken Marika and is setting up his next move. My hacking team has tracked his location—"

Lilliana laughs again, more bitterly this time. "Hackers. Tracking. God, I wish I'd never been born into this life. I'd rather be a cashier at a fucking supermarket than have to deal with this shit."

I look at her, at the hollow expression on her face, and I make a decision that I hadn't known I was capable of making. "Alright, *krolik*," I tell her quietly. "If that's what you want, then when this is over—you can have that."

She blinks at me. "What do you mean?"

"I'll let you go. Give you a divorce. You can live whatever life you want. You can be a cashier or a waitress or a student or a singer. Pick. Have the freedom you want. The life you decided you'd have after you did what your father ordered you to do. You've done it, haven't you? So once this is settled, and I know you're safe—" I spread my arms. "I'll open up the trap, little rabbit. You can go back to the woods."

Lilliana swallows hard. "I don't believe you," she says softly.

"I don't really expect you to. But it's the truth." I let out a slow breath. "Your father is a dead man, Lilliana. I will get revenge for both of us. Mine and yours—for my father's death and my sister's pain, and yours too. And then you can do what you like."

"I don't think you can do it." Lilliana meets my gaze, that hollow expression still lingering on her face. "Your father had security. Power. Everything you have. And we found him rotting in his office. I think mine has found an upper hand over you, and now he'll get what he wants. And at the end of the day, it *is* my fault, even if I didn't know about it—because I was the key. I was used, but I still opened the door. So why would you let me go? This is the end of everything he's been plotting for years, and I was what made you and your father agree to let him in."

"I *will* do it." I look at her evenly, wanting her to understand that it's not a matter of *if*. That revenge against her father isn't something I'll leave up to chance, or the rescue of my sister. It will happen, however I need to accomplish it.

Lilliana shakes her head. "Fine. You know what? If you manage it—"

She steps a little closer to me, and then closer still, close enough for me to smell the scent of her skin, sweet soap, and a little sweat. A scent that makes my cock twitch in my pants, and my mind briefly flip to ideas of bending her over the railing, her knuckles turning white from clenching it while I pound into her, making her scream her pleasure out over the Chicago skyline. The image does more than make me twitch. I feel my cock swell, throbbing against my thigh, and it takes all my self-control and resolve not to reach out and touch her.

"If you manage it," she says softly, "I'll give you what you want. A night where I pretend to be entirely yours. I'll moan your name and beg for your cock and plead for you to make me come. I'll do anything you want. I'll be your good little rabbit. How does that sound, Nikolai?"

She almost purrs my name, her hand on the railing suddenly very close to mine, and I'm rock-hard, the ache spreading through me until I'm not entirely sure how I'm going to walk away from her without having sunk myself inside of her at least once more.

But I don't want her pretense. I don't want any more lies, and I don't want to hurt her any longer—I *never* wanted to hurt her in the first place.

"No," I tell her quietly, and her eyes widen.

"No? Is that not what you want now?"

"It's not good enough." I see the startled look on her face, and I keep going, talking more quickly before she can interrupt me or get the wrong idea. "I want that to be a reality, *krolik*, not a game you play for me."

I step a little closer, close enough that our bodies are almost touching, but not quite. She looks up at me, those blue eyes widening, and I think to myself that I've never in my life seen a woman as beautiful as she is.

How did I not see how perfect she is for me until now? How perfect —she *is*?

I reach out, brushing a lock of blonde hair gently away from her face. "I want you to moan my name because you're aching for me, *krolik*. I want you to plead for my cock because you can't bear to go a moment longer without me filling you up. I want you to beg for my tongue on your pussy because you need me to make you come so badly that you can't stand it. I want all of that to be real. And if it's not real, little rabbit, then I don't want it."

I whisper that last, leaning forward so that my lips brush against the shell of her ear, and then I pull back, still looking down at her, close enough to touch.

"I want you forever, Lilliana," I tell her gently, and I do touch her then, the ghost of my fingertips brushing against her cheek. I've never touched her so gently, and I can feel the shiver that goes through her. "Knowing who you are only makes me want you more. Knowing what you've been through makes me see you in a different light. I haven't done anything yet to deserve you. So it's time for me to try."

My hand presses against her cheek, feeling her warmth sinking into my skin. I lean forward, my lips against hers, and I ignore the ache in my cock, the throbbing, urgent need to spin her around and take her, to fill her up with my cum, to make her mine again and again. I focus on the kiss and only that, on her mouth against mine, the soft fullness of her lips—the way I feel them part for me, her body softening towards mine despite herself. I feel the hot, wet brush of her tongue against mine, feel her tremble, hear the tiny sound in the back of her throat, and *god*, I'm so hard that it hurts. But all I do is kiss her, my hand touching her cheek.

I feel her arch towards me. I could push, and I think she would give in. I think—no, I *know* that she wants me, despite what she says. I know that it wouldn't take much to make her go over that line.

But I want her to walk towards me instead.

So I pull away, taking a step back and another, until I can no longer touch her if I wanted to.

"The next time I touch you like that, *krolik*—the next time I take you to bed, it will be because you want me," I tell her.

And then, before she can say a word, I turn and walk away.

The next time I see her, it will be with her father's blood on my hands and the proof of his demise to show her.

—

Everything is a blur.

I have bursts of memory as I come back to consciousness—the moment when the one alarm that my hackers missed went off, the sound of shouts and gunshots, and the sight of the trusted men I had with me crumpling to the concrete floor. Knowing I was outnumbered, that Lilliana's father had managed to outmaneuver not only my father but me—and the blind rage that came with that.

I'd fought hard not to let them take me. But it still ended up the same way. And I know what's coming even before I wake up to the pain of the impact against my face, enough to jolt a man out of a deep sleep—and me out of black unconsciousness.

. . .

I've tortured enough men that it takes only a moment, after the initial burst, to understand what happened. A fist to my jaw, hard enough to loosen teeth, to break the skin at the corner of my mouth from a ring on the hand that struck me. I know, because I've done it before. But I've never been on the receiving end, not like this. Not restrained, in the dark, the taste of blood in my mouth where a moment before there was only unconscious nothingness.

A light comes on. Bright, overhead. Glaring. I know this tactic, too. The shock of it, turning everything into sharp focus all of a sudden. A face looming over me, that same hand in my hair. I twist against the restraints and feel leather creaking against my skin. Straps, holding me to a chair.

Looking sideways, I see the all-too-familiar worktable of implements. The thin knives, the rough-edged hand grater, the tried and true pliers, the battery cables. Another leather strap, and I wince, remembering how roughly I'd once applied one of those to Lilliana, under the guise of an acceptable punishment.

The man looming over me is Lilliana's father. I recognize him immediately, even with my eyes still adjusting to the abrupt light. I sneer up at him, refusing to let him see that anything about that hurt me.

"I'm going to need information from you," he says, his voice hard and flat. "Account numbers. Names. Men I can rely on and the ones who are so loyal to you that I'm going to have to put them down like dogs so they don't bite me. You give me what I need, and it'll hurt less."

"Fuck you." I spit at him, the glob of saliva striking his cheek and sliding down his jaw—and I don't see the fist coming before it strikes my cheekbone almost exactly where the spittle hit him.

"It'll hurt your sister less, too," he snarls, hitting me again, and I feel the sharp sunburst of pain where the ring hits bone. "I have a lot of men interested in sampling that. A lot of men who might like to introduce her to all sorts of things. I could make you watch. Would you like that, Vasilev? I heard you always were really protective of her. Got a little crush on someone you shouldn't?"

"You're a sick fuck." I twist my head away from him. "I know all the tactics, Narokov. I wrote the book on some of them myself, so to speak. I can already think of all the things you're considering doing. So go ahead. I suggest starting with the strap, so you can use the knives on the welts, for maximum pain."

For a brief moment, he looks taken aback, and that feels like a victory. Not one that won't come with fresh pain, I'm sure, but a victory nonetheless, and I'll take what I can get. I don't regret it, not even when I see him reach for the thin knives instead.

"I think I'll mark where I want the welts to go with these," he says thoughtfully. "And then see what kind of patterns the blood makes. Unless, of course, you feel like starting to talk. You can start with the account numbers that have over seven figures in them."

I don't talk, of course. Not through the blades carving into my skin, or the leather strap hitting the tender flesh, or the angry fists he applies to me afterward, furious that I'm not breaking. I don't think he understands that a man like me can't be broken. I break others. I've spent a lifetime preparing for someone to try to give back what I've always dished out.

Until the door opens, and two men shove someone inside. A woman. A beautiful woman with honey-blonde hair and terrified blue eyes that instantly land on me—and I think maybe there's a way to break me after all.

That she's more of a key than she knows. Not just to the door her father wanted to walk through, but the lock that holds my lips sealed.

Lilliana

I feel hopeless, when I'm dragged into the compound.

I hadn't felt safe, exactly at the penthouse—but I hadn't thought they'd be able to get to me. *Nikolai* had been so sure that they wouldn't be able to get to me—and yet they did. My father must have done his work meticulously, to know how to get inside Nikolai's defenses—or there were more traitors in the mix than Nikolai knew.

I suspect it's the latter.

I'm still in my pajamas, my hair a tangle, feet bare. They didn't even let me bother with shoes as they hauled me out of the bedroom and out to the waiting car. The only thing that makes any of it better is that they at least didn't tie me up—but then again, why would they? I'm no threat to any of them. Even armed, I couldn't have gotten more than a few.

The warehouse is cold, and they march me down the hallway so fast that I almost trip over myself, all the way to a heavy door that two of the men shove open and push me inside of. I see my father out of the corner of my eye, blond and imperious and watching me like a hawk, but I can't even look at him, because of the horror in front of me.

I can't believe what I'm looking at.

The man in front of me barely resembles Nikolai, at least when I first look at him. His face is swollen and bruised, his mouth puffy, his lip split and trickling blood down his chin. One of his hands looks as if a few of the fingers have been broken, and I can see purple-black bruising across his bare chest. He's wearing nothing but a loose pair of sweatpants, and I can see bloody lines across his skin, as if someone has cut him with a knife, welts that look like someone has beaten him.

I told him I wanted nothing to do with him, and I meant it. I told him I couldn't forgive him, and I meant that too. But I never wanted to see him like this. I never wanted any of this to happen to him.

"See what I do for you?" My father grabs my chin, forcing me to look straight ahead, so I have to see what they've done to him. "This man demanded your hand in marriage. *Raped* you. Forced you to be his wife. See how I've punished him? He thought he deserved you as a wife, rather than just something to stick his cock in."

He lets go of my chin, running his fingers through my hair in a twisted mockery of a father reassuring his daughter. "Do you want me to cut it off, Lilliana? Let you crush it under your heel, maybe? Do you want to do it yourself?" He grins at me, reaching for a knife. "You can't do it just yet. A man can only take so much, and we've got steps to take before we get there. But you can hold the knife if you want. Feel the weight of it. Think about how it will feel cutting through his cock."

"If I had a knife in my hand, I'd use it to stab you," I hiss, and he pulls it back, *tsking* as he shakes his head.

"Is that any way to talk to your dear father? The man who gave you everything?"

"You *took* everything away from me." I swallow hard, unable to keep looking at Nikolai, at the horrifying sight of his tortured face and body. "My childhood. Any innocence that wasn't physical. My choices. You took all of it away. You can't tell me otherwise."

"It was for us." His hand strokes over my hair again, and it takes everything in me not to pull away. "For *us*, Lilliana. Once I'm in charge, you can have anything you want. You'll be a rich widow. And then—" His hand presses against the back of my head, fingers curling against my skull. "You'll be all mine again, *sladost'*."

Nikolai jerks against the straps holding him to the chair. "Fuck off, Narokov," he spits, and my father shakes his head, letting go of me just long enough to step forward in two quick strides and punch Nikolai hard, right in his already swollen mouth.

"Stop it!" I cry out. Nikolai doesn't make a sound, but from the way he jerks backward and shudders, I can only imagine how much it must have hurt him. "Stop. Please—"

My father turns towards me, his brow furrowed. "So you care about him?" He shakes his head. "I'm sorry for that, Lilliana. I thought you were stronger than that. Tough enough not to let your feelings get involved. If anything, I thought this would be a gift to you. Something to show you how I've thought of you even while you were being ruined by this brute. It's a shame I had to do it this way. I would have rather you stayed with me, untouched, until *I* decided when it was the right time to teach you myself. But there really was no choice. And now you don't appreciate what I've done for you." He clicks his tongue again. "Maybe some correction is in order for you, too."

Nikolai lets out a strangled roar, jerking against the straps again. "You fucking bastard," he snarls. "Your own daughter? Sick fuck— it's me you want to hurt. So come back here, and make yourself feel like a man by picking on someone who can't fight back."

He spits out blood, spraying it over my father's face as he turns back towards Nikolai, another fist landing on Nikolai's jaw.

"Please," I whisper again. I don't have any idea how I want things between Nikolai and me to go, how I see this all turning out, but I know this isn't it. I know I don't want to see my father beating him to a pulp.

I know, above anything else, that I don't want my father to have the kind of power he's grabbing for. And I know I don't want what he has planned for me. "Please stop."

My father jerks his head towards something behind me, and I turn around to see two huge guards in cargo pants and black shirts coming toward me. "Put her in a cell with the other one," he says sharply. "She can think about her loyalties there."

"What?" I gasp, trying to step out of their reach, but there's no chance of it. "No, I—stop it! Don't touch me."

"Leave her alone!" Nikolai roars, but the words are cut off in a groan of pain. I don't see what's happened to him, and I'm ashamed to say that a part of me is glad I don't. I'm not sure how much more of this I can take.

The two guards grab me, dragging me out of the room, even as I twist and kick in their grasp. I know it's useless—there's no way I'm getting out of this.

They're not overly rough with me, but I can't bring myself to care one way or another. All I can think about is Nikolai, tied up in that room, at my father's mercy—and it doesn't seem as if he has much of it. I don't know why that surprises me a little, after all the years I spent on the other end of his "teaching." But I hadn't known *this* much violence was in him.

If he succeeds at what he's trying to do—

I can't let myself think that's possible. If it is—then there's no hope for any of us. I'd rather die than give in to what my father wants from me—and I imagine I will, if I fight him for too long and too hard.

Or he'll lock me up and take what he wants.

I feel sick at the thought. The guards march me down the hall, down to a row of cells, and I gasp when I see inside of the one we stop in front of.

I don't recognize the girl sitting inside at first, the same way I hadn't recognized Nikolai. But this time, it's not because she's physically hurt so much as that it just seems as if everything has been drained out of her. Her long blonde hair is hanging limply around her face, stringy and greasy, and her face is so pale that it looks almost translucent. She looks thinner than before and so utterly exhausted that I half-expect her to pass out at any moment.

"Marika?" I whisper her name, and she looks up tiredly, her eyes widening a fraction when she sees me, as if that's all she can muster.

"Lilliana." She breathes my name sadly, and one of the guards yanks the cell door open, the other one shoving me unceremoniously inside.

"The two of you can catch up. Have fun, ladies." He slams the door shut, and I flinch as I hear the lock turn.

If we get out of this, I never want to be locked in another room for the rest of my life.

"Are you alright?" I go to her immediately, sitting on the thin cot beside her and gently reaching out to push her hair out of her face. She flinches away from my touch, and I instantly wish I hadn't tried. I should have known better.

"Compared to Nikolai?" she laughs bitterly. "They showed him to me this morning, you know. I saw what they've done. I can only imagine how much worse it's gotten since then."

"I just saw him, too," I whisper. "I'm so sorry, I—"

"It's not your fault." She turns her head and sees the expression on my face. "You really think I thought you had anything to do with this? I know men like your father, Lilliana. I've grown up around them my whole life. Men grasping at straws, at power any way they can get it. Nikolai is a violent man, too. But he never needed to reach for power. Your father is a small man, and he can't get high enough to grab it without making a tower of bodies underneath him to climb up and stand on."

She swallows hard. "I'm sorry. I shouldn't say that about—"

"No, you should." I reach for her hand, squeezing it lightly. "My father is a horrible man. He always has been. He raised me to be sent into your father's bed, knowing I might not make it out alive—and the first part of that would have been bad enough. I spent my whole life being groomed for one man's pleasure and another man's ambition."

"Oh, Lilliana." Marika looks at me sadly. "I can't even imagine. And then Nikolai—"

"I know he was trying to keep me out of your father's hands. And I don't want to speak ill—"

"It's alright." Marika gives me a small, sad smile. "I've already been told he's dead. I'm sad, of course—he was my father, and he wasn't the worst one. There *are* worse in our world. You know that; I understand now. But he wasn't a good father either. I can't say I'll grieve him for a very long time."

Her shoulders slump, as if saying all of that took something out of her, but she doesn't let go of my hand. "I don't know what's going to happen to us."

"I know what my father wants to happen to me," I tell her what he said, in the room with Nikolai, and Marika winces.

"I don't even know what to say. That's—"

I nod, swallowing hard. "Someone will help." I try to find some conviction to put into my voice. "Nikolai must have people loyal to him. Someone who will come."

Marika nods. "He has plenty. My brother has always been brutal when it comes to our enemies—but anyone who is loyal to us has reason to respect him." She looks at me as she says it, frowning a little. "I know this is probably hard for you to believe. I know you have reason to hate him, I'm sure. I don't blame you—you didn't ask for any of this. But he's a good man, in his own way. He looks out for the men underneath him. He ensures their families are taken care of. Their widows, their children—if it comes to that. He doesn't ask things of them that he isn't willing to do himself. And that matters in our world."

She's silent for a long moment, breathing slowly, in and out. It makes me wonder what's happened to her while she's been here. "He has always had a code. I can't say I've always thought it was enough. He's done things I can't say are forgivable—at least to those he's done it to. But I know he's always tried to be better—than the world around him. Our world."

I can hear the conviction in her voice, and it makes me want to believe it, too, just a little. I think of him on the balcony, the worry in his face and voice when he'd thought I might have been considering jumping, the gentle way he'd touched me, the way he'd turned down my offer of a night where I'd gratify his every wish. I'd meant it—and I think he knew I meant it. But he'd said no.

He said he wanted it to be *real*.

Could it ever be? A small part of me, a part that doesn't feel strong enough yet to be certain, thinks that he really might regret the things he's done. That he might truly want to earn my forgiveness. But even so—

Could I ever possibly give it to him?

"I'm tired," Marika says softly. "I'm sorry. I think I want to try to sleep—"

"No, that's fine." I get up, moving to the cot on the other side of the small cell. "Get some rest. I don't know what's going to happen tomorrow."

"Neither do I," she whispers, her voice faintly broken, and then she rolls onto her side, facing away from me.

I lie there awake for a long time, thinking about what she said, about Nikolai, about his reaction to everything I told him. About his insistence that he wanted me to forgive him, if I could. About how it felt, seeing him like that, bound to a chair and tortured.

Could I have feelings for him?

I don't know if now is the time to figure it out. But I might not have any other chance.

He might not be as bad of a man as I imagined. Not a good man, not by any stretch of the imagination, but not the cruel brute I'd painted him in my head. Marika's explanation of him had been of a man who is a product of the world around him, but trying his best to be decent, in spite of that. I'm not sure I buy it entirely. But I can see where she's coming from.

I saw glimpses of someone who I could like. Perhaps even love, if I had more of it. More of that part of Nikolai, more time, more *everything*.

If there's no way out of this marriage, could there be a way to be happy in it?

I close my eyes, feeling tears leak out of the corners at the thought of what my father did. It's all worse than I could have imagined. And now, at the end of it, it's too late for me to change anything—as if I ever really could have.

I wouldn't have thought I could sleep on the uncomfortable cot, in a cold cell, with only one thin blanket and pillow. But I'm exhausted, and sleep creeps over me eventually, pulling me gracelessly under into chaotic dreams.

I dream of Nikolai, pinning me down in the snow by the tree stand, both of us naked but somehow not freezing, his hard, hot, muscled body pressing against mine as I feel the unrelenting slide of his cock inside of me, his voice groaning my name in my ear.

Lilliana, god, you feel so good, Lilliana, take me, little rabbit, take me, fuck, fuck—

A stream of consciousness, words sputtered out in the strange way they so often are in dreams, and the feeling of my body tightening, liquefying, coming apart around him. The snow melting, draining away in rivers of blood, and then Nikolai is gone, and it's only me, lying in wet mud, and all around me is my own blood, my hands and feet caught in animal traps.

My father is looming over me, malicious lust on his face, face twisted in a sneer. *Little rabbit, little rabbit,* he mocks. *What a stupid nickname. But you're trapped anyway, aren't you? And the big bad wolf—*

I jolt awake, gasping, crying, my stomach twisted with a sick nausea that sends me half-stumbling, half-crawling to the toilet in the corner to throw up everything in me. It stinks, and that only makes it worse, making me heave until there's nothing but bile for me to spit out.

The dream—

I liked it, in the first part. When Nikolai was there. In the dream, I wasn't fighting to get away. I wasn't twisting my mouth away from his or telling him to go fuck himself, or trying to pretend I didn't want to come. I was arching underneath him, hips angling for more of his cock inside of me, nails clawing at his shoulders as I chased the pleasure that built with every stroke, every jolt of him deep inside of me. I wanted him. I wanted what he did to me. Until it faded away, and then—

A rabbit, caught in a trap.

The trap was never Nikolai's. It was my father's. Nikolai married me to save me from himself. To find a way to have me without violating me, in his own twisted way of thinking. And not just that—but to keep me away from his father. From being sent back to mine. He's no white knight, no prince Charming, but he tried to rescue me in his own way.

But my father is the one who wants me trapped and at his mercy. And now he has exactly that.

He's going to try to use me to break Nikolai.

And knowing what I do now—I'm very worried that he might succeed.

Lilliana

First thing in the morning, I'm woken up by the sound of keys in the door. "You," the guard snaps, pointing at me. "You're staying here," he adds, glancing at Marika. "Better hope he doesn't give me permission to come back in and tell you good morning."

She winces, flinching back, but she says nothing.

I'm not offered breakfast or even a cup of water. I'm marched directly back to the room where Nikolai was the night before, and when the door is opened, and I'm shoved in, I see that he's still there.

He looks terrible. His face is still swollen, heavy, exhausted bags under his eyes, the cuts on his body crusted over with blood, and the bruises a sick shade of purple-green. He lifts his head slightly when I'm pushed into the room, and I see the look of horror in his eyes.

"Leave her alone," he says thickly, and I see my father push off of the wall, striding towards me.

"Then tell me what I want to know," he says simply, and Nikolai lets out a long sigh that seems to come from somewhere in the very depths of him. His blue-grey eyes turn to me, more grey now than anything else, and the expression in them is both sad and resigned.

"I'm sorry, *krolik*," he says quietly. My father lunges towards him, his fist connecting with Nikolai's shoulder, where deep lacerations run over his skin. I can see from the swelling that it's likely already been dislocated.

Nikolai lets out a low grunt, and that's all—though I can only imagine how much it must have hurt.

My father steps behind me, and I feel the prick of a blade at the back of my neck. "Don't move," he warns, and a moment later, I feel it slicing through the fabric, tearing through the thin material of the tank top I'd been wearing to sleep in when I was snatched last night. He shoves it off of my shoulders, leaving me bare from the waist up, and then shoves down the loose pajama bottoms I'd been wearing. My panties go with it, and I'm left standing in a pool of clothing, shivering, looking at Nikolai as he stares at my father with a venom that I've never seen on his face before.

"Don't you fucking dare," he snarls, his hands curling into fists, as if he'd break through the straps to get to him and stop what I'm terrified is about to happen. "Don't you touch her—"

"I'm not going to." My father shakes his head. "Not like that, anyway. Get your mind out of the gutter, Vasilev."

"I heard what you said you wanted. You sick piece of—"

"Of course. It's what I've always wanted from my pretty Lilliana. So much more beautiful than her mother. She really took after me in the looks department. But I'm not going to waste the pleasure of *that* first time by doing it in front of you. Especially not when I've already had to sacrifice so much of her to you. No, I'm thinking something else."

He reaches for the leather strap, which I see with a sickening twist of my stomach is crusted with dried blood—*Nikolai's* blood. "Since you seem to be able to take your punishment so well, let's see how she does, taking it for you."

Nikolai's helpless roar of fury mixes with the sound of the leather striking my bare skin. I stumble forward, nearly falling as the strap hits the side of my ass, swung with the full strength of the arm wielding it, hot pain bursting over my skin. I cry out, unable to stop myself, and I grip the back of a wooden chair near me, tears already filling my eyes.

"You must have trained her well." My father clicks his tongue. "Look at her, on the verge of bending over like a good girl for her punishment. I haven't had to spank her in years. But I think she's earned it. Or rather—you have, and she's going to take it."

The belt comes down again. Nikolai is thrashing in the straps holding him, cursing, raining down threats on my father, but it doesn't matter. There's nothing but pain, the belt coming down onto my skin over and over, hot lines of pain welting my flesh, marking me, drawing blood. I sob, knowing it won't matter, knowing that there's nothing that can help me, and a small part of me wishes Nikolai would just give my father what he wants, so that it would stop.

The more rational part of me knows that if he does, it will all be so much worse, anyway.

I don't know how long it goes on for. I don't know how I'll walk when it's all over. All I know is that at some point, the blows stop, and my father's hand is on the back of my neck, yanking me backward as he throws a towel at me. It smells faintly musty, but I'd take anything at this point to cover myself.

I wrap it around my shaking body, my knees turning to water, and I feel like I might pass out. Pain radiates up my legs and my back, curling into my belly like hooks threatening to tear me apart. I feel like I'm going to be sick.

My father grabs my arm, marching me out of the room and slamming the door behind him. He has to half-drag me, my legs threatening to give out as he pulls me into another, empty room.

"You can make this all stop," he says, looking at me. "Figure out how to break him. Make him tell me what I need. And then I won't have to hurt either of you any longer."

I stare at him. "Is that supposed to be an incentive? Give you all the power you want, and you won't continue to torture me and my husband? Do you *hear* yourself?"

"You always knew what I wanted, Lilliana."

"No, I didn't!" I blink back the threatening tears. "I never knew *this*. I only knew that you wanted to go higher. You were ambitious, but I didn't think you were this stupid—"

He slaps me so hard that when my head flings to one side, I almost think he will have broken my neck. As it is, I can feel something pull that I know will hurt later.

"I won't help you," I hiss, tears leaking down my cheeks. I'm in too much pain to stop it. "You lied to me. I was supposed to have my freedom after the night with the *pakhan*. I went along with all of it, endured, did as I was told, because I was promised that I could do what I wanted afterward. And instead, I ended up a fucking bride."

"Is that your answer?" he asks coldly, as if I never spoke. "You won't help?"

"I won't do a goddamn thing for you that you don't force out of me."

A cold, evil sneer twists his face. It's something unrecognizable—but then again, I don't think I ever really knew him at all. "Then you'll die along with him," he says coldly. "After I enjoy what should have always been mine, anyway. Unless you please me, of course. Then I might keep you alive a little longer, daughter."

This time, I can't stop from being sick.

Lilliana

I'm thrown back into the cell with Marika. She's too weak to talk very much, and I can't find the energy either. I'm a swollen mass of pain, nothing other than the towel to protect my modesty, and the rough terrycloth chafes against the bloody welts on my skin. Marika is so far untouched, and I'm terrified of what might come in the morning for her. If my father thinks that I won't be the key to breaking Nikolai, I have no doubt that he'll try her next.

I'm correct in that. We're both dragged into the room the next morning, where Nikolai is bound in the same chair, his torso a further mass of cuts and bruises, his mouth so swollen that I'm not sure where his lips end, and his flesh begins. It's horrifying, and I start to cry the minute we're shoved into the room, a sinking hopelessness spreading over me.

Marika is stripped, just as I was yesterday. She stands there, looking at her brother, as the leather comes down on her flesh. "Don't tell them a fucking thing," she whispers, before she's jolted forward, down onto her knees, too weak to stand up under the rain of blows. She stays like that, crouched on the floor as Nikolai watches in utter misery, his expression one of a man who wishes for death.

"You can stop hurting them," he growls out through gritted teeth. "It won't change a fucking thing. I won't tell you what you want to know. It's all wasted—"

"Oh, I'm pretty sure I've figured out by now that you won't," my father says, as he brings the strap down hard across Marika's back. "But it's not wasted. It's just for my own enjoyment now."

He kicks me down next to Marika, both of us crouched on the floor as he stands behind us, the belt coming down on my skin, too, marking all the flesh left untouched yesterday. I feel tears leaking down my face all over again, and I want it to be over, too. I'd rather just die and let it be finished. After everything, this is too much.

I'm so lost in my misery and pain that I don't hear the sound of the door being kicked open at first, or the shouts. It's not until I hear the burst of gunfire and fling myself to the floor in anticipation of feeling the sharp pain of a bullet that I look to one side and realize that it's not Marika and I that are being shot at, that my father didn't decide it was finally time for our execution.

Someone has come to rescue us.

A bullet goes wide, and I hear Marika scream, blood spattering across the floor as it strikes her calf. The workbench full of tools is toppled over as two men grapple across the room, and Marika flings herself forward, a streak of blood following her as she grabs for a knife. For one wild moment, I think she's joining in the fight—and then I see her cutting at the straps holding Nikolai, getting him free.

He bursts out of the chair like a wild thing, his face so full of a dark rage that it terrifies even me. I can't hear anything over the gunshots, and soon the room is a haze of smoke, blood spattering in every direction, a fight like nothing I've ever seen or imagined breaking out all around us. I feel a booted foot drive into me, kicking me aside, and then something heavy lands near me, making me cry out.

I can't breathe. All I feel is pain. I reach for Marika, but I see a muscled man in cargos and a tight shirt lifting her, a sheet wrapped around her body as he cradles her in his arms. I can't see Nikolai, and suddenly I *want* to see Nikolai, to know he's there, but I don't see him at all.

The room is spinning. I feel someone picking me up, cool cloth wrapped around my body, and I cry out anyway because it hurts, even as gently as I was touched. I don't know where I'm being taken or who is holding me. I hear Nikolai's name on my lips, numbly, feel the shape of it—and then everything is black, and I know nothing.

Lilliana

I've never been glad to wake up to Nikolai before.

He's not in bed with me this time. He's sitting across from the bed, in a chair near the glass doors, and I realize we're back in his penthouse. *Our* penthouse, I suppose, technically, since we're married. It's a strange thought.

"How long was I out for?" I whisper, my voice coming out cracked and hoarse, and Nikolai jerks in his seat, turning to look at me. He's dressed in loose sweatpants and a t-shirt, and the skin that I can see is still mottled with bruises. His face is bruised too, the cuts on his cheekbones and jaw scabbed over, and his lips are still swollen, though not as severely. I'm afraid to see what I look like. "Marika, is she—"

"You've been out for a few days," he says quietly. "A doctor hooked you up to an IV for a while, to keep you hydrated." He nods towards my arm, and it's then that I see the bandage in the crook of it, stark white against all the bruising. "Marika is—well, I hesitate to say she's fine. But she's alive. And she will be fine, in time."

"And you?" My voice sounds like a croak. I can see that he's alive. It makes me happier than I would have thought it would, and I try not to let it show. I don't want him to know that I'm glad, not when I don't know how I feel about everything else involving him and our marriage. Not when I don't yet know what I want to do.

"I'm in one piece." He holds up his left hand, which is splinted, the fingers individually wrapped in gauze and metal. "But I've definitely felt better in my life."

I push myself up a little against the pillows—or try to—and he's on his feet in an instant. I can see from the stiff way he moves that he has a good bit of healing left to go himself, but he walks to the side table closest to him, pouring me a glass of water out of a pitcher.

"Here," he says, handing it to me as he helps me bolster myself with the pillows. "This should help."

I'd never known how good water could taste. It's clear and cold, and I force myself to sip at it. I'm glad, too, that it gives me something to do that doesn't require me to speak. He stands there for a long moment, looking at me, and I don't have the slightest idea of what to say.

"I'm sorry for what happened to you," he finally says, his voice low and quiet. "It was—unconscionable. Your father—" He clears his throat. "He escaped. I have a manhunt out for him. He won't get away forever, and when he does—"

Nikolai doesn't have to finish that sentence. I can see the anger in his eyes, the carefully controlled rage, and I know that my father won't escape him forever.

"I meant what I said before I left," he continues. His voice flattens, growing emotionless, but I have the strange feeling that it's that way because it has to be for him—because he would be *too* emotional otherwise. "When I'm sure it will be safe for you to leave, you can. I'll give you a divorce."

He pushes his unharmed hand into his pocket, and he finally meets my eyes. I can't read the emotion there, but it looks—resigned. "I should never have kept you against your will. I can't change what happened, but I can let you choose your own life going forward. I'll avenge you and Marika—and then you can be free."

I hadn't expected him to keep the promise. I hadn't expected him to really mean it. He sits slowly on the other side of the bed from me, and I do something I know I shouldn't. I lean forward, slowly and carefully, and I touch his face as gently as I can manage.

Leaning forward, I brush my lips over his.

He groans at the touch, and I pull back instantly, but he shakes his head. "That wasn't pain, *krolik*," he murmurs, and I hear the tinge of lust in his voice. "It's been days. I'd have to be more badly hurt than this to not want to be inside of you."

A rush of sensation tingles over my skin at that, prickling every hair, my pulse leaping into my throat. I shouldn't kiss him again. I should tell him to leave. But I find myself leaning forward, my lips brushing against his again, still careful of the swelling.

His good hand comes up, brushing against the curve of my breast. "I don't want to hurt you." His voice is hoarse now, and I can hear the desire in it. I don't hate it like I used to. I can feel myself wishing he felt better. That we both did.

Nikolai leans into me, his hands gently on my waist as he lays me back against the pillows, and I shake my head. The instant I do, he stops touching me, and I blink at him in surprise.

"I told you. No more unless you want it."

"I—" I can't make myself say it. But I *do*. I can feel a pulse rippling under my skin, spreading through me, an ache that I haven't felt before, even with him. I want more. But I'm under no illusions that we could go all the way, even if I told him flat out that I wanted it. He might be willing to try, but I know we're both too injured. I lick my lips, feeling that urgent, thrumming electricity again as I look at the tense expression on his face, waiting to see what I'll do.

"Watch me," I suggest, nudging back the blankets. "Since you only have one good hand."

His eyes widen a little as he realizes what I mean. I'm naked beneath the blankets, and I try not to look at the mottled bruising on my skin. I've always known I was beautiful, but the tapestry of purple and yellow and green blooming over most of my body makes it hard to feel that way.

But when I look up and see Nikolai's face, there's no change in it. He's still looking at me as if I'm the most desirable thing he's ever seen. His good hand drifts to the waist of his pants, and I nod breathlessly, my own hand slipping between my thighs as my pulse quickens.

"You want me to watch you?" The rasp of his voice feels like velvet rubbed the wrong way. "You want to watch me?"

I nod, and he narrows his eyes at me.

"You have to say it, Lilliana. I won't believe you unless you say it aloud."

"I want us to watch each other," I whisper. Then my breath catches in my throat as he pushes his pants down around his hips with one hand, his cock slipping free, and the sight of him wrapping his fingers around his hard length makes me feel dizzy with lust.

His gaze sweeps over me, all the way down to where my fingers are between my thighs, parting myself for him to see, and I see his cock throb in his hand as he starts to stroke. "You're so beautiful," he murmurs, his voice thick with desire, and I can feel how wet I am already.

"Still?" I hear the tremor in my voice despite myself, and it's not only desire.

"Always." Nikolai's gaze is hungry, flicking from my face to my breasts to the soft wetness between my thighs and back up again. "You don't know how hard it is not to be inside of you right now. If I thought I wouldn't hurt you—"

He groans, his cock jerking in his fist, and I see the muscles in his thighs tighten. "Fuck, Lilliana—" he breathes. "It's been too long. I don't know—"

"I won't take long either." To my surprise, it's true. I don't know if it's how long it's been since he's fucked me, or the lewdness of willingly showing myself off to him, or just the close intimacy of what we're doing, but I'm on the edge too. I can hear my fingers wetly stroking against my clit. As Nikolai squeezes his cock, his breathing coming faster as I see his shaft glisten with his dripping pre-cum, I know I'm close to the edge.

"I want you to come on me," I whisper, and Nikolai groans, his eyes closing as his cock jerks and shudders.

"*Fuck*—just hearing that is going to get me off." He grits his teeth, slowing his strokes, his fist gliding down to the base of his cock and resting there for a moment as he leans forward. "Where do you want it, little rabbit?" His voice is thick and rough, and I know he's going to come at any moment. "Where do you want me to come, *krolik?*"

"Right where I'm touching." The words come out of my mouth before I can think about them for too long, but it *is* what I want. I spread myself open with my fingers, still rubbing tight, quick circles over my clit, and I hear Nikolai's groan as he leans closer. "I'm so close—" I suck in a breath, feeling my thighs tense. "I'll come when you do. When I feel—"

"Oh *god*," Nikolai moans, and his cock swells in his fist as he angles it downwards, the first hot spurt of his cum shooting over my pussy, drenching my folds and my fingers, the heat of it against my clit, the last thing I needed to push me over the edge, too.

"Nikolai!" I cry out his name for the first time of my own accord, my thighs falling open as my hips buck upwards into his hand, and he's still coming as I do, his cum splashing over my hand and my clit, his face tight with pleasure as we both come together, and the pleasure is dizzying. It keeps going for longer than I've ever come like this, until he's squeezing out the last of his cum with a shaky hand, and I feel as if I can't catch my breath.

He leans back, tucking himself away, and gets up as quickly as he can. "Just wait," he tells me, crossing the room and disappearing into the bathroom, and a moment later, he comes back with something in hand.

I don't quite believe it until he's actually doing it—gently wiping away the cum from my skin with a warm cloth. I don't think to stop him, I'm so startled, and when he steps back, it takes me a moment to speak.

"You didn't have to do that." I've never known him to do anything so tender.

He looks at me quietly for a long moment. "I know," he says finally, and turns to go back into the bathroom.

When he returns, I'm already nearly asleep, still exhausted from my injuries and the orgasm. But before I fall asleep, I feel him gently tug back the covers, sliding into the bed next to me.

"I'll leave if you want me to," he says quietly. And for the first time, I actually believe he would.

"No," I whisper, between sleep and wakefulness, knowing that I want him to stay. I want to wake up next to him. And right now, I don't want to think too much about why that might be. "You can stay."

I feel him settle into the bed on the other side of me. A moment later, I feel his uninjured hand touch mine.

And then, together, we fall asleep.

Nikolai

I'm woken in the morning by a heavy knocking on the door.

I can't move quickly, but I get out of bed as fast as I can, not wanting it to wake Lilliana. She's sleeping peacefully, and she needs all the rest that she can get.

I'm still shocked at what happened between us yesterday. I hadn't expected her to even kiss me again, let alone—

It makes me think that there might still be a chance for us. That I might get to earn her forgiveness after all.

When I crack the door, I see Adrik on the other side—the guard who helped get Marika out of the compound. "I have something for you," he says quietly, and I step out to meet him in the hallway, closing the door carefully behind me.

"What is it?" I can hear the touch of impatience in my voice, but I'd been sleeping well for the first time in days, and next to Lilliana. I'd rather still be there than talking to him right now.

"We have Narokov," Adrik says simply, and that's all I needed to hear.

"Where is he?"

"We have him in one of the warehouses down by the docks. He's not going anywhere."

"Good." I glance back at the door. "I'm going to see if Lilliana is able to come with me. Give me a few minutes."

"I serve at your pleasure," he says formally, stepping back as I turn away to go back into the bedroom.

Lilliana is still asleep. I don't like waking her, especially not when she needs the rest, but I know she'll want to be there to see what becomes of her father. And I want her to have the chance to take her vengeance herself, if she wants it.

Gently, I reach down, brushing her hair away from her face. "*Krolik*," I murmur, touching her cheek. "Lilliana. Can you wake up?"

It takes her a minute to stir. She rubs the sleep out of her eyes, looking up at me with an expression that makes my heart briefly beat faster in my chest. I've never had a woman make me feel that way with only a look. Hell, I'm not sure one has ever made me feel that way at all.

"Nikolai?" It's the second time in two days that she's said my name without rancor or acid on her tongue. It sounds the way I think I'd like to hear her say it every morning, and it makes me ache. "What is it? Is something wrong?"

"We have your father," I tell her quietly. "I thought you might want to be there, to see what happens."

Her eyes open immediately, and she pushes herself up halfway, wincing as she does. "What do you mean—you found him?"

I nod. "My men did. I thought you should have the choice, if you want to come with us. Or if you want me to—take care of it, without you having to see him again."

She shakes her head, swallowing hard. "No—no, I do want to be there. I need to see him before—"

Lilliana can't finish the sentence, and I understand. It's not an easy thing to think about, when you've never faced death so closely before—especially not the death of someone close to you.

I reach for her, helping her sit up. Her teeth sink into her lower lip, and I can tell she's fighting back the pain. "You don't have to go," I tell her again, hating the sight of her hurting like this. I'm going to revisit every one of these bruises on his body. "It won't be pretty."

"I know," she whispers. She holds the sheet to her chest as she sits up fully, breathing slowly to manage the pain. "Can you help me get dressed?"

Something about the way she says it, the vulnerability that I've never heard from her before, breaks my heart. At this moment, we're not adversaries, the way we've been since that night she was led into my father's study. We're husband and wife, and my wife is in need of my help.

I find a soft, loose cotton dress in the closet and bring it to her, helping her pull it over her head. She smiles wanly at me as it falls around her hips, her eyes tired and sad.

"I can't imagine you find me very attractive like this." She gestures at the loose black dress, the bruises littering her arms, her pale face, and my chest aches all over again.

Gently, I reach out, my fingers brushing the edge of her jaw. Her face is the only part of her that's unmarked, except for a bruise on her left cheek where he struck her. A cold rage fills me again when I see it, and I remind myself that he's in our custody now. He will pay for all of this, but I need to make sure Lilliana is taken care of first.

"I find you every bit as beautiful as the night I met you," I tell her gently. "I want you every bit as much. The only reason you're not on that bed right now with me between your legs is because there are other things we have to do right now—and because I don't feel certain that you want me there."

There's an expression on her face that I can't quite read. She looks at me as if she's not quite sure what to make of me, and I wish I had time to find out what she's thinking. But we need to go.

"Can you make it to the elevator?" I ask her. "I'll help you."

She nods. "I don't like feeling so helpless," she says softly, not looking at me. "This feels—"

"I know." And I do. No physical pain could ever have been as terrible as the mental torment of being strapped to that chair, watching as Lilliana and Marika were hurt, and I could do nothing about it. "It will get better. Knowing he's gone will help."

"I hope so." Her hand is on my arm as we make our way out into the living area of the penthouse, to the front door, and past my security to the elevator. It's slow going, but we get there without any major mishaps, and my security joins us downstairs before we go to the cars.

It's a silent ride to the warehouse. Lilliana's hands are knotted in her lap, her lips pressed together, tension running through every inch of her body. She looks like a statue, sitting there frozen, like she might shatter at any moment with a word or a touch. I want to reach for her, to comfort her, but I know that might do more harm than good.

I help her out of the car when we get to the warehouse, and she stands there for a moment in the sunlight, trembling. "Are you sure you want to go in there?" I ask her, and she nods stiffly.

"I don't know if 'want' is the right word," she whispers. "But I know I have to. So let's get it over with."

I'm impressed by her bravery, by the sheer tenacity of her putting one foot in front of the other all the way through that door, into the warm, fetid air of the warehouse to where her father is sitting tied to a chair, facing us and surrounded by guards.

They weren't gentle with him, and I'm glad to see it. His blond hair is dark with sweat and matted with blood, and bruises are already blooming over his face and jaw. He looks up, glaring at us both, but I can see the terror in his eyes. He knows what's coming for him, and unlike me, he's not a man who can take what he's served to others.

I see the dark, spreading stain at his groin, and I laugh.

"I haven't even touched you yet, and you've already pissed yourself. Some man. Some future *pakhan*." I laugh again, and I see his gaze flick to Lilliana. "No. Don't you fucking look at her. Look at me, you traitorous son of a bitch."

But his gaze is fixed on his daughter, wide-eyed and pleading, as if there were a chance in hell that she'd ever help him now. "Lilliana. You can't stand there while he hurts your father. Where is your loyalty? Where is your loyalty to *me*?"

Her body stiffens, jerking with a sharp flinch as she stares him down. "You mean like you hurt me?" she asks quietly, her voice a harsh whisper, rasping out of her dry throat. Like you made Nikolai watch while you beat me half to death, while you threatened me with things that no father should ever *think*? Except—" Her mouth twists in a smile so vicious that I never thought I would see anything like it on her face. "It hurt Nikolai, to see me treated like that. It won't hurt me to watch him do the same to you."

She steps back, and I know that for what it is, her tacit agreement that whatever I want to do to him, she has no argument with.

And I do plenty.

It's not hard to get the information out of him that I need. Ivan Narokov is not a man who was built not to break. He was never meant to withstand pain. It only takes a few broken fingers and a nail before he's telling me his entire plan—most of which I know already, since it hinged on using Lilliana to achieve his in, and then using that position to discern the information he would need in order to stage a coup.

What I really want are the names of the men who helped him. The other traitors, the ones that I will take apart piece by piece for helping Narokov kill my father and hurt my wife and sister, for their willingness to betray us in such a way.

He gives them up easily. I could likely have gotten the information from him without any further pain, but at this point, I'm hurting him for my own pleasure as well as for what it will make him say. When he's a bruised and bloody mess, face swollen from my fist and his crying, his clothes stripped away and every inch of him marked with the bruises and wounds that he gave me, my wife, and my sister —I turn to Lilliana.

I hold out a knife to her, as he did, my expression calm. "Do you want to do it? It's your right, if you do."

Lilliana stares at it for a long moment. I see her lips tremble, her hands shaking at her sides. I can see her thinking, imagining how it would go, how it would feel to be the one to end her father's life. She looks at him, almost unrecognizable now, a bloody lump of so much breathing meat. And then she looks back at me and shakes her head, slowly.

"I can't," she whispers, and I close my hand around the handle of the knife, holding it at my side.

"Do you want to leave while I do this?" I ask her, giving her a moment to think, and she shakes her head again.

"No. I need to see—I need to see that he's dead. I just—I can't—"

"I know." I turn to him, and I see the terror in his swollen eyes, see his lips form pleas that he can't find the strength to say any longer. I step forward, grabbing a fistful of his bloody hair and yanking his head back, pressing the blade to his throat.

I give him a moment to realize what's about to happen. I draw it out, letting the fear sink in, letting him take in the fact that he's going to die in a moment. Even with all the pain I've inflicted on him, he still looks like a man who wants to live. Who thinks that somehow this can all be undone, and he can go back to who he was before.

I drag the knife across his throat. Slowly, so he feels every inch of the blade parting his skin. I don't flinch when the blood sprays across me. I don't stop until his throat is laid open, and then I step back, watching him stare at me and Lilliana in mute horror as his life drains away from him.

I look at my wife, standing there shaking, her fists clenched at her sides. "He'll never hurt you again," I tell her quietly.

And then, I walk with her, back out to the waiting car.

Back to the home that will only be ours for a little while longer.

Lilliana

I've never seen Nikolai like this before. He stands in the entryway, still covered in blood, his hands trembling. When he looks up at me, there's an expression of such desolation on his face that I don't know how to begin to understand it.

"You can leave in the morning if you want," he says quietly, his voice low and flat as death. And then he walks past me in quick, long strides, disappearing into the bedroom with the door slammed shut behind him.

I don't know whether to follow him or not, at first. I'm still shaking, too, stunned by the sight of seeing my father's throat laid open in front of me. There had been so much blood. He'd looked right in my eyes as he died. But what feels worse is that I don't wish he were still alive. I don't regret not trying to stop Nikolai.

If anything, a small part of me regrets that I didn't do it myself, the way Nikolai offered. But—I couldn't.

I've never killed anyone. Never *hurt* anyone. I didn't think I could start with my own father.

What do I want from Nikolai?

I don't know the answer to that. I believe him when he says I'm free to go. That I could walk out of that door tomorrow morning, and he would give me the divorce he promised and probably a generous settlement as well, and I can have whatever life I please.

But standing on the cusp of that, I no longer know if I want to go.

Nikolai has done things that were wrong. Things that hurt me. But I believe that he wants to make it right. And I—

I think of the man who threw snowballs at me in the forest, who cooked me dinner, who went to the trouble of arranging a dinner and romantic drinks for us, even though he had no need to. Who asked me about myself—the first person who ever really had. Who tracked me down in the snow, who cared for me, who kept me alive.

Who, I think, might be falling in love with me—if he isn't already.

And I—

What do I feel for him?

He makes me angry sometimes. He frustrates me, others. But he also matches me, wit for wit, and never makes me feel as if I have to be less than myself. If anything, I think he wants to help me *find* the parts of myself that I don't yet know about. The things that I've never been able to discover, because of the life I've led up until now.

I hear a shattering sound from the bedroom, and that's what spurs me into action and gets me to move quickly from where I'm frozen in place by the door into the room that I share with Nikolai—*our* bedroom, which is still a thought that I can't quite wrap my head around. Nothing in this penthouse feels like *ours*—but maybe I could change that, if we made this real.

If I decided to stay.

He's not in the bedroom. I walk carefully, quickly to the bathroom, pushing open the door—and that's when I see him.

He's standing over the sink, surrounded by glittering glass. The mirror above it is shattered, and I can see from his bleeding knuckles and the bloody glass on the counter that he punched it.

"Nikolai?" I walk towards him with the same quiet, carefulness that he approached me on the balcony. "Nikolai, are you alright?" I feel like the rabbit approaching the wolf, but I'm no longer quite so afraid that he'll bite me.

Sometimes, now, I think I want him to.

He's cradling his newly injured hand in the splinted one, and when he looks up at me sharply, an expression of surprise on his face, I see tears shining in his eyes.

It's not the pain of his hand. It can't be. Nikolai has endured pain far worse than this and has not made so much as a sound. I've seen it myself.

"Lilliana." He says my name in a whisper, like he wants to beg me for something, when once he was the one who said I would beg him. His eyes are damp, the lashes trembling with tears, and I can't imagine seeing this man cry—but he's on the verge of it. "I don't know what to say."

"You could start with why you've shattered the mirror." My voice is calmer than I expect it to be. "If you're angry with me, I can leave tonight—"

"I'm not angry with you." The words come out flat, almost hopeless. "I'm angry with myself."

"Why?" I look at him confusedly. "You got what you wanted today. My father is dead. He can't threaten your family or your position any longer. Your sister is safe. And I—"

"—are no longer mine," he finishes, and I stare at him.

"*That* is what this is all about? Me leaving?"

Nikolai glares at me, and for a moment, I see the fire that I'm used to, his typical reaction to me. It's almost a relief. "Of *course*, that's what this is about," he growls. "You're leaving in the morning. And I—"

For a moment, I can't speak. I think I'm beginning to understand what it is that he's going to say. And since I have no idea what to say in return—I simply wait.

"I don't want you to go," he finishes. "And I'm angry with myself, because it's my fault that you are. Because I have pushed you away. Because I had a chance to have a woman as my wife who is stunningly beautiful, intelligent, brave, and tenacious, and I have driven her away every chance that I had, because I was so arrogant and stubborn that I wouldn't see what it was that she needed from me."

For a moment, I can't breathe. I can't think of what to say. "What did she need?" I ask softly, my heart beating in my throat, and Nikolai looks at me sadly.

"Patience. Kindness. Understanding. I gave her none of that. And now—" He swallows hard, his bleeding hand curling into a fist. "Now it's too late."

Slowly, I step forward, watching for the glass. I bend down when I'm close to him, opening up the cupboard beneath the sink to find the first-aid kit I know is there. And without a word, I take it out and set it on the counter, opening it up to find alcohol pads, gauze, and medical tape.

"Lilliana, what are you—"

I ignore him for a moment, ripping open one of the alcohol pads. "You called me tenacious and yourself stubborn." I press the pad against his knuckles, hearing the quick hiss of his breath. "But those words both mean the same thing, Nikolai. It's just one sounds better than the other." I make another pass with the alcohol pad, before setting it aside and reaching for ointment to rub over the wounds. "We're both stubborn. We both butt heads, and often. And yet—"

"What?" He swallows hard, looking down at me as I start to wrap his hand with gauze. "What else is there, Lilliana? You told me over and over that I was hurting you. That I *had* hurt you. And I didn't listen. I couldn't seem to hear you. I wanted to earn your forgiveness, but I don't think—"

"That's not for you to decide." I secure the gauze, but I don't let go of his hand. "I wasn't going to stay, Nikolai. But then—so much has happened, since you walked out on that balcony and told me that you would let me go. I've learned more about you. I've seen—certain things—in a different light. And I see that you are trying."

I breathe in slowly, measuring my words as I look up at him. "Isn't that what marriage is supposed to be? Continuing to try, even when you fail?"

"A normal marriage, maybe." Nikolai's jaw is still tense as he looks at me. "A marriage where two people love each other."

I can feel the stutter of my heart in my chest. "Do you love me, Nikolai?" I ask softly, and he lets out a breath that I hadn't realized he was holding, his gaze fixed on mine.

"I do," he murmurs. "I'm not sure when, Lilliana. I can't say for sure. But I do love you."

"And I—" I look at him, and I can't say for sure when, either. I can't say if it was when he cooked me dinner that night in the cabin, and I saw a different man than the one that I'd thought I married, or if it was the snowball fight in the woods, or when I woke up thinking I'd frozen to death in the snow only to find him at my side.

It might have been less than an hour ago, when I watched him take vengeance on the man who controlled my whole life—who never stopped controlling it, really, until Nikolai opened his throat with a knife.

It might have been when he set me free.

"I think I love you, too," I whisper. "I do. I do love you. I don't know how, but—"

Nikolai steps forward. I feel the brush of gauze against my cheek as he touches my face, lifting it up to his, and his mouth comes down on mine.

It's slow and gentle, and it's what I want. His lips brush over my mouth, again and again, as if he's trying to memorize the feeling of my mouth against his, the shape of my lips, their fullness, their taste. As if he's a blind man learning me with touch. He stands there for a long time, simply kissing me, until his tongue flicks out to taste my lower lip, and I gasp, a shudder of desire running through me.

"I need you, Lilliana," he murmurs against my mouth. "I'll be careful of us both. But I need—"

"I know," I whisper. "I do too."

He walks me backward towards the bed, his hands already bunching in the loose dress despite his injuries, pulling it up over my head. I don't feel fear, this time, that he doesn't like what he sees. I can tell from the look on his face, the way his hands roam over me, gentle but urgent, that there's nothing about me that he doesn't want. That he wants *all* of it, all of me.

"I need to taste you," he whispers, his fingers tracing patterns over my skin as he kisses me over and over, his body tense with the restraint that it takes to do so gently. His mouth drags down my throat, over my collarbone, lower still, his mouth pressing kisses to every inch of bruised skin, until his hands are gently pushing apart my thighs, opening me up for him.

"Nikolai, you're hurt too—" I whisper, and he shakes his head.

"I've been in pain for much worse reasons than this," he murmurs, and then he lowers his still-faintly swollen mouth between my thighs.

His tongue feels like heaven. He was right all along—the pleasure is magnified a hundred-fold when I give myself up to it. He slides his tongue over my outer folds, teasing me for a brief moment before he delves between them, too hungry to draw it out for long—and I don't want him to. My entire body feels like it's throbbing, aching with the need for release. I cry out as his tongue flutters over my clit, his lips wrapping around the swollen flesh as he sucks it into his mouth, driving me toward the edge quickly.

"Nikolai—" I pant his name, no longer caring what sounds I make, what I say. It doesn't matter any longer, and that's a kind of relief, too, to let go of my fear of letting him know that I want him, to stop fighting my own desires. I give myself over to it, to the heated pleasure, the feeling of his mouth sucking, his tongue swirling over my most intimate flesh, his hands pressed against my thighs, and I cry out as he presses his tongue against the most sensitive spot—and I come unraveled against his mouth.

I scream his name, my hips bucking against him, an orgasm stronger than anything I've had before crashing over me. He holds me in place, still sucking, licking, driving me higher, and I think it's never going to end. I'm never going to stop coming on his mouth, never going to stop feeling as if the world is dissolving around me in liquid heat, and then, as it starts to fade, he slides up my body, and I feel the thick press of him against my drenched entrance.

"You can tell me to stop," he whispers hoarsely. "I'll stop if you want, Lilliana. But *god*, I need to be inside of you."

"I need you too," I whisper, and I see the look on his face, it's everything he's ever wanted to hear. "I need you. Please—"

He pushes into me slowly, careful of my bruised and battered body. Each inch of his swollen cock almost feels like too much, stretching me past my limits, but it feels good, too. I love the way it feels when he fills me—I always have, even when I hated it, too. And now that I've given in to it, it feels so much better.

Just like he promised me it would.

"Nikolai—" I breathe his name, and he groans, pressing his lips against my shoulder, his hips shuddering as he sheathes the last inches of himself inside of me, and I clench around him, wanting to keep him there.

"I don't know how long this is going to last," he whispers against my skin. "It's been too long—*god*, you feel so fucking good—"

"So do you." I run my hands through his hair, my hips arching under him, my body heedless of the bruises. I can feel the soreness, the aches in me that have nothing to do with pleasure and everything to do with pain—but I don't care. I need him. I need this.

Slowly, I move against him, feeling myself tighten and ripple along his length, the slow, hot slide of him inside of me. I feel his breath against my skin, quickening as the pleasure builds, higher and higher, until I know that both of us are going to come apart, and neither of us can hold back any longer.

"Oh *fuck*, Lilliana—" he groans my name, his face turned into my neck, lips dragging over my skin, and then he kisses me, his tongue sliding into my mouth as his cock slides deeply into me once more. I feel him start to shudder as the hot rush of his cum fills me, his cock throbbing as I squeeze around him, my own orgasm pulsating through my body in waves as I sink my fingers against his shoulders and cling to him.

I whisper his name against his mouth, the sounds lost in the kiss, the two of us arching and straining together as the pleasure throbs through us both, and I can feel him trembling against me as it finally starts to ebb.

Nikolai collapses to one side, breathing hard. "It's going to be a little while before I can manage that again. But as soon as I can—" He reaches out, trailing his fingers over the side of my breast. "You're sure you want to stay, Lilliana?"

I nod, reaching for his hand and threading my fingers through his. "I'm sure," I tell him softly. "I want you. And I–I love you."

He turns towards me, lifting my hand to his lips. "I love you too, Lilliana. And I'll make it up to you, every day of my life."

I give him a soft smile, moving carefully to lie as close to him as I can, almost in his arms. "You already have."

Nikolai
One month later

A month ago, I wouldn't have imagined this was possible.

I look down the beach as I stride towards the slender figure lying on a lounge chair, drinks in my hands, and I feel a little as if I'm in a dream. My wife is smiling at me, eager to see me. This morning, I heard her scream my name as I made her come three times over—with my fingers, my mouth, and finally, my cock. And now I can see her waving at me, motioning me towards her, eager to have me back at her side.

I had never thought Lilliana and I were destined for love or happiness. I had thought the best that I could do was save her from a fate that she didn't deserve, and then tuck her away where neither of us would have to be bothered with the other. But instead, I've found something that I never knew was possible for a man like me—a brutal man, a Bratva *pakhan* now, a man taught all his life that what I feel for her only leads to loss and failure.

Love.

There is no one for me besides Lilliana. I told her that, a week after she said she wanted to stay, with a ring I'd bought for her in secret—and just the memory of that morning makes me hard all over again.

I'd woken her up with soft kisses on her mouth, her jaw, her throat, until she was squirming under me, half-asleep still and eager for more. I'd had to be so careful with her as we both healed—still did, really—but if she was begging for it, I wanted to give it to her.

I loved the taste of her. I didn't think I'd ever get tired of it. I kissed my way down her body, taking the time to play with her breasts, licking and sucking her nipples until she was fully awake and her hands were buried in my hair, her hips squirming beneath me. I was rock-hard, aching to be inside of her—but I had other plans before I fucked her.

I made her beg a little that morning. I kissed her hipbones, her inner thighs, sliding my tongue along the crease of them, nibbling and sucking the outer folds of her pussy until I could see her dripping and she was breathless, whispered pleas drifting down to me. Please, Nikolai. Please. I need you to lick my pussy. Please.

I hadn't yet gotten used to the sound of Lilliana begging for me, of those filthy words coming off her tongue without me forcing them. It was enough to make my cock drip pre-cum, to make me thrust against the bed as I pressed my mouth between her legs, wondering if I'd make a mess of the sheets before I could even get inside of her. I'd slid my tongue inside instead, imagining it was my cock, the hot wet velvet of her squeezing around me as I fucked her with it, curling my tongue inside of her and rubbing that sweet spot that made her twist and writhe, her fingers digging into my scalp as she tugged on my hair.

"God, Nikolai!"

I did think I was going to cum then, from the sound of her crying out my name, begging me. My cock throbbed, and I thrust against the bed helplessly, reaching down with my barely-healed left hand to stroke myself. I needed my right hand for her, but I couldn't go another second without touching my cock. It was aching, on the verge of exploding.

I ran my tongue up the dripping folds of her pussy, up to her clit, rolling my tongue over that hard pebble of flesh the way I knew she liked. I found the rhythm, circling, rubbing, my hand squeezing my own cock to stave off my climax as the taste of her flooded my mouth, and I found I couldn't hold off.

"I'm going to come just from licking your pussy," I groaned against her flesh. "I'm going to make a fucking mess all over my hand just from the taste of you. God, Lilliana—holy fuck—fuck—"

I sucked her clit into my mouth as I felt my cock swell and erupt in my hand, hot cum spilling over my fingers and onto the sheets as I sucked and licked at her pulsing flesh, and I felt her arch up, heard her crying out my name as she came hard, drenching my mouth and chin with her arousal—and more of my fucking cum spurted out of my cock, like I couldn't stop coming until she did.

I was still fucking hard when she relaxed against me, and thank fuck, because it would have ruined my plan, otherwise. I hadn't been able to keep control of myself, not with the way she tasted, how good she felt—but I leaned up, pushing my cum-covered cock into her drenched pussy as I reached under my pillow, and as I started to thrust inside of her to the sweet sounds of her moans, I reached for her left hand.

"I should have done this from the beginning," I told her, my voice hoarse as I thrust again, holding myself deeply inside of her as I spoke. "But I'm doing it now. You're my wife already, Lilliana. But I want you to choose to be."

I opened my palm to let her see the ring there, a rose-gold ring with a brilliant round diamond, the band encrusted with smaller diamonds, sparkling in the light. "Will you marry me again, Lilliana?" I asked, and she stared up at me, her eyes wide.

"You're asking me to marry you while you're inside of me?" she breathed, as if she couldn't believe it, and I grinned at her, rocking my hips so she could feel the hard swell of my cock buried inside of her.

"It felt like the right way to ask."

"You're insane," she whispered. "But I can't tell you no." She reached up, taking the ring out of my hand, and slipping it on her finger, before she wrapped her hand around the back of my neck and pulled me down to kiss her. "I don't want to tell you no. So—yes, Nikolai. I'll marry you again—"

A small, wicked smile played over her lips, and I could feel it against mine. "As long as you make me come at least twice more before you do."

I slid my fingers between hers, feeling the new sensation of the ring on her hand. "Deal," I whispered—and then I started to fuck her again, just the way I knew she liked.

I saw that ring sparkle in the sunlight as she waved to me, and I reached the lounge chairs, setting down our drinks. Her smile is almost as brilliant as the diamond, and I lean down, grazing my mouth over hers as I kiss her softly.

"Is this sunny and warm enough for you?" I ask her teasingly. I'd promised her a honeymoon after we'd renewed our vows, just the two of us with Marika there. She'd told me only if we went somewhere with no chance of snow this time.

"Oh, it's definitely warm enough." Her hand curls around the back of my neck, pulling me down for another kiss. "But we can heat it up even more later, if you'd like."

"I like the sound of that." Her mouth tastes like pineapple and the hint of the tang of vodka, and I consider whether or not we ought to go back up to the room right now.

"I was thinking about what we do when we get back home," I tell her, sitting back on my own chair as I reach for my drink. "Do you want to continue living in the mansion? Or the penthouse? Or would you prefer something else? I can call someone, have them be ready to give us some options as soon as we're back—"

Lilliana pauses for a moment. "I think the mansion has bad memories for both of us," she says softly. "And your penthouse—it's beautiful, but it's *yours*. It's never been ours. So I think maybe— maybe the best thing would be if we chose something together. A fresh start. Something we can make our own from the very beginning."

Her hand is resting on my leg, and I reach down, taking it and running my thumb over her knuckles. "I like the sound of that," I tell her, and I mean it. The idea of making a home with her—of a place that has only our memories and nothing else—sounds like a dream that I never thought to have. Something new to achieve that I couldn't possibly have known I would want.

She stretches on the lounge chair, her breasts moving invitingly beneath the thin black material of her bikini top—there's hardly anything there, only the smallest strips of fabric attached to gold chains draped over her pale skin, and it makes my cock hard just looking at her. "We could take these drinks up to the hotel," she murmurs, her back arching, and I know she's teasing me on purpose. "And you could see about making good on some of those promises you whispered in my ear this morning."

"About how I was going to make you scream my name?" I lean forward, my lips brushing against the shell of her ear again. "Or about how I'd fuck you on the balcony overlooking the beach, so everyone could hear it?"

"Both." She turns her head, capturing my lips with hers.

It's only a short walk to the hotel, but we're there in half the time, the drinks forgotten in our hurry. It's for the best, because once I have her in the elevator, I pin her against the mirrored wall, lifting her hands over her head as I grind my cock against the thin strip of fabric covering her pussy. I hadn't minded being gentle with her while she recovered—I knew it was what she'd needed, for more reasons than one—but I want her ravenously, and it's good to be able to touch her the way I want to.

It's even better, knowing that she wants it just as much in return.

"Nikolai—" She gasps my name, panting it against my lips as I kiss her, rocking my hips into hers. I'll never get tired of how it sounds on her lips, hearing her moan and scream and whimper my name, the way I'd once told her that she would. She's always driven me mad with desire, but nothing gets me harder than knowing that she wants me—truly and absolutely. That she is *mine*, that she has given herself to me.

That when I take her, it's because she wants me to.

I slip my fingers under her bikini bottoms, feeling the slick wetness already gathering on her outer folds. "Someone could come in," she whispers, glancing towards the doors. We have the penthouse suite in the resort, and there are several floors between us and it. "Someone could see—"

"Let them." I slip my fingers in between her lips, feeling that slick heat coat them. "They can watch while you come all over my fingers, *krolik*. They can watch my little rabbit squirm in her trap."

"Is it a trap if I want to get caught?" Her voice is breathy, her hips moving, pushing herself down onto my fingers despite her protests. "Oh god, Nikolai—"

I slide my middle finger into her pussy, and she tightens around me, a sharp whimper coming from her mouth. "We could get in trouble—"

"No one will say a word." I curl my finger, stroking it inside of her, my cock aching at the feeling of her wet, tight heat. "And if they do, they'd regret it. And you, my little rabbit—" I add a second finger, knowing it can't come close to the stretch of my cock, knowing it's still a tease even as she writhes on my hand. "If you don't let me enjoy you like this, you might end up with my mouth on your pussy instead. How would you feel if someone came in and saw *that*?"

I stroke my fingers inside of her, enjoying the sound of her whimpers, the tight press of her lips as she keeps glancing anxiously at the door. "Or I could fuck you. Would you like that better? Bent over with my cock in your pussy while someone else watches? While they watch you come all over it?" I lean closer, pushing my fingers deeply inside of her, my thumb finding her clit. "Or I could fuck you in the ass—"

"Nikolai!" She cries out, and I feel her tighten on my fingers, a flood of arousal gushing over my hand as she comes hard. I feel myself harden to the point of pain at the thought that she came because I'd mentioned fucking her in the ass.

Oh, do I have plans for you, my little rabbit.

I keep my fingers in her as the elevator keeps going up, stroking inside of her, idly grazing my thumb over her clit to keep her on that edge of the climb upwards to pleasure again. I press my own hand against my cock through my swim shorts every so often, trying to keep my aching erection at bay until I can have her in our room and all to myself.

I watch the number creep upwards. No one comes into the elevator, and I can see Lilliana's look of relief as it reaches the floor just before the penthouse. I thrust my fingers into her once more, making her gasp, and then slip them free, raising them to my lips as I lick her off, just as the doors open.

Lilliana's face is flushed bright red as she follows me out into the penthouse, and I pick her up, swinging her into my arms with a small cry as I carry her out to the balcony.

"I told you I'd fuck you out here," I breathe into her ear as I turn her around, placing her hands on the railing. "I want you to scream my name so loudly they hear you all the way across the beach."

And then I drop to my knees behind her, pulling the fabric of her bikini bottoms aside, and press my mouth against her dripping pussy.

She cries out, arching her back as I urge her legs wider apart with one hand, my tongue delving between her folds and inside of her, up to her clit, licking her in long strokes that leave her writhing backward against my face, her oversensitized nerves keeping her there on the knife's edge of pleasure. I hear her moan, her hands clutching the railing, her ass grinding back onto my face as I make her come for me again with my tongue, wanting the taste of her filling my mouth as I rub my tongue over her clit, and she cries out.

I keep her swimsuit to one side as I get my cock out, stroking myself once with a firm grip as I nudge the swollen head against her entrance, pushing inside of her. She feels so fucking good, tight and hot and wet, and she moans again as I thrust hard, sinking all of myself into her in a long stroke. "Nikolai!" she cries out, and my cock throbs, hearing my name on her lips like that.

"I'm going to take your ass out here on the balcony," I murmur in her ear, thrusting again. "Out here where everyone can hear the sounds you make. Do you want that, *krolik*? My big cock in your ass, filling you up with cum, making you mine in every way while anyone could look up here and see you getting fucked?"

The moan she lets out reverberates through her entire body, shuddering back against me as she writhes on my cock, and I reach to rub her clit, wanting to feel her come one more time. I love making her come, now more than ever, when I know she wants it too. "Tell me yes." I thrust again, hard and deep. "Tell me you want me to fuck your ass. Tell me you want my cock in the only hole you haven't let me take yet."

Her head drops forwards, her ass grinding against me as I fuck her, and for a moment, I'm not sure that I'm going to make it long enough to come in her ass. Her clit is throbbing under my fingers, swollen and sensitive. She lets out a helpless moan as she starts to come again, shuddering against me as her back arches deeply and she cries out.

"Yes," she breathes through the moan, letting out a small whimper as I stroke her clit again. "I want you to fuck my ass—I want you to fuck all of me. Please—"

I slip out of her, relishing the small cry that she makes when I'm no longer filling her, and I slide my fingers through her drenched pussy, using her own arousal to lube her small, tight hole as I push the head of my cock against it. "It will feel too big," I warn her. "But you can take it. My good little rabbit. You can take my cock, Lilliana."

She nods breathlessly. "I can take your cock," she whispers, her ass nudging backward against me, and I feel myself throb with anticipation.

I have to go slow—excruciatingly so. She's so tight, almost *too* tight, and it's a struggle, even as wet as she is, to get my cockhead inside her ass. I push into her, spreading her open, and the shriek she lets out when my cock pops inside of her is enough to make some of the beachgoers below look up at our balcony.

I hope they can see me fucking her.

"Good girl," I murmur, running my hand down her back. "Such a good girl. That's just the first inch. You can take all of it."

She gasps, breathing hard, but she nods. Her acquiescence makes me harder than ever, and I thrust forward a little more, sinking another inch into her tight ass as she cries out.

Slowly, a little at a time, I make her take all of it. She's panting and moaning by the time I seat myself fully against her perfect ass, my fingers stroking her clit to make it easier, and I give her a moment to adjust as I throb inside of her, the tight heat so good that I know it will only be a few strokes before I fill her up.

She cries out again when I start to thrust, moaning so loudly that I can see people below fully watching us now, and that only turns me on more. Again and again, I sink inside of her, until I hear her moaning my name, feel her clit throb against my fingertips, and she screams out that she's coming.

The orgasm is so intense it's almost painful. My cock swells and hardens in her ass, filling her up with cum as I hear her begging for it, pleading, her own orgasm taking over until her knees nearly buckle and she's clutching the railing, and I'm not sure I've ever come so hard or so much in my life. I can see it dripping out around my cock, trailing down her skin, and I can still feel it throbbing, shooting out of my cock long past when I normally would still be coming.

When I slip out of her, collapsing back on one of the lounge chairs, she doesn't move for a moment. All I can think is how fucking gorgeous she looks, her bikini bottoms still displaced, her pussy pink and puffy and swollen, and my cum dripping out of her ass, her chest heaving as she clings to the railing and tries to catch her breath.

A moment later, she turns, coming to join me on the lounge, and she leans against my chest as she curls into my arms.

"I liked that," she says softly, leaning up to plant a kiss on my neck. It makes my heart skip a little, hearing her say it. There was a time when she would never have admitted that she liked it, that I made her come, that she wants me to do it again. "I love you, Nikolai."

She looks up at me as she says it, and I slide a finger under her chin, bending down to kiss her. "I love you, too, *krolik*."

There was a time when it felt like I was hurting her every time I touched her. Like my lust for her was poison in her veins, killing her slowly.

But I found a way to heal her—and she healed me, too. And now I'll get to have her forever.

Just the way I vowed I would.

Epilogue
Lilliana

It's another month after we get back that we have our new house. We took our time choosing it, wanting it to be perfect—and it is.

The new house is everything I could have dreamed of—everything I never thought to dream of, really. It's a massive stone mansion outside of the city, on beautifully landscaped grounds—practically an estate. The house itself is four stories, full of so many rooms I don't know how we're ever going to fill them, and a sunroom with a huge windowed wall so like the one in the cabin we stayed in that I ask Nikolai if we can put a heated pool and wet bar in the way there was in the cabin.

He says yes, of course. There's not much that he doesn't give me, if I ask for it. His reticence to get too close to me has been replaced by devotion, by love that startles me with how much he seems to be able to give—and so something that once would have felt like a curse is now something that I'm excited to share with him.

I wait until the first night in our new house, already mostly furnished by the decorators we hired and worked with, to tell him. I'm sitting at the island in the kitchen—not unlike that first night in the cabin—while he makes me dinner, and when he goes to pour me a glass of the red wine he knows I like, I shake my head.

Nikolai frowns. "Are you sure? You love—"

He freezes, looking at me. "Lilliana—"

I nod, a sudden lump in my throat. "Are you sure?" he asks, and I nod again, trying to find words.

"I'm very sure," I whisper. "Nikolai, are you—"

"Happy?" He drops his tongs, coming around the island to lift me off of the seat and up onto it, his hand sliding over my still-flat belly. "I'm ecstatic. I can't believe—oh fuck, Lilliana. I'm so fucking happy."

To my shock, he bends down, kissing my stomach through the thin chiffon of my blouse. It's such an unexpected gesture that it brings tears to my eyes, and I run my hand through his hair, trailing my fingers over his scalp as his hands slide up my thighs.

"When?" he asks, and I laugh softly.

"I think it might have been our honeymoon," I admit. "We had a *lot* of sex."

"We did," he agrees, and I see a sudden heat in his eyes, his hands nudging up the black pencil skirt I'm wearing. The island is at hip level for him, and I can see the bulge in his trousers, the thick ridge of his suddenly hard cock. I let out a small, breathy moan at the sight, biting my lower lip, and his hand instantly goes to his belt.

He leans forward, kissing me as he frees his cock, pulling me to the edge of the island as he pushes my skirt up the rest of the way with his other hand. "Just in case," he says teasingly, his cock nudging at my entrance, and I laugh.

"I think anything else is overkill," I tell him, but my thighs are already spreading open, my pussy wet for him as I feel him start to push into me. He feels so fucking good—he always feels so good—

and I wrap my legs around his hips, pulling him closer as he starts to thrust.

I can smell dinner starting to burn. But his fingers are on my clit, my own orgasm close, and as he grazes his teeth over my neck and starts to fuck me harder, murmuring in my ear how much he wants to fill me up with his cum, I decide I don't care. We can always make another dinner. And right now, Nikolai is all I want.

He's all I'll ever want. Forever.

Keep reading for a sneak peek of my next Bratva romance, Dangerous Vows! Or click here to begin enjoying all your favorite tropes now!

✓ *Age-Gap*

✓ *Arranged Marriage*

✓ *Enemies to Lovers*

Can't get enough of the sexy Nikolai and Lilliana? Click here for a bonus scene.

And don't forget to click here to join my Red Hot Diva's reader group on Facebook for exclusive sneak peeks and giveaways.

Preview of Dangerous Vows
Marika

I sat alone at my vanity, contemplating the night ahead.

It had been a little while since I'd seen my brother, Nikolai Vasilev, and his wife. I saw him less often now than I had before—before his marriage, our father's death, my kidnapping and his wife's…all of the events that had made the last months feel as if they'd taken up a much greater span of time than they already had. It had all ended with the threat neutralized, Nikolai and Lilliana happier than they had ever expected to be together—and me here, in our family's mansion, trying to find a way to piece back together who I was, and who I am now.

I liked the solitude, if I was being honest. It felt a little strange—the mansion had been too big even when it had been only Nikolai, our father, and I—but it fit my mood these days. I could wander around most of it without so much as even running into a staff member or any of the security, who kept themselves always ready but out of my sight for the most part. I know they worried about me—I could see it in their faces when I did run into them on occasion—but I put it out of my head most of the time.

I had never been alone in my life, and now I was more often than not. Nikolai and Lilliana came by about once a week—usually together, sometimes apart—but they had other things to occupy them. Nikolai had the Bratva to put back together in the wake of our father's death and his marriage to enjoy, new as it is. He'd renewed his vows with Lilliana and taken her on a honeymoon, and then instead of moving back into the mansion with me or returning to his penthouse, they'd purchased a new estate of their own, ready to fill it with the family they'd already started creating.

Tonight was one of those nights. We had a 'family dinner' planned, the three of us all that remains of either of our families for now, and I'd been trying for over an hour to get ready for it.

The day had started out difficult. I'd planned on visiting my father's grave this morning, and had gone, but it had been rainy and wet, the end of winter turning into the first damp chills of oncoming spring, and I'd stood in the graveyard for a long time under my black umbrella, staring down at the gravestone and shivering in the wet cold until Adrik had finally come and urged me back to the car, solicitously convincing me to go back home.

Adrik. I touched my lower lip, glancing over at the rumpled sheets of my bed. I had never had a secret like Adrik before. For a little over a month, I'd kept it. And now I didn't know what to do.

It had happened while Nikolai and Lilliana were gone on their honeymoon. I had spent a month convaelescing, trying to heal from both my physical and emotional wounds, with Nikolai and Lilliana both doing their best to help me while they recovered themselves. Adrik had asked to stay on my security detail at the mansion, and Nikolai had agreed. He owed him a favor after all—it was thanks to Adrik that I'd gotten out of the compound where I'd been held prisoner at all.

I shivered, getting up from my vanity to walk acros the room to my closet and look at the clothes hanging there for the tenth time since Adrik had left. There was no real need to dress up, but our father had always insisted on us dressing for dinner, a tradition held over from the old world and how his family had done things. Nikolai and I had unspokenly kept it up, even after his death, when the three of us had started this new tradition of weekly family dinners, now that we no longer lived together.

I ran my fingers over the fabric, feeling off-balance and tired. I would have liked to fall asleep after Adrik left, but that wouldn't have left me with enough time to get ready. As it was, I'd had to shower again to get the scent of Adrik's cologne and the mingled scents of male sweat and sex off of my flesh, but they still hung in the air of my room, sending a shiver of desire through me all over again.

I should have told him no. And now that it's too late, I should tell him no, the next time he wants to come to my bed.

Even now, it's hard to piece together exactly how it all happened. I had been lonely while Nikolai and Lilliana were gone on their honeymoon, with strict instructions from Nikolai not to leave the house unless I was closely guarded, and no real desire to go anywhere or do anything. I had remembered that Adrik was the one who had gotten me out, that he had helped rally Nikolai's remaining loyal men and rescued the three of us, and that I owed him thanks. So I'd invited him into the informal living room, offered him a drink. He'd been hesitant to accept it, at first.

"I'm on duty, Ms. Vasilev. I shouldn't be drinking."

"Just one. And you can call me Marika. It's the least I can do, after you saved my life." I'd held out the crystal glass of vodka, another in my other hand for myself, and I saw the brief moment's hesitation before he stepped forward and took it from me.

Had I been flirting? Even now, I'm not entirely sure. I had been alone and lonely. Adrik was gorgeous—*is* gorgeous—six feet four inches of muscled, chiseled, tattooed perfection, with light blond hair cut short on the sides and long on top, bright blue eyes and a face that would catch any woman's eye. Dressed in the black cargo pants and fitted black t-shirt that made up the uniform of Nikolai's security, he was mouth-watering. Especially for me, innocent and curious, no longer sure what my future held and aching to take some of it back for myself.

He had asked how I was doing. If I was healing well. We'd ended up on the couch, sitting side by side, drinking a second glass of vodka, and I had felt his eyes on me as I told him I was physically better, but still struggling some days with the memories of what had happened. I had nightmares. I wasn't sleeping well. I don't know what came over me, to tell someone who was essentially a part of the staff so much—but he had saved me. He had picked me up himself and carried me out of the compound, bleeding and injured, half-dead from the beating I'd been given, and fought his way out with me in his arms.

How can I blame either of us, for feeling like it had created some kind of intimacy between us, as inappropriate as it was?

He had asked, hesitantly, how badly I'd been hurt. I understood what he meant, the delicate question he was dancing around. *"They didn't assault me in* that *way, if that's what you're asking,"* I had told him, and I saw a strange expression cross his face.

"That's good," he'd said finally. *"I'm glad you weren't hurt worse than you were, Ms. Vasilev."*

I'd frowned, eyeing him with a feeling that was something between curiosity and discomfort. *"You seem disappointed with that answer,"* I said. *"That's a strange thing to be disappointed about. And I told you to call me Marika."*

He shook his head abruptly, setting the glass aside. *"Of course I'm not disappointed that they didn't—violate you."* His voice had a tinge of horror to it. *"I'd never wish such a thing on anyone. Especially you."*

I still didn't understand. The last words sent an odd flush of heat through me—*why especially me?* I realized how close he was sitting to me. Our knees were almost touching. It felt ridiculous, like I was in some sort of staged Victorian play, being faintly aroused by the inch of space between my knee and Adrik's. But I was suddenly very aware of everything about him.

"Your brother will have plans for who you're supposed to marry," he said suddenly, as if he'd been thinking the words for a long time, and only now found the nerve to say them. *"If things were–different, he might not marry you to anyone. And then–"*

I had stared at him, pieces clicking into place, wondering if he was really saying what I thought he was. It seemed absolutely absurd. But the way he was looking at me, an intensity in those blue eyes–a *hunger*, as if he'd been holding something tightly in place for a long time, and was now losing his grip on it.

"What are you trying to say?" I breathed, and Adrik's hands clenched on his thighs. I could see the moment he made a decision.

"I'll show you instead," he said, and then one of those hands was on my jaw, tipping my chin up, and I was being kissed for the first time in my life.

It was slow and sweet and breathtaking. I had known, dimly, that I shouldn't allow it. That even this was a risk. That I still held value to our family–that my *innocence* had value–and I was dancing a dangerous line. But Adrik's mouth was full and soft and warm, the kiss eager and careful all at once, and I could feel that the desire in it had been there for a long time. Maybe even before my kidnapping, before my rescue. I thought of him watching me over months and years, wanting me, pining for me from afar, and it was all so romantic that I let myself be swept up in it without even really knowing if it was all true.

Nikolai was somewhere far away, in a warm place with his wife, and there was no one to stop me, no one to worry about finding out. I breathed against Adrik's mouth for him to lock the door, and he hesitated–but his desire won out, too. He came back to the couch and kissed me again. I let him do more than kiss me. He paused at every moment, at every choice–but I wanted to reclaim my body for myself. I was still a virgin–my kidnappers hadn't taken that from me—but they had hurt me, shamed me, stripped so much else away from me. I could feel Adrik's hands piecing that back together, smoothing away the cracks, and I decided in a whirlwind of emotion and sensation that I would give him the one thing I had left to give.

It was good. Better than I'd expected. Afterwards, he got dressed, looking at me with worry on his face. *"I'll keep it a secret,"* he said, bending to kiss me. *"But while your brother is gone, I'd like to see you again."*

I had looked at the bloodstain on the couch for a long time afterwards, wondering if I'd be able to get it out, and if anyone would even notice.

I had seen Adrik again—most nights, while Nikolai was gone. I'd expected it to have to end when he and Lilliana came back, expecting them to move into the mansion with me. But they hadn't. I had the mansion mostly to myself, protected behind two sets of iron gates with a triple guard now on each, all of them warned about what would happen to them if there was another betrayal like the one that had led to our father's death and my kidnapping, and there was no one to stop Adrik and I.

So for over a month now, he's been in my bed. And every time, afterwards, I ask myself exactly how I think this is going to end.

Maybe there won't be a marriage at all, I think to myself as I take a pair of black slacks and a white silk blouse out of the closet, laying them out on the bed as I start to take my hair down out of the pin curlers it had been in. *Our father is gone. Nikolai doesn't hold with all of the old ways, I know that. Maybe things will be different.* Nikolai himself had seen the trials that came with an arranged marriage, how close his and Lilliana's union had been to being one of endless contention or at best, a frigid truce. He might let me make my own choice, find other ways of making alliances or strengthening his power and hold over the territory. And if so, I might be able to convince him, in time, that there was no harm in it—even if that choice turned out to be a member of his own security team.

Adrik had saved me. Nikolai ows him for that. And if Adrik and I could managed to convince him that what we have is worth bending the rules for, I might be able to hope that my brother could find it in his heart to do things differently.

I check the clock; twenty minutes until Nikolai and Lilliana arrive for dinner. I have just enough time to finish my makeup and meet them downstairs. I spent too long daydreaming, something that seems to happen more and more often since I was rescued. I've always had a tendency to get lost in my own head, ever since I was a child, but it's been harder than usual to focus and not lose track of time since I came back.

I reach for my makeup case, pushing thoughts of the past and of Adrik out of my head. I want to enjoy the evening with my brother and sister-in-law, and I don't want anything to spoil it.

Of course, I didn't know what it was that Nikolai planned to talk to me about, when I had that thought.

—

Nikolai and Lilliana arrive right on time, and I let them in, leading the three of us to the informal dining room–having dinner in the formal room, at a table that could seat an entire dinner party's worth of guests and then some, feels a little too ridiculous.

"How is the new estate?" I ask them as the first course of dinner is served. I'd spent a lot of time planning the menu–something to occupy my time–and there's a salad studded with cranberries and goat cheese and a pumpkin-crab bisque for the first course.

"We're rattling around in there a little," Lilliana says with a smile, reaching for the pitcher of sparkling water instead of the wine Nikolai and I are drinking. "But we'll fill it up soon enough." She pats her still-flat belly with a smile at her husband. "Although it might always feel a little too big. I would have been happy with something smaller, but you know–"

"Can't have the *pakhan* of the Bratva living in a two-story brownstone," Nikolai says with a smirk. "You'll be glad for that space when we start having dinner parties."

"What makes you think I'll be excited to have dinner parties?" Lilliana asks teasingly, and I watch their banter, glad to see them teasing each other playfully, without the acid bite that there used to be to it. They've both come a long way since the rocky start of their arrangement.

"You've got to be getting lonely here," Nikolai says, glancing at me as we finish the first course and one of the staff members brings the second. "This place is too big for one person."

"It's not one person." I feel my stomach tighten a little at the tone of his voice–it sounds like he's leading up to something, and I'm not sure that I'm going to like it. "It's me, and an endless amount of security, and the staff besides."

"That's still lonely." Nikolai dips one of the shrimp served on the chilled plate into a small crystal bowl of cocktail sauce. "But I think that might change soon, Marika, if you're open to hearing what I have to say."

I know well enough that I don't really have the option. Nikolai is my brother, and he loves me dearly, I know that. But I can hear the tone in his voice–the *pakhan*'s tone–and it's one I'm not accustomed to. I don't like the sound of it, and I do my best to keep calm as I answer.

"I think you're going to tell me one way or another," I tell him simply. "So you may as well."

I don't miss the glance Lilliana gives Nikolai, and it makes me wonder how much he's told her of whatever it is that he's about to say. There was a time when he never would have shared any sort of information that might be held in confidence with a woman, not even his wife, but things are different now. *Nikolai* is different, softened by what he's found with Lilliana. I'd hoped that newfound softness might extend to my own situation, but I have creeping sense of unease that that's not the case.

His next words confirm it.

"Theo McNeil is looking for a wife," Nikolai says bluntly. "He's gone on too long without an heir, and from what I've heard, the other Kings are starting to pressure him about it. Most of them have heirs, and they don't want a civil war breaking out if he were to die without someone to take over for him."

I frown. "He's not that old, is he? Not on death's doorstep, anyway."

Nikolai chuckles. "No. Forty-three, I believe. But he needs to find a bride first, wed her, produce an heir and let that heir get old enough to comfortably take over in the circumstance of his passing–and that's a lot of things to happen when a man in our line of work can find himself on the wrong end of a bullet at any time. They're taking all that into consideration. We don't always get the pleasure of growing old."

Those words aren't unfamiliar to me, but they hit harder now, in the wake of my father's death and my own brush with mortality. I swallow hard, holding my brother's gaze as I ask the question that I feel fairly certain I already know the answer to.

"What does that have to do with me?"

Nikolai's expression was guarded as he looked at me. "Theo's organization is the only one more powerful than the Vasilev Bratva," he says finally. "The Kings have resources beyond what we do, coming in not only from their home organization in Dublin, but plenty of other places as well. Theo has turned his attention to our territory, and I have it on good authority that he's considering moving in on us. Trying to take our contacts, our territory, our business."

"That would start a war." I stare at Nikolai. "That–"

He nods. "And if he's considering it, it means he feels fairly certain he can do so and win. That puts all of us in danger, and everything our family has built."

"So you're going to try to make an alliance with him." It's not even really a question. It's how this always goes. An alliance needs to be made, and the innocent, unmarried daughter is how it's brokered—or in this case, the innocent, unmarried sister. I'm no longer innocent, but Nikolai doesn't know that.

For the briefest moment, I consider telling him—shouting it out over rack of lamb and roasted potatoes, just to see the expression on his face. *I'm not a virgin. Adrik fucked me on the couch in the living room. Yes, the informal one. You can see the bloodstain if you like, I never did manage to get it all the way out.*

I really do think about it, just for a second. But I can't. Not only because of the punishment that would undoubtedly be visited on Adrik if I did, but because after everything, I can't bear to see the look of disappointment on my brother's face. He's the only family I have left—the only *blood* family—and the idea of him seeing all his plans wither because of my foolishness feels like too much to bear. He's my big brother, and he's never been disappointed in me in all my life. I hate the idea that he would be, now.

"Yes." Nikolai still has that guarded expression on his face, as if he's waiting for my reaction. "I think you know how that will be arranged, Marika."

Lilliana is very quiet, across from him. I wonder if they had this discussion before, if she tried to talk him out of it, or if she understands *the way things are* now. If she's come around to the way that the Families do things, now that she's chosen to accept her place in it—if she'll be as accepting one day when it might be her own daughter handed over to broker a business arrangement.

Love has a funny way of making people see things very differently than they used to.

"With a marriage." My voice sounds flat and distant, like I'm hearing it down a hallway. "Between Theo and I."

Nikolai lets out a breath, as if he were expecting a tantrum from me, and nods. "That's exactly it. But Marika—" he pauses, considering his next words. "It won't be forever."

"What do you mean?" I look at him confusedly, and he glances at Lilliana before returning his gaze to me.

"This is an arrangement that has an end date," he says. "I'm planting you as his wife, Marika. You will go through with it in reality, of course—the wedding, the consummation, all of it. But I intend to have you find information that will enable me to put an end to Theo and his branch of the Kings before they can do the same to us."

I stare at him. "You want to use me as a spy?" The possibilities feel different now. I still don't *want* to marry Theo McNeil, or go to bed with him, or pretend to be his happy wife—but this isn't the same as saying *til death do us part* and meaning it. This is something else.

"I want you to be careful," Nikolai says firmly. "But essentially, yes. I want you to find whatever you can—get him to talk to you, any means you can devise of finding out what's going on that I can't access. You will be able to get closer to him than I or anyone else possibly could, especially if he thinks you're happy with him, and you please him."

I see Lilliana wrinkle her nose at his phrasing, but she says nothing.

"Once he's taken down and his organization disbanded, you'll be a widow," Nikolai continues. "I'll write the deed to the mansion over to you. You can do as you like after that—marry, or not marry at all, sell the house or keep it, whatever you choose."

I look at him for a long moment, unsure what to say. "This is a dangerous plan," I say finally, picking at a loose thread on the seam of my pants. *What will Adrik think?* It shouldn't even be a consideration—it shouldn't matter. But I think, for a moment, of his hands and mouth on me, the eager passion every time he takes me to bed, and I wonder if he'll be willing to stand idly by while I marry someone else, even for a little while.

But I haven't made him any promises, and I'm not even sure if there's a future for us. That's not a choice I've made. It's not one I'm ready to make anytime soon.

This is a choice I have to make now—if I even have one.

"What if I say no?" I ask Nikolai softly, and he sighs.

"I'm not going to force you, Marika. I'm not Lilliana's father, or ours. I am going to give you a choice in this. But I think you know the choice that I want you to make."

I do, of course. And I also know that I don't really have one. My purpose has always been to marry for the advancement of our family, and that hasn't changed just because our father is gone. I was a fool to think that it might have.

I don't think there's a single future where I don't end up married to someone to benefit our family's future. At least with Theo, there's a purpose to it beyond just warming the bed of some crime organization's heir and providing him with children. I can keep our family from being hurt by this man. And then—

Maybe there's a future for me with Adrik. I have no idea. But I might at least be able to find out. It seems better than the other options that I can see unfolding in front of me, if I tell Nikolai no this time.

"Alright," I tell him quietly, the food in front of me forgotten. "I'll do it."

Click here to get the full length standalone of *Dangerous Vows* now!

Printed in Great Britain
by Amazon